I0700226

NIGHTWALKER

NIGHTWALKER

DEMONIC WAR

NIGHTWALKER

BOOK 1

NATHAN MANIOCI

To all those who believe in monsters and magic. The only things that truly exist are the things you believe in. Remember, the only limit is your imagination.

Contents

"Monster? Who's the monster here? I have done nothing wrong, and yet you and your kind all wish me dead!"

— Frankenstein's monster, Van Helsing

Prologue

If someone told you monsters were real, would you believe them? The creatures only featured in myths and fairy tales, all the things that go bump in the night, walking among people. For fifteen-year-old Ren Nightwalker, stories of monsters being real would sooner put him to sleep than keep him awake. Living in a coffin of darkness, he was sure his life couldn't get much worse than it already was.

Ren walked down the hallway with his hands in his pockets. Every step he took seemed to echo through the hallway. As he passed, the other kids in the hallway ran out of the way, clinging to each other in fear. They avoided him like the plague, afraid of being his next target.

His famously bad reputation was plastered throughout the town, evidence of the unfathomably bad company he kept. However, it was his sheer capability of violence that made him feared. But for Ren, his company and aggressive attitude were merely a way for him to escape a dead reality.

The year before, Ren's mother had died in an accident. Not the typical car crash kind of accident either. The kind of accident where a clean apartment suddenly bursts into flames and explodes.

Most people thought it was your accidental kitchen fire that spread out of control. But Ren knew it was no accident. There was not a single lit flame in the place when it happened. The dining room had just burst into flames out of nowhere, and the fire spread almost too fast. It took only a minute before two other rooms were engulfed in flames. Then the fire exploded outward. The windows shattered as the flames shot out into the cool winter air.

Ren's mother pushed him away from the fire just as the windows exploded. He watched as he fell three stories, hitting each level of the fire escape stairs on his way down.

For most of Ren's life, it had been just him and his mother. His father's job always kept him away from them. Being just the two of them, Ren was very close with his mother, so when she died, it hit him hard.

No one believed him when he said there was no way it could have been an accident. It wasn't just the fire that made him believe that either. It was the figure he saw looming next to one of the door frames. Everything had happened so fast that he barely had a chance to get a good look, but he still saw them.

After she died, Ren's life just spiraled out of control. He had nowhere to go and no relatives to call on. He was utterly alone in the world. With no way out, he took those who had been his enemies and used them to his advantage. Now, his only closure was in a single girl he'd known since they were infants.

Ren walked into the classroom and threw his bag to the floor next to a seat. The kids in the class turned their heads to avoid making eye contact. A nervous tension filled the room. He sat down and propped his feet up on his desk. Leaning back, he stared at the ceiling momentarily before closing his eyes.

A tap on his shoulder forced him from his rest. His childhood friend Kelsey stared down at him. "Hey, Ren, moody as usual, I see." She pinched his cheek.

"Stop it," he said, gently smacking her hand away. She laughed and sat down on his desk. He moved his feet to the side for her. He wished he had more classes with her than just this one.

Once school ended, Ren walked Kelsey home before heading to the south end of town. Winter in Florida was still winter, just without any snow. The cool winter wind blew down the road, wrapping around him like a blanket. He hated the cold.

Ren came upon an abandoned building off to the side of the road. He unlocked the chain and slid the rusted iron door to the side. This building belonged to the relative of one of his unsavory companions, and they let him crash there since he had nowhere else to go.

Turning on the lights, he headed up a set of stairs. What was once an office was now his bedroom. A single bed, a nightstand with a lamp, a bookshelf full of books, a beat-up desk with an old office chair, and his own personal bathroom. It wasn't much, but it was home.

Setting his bag down, he headed back downstairs and entered a dark room. He flicked on the lights and turned to see a man with bleach-blond hair and a goatee sitting at the table. Ren looked for the knife he kept nearby but couldn't find it.

"Looking for this?" the man asked. He held up a spring blade knife. Damn. "Sit," the man told him.

Ren walked over and sat down across from him. The man put the knife on the table. "So, this is where you've been staying. I'm sorry I haven't been around. You've done well for being alone, all things considered."

"What do you want?" Ren asked the man.

"Is that how you talk to your father?" Ren ignored him and pressed him for more information.

"How did you find this place?" Ren asked, ignoring his comment.

"I have my ways. As for why I'm here, I've come to get you. I took some time off from my job. I'm taking you back to India. You can live with me there," his father said.

"Why bother coming to me now? Where were you when I needed you a year ago?"

"You want to keep living in this dump? Alone?"

"I'm not alone; I still have Kelsey," Ren reminded him. "I'm doing fine without you."

The man released a heavy sigh. "This is my fault. I shouldn't have left you alone. You're coming back to India with me, no exceptions. I'm giving you your life back, and all your vampiric powers with it. Pack your things; our flight leaves in two hours."

His father got up and walked out of the room. Ren sighed before heading upstairs to pack what little belongings he had. His father came upstairs carrying a suitcase. Ren filled it with his already minimal possessions, so there was plenty of room left.

Next, he sent Kelsey a message. Since she was all he had left, he at least wanted her to know. He couldn't leave without telling her.

Downstairs, Ren turned off all the lights and headed out the door. He locked it behind him and walked to the car parked at the side of the road with the back door open. His father sat in the front seat, talking on his phone. Ren put his things in the back before looking back one last time at the place he called home. He opened the passenger side door and sat down in the seat, a new life ahead of him.

☦

"Targets sighted," Ren said through his earpiece.

"Copy that," a voice on the other side of the earpiece said back. "The rest is up to you. Good luck." There was a click, and the voice was gone.

Ren leaped onto the tiled roof of a house and made his way to the other end. A man and a woman stood on a balcony overlooking the ocean. They were engaged in conversation. Ren jumped down, landing behind them. They whirled around in surprise, and he quickly slit their throats and threw their bodies over the railing. They fell into the water below, sinking to its depths.

Using his earpiece, he notified the person on the other side that the mission was complete. There was a brief silence before the person on the other side informed him of a potential new mission. A new mission, so soon after this one?

Curious, Ren requested details, inquiring as to the objective. He never would have guessed that by accepting it, it would change his life forever. The new mission was set to occur in America, in the city where he used to live no less. It was time for him to return home.

"Anything seem out of the ordinary?" Ren asked.

"Not out of the ordinary, no. But there are a lot of shades here," Marcus said. Ren and Marcus looked out at the city from the window of their plane. From the palm trees to the busy streets and the towering skyscrapers, it was just as they remembered it.

Silence passed between them as they took in the city they used to call home. "It's been three years. Time to find out what's changed," said Ren.

One

The Day the Past Returns

Kelsey looked up at the sky. Two girls who were walking with her stopped. "What is it?" one of them asked.

"It's nothing. My mind just wandered off," Kelsey said.

"Have you heard from him?"

Of course, they knew what she was thinking; they always did. Kelsey shook her head. "It's already been three years without a word. I don't think he's coming back."

Her two friends exchanged insecure glances. "Kelsey, listen," one of them said. "Maybe, you know, maybe this is a sign. It's been three years since he left, after all. Maybe it's time you let go and forget about him. You're only hurting yourself like this."

She didn't want to. She really, really didn't want to. Forgetting about Ren was something she didn't think she even could do. But perhaps they were right. After all, he had probably already forgotten about her. Ren was gone, and he wasn't coming back.

Kelsey's phone started ringing. She took it out of her pocket but didn't recognize the number. For whatever reason compelled her to, instead of ignoring it as she usually would, this time she answered.

"Hello?" she asked. No response.

"Kelsey?" the person on the other end finally asked.

The moment she heard his voice, the whole world seemed to stop. She gasped lightly. The softness it contained, the way it soothed her worries, the way it said her name, she'd recognize that voice anywhere. "Ren?"

"It's been a long time. How have you been?" Ren asked.

"I suppose aside from the fact that you just left out of the blue, and I haven't heard from you since, I'm fine," Kelsey said back.

"Yeah, I'm sorry about that," Ren said back. "Really, I am. I wish we could have had more time together. And it's not exactly easy to get a hold of you from the other side of the world."

For a brief moment, all the rage that had built up, all the emotions she'd been holding back surfaced. But they quickly faded after Kelsey realized he meant the things he'd said for her sake. "You still could have called once you know. Even an email would have been fine."

"I know; I'm sorry. I mean it."

"So, why now?" she asked. "Why call now?"

"I miss you," he confessed. She forgot to breathe for a moment when she heard that.

"I miss you," she confessed. "Do you ever plan on coming back? If not, we should video chat. I, I want to see you."

Kelsey heard him chuckle from the other end. "Actually, that's one of the reasons I'm calling."

She felt her heart begin to beat rapidly. She could see him again.

"Look up," he told her. It was a strange request. Kelsey looked up, not sure what to find. Sitting on top of a large stone wall to her left was a boy with long bleach-blond hair. In the light of the sun, even with the distance away that he was, she could see the blue of his cobalt-colored eyes. All the strength left her hands, causing her phone to hit the pavement.

Ren jumped down from the wall and walked over to her. The closer he got, the faster her heart beat.

Finally reaching her, he wrapped her up in a warm embrace. He released her but kept his hands on her waist. She still couldn't believe he was here.

Kelsey took in Ren's new appearance. His once short bleach-blond hair was now very long. Parted in three sections, his long bangs curved right, ending at his nose and exposing his face. Oh man, those eyes. They were so blue.

"It's really you," she said, a little skeptical.

"It is," he confirmed. "I'm here for work. We just opened over here, and many of us haven't arrived yet. My father sent me here ahead of everyone to secure any last-minute necessities and prepare for their arrival."

"So, you're here on work. For how long?" she wondered.

Ren stared into her green eyes. She was worried, worried he'd be gone as fast as he'd arrived. "For a long while," he said. He saw the change in her expression when he said that, whether it was happiness, relief, or even both.

Ren stared at Kelsey, a rather curious smile on his face. "You've grown up. And you've gotten beautiful." Her freckled face was beet red, and he loved it.

"If anyone's changed, it's you," she told him. "I barely even recognized you. Your hair's gotten so long, and you've gotten taller than me."

Kelsey's two friends approached awkwardly. "Ren, this is Jessica and Lisa," Kelsey introduced.

"Pleasure," he said, giving a brief but natural introduction.

"Likewise. Kelsey's told us much about you," one of them said. Ren deemed that she was clearly the outspoken one between the two.

"Doesn't surprise me," he said with a smile. No, it definitely did not surprise him.

"Are you working today, or are you off?" Kelsey asked Ren.

"A little of both, actually," he replied. "These remaining items are work-related, but it's at my leisure. I am on call should work come in, though."

At his leisure. How Kelsey wished she had work at her leisure. "Where are you staying? Do you need a place?" she asked.

"No. I've got a hotel at the moment, and the construction for my new house is almost completed. Which reminds me, another reason why I initially called you," he said. "You interested in a career change, by any chance?"

"Me, work with you? I'd be grateful, thank you!" she responded, ecstatic over his offer.

"Ah, I owe you anyway. Call it a little appreciation from me for being there when no one else was."

Kelsey looked at him with concern, but he only smiled. Her eyes dropped to the ground, unable to meet his own. Ren raised her head, forcing her to look at him.

"I'm fine, Kelsey. I've put the past behind me and come to terms with everything." He ran his index finger along her cheek. He said that with honesty in his voice, but she still didn't feel fully convinced.

"Kelsey told us you guys have a lot of history," Lisa said, "but never how much."

"We grew up together," Ren said back. "She helped me out a lot in the past. I wasn't exactly the best of kids. But Kelsey never left my side, no matter what. And for that, I'm eternally grateful."

"I didn't do anything, though," Kelsey said back. And it was the truth. She hadn't done anything. She regretted it every day.

"You did more than you know," Ren said back. "It takes a special kind of person to do what you did for me."

"What do you do for work, anyway?" Kelsey asked, suddenly interested in changing the subject.

Ren pondered how to explain it to her. "It's complicated," he said. "But I guess in simple terms, we're something like bounty hunters."

"Isn't that really dangerous?" she asked.

"It can be, but we take that risk," he said back. Guess that was the nature of the profession. They all came with their own set of troubles and dangers, after all.

"Bounty hunting. What would I even do in a place like that?" Kelsey wondered.

"You'd be an assistant. We have many more jobs than just the hunting part, believe me. There are a lot of logistics that go into it."

"An assistant? I guess that makes sense. Have to start somewhere."

"I think you misunderstand." She looked at him in confusion. "You'd be *my* assistant. And I really need the help, too," he added.

"Oh," she said, her cheeks turning red with the heat of embarrassment. "What do I do about school, though? Are you even going?"

Ren released a heavy sigh. "Unfortunately, yes." Kelsey couldn't hold back her laughter. "I'll be finishing up the remainder of my studies while I'm here," Ren continued. "I've already done the paperwork. Back to the same school I left in the first place. Although transferring in in the middle of senior year isn't the best idea, my father said I 'absolutely had to finish.'"

"I can already tell this is going to be a blast," he said sarcastically. "People don't forget things as easily as you might be thinking. I'll likely only have you and Marcus to rely on."

Kelsey could tell the whole thing was weighing heavily on him. Wait, did he say Marcus? "Marcus. You mean Marcus Allagash?" she asked.

"Yeah. You know him?"

"I've got a couple classes with him, though we haven't talked much." She was about to say something when Ren's phone rang. His expression immediately grew serious the moment he looked at the number.

"Talk to me," he said, answering the phone.

"The target's been spotted," the person on the other end answered. "Just south of your position. I'll send everything to you now. Doesn't look like he'll be any trouble, just pissed off the wrong people."

"Got it. I'll take care of it."

"Ren, watch your back. Something doesn't feel right. There are far too many shades here. It's like they're all gathering."

"I noticed. I'll be sure to keep a lookout. See you back at headquarters."

Ren quickly texted Marcus before putting his phone back in his pocket. "Sorry girls, duty calls," he said. "Kelsey, I'll pick you up tomorrow. We have a lot to catch up on. It was nice to meet you," Ren said to Jessica and Lisa. And just like that, he was gone, only this time, his return was already assured.

Two

Making Up for Lost Time

"I haven't been back in three years," Ren said to himself. "Alright, let's get this over with."

He walked through the front door and made his way to the principal's office. He didn't spot a single person in the hallways on his way there, which was odd. This was a high school. There were always people hanging out in the halls. He couldn't tell if this was a good thing or bad.

He had to remind himself of what Kelsey told him. He's changed a lot in these last three years. No one would probably even recognize him anymore.

Ren knocked on the door to the principal's office. "Come in," the principal said. Ren opened the door and stepped into the room.

The principal sat at his desk, looking at some papers. He looked the same as Ren remembered. Dressed in a black suit, his slightly large stomach protruded out just a bit. His brown hair was cut short, and his beard trimmed.

"You haven't changed a bit," Ren said to him.

The principal looked up from his paperwork. "Do I know you?" he asked.

"I guess Kelsey was right; no one will recognize me." The principal just stared at Ren.

Ren motioned to the chair, and the principal gestured for him to sit.

"What can I help you with, young man?" the principal asked.

"It's been a long time. I guess I should start by apologizing for all the trouble I caused you back then. James, it's me, Ren Nightwalker," surprising him with the first name basis. "Powers, memories, and all."

The principal's eyes went wide. "I see. Then you've finally returned." The principal came around and dropped to one knee. "Welcome back, Your Highness."

"James, you know how I feel about the bowing in the human realm. I may be the prince of the vampires, but monsters don't exist to humans, remember? If they catch wind of our existence before they are ready, then who knows what catastrophe will occur."

"I know, but it's been a while. Thought I was overdue." Ren grinned at his snarky remark before handing him a stack of paperwork. His transfer documents. The principal took the paperwork and examined it quickly.

"If it's okay, I want to pick your brain a bit," Ren said. "As I have just returned, I'm still lacking in information. There are many things I don't know yet. What's going on around here lately?"

"You mean that increase in shades?" James asked. It could only be about that, so he was certain it was the topic of Ren's conscience. And in response, Ren nodded, confirming his belief.

"To be honest, I have no idea why their numbers started increasing. It's like something is gathering them here," James admitted.

"Do you think Verin could be planning something?" Ren wondered.

"You think he's making a move?"

"I'm not sure. He's been sticking with the same tactics for a while now. But the number of shades has been increasing drastically. Soon we won't be able to hold them all off."

"Their numbers are becoming a problem. Only my magic keeps them away from the school, but Beastkin aren't the strongest magic users, as you know," James said.

"Yeah, I know. You're extremely gifted for your race. If it was anyone else, they wouldn't be able to handle protecting the school."

"Do you have a plan?" James asked him.

"I'm going to talk to my father. I'm not sure what's going to happen, but we need to start making bigger strides in this war. We need to take the fight to them."

"Isn't that what you guys in Trinity are doing?"

"It's not enough. Our victories thus far are like small ripples in a vast ocean."

"It worked in India. That's why you guys came here, isn't it?" James questioned. The conversation was starting to turn.

"It worked in India because the shades were never this numerous, and Verin was pretty quiet."

The room was silent for a moment. A heavy air loomed over them.

"That doesn't bode well for us then. I'll think about the situation and let you know if I come up with anything," James said.

"Thanks, we need the help."

"You should let Marcus know too."

"I already did. We're meeting later to discuss it."

Ren got up from his chair and walked to the door. "See you tomorrow," he said and closed the door behind him. He walked back to his car parked in the parking lot. A silver Lamborghini Huracan. He opened the door, pushed the start button, and drove off.

His next destination was the house he had built. Okay, maybe the word house was a bit of an exaggeration. Ren pushed a button on his rear-view mirror, and a large gate with tigers on the posts swung inward.

He drove down the single road with a line of trees with pink leaves on both sides, following it until it circled in front of a large two-story Spanish-style mansion. In front of the house was a fountain of a tiger sitting proudly.

Ren parked the car out front and walked into the house. He walked around to check everything out. A group of men had just finished moving all the remaining furniture into place.

Seeing everything in order, he examined the remaining rooms. A full-grown tiger was lying on the carpet in one of them. Its white fur was like touching a cloud.

"Nidar, there you are," Ren said, scratching him on the side of the face and under his chin. The tiger purred with pleasure. "I just stopped by for a minute to check-in. I'll be back later."

Ren gave the animal he called his companion one last touch before leaving. Trinity was located at the edge of town. It was easy to miss if you weren't looking for it. The empty warehouses next to it were abandoned and completely inaccessible. All the doors and windows were boarded up.

Ren parked behind the building in a spot that had a sign displaying his name, and his wasn't the only one. Every spot in the lot had one. Out front, the sign above the entrance had no words, only a symbol. A flaming bird with its wings extended out. A phoenix, the symbol of Trinity.

Ren entered, and everyone greeted him. He sat down at the counter and ordered a drink. On the surface, it appeared as a normal bar. In truth, it was anything but.

Trinity was founded by Ren's father, some three hundred years ago. It was through Trinity that Ren and all its members found work. They were the resistance. And Ren was no teenager. His youthful appearance only disguised him like so.

"Hey, Jay," Ren said, greeting the bartender.

"Hey, Ren. I wasn't sure if you were going to show. What have you been up to today?"

"Making the finishing arrangements for when the others arrive. Is my father here?"

"Nah, he left a while ago. Something about business he needed to attend to. Any words on the shades?" Jay asked.

"Nothing so far. James Wilson said he's looking into it."

"So you met with him?" Jay asked. James was well-known within Trinity's ranks, so it boasted no surprise.

"He's the principal at my high school," Ren told him.

"Don't you think you're a little old to be attending high school, Ren?" asked one of the people in the bar.

"Not my idea! It was my father's, for who knows what reason. I should be here fighting instead of attending a school for human children."

"I don't blame you," said Jay. "You complete all your jobs perfectly. And you've still got the most rifts of anyone in Trinity."

"I'm sure Leo has his reasons," a familiar voice said. Marcus Allagash walked into the bar. He clapped Ren on the back and sat down next to him. "If he wants you to go, it's for a reason. He knows what he's doing. After three hundred years, we know that better than anyone."

"I don't disagree. It doesn't make it any more irritating, though. It's good that you're here, actually. I wanted to talk about finding a new solution to dealing with the shades. We're already rifting them as fast as we can, but there are just too many. They only keep coming. We won't be able to rift them all like this," Ren said.

"I know; I've been thinking the same thing," Marcus said back. Like always, he and Ren were on the same page.

"James said he'd help and look into it," Ren continued. "He's noticed the increase and agrees it's a problem. At this rate, we won't be able to withstand them."

"James? James Wilson? If anyone can help, he can."

"We came back to America to start forcing Verin's hand. We came here so we can finally win this war," Ren said, and Marcus nodded in agreement. "We can't do that if we don't change our approach."

"That's easier said than done."

"Not if we wipe out his entire army and take out his leading forces. If we dwindle him enough, he'll have to surrender eventually."

"If we're to force Verin's hand, we'll need more information on his plans. We're at a total disadvantage without it, and that's even harder to do than take out all the shades," Marcus added. "The dude's a ghost. No one knows what he's up to or even where he is."

"Problem number two," Ren said back. "Which I think we'll solve along the way."

"Problem number one, then. Wipe out his forces. You got any ideas on how to do that?" Marcus asked.

"A couple, yeah. We find a way to gather them in one place."

Ren laid out his plans for finally taking down Verin and ending the war. They were thorough and well thought out, but not without holes. Holes that currently were impossible to fill.

Luck was probably on their side the entire time because a phone call with an auspicious job opportunity came while they were discussing. Jay answered the phone and wrote down all the information he could get before it was transferred to them.

"Hey Ren, I think I found a start to your mass takedown plans," Jay told him.

"A job?" Ren asked.

"The target is Alexander Nickleson: international terrorist, drug dealer, and murderer. He's also got his hands in prostitution and human trafficking. This guy's the real deal. According to the intel, he's in this town on business. Probably something illegal. He's on his luxury yacht just off the shoreline. Expect heavy resistance, though. You're free to take them out as you please. You're only confirmed death is Alexander's."

"How much?" Ren asked.

"A lot?"

"How much a lot?"

"One hundred million."

Marcus whistled, and the rest of the people in Trinity looked impressed too. One hundred million dollars made this job one of their biggest yet and came with the danger necessary to back it up.

"We use the boat," Ren quickly realized. "Load it with as many shades as we can get after killing Alexander and his help, then we send it out to sea and blow it sky high."

"My thoughts exactly," Jay said back. "Alexander moves around a lot to avoid being tied as expected. I suspect we have tomorrow, the day after at the latest, before he disappears. So, let's get to work, shall we?"

Three

Targets

R en hid behind the wall. His target was pacing back and forth and talking on the phone. He appeared to be arguing with whoever was on the other end of the line.

Ren reached down and drew a dagger he had hidden in his combat boots when the target moved into the kitchen, tossing his phone onto the table.

In seconds, Ren closed the distance between them. He put one hand over the man's mouth, and the other plunged the dagger into his temple.

His target dropped to the floor in Ren's arms. Ren leaned him against one of the base cabinets, then wiped the blood on his sleeve and sheathed the dagger back in his boot. Lying there as nothing but an empty husk, Ren still found no fault in his lack of emotions. He didn't bear any grudges; it was just business.

With a snap of Ren's finger, the body suddenly erupted into flames. The flames lasted only a few seconds, spreading over the corpse until it was a pile of ashes. Then, the fire disappeared, leaving not a trace of its presence. Magic.

Ren immediately contacted Trinity to report the mission status. Jay answered, as he always did, their conversation brief but direct.

"Jay, it's me. The mission is complete," Ren told him.

"Already? You must be looking forward to the mission. That was fast. Faster than usual, even."

"I always am. Is everyone ready?"

"We're all good on our side. We'll be waiting on you and Marcus. Be here at fifteen hundred."

Ren looked at the time. "Fifteen hundred," he repeated. "I've got to go. I start school soon. See you then."

Ren's car was parked two streets over to avoid suspicion. He really didn't want to deal with this, but his father was adamant about it, so he'd just have to deal with it. Today was officially his first day, and being late or merely not showing up wouldn't look good, not that he cared. But he didn't want to make James's life more difficult either.

He pulled into the parking lot with ten minutes to spare. After finding a spot, he headed to his first class. The room was already full when he got there, and a woman he knew to be the teacher stood in front, writing something on the smart board. Technically, the class didn't officially start for several minutes.

Ren opened the door and walked into the classroom. All eyes turned to him, and everyone dove into hushed talk among each other. Rumor had spread fast of Ren's return, especially after he made an appearance in person. As he promised Kelsey, the day after his arrival, he picked Kelsey up so they could catch up. That happened to be right after school, when everyone was leaving. There was a huge crowd, and it caused quite a stir.

As far as he knew, many of them had put Ren's past actions behind them, especially after he directly apologized to them. He'd hoped to make amends and, therefore, the situation less awkward. That's when they found out he was taking classes there. He just hoped it remained as such.

Yup, here we go. Just wonderful, Ren thought. His only solace came from a close relationship with the teacher of this class, Genene Perkins. She used to be friends with his mother, which meant she and Ren went way back. And, of course, there was the whole monster thing.

"Genene," he greeted, giving a slight incline of his head.

"There you are, Ren. I was worried you weren't going to show. Take a seat. There's an empty one next to

Kelsey." Kelsey waved at him, and he smiled, before finding his seat next to her.

"*Shubh prabhaat,* Kelsey." His use of strange words surprised her and the rest of the room. "Oh, sorry. Old habit," he said after realizing.

"You speak other languages," she asked. But if she thought about it, it really wasn't all that surprising.

"A lot. That one happened to be Hindi. I learned it back in India, obviously."

"Let me guess. That means good morning, right?" she asked.

"Bingo," he said back.

"You have got to drop that habit, man," Marcus said, walking into the room. He set his stuff down in the seat in front of Ren, and they bumped fists.

"Yup, working on it. Old habits die hard," Ren responded. And it was the truth. Speaking in other languages was a habit from working in Trinity after all.

Before Ren and Marcus could distract the class any further, Genene got started. It wasn't halfway through that she handed out a worksheet. The scores they received would demonstrate their understanding of the subject.

"Ren, what are you doing?" the teacher asked him. He was talking to Kelsey and doing something with his hands. "Stop flirting and do the work I assigned, please."

Ren looked at her with confusion. "I'm not flirting. I finished like five minutes ago. I noticed she was struggling, so I'm helping her figure out the answers."

"You're done already?" she asked, shocked. He got up and handed her the paper and turned to look at Marcus.

"I'm surprised you're not done yet," he said to him.

"Oh, I am done. I finished around the time you did; I was just too lazy to get up and give her the paper." Ren shook his head, like he'd been expecting to hear that.

He got every question correct. Not that I expected any less, the teacher thought. She released a heavy sigh.

"Alright, fine. I know how close you two are. If you plan on helping her, do so; just try not to distract the rest of the class. Otherwise, I'll have to separate you two."

The look on Ren's face was full of disdain. He was being treated like a child, even when Genene knew he was several times her own age. It was an act to keep up with the high school facade, but he didn't like it. Humans.

"We'll keep to ourselves, promise," Kelsey said.

"You two have always been close," one of the students said. "Ren's not even back a week, and you're already all over each other."

Kelsey's entire face turned bright red as the class burst out laughing. Ren just looked at Marcus, and the two shrugged at each other.

When the last bell of the day rang, the other kids rushed out of the building. Ren and Marcus exchanged looks, then nodded. With a quick goodbye to Kelsey, they grabbed their things and headed for the parking lot.

Ren pulled out of the parking lot and off to the side of the road. Marcus pulled up behind him in a matching black Lamborghini. Besides the black body, the only difference between the two were Marcus's spoiler, and shade of headlights.

"Let's go," Marcus said. "We have a half hour until the meeting time. We have to hit the boat at three."

Ren put his signal on, put the car into drive, and pulled forward. Marcus followed behind Ren for the entire half-hour drive to Trinity. They pulled into the parking lot behind the building and headed inside.

The four other team members accompanying Ren and Marcus on the mission were already gathered and ready. Nathan Adams, Trina Heely, Nicolas Carry, and Juliana Haynes were chosen among the volunteers. A solid team with lots of experience with rifting shades, high-end target assassinations, and explosions.

"Good, you made it," Jay said when he saw them. "Everyone's gathered and waiting."

"Perfect," Ren said back. "Marcus and I were thinking about starting early. Things got done faster than I thought. I want to go over the plan one more time with everyone, and then we can get started." The team gathered around a table, and Ren began reciting the plan.

"First, Marcus and I will tie off the ship to keep it in place. Meanwhile, Trina, Nate, Nick, and Julie will provide cover from any incoming shades which will most likely be gathering."

"Once the coast is clear, Julie will use her magic to lure in the shades, and the others will board the ship. Nate, you stay behind until Julie is finished, then you two will join up with the others on deck. I will find and kill Alexander. Julie, I want you with me as backup. I don't know how many guards he has; I want someone at my six, just in case. Nick and Nate will plant the GPS and explosives. Finally, Marcus and Trina will kill the guards on the boat as they come. Do whatever you can to draw those shades in."

"Once the boat is filled with shades, we cut the lines and send it out to sea using the GPS. When it's out far enough, flip the switch and send it to oblivion. Any questions?"

He looked around the room, but no one said anything.

"What if something goes wrong, and we have to improvise?" Nathan asked.

"If you need to, you have my permission to act of your own accord. I trust each of you to make decisions where it's necessary. And if the plan does fall apart, do whatever you need to do. Is everybody ready?"

"We just have to finish sorting all the explosives," Nick said back.

"I want to double-check the surrounding area around the target," said Trina.

Ren nodded. "You've got fifteen minutes, then we're heading out. I need to change anyway. Get to it."

Marcus checked on the others while Ren went to his father's office to change. Trina had finished going over the area on a map. It was covered in red marks and circles and notes.

"Anything interesting?" he asked her.

"This is the best vantage point," she said, pointing to a spot on the map. It's got a high elevation and provides protection from the buildings surrounding it."

"We should hit the bridge," Marcus suggested. "It passes beneath the elevated railway. If we come from there, we don't have to worry about watching our backs, and it's good cover. We can sneak around the side undetected and secure the boat. With the right timing, that sector is one big blind spot. They won't even see us coming."

"The hardest part is drawing the shades," Trina said. "I'm not sure how we're going to be able to draw all those shades in that fast."

"The death and bloodshed will draw them no problem," Marcus said back. "Shades are naturally drawn to monsters. All six of us together in one place is going to draw a lot of attention, especially with Ren and me there. We're like an open faucet when we want to be."

"I don't understand how you two have such strong control over your energies, especially when they are as strong as they are."

"The older you get, the easier it is to control your ki."

"Right," she said after a brief pause.

Marcus started laughing. "When you get to our age, then you'll understand."

Nick and Nate came over carrying six pouches each. They were attached to their belt with three on the left side and three on the right.

"We're done sorting the explosives," Nick said. "Nate, you, and I get six pouches each," he said to Trina. Nate handed six pouches of explosives to her. "These are top-of-the-line and very hard to notice. They're small in size but pack a big punch."

Ren walked toward them in an outfit they were all very familiar with. A white t-shirt adorned his bodice. The t-shirt had strands of light brown thread that seemed to mix with the white. It hugged tight, revealing the lean, solid layers of muscle along his upper body.

Black pants and black leather combat boots decorated his lower body. A brown belt with a golden square buckle covered his waist over the t-shirt.

A deep mahogany leather jacket with a high collar sat open on his frame. The inside was lined with gray hare fur with a peppering of hazel. A hood rested comfortably behind him, the back of the jacket stopping behind his knees and the front just below his waist.

Ren loaded two Berettas and placed them in the holsters on the sides of his legs. Weapons he did or did not use for assassinations depending on the target. Why? Because of the noise, why else. And silencers only worked so well.

Strapped to his back was a golden one-handed longsword layered in intricacy. Its design had clearly been painstakingly sculpted and crafted.

"Let's go," Marcus said. "Julie, you ride with Ren. Trina, you'll ride with me. Nate and Nick, you two are together."

The six of them loaded their gear into their respective cars.

"Ready?" Ren asked her.

"Let's go," she said back.

Ren turned it over and put it into drive. They flew down the roads at speeds that were definitely illegal. Once their destination was near, Ren slowed down and came to a stop on a curved road at the end of the tunnel. The outside of the tunnel was open and supported by columns, which gave a clear view of the ocean below.

Marcus and Trina pulled up next to them. Ren motioned to Marcus, who seemed to catch the drift. Just within view, near the shoreline, was a large black and white yacht.

Four

The Beginning of the End

Ren and Marcus drove out of the tunnel and pulled over to the side of the road.

Ren opened the trunk and pulled out two rolls of rope, handing one off to Marcus. "Help me tie these ropes. Nate, hand me one of those EMPs," he said. Nate reached into one of the pouches attached to his belt and pulled out a small, thin, black disk, tossing it to Ren, who put it in his pocket.

Alexander's yacht was visible just off the shoreline, with the sun still long off from setting. "Ren, we're sitting ducks out here," Marcus said.

"I know. Get ready to move," Ren said back. "We hit fast and hard. Marcus, if you would."

Marcus proceeded to the water's edge, already aware of Ren's motives. Like Ren, he, too, had a golden sword. It remained sheathed at his hip rather than his back, where a silver and blue bow was strapped. He had no quiver, no arrows, only the bow. Drawing it, Marcus twisted both limbs in opposite directions in the middle. The bow split in two and shrank into a pair of daggers with a blue blade and silver edge.

Dipping the blades into the water, he slashed upward, and a path made from ice formed following the slash.

"Move!" Ren said. The six of them took to the ice and headed for the yacht. The ice path they ran on stopped before it could reach their target, leaving Marcus to extend the path. Now, with the yacht in reach, it was Ren's turn. In one quick motion, he reached into his pocket and threw the EMP device at the boat. It hit the stern, just below the water. A flash broke through from beneath the water, and the boat came to a stop.

Ren jumped into the air, his feet hitting the starboard side of the yacht, and stuck. Running vertically up the side, he leaped over the rail and touched down on the deck. At the same time, Marcus suddenly started growing, his face elongated, and his fingernails extended into claws. Light hazel brown fur appeared over his entire body, his clothes disappearing, and he grew ears and a tail. A werewolf.

Digging his claws into the yacht, Marcus climbed up the yacht, reaching the top around the same time as Ren, returning to his human form on the deck.

"Everyone, get to your positions," Marcus ordered. The six of them paired up and separated.

"Come on, let's find Alexander," Ren said to Julie. He drew the guns holstered at his legs and flipped the safety switches off, then kicked open the nearest door.

Onward they went through the boat, taking down guards and drawing in shades with their ki.

Without even looking, Ren held his arm out to the side as they passed a hallway and fired his gun. There was a thump, and a body hit the floor. Ren closed his eyes. The flow of blood flooded his senses, overcoming his sound and smell. Even with his eyes closed, it was like seeing completely clear.

He moved his arm around the corner and fired his gun three times in quick succession, killing three more guards. Then, they turned and started running.

"How's our time? Are we almost to Alexander's location?" she asked.

"Nearly there," he responded.

"Do you sense him?" she asked, referring to the use of his vampiric powers.

"His blood flow, yes. The number of hired guns makes it difficult to pick him out, but I've still got him. Thankfully Alexander is such a pig that his blood flow gives away all of his emotions."

Ren stopped in front of a bare wall. Julie readied her weapon as he shot at the wall, then rushed right through it. The wall gave way like paper, and he stood inside a hidden room with a single wooden door. It was dark and empty, save for the single desk, chair, and a lit oil lamp.

"He's getting away, come on," he said. Exiting the room, the two of them turned left down a hallway before stopping at a window.

Ren broke the window by shooting it with his gun and held his arm out the window. Blood, three different flows, and moving fast. From the erratic flow of one in particular, he knew it had to be Alexander. "Three… two… one…" he fired as a raft came into view with three people on it.

A man in a white suit suddenly lurched and dropped into the water. Even from the back, he matched Alexander's description exactly. The two guards on the raft ran over to the side to grab him when Ren fired again, and the raft exploded.

Out of nowhere, a heavy impact into the side of the yacht sent it gliding across the water, and a wave of water came crashing up the side. Ren turned quickly and draped his jacket over him. Julie covered him with her body, shielding him from the water that got in.

Ren looked up at her. "Thanks," he said.

"You're welcome."

"That impact would have been the rest of the team luring the shades onto the boat. We need to get back to the deck and regroup," he suggested.

"Do you remember the way back?" Julie asked. Then she noticed his intense focus on the broken window. "What's wrong? Did the water hit you?"

"No, I've got a better idea than running all the way back."

Placing his hand on the wall, a pulse of blue energy rippled down his arm, into his hand, then to the wall. The wall exploded outward, leaving a giant hole in the side.

"Are you insane?" Julie asked. "If that amount of water touches you, you'll die!"

Ren knelt down with his back to Julie and put his hands behind him. "I know. But it's the quickest way. Now climb on and wrap your legs around me." With a frustrated sigh, she climbed on, and he stood up, allowing her to tighten her grip.

Mere feet below the edge of the hole, water churned violently. With one mighty leap, Ren cleared the opening, grabbing the edge to swing himself around. His feet hit the side of the yacht, and he immediately began running vertically up to the deck. If only he could fly. Sometimes he really wished he had his wings.

Atop the deck, Ren and Julie found the remainder of the team. They stood by the starboard side railing, the same side they'd first boarded from. Whatever was happening below, it had all their attention. A literal army of shades poured onto the ship through a massive hole. Well, now the shaking made sense. However, their plan may have worked a little too well. There were far too many shades for this one boat to hold.

"This yacht isn't going to hold," Ren said. "We need to get to shore before we're overrun."

"Exactly how do you plan on getting back without the remainder of them coming after us?" Nick asked.

"Marcus," was Ren's only response.

"Already working on it," Marcus said back. He placed the ends of his two ice daggers together and twisted in opposite directions, but in reverse from when he did it to separate them. The daggers merged and formed back into a bow. The only problem, no arrows.

Drawing the string, an icy blue arrow formed out of thin air. In bow form, Marcus had an unlimited number of magic arrows, so long as his own magic lasted. He shot the arrow down at the water. It pierced through and disappeared. Moments later, a pillar of ice wide enough for all of them to squeeze on shot into the air, just within reach.

"Go, move!" Marcus said anxiously. They were cutting time too close for comfort. With everyone on the pillar of ice, Marcus fired another arrow and created another pillar. All six of them moved to the new pillar simultaneously, watching as the one they had just been standing on cracked and shattered afterward.

There were so many shades it was disgusting. By now, the yacht was entirely full of them. They swarmed the deck like insects, spilling off over the side and into the water below. It was a good thing water killed shades, thanks to its purity. Even still, there were so many remaining that hadn't yet boarded.

"We can't wait any longer. Nick, take her out," Ren said.

"We're almost to the shore," Marcus said over them.

Nick grabbed a remote control consisting of a switch and a single nob from his equipment. Once all six of them were safely on solid ground again, he flipped a button, and the engines on the yacht roared to life. It inched forward, and Nick turned a nob to the left. They all watched as the boat turned left out to sea.

"Shades, incoming!" one of them said.

"Ren!" Marcus called.

"On your six!" Ren said back.

The two of them got back-to-back as the remnants of the shade army surrounded them.

The rest of the team set their gazes on Ren as he reached behind him for the golden sword strapped to his back. They knew what that meant and got right beside him. He drew the blade and spun it in his hand in one smooth rhythm. The blade had an extra-long golden collar, with unreadable inscriptions formed into it on the top. Even more of them were pressed into the fuller of the blade, which was nearly the size of the sword itself.

Simultaneously, Marcus placed one hand on the handle of his sword and the other on the sheath near the habaki: the blade collar. Unlike Ren's double edge sword, Marcus's was a katana with a golden blade with a single curved horn in the center of the spine. It more resembled a lightning bolt in style.

He took a stance like a quick draw and drew his sword in a flash. Spinning right, Ren spun left at the same time. The pommels of their swords struck each other, and a spinning golden blade of energy shot out from where they touched.

The golden energy released from Ren's and Marcus's swords ripped apart the shades surrounding them. But it didn't wipe out all of them.

Ren backed up, making the others back up along with him. The shades started gathering together. He looked at Marcus, who nodded. Ren swung his sword, and a wave of golden energy raged through the shades, obliterating the ones in its path.

Julie and Trina, who were busy guarding Nate and Nick, found an opening after Ren's and Marcus's attack and used it to take out countless shades. Their combined attacks left little for improvement, however, as the shades started closing in on them. There were just too many.

"Hold strong!" Ren said. He and Marcus swung their swords and released another powerful attack, thinning the shades' numbers.

Ren momentarily turned to catch a glimpse of the yacht. It was almost out of sight by now. Far enough away to not cause any trouble or draw more attention than it needed to.

"Nick, blow it," Ren ordered.

Nick pressed the switch on the detonator. There was a flash followed by the sound of an explosion as a giant ball of fire shot into the air.

The explosion caused a much-needed distraction as it got the shades' attention. Working together, all six of them now joined the battle, rifting every shade in the area until they were gone.

Ren and Marcus sheathed their golden swords, and the golden aura that bubbled off them disappeared. Said to be made by gods, those were two of the most powerful weapons in existence. That which was known only as a 'heaven's blade,' of which there were only thirteen in existence.

So, this is the power of a Heaven's Blade, Nick thought. *Their strength is off the charts.*

And it was true. With powers like theirs, Ren and Marcus were literal monsters, not just in terms of species. As one of only thirteen existences in the world, their powers and responsibilities had to be just as heavy to match the weight. One did not simply obtain the title of Heaven's Blade for nothing. You had to be chosen, as the weapon that chose you was proof of your strength.

Ren looked around but felt nothing out of the ordinary. There were no shades remaining or spectators that shouldn't be there. In order to be absolutely sure of the state of the yacht, the shades, and the mission target, the six of them watched the yacht burn in a large ferocious roar of flames. Slowly it sank below the surface of the water and disappeared, leaving a trail of steam in its wake.

Marcus rubbed the back of his head. "Maybe we used too many explosives," he said.

"It's fine. They got the job done," Ren said back.

"Only you would say that, you pyro," Marcus responded.

Ren shrugged off the comment. "Let's just return to Trinity."

"Ren, you're bleeding," Julie noticed.

Ren felt the warm touch of liquid drop onto his hand. With the color of deep crimson, it could only be one thing, blood. It dripped from his nose, and he wiped it away before reaching behind him. Three loops were sown into the leather of his belt. Each loop held a vial filled with the same crimson-red liquid.

Ren pulled one out, uncorked it, then poured the contents into his mouth. He put the cork back on the vial and put it back in the loop.

"Are you alright?" Nick asked. "Do you need to rest, go to the hospital?

"I'm alright, don't worry. No injuries here," Ren lied. True, he may not have been injured, but that wasn't why he was bleeding.

Marcus stared at Ren with an intense gaze. Ren wasn't fooling him; they'd known each other far too long for that. He wasn't injured, but something was definitely wrong.

Five

Where Evil Sleeps

Ren pulled into Trinity's parking lot after the long drive back from the mission. It was dead quiet as he and the rest of the team walked inside, the anticipation of hearing the news keeping them on the edge of their seats.

Ren reached into his pocket and pulled out his credit card. "Warriors of fortune, drinks on me!" he shouted. The bar erupted into cheers.

"Well done, everyone," Jay said. "We made a grand effort today. And Ren, your father is here. He's in the back. Said he had to grab something and use the can."

"Like, like in that order?" Ren asked, overly curious.

"I hope so," Jay responded. They started laughing.

A man with bleach-blond hair the same as Ren's walked into view from behind a doorway. A clean, trimmed goatee and eyes the color of emeralds made him unforgettable.

Ren approached his father, and they embraced. "Hey, Dad."

"Ren, how did the mission go?"

"It went well." Ren gave him the details of their actions. His explanation took them to the bar, where they sat with a drink in their hand.

"I see. It sounds like we really dealt a heavy blow to Verin's ranks. That's something we haven't been able to accomplish for some time."

"Maybe not," Ren said back. "Julie and I were talking on the car ride back. She felt the whole thing was a setup. There were too many shades even for us. Almost like Verin wanted us to draw them in and kill them. I know regular shades aren't capable of following too many complicated orders at once, but if they were being controlled directly, that would be different. We have no idea how large their forces actually are."

Ren's father released a rather heavy sigh. "That doesn't sound good. If Julie's feeling is correct, Verin might have had a goal behind today. He's starting to calculate and make his move, the same as we are."

Ren slammed his fist on the bar top. "Damn it! Are we just playing right into his hands? Is that what we've been doing this whole time?"

"Their forces far outnumber ours. If we go at them head-on, we'll lose too many of us. It's not worth the risk. We need to find another way. Perhaps it's time we cut the snake off at the head. We start taking out their leaders."

Ren set his new half-empty drink down. "Are you talking about Verin's four generals? They're not ready for that. Only you and we Heaven's Blades can fight them."

Ren's father set his gaze on him. "I know," he said.

Ren understood exactly what his father was saying. "I see." There was a long pause from Ren before he spoke again. "Okay, I'll grab Marcus. You're right about his generals. We're Heaven's Blades for a reason. It's time to show why. We take down his four generals."

"You should let Kelsey know," Ren's father said. "You'll be away again. She'll go nuts if you pull another disappearing act and don't tell her."

Ren grinned at the thought of Kelsey scolding him for leaving without telling her. "That's a wise idea," he said. "I don't want to die just yet." His father started laughing. "Besides, I made a promise that I have to keep."

Click. The sudden sound drew Ren's and his father's attention. Jay was leaning over the phone, now on the receiver. Based on his expression, it wasn't a good phone call.

"This... could be troublesome."

"What is it, Jay?" Ren's father asked.

"A job. And by the sounds of it, a shady one. A house in Jerringtone Heights. It's gone dark. No lights, no sounds, no traffic. Empty, abandoned."

"Miasma?" Ren asked curiously.

"Worse. It's what's inside. Men go in, and they don't come out. And I mean *only* men."

The hair on Ren's arms suddenly shot up. "Shit. Marcus!" he called.

Marcus walked over to them from his spot. "What's up?" Then he noticed their serious expressions. "What's happened?"

"We've got a job. Jay, send the client my way."

"Ren, I mean it, be careful," Jay said. "If what's in that house is exactly what we think it is, Julie was right. Verin's making his move."

"Ren, just what the hell kind of job is this?" Marcus asked.

"A house flooded by miasma. Men who enter never leave."

Marcus's senses suddenly went wild with worry. "Men? Ren, you don't think…." His instincts were no doubt telling him the exact same as Ren's were telling him.

"I think so, yeah. And I really hope not. For all our sakes, pray that I'm wrong."

The house they were looking for was a two-story colonial made of brick. It had a two-car garage and a porch supported by four columns.

Ren and Marcus pulled to the side of the road a few streets away from the house. They crossed through yards until they came to the back of the house. Ren ran up the wall to the roof, and Marcus took the back door. He picked the lock and stepped into the darkness of the house, closing it behind him.

Ren dropped onto the roof of the garage, never making a sound. He grabbed the dagger strapped to his side and jammed the blade into the window where it locked. With one quick motion to the right, the blade easily cut through the lock. Then he lifted the window up and climbed through. He stood at one end of a bedroom that was completely empty. There wasn't a single piece of furniture in it.

Closing his eyes to concentrate, he searched for the flow of blood. There were two, one which he recognized was Marcus, still downstairs. The other, he didn't recognize. Someone was in here.

Ren opened the door at the other end of the room and stepped into the hallway, never making a sound. He sensed Marcus coming up the stairs, and when Marcus saw him, he walked up to him.

"I searched the first floor of the house but came up empty. There was no one down there."

"They're in there," Ren said, pointing to a room.

Standing outside the door, Ren readied his pistols and Marcus his ice daggers. Ren turned the nob. The door was unlocked. He opened it and stepped into the room, Marcus right behind him.

The outline of a figure in the bed was the first thing they saw. This was the person whose blood Ren had sensed, but something was wrong. The size of the outline was small, very small. Could it really be? Was their target a child?

Ren walked over to the bedside and gently peeled back the blankets. A small girl, not even in her teens by the look of it, was fast asleep. He bit back a heavy curse and raised his dagger.

Marcus's hand found Ren's wrist, stopping him. "Wait," he whispered.

"It has to be done, Marcus."

Of course he knew it had to be done. But part of him wouldn't let it. "She's a child."

"She *looks* like a child. Do not be deceived. She could be as old as either of us or only take on the appearance of a child. We need to rift her before she wakes."

The sleeping girl opened her eyes to see Ren and Marcus standing there. She jumped and moved away, throwing the blanket at them. "Stay away! I don't know where she is! Stay away!" She?

As if on cue, the door to the room slammed shut. They turned in the direction of the door, and the lights burst to life.

Six

The Demon of Lust

A figure appeared in the room next to the door. A woman, probably in her late thirties, with brown hair cropped to her shoulders. Her outfit was entirely erotic and completely revealing, leaving only the most private places covered. It was true, all of it. Verin was on the move. A monster subspecies to the demon race. Known for bewitching and sucking out the vitality of men, this woman was a succubus — an A-rank monster.

Wings shot out of her back, and she flew at them. Marcus intercepted her, using his bow to block her before her weight and momentum forced them to the ground. She pinned Marcus down, but he still resisted.

"Get the girl out of here. Go. I've got this!" he told Ren.

Ren immediately picked the girl up, holding her tightly. "We're getting you out of here. Do not let go of me, no matter what!" he told her. She held on to him like he was a lifeline, gripping his jacket tightly in her tiny hands.

With Marcus still holding back the woman, he ran for the door. Before he could get there, the woman managed to throw Marcus off and struck Ren with her claws. A wave of power overcame him, sending him flying into the wall. A-rank monsters were no joke, and she proved it. He tucked the girl close to him, careful to protect her from harm.

Marcus grabbed hold of her wrists from behind and threw her to the ground, pinning her below him. An evil smile escaped her pink lips before her eyes settled on him, and a pulse of magic released. A succubus's signature ability: charm. It made whoever she cast it on, man or woman, obey her.

Cocky brat. You were dead the moment you entered this house. Give me all of you.

"Now, release me." She waited for Marcus to let go, but he never moved, only further tightening his grip. *It's not working!*

She pushed him off her, and Marcus was on his feet before she could even come up with her next thought. Her instincts took over, and she leaped backward onto the bed.

"What did you do? Why can't I charm you?"

Marcus surprised her by responding with laughter. "Can't? No, it's not that you can't charm me; I simply didn't let you. I've had a thin barrier of magic around my body since before we even entered this house. Your little charm spell can't break through."

"When we came here believing we would come in contact with a succubus, we prepared ourselves for all of your tricks," Marcus continued.

Black energy started pouring out of the woman's body. Her magic enveloped the whole house in its tight embrace.

The sound of a gunshot suddenly rang out, followed by a cry of pain from the succubus. She fell to the ground, clutching her wounded shoulder. Ren had one of his Berettas pointed at her.

"Marcus, take the girl," he told him. "You're faster than me. Get her out of here, and I'll hold the succubus back." Ren was right. Marcus was the faster of the two of them being a werewolf. With his speed, he could get the girl out of danger faster, which meant a huge liability was gone.

The succubus shifted, ready to lunge at him, when Ren drew his remaining pistol and pointed it at her, stopping her in her tracks.

There was a moment of hesitation which Marcus took advantage of. He moved with incredible speed, taking the girl from Ren's protection, and disappeared through the door.

"No! Give me back my prey!" the succubus yelled.

"Prey? She's a child!" Ren yelled back. "Besides, succubi don't hunt women; only an incubus does."

"I'll have you know that I take no allegiance to men alone. A woman's vitality is just as satisfying. That child is an unripe fruit, but she'll grow into the perfect nutrition source."

Anger flooded through Ren's very being. With his ki cut off, so too was his monster energy. As a result, most monsters assumed him to be weak while they flaunted their own power. It made dealing with ones like this succubus all the more fulfilling.

"I've taken out a few Succubi in my time," he said. "But never have I wanted to kill one more than now." A wave of immense fear suddenly rushed over the succubus as Ren's monster energy exploded.

The woman was crushed under the fear, drowning in an ocean of his monster energy. His canines elongated into fangs and his eyes practically radiated power.

"It can't be. A real S-rank monster. A vampire!"

The whole room was swallowed in a blinding light as Ren unleashed his magic, obliterating the succubus. When the light faded, not even her body remained.

Marcus was waiting outside by his car when he saw Ren walking towards him. The guy was pissed, he could see it in how he walked, and he didn't blame him. The girl they rescued sat silently in the passenger seat of his car.

"How's the girl?" Ren asked. He was more worried about her at the moment.

"Quiet. You okay?" Marcus asked. Ren nodded back. "What do we do about her?"

"The only thing we can do. We find out where her parents are and hand her over." He knocked on the passenger window, and the girl stepped out. "What's your name?"

"Ellie," the girl said.

"Where are your parents? That woman took you, didn't she?" The girl shook her head, surprising him. But her next comment surprised him even more.

"That was my house. That woman came and killed everyone. She killed my mom and dad. I've been locked up there since, too afraid to leave."

When she started crying, the only thing he could do was put his hand on her head in an attempt to comfort her.

"You shouldn't have had to go through that. Who's willing to take care of you then?" Ren asked next. "Grandparents, aunts, uncles, even friends?" She shook her head.

"Daddy's mom and dad died a long time ago. Mommy's mom and dad don't talk to them anymore. They didn't like them being together, so mommy ran away with daddy. Daddy had a brother, but they don't know where he is. I've never met anyone else."

Damn. That made things much more complicated. Ren looked at Marcus, then he and Marcus knelt in front of her.

"We're really not supposed to do this, but if you don't have anyone else who can look after you, you can stay with one of us for the time being," Ren said. "Just know that there's a chance that someone from your family may come looking for you. Should that happen, you have to go with them." The girl just nodded, wiping her eyes with her sleeve.

"Would you rather stay with Ren or with me?" Marcus asked gently. "Either of us would be more than happy to look after you." The girl grabbed the lapel of Ren's jacket with her tiny hand. "I guess that settles it then."

Ren gently rubbed the top of her head, but she never let go of his jacket. Perhaps it had something to do with him being the first one to take her after the succubus appeared. After what she had just gone through, Ren's presence likely made her feel safe.

"Ren, if you're going to be taking her in, you should let everyone know and make the proper arrangements," Marcus said.

"I know. I'll need to talk to the proper authorities and agencies too. If we can't find someone to take her in, and only if she decides to stay with me, I'll adopt her."

"Then I think it best if we get going. We should get her out of here and bring her somewhere she'll feel safe."

"I agree, that's a good idea. It's getting late anyway. And I still need to report the success of the mission. You can crash at my place too," Ren said. "Come on, Ellie."

He helped her into the passenger seat of his car and buckled her in before getting in the driver's seat. Marcus pulled out first, and Ren followed behind him. He looked over to check on Ellie several times throughout the drive. With what she had gone through, he wasn't sure exactly what her mental state was at the moment.

That kind of thing can scar a child for life, especially losing her parents like that. She was a sweet kid, and he didn't want her to suffer any more than she already had. He had to navigate carefully.

They pulled up to the gate, and Marcus opened it with the opener Ren had given him. Being best friends and partners most of the time, Ren and Marcus always had a spare gate and house key for each other's place. That way they could come and go as they pleased.

Ren pulled into the four-car garage. It was already filled with two other vehicles, his favorite car, and a motorcycle. He helped Ellie out, and the three of them walked inside. A closet stood to the left, and a coat rack to the right. They took their shoes off and walked into the next open room, one of the many nodes within the house. It had a sofa and a recliner, along with a small table. Then, they continued on until they reached the living room.

Laying on the floor next to the couch was a fully grown white tiger. It raised its head when they entered. "I'm home Nidar," Ren said. "And I brought guests."

The tiger got up and walked over to them. Marcus scratched his head and underneath his chin. Nidar nibbled gently on his hand. "Yeah, I missed you too, bud."

"Nidar, this is Ellie. She's going to be staying with us from now on," Ren said. The tiger turned its blue eyes on her. She looked terrified and amazed at the same time. Ren placed his hand on her head and nodded, indicating that it was safe. That seemed to help calm her down.

Nidar rubbed his head against her. The tiger was unbelievably smart, so it was likely he had already sensed the tension and Ellie's emotions. "He likes you," Ren told her.

"It's a real tiger!" she said. Her expression was one most people had when they first met Nidar.

"I found him as a cub. For now, though, let's get you to bed; it's getting late," he said to Ellie. "You can sleep with Nidar if you want."

"You'll let me? Thanks Ren!" Ren chuckled, glad to see that she seemed happy. He just hoped that tonight would be the same for her.

"Come on. I'll show you to your new room." He led them away, Ellie's hand grasping a fistful of Nidar's fur.

Seven

Hunting Prey

Ren woke up as the first streaks of sunlight passed through his window. He looked at the time; six in the morning. His alarm was set for seven, so he climbed out of bed and checked on Ellie. She was asleep on her bed with her arms around Nidar. The peacefulness of her sleeping was a huge breath of relief. He really had been worried that she would be too scared to sleep.

The tension had taken its toll on his body, leaving him tired and hungry. For now, he would settle the latter and headed to the kitchen. Marcus walked in halfway through his meal.

"You're up earlier than usual," he said to Ren.

Ren sat his fork down on the table, leaning it against his plate. "Yeah, to be honest, I was pretty worried. I didn't sleep much."

Marcus sat down next to him. "Me neither. She's a good kid. No one should have to go through what she went through, least of all a child. I checked on her just before I came in. She's still asleep, with Nidar to boot."

A wave of relief overcame Ren when he heard that. "Same as when I checked on her then. Good."

Marcus helped himself to breakfast while Ren finished his own. Their entire conversation that followed was a discussion on the content of the mission with the succubus before Ren went to wake Ellie up.

Outside Ellie's room, he gently knocked on the door. "Ellie, are you awake?" There was no answer. "I'm coming in." He opened the door and entered her room. She was still asleep in the same position as before. Ren rubbed the top of Nidar's head. The white tiger opened its blue eyes.

"Come eat breakfast. Marcus is down there now. I'm going to wake Ellie." Nidar licked Ren's face, then climbed off the bed, stretched, and headed for the kitchen.

Ren gently roused Ellie from sleep. She stirred, then opened her eyes. "Ren?" she asked before yawning.

"How'd you sleep?" he asked. Admittedly, he was still worried she would tell him the opposite of how she looked.

"Good. The bed is comfortable." Relief filled him again. He only hoped it remained.

"I'm glad. You want breakfast?"

"Yes, please." She sat up and climbed out of bed. Ren took her hand and led her to the kitchen, as she hadn't been there before.

When Ren and Ellie got there, Marcus and Nidar were waiting. Ren sat Ellie down at the table. She sat comfortably in her chair, swinging her legs back and forth.

When breakfast was done, Ren placed it in front of her and Nidar and took a seat at the table again. Marcus took Ellie around the house after they finished, showing her all the rooms while Ren called his father.

"Hey, Ren," his father greeted. "It's unusual for you to call me in the morning."

"I know, but I need your help with something. Something happened with the mission yesterday. We were right. But this situation is a little delicate right now. It's best that you come over."

His father was quiet on the other end of the line. "Alright, I'll be there in twenty minutes."

"Thanks. See you when you get here." If anyone could help him, it was his father.

Only seconds after the call ended, Ren started coughing. Droplets of blood covered his hand, a trickle running down his nose. He returned to his room and opened the double doors to a wardrobe. Inside was a mini fridge filled with bags and portioned vials of a viscous red liquid: blood, the kind used for transfusions. He ripped the cork off one of the vials and gulped it down.

The side effects slowly faded. His breathing was still heavy, but he was mostly back to normal.

Damn it, he thought. *They're losing their effect. Not good. I'm reaching my limit.* Tossing the empty vial into a bin next to the fridge, he headed for the living room. He needed to calm himself and let the transfusion blood do its job of suppressing his urge to feed.

At some point during Ren's rest, his father walked into the room. The desire to feed had now been near entirely suppressed. He hated when his urges took over. They were so strong they actually overpowered everything in his mind, forcing him to focus only on them.

Ren got up to greet his father. He was dressed in loose-fitting clothing, evidence of his day spent at home rather than at Trinity.

"So, what was this problem you wanted my help with?" his father asked. "It sounded pretty important on the phone. Especially for you to call me so early in the morning."

"Follow me," Ren said. "They're around here somewhere."

Ren led his father through the house in search of Marcus and Ellie. He found them in one of the family rooms, looking over a stack of books on the coffee table. Recognizing Marcus, he and Leo exchanged a quick greeting. It wasn't a surprise at all that Marcus was there, especially after they left Trinity together for a job the night before.

"Ellie," Ren called. Ellie turned at the sound of her name.

"Ren, there are so many books here!" Ren chuckled at her excitement.

"Come here, munchkin; there's someone I want to introduce you to." Ellie set the books down and walked over to them. "Ellie, this is my father, Leo." His father looked at him with a surprised expression.

"Ren's daddy?" Ellie asked, looking at him. "It's nice to meet you," she said, sort of shy.

Leo knelt down so he was eye level with her. "It's nice to meet you, too," he said. "I take it this is why you called me."

Ren motioned him over to the couch. All four of them took a seat. Together, he and Marcus told his father everything that had happened the night before.

"I see. So that's what happened," his father said. "If she truly doesn't have any family, then I think you made the right decision letting her stay with you."

"I couldn't just leave her," Ren retorted. Human or not, leaving her there wasn't in the cards.

"No, that would be wrong," his father agreed.

"I'm contacting the proper agencies so I can look after her, but I'll need your help figuring out what to do while I'm at Trinity. I also need to figure out where she went to school."

"Don't forget your other problem," Marcus reminded him. "What you're going to do while you're out on missions? You can't leave her at Trinity."

"I know, and I'm not sure, honestly. I'll have to find a babysitter. I have no idea who would look after a kid for days at a time, though."

"I can look after her," Ren's father said. "Unlike you two, I'm not in the field anymore. I can do my job and take care of her at the same time. It shouldn't be an issue at all."

Ren's phone started ringing. He looked at the person calling. The name read Trinity; it was a job. Ren answered the phone and Jay's voice appeared on the other end.

"Hey, Ren. Got another job for you."

"I've got Marcus and my father with me. I'll put you on speaker. Give me the details."

"The target's name is John Alger. He owns a fruit shop in town, divorced with one kid. This guy is constantly popping in and out of the radar. We last had record of him being in town. Hopefully, he's still here."

"We learned that he has a fruit shop in the shopping district. I don't need to tell you to be cautious about doing your work in such a crowded area. The pay is your standard one million."

"I can handle that. Getting him out or taking him down when no one is around won't be a problem. I'll start later today. And Jay, I'll stop by later to discuss yesterday's mission with Marcus. I'm afraid it's bad news." He heard Jay curse on the other end.

"As I feared. Marcus, I've got other assignments for you and the rest of the Heaven's Blades," Jay said, switching over to him. "So you won't be joining Ren on this one."

"Right, call me later with the details, Jay," Marcus said.

"Good hunting, guys. And be careful. More so than ever."

"I'll head out now, then," Ren's father said. "I've got some errands to run. I'll be back to watch Ellie while you're gone. It's best not to leave her alone right now."

His father got up from the recliner and bid them farewell before leaving. It was hours later that he returned, allowing Ren to make his move on his target.

There was no doubt in Ren's mind that this guy was still hiding out in the city. He pulled into the entrance of a parking garage. One of the primary workers on duty there was a supporter of Trinity, so Ren had free access for missions.

He drove all the way to the top and stopped in front of a metal door big enough for his car. Ren held a card underneath a scanner. The scanner's red light turned green and buzzed. The metal door rose, and Ren drove through, closing behind him. He was inside a small section of the parking lot inaccessible by regular people.

It was surrounded mostly by glass on all sides. There were fifteen spots, but only three were being used.

Ren pulled into a spot in the far corner. He walked to the side closest to him and held his card underneath another scanner. It turned green and buzzed, just like the other one. Ren opened a door and stepped out onto the rooftop.

"The shopping district. That's downtown. Good, this makes things easier. Let's see if he's still there. If I get lucky, I'll be back home in time for dinner."

Backing up all the way to the glass parking garage, he shot forward and ran full speed to the edge of the roof. Pouring his ki into his legs, he jumped and landed on the roof of the next building, then kept running. He reached the end and jumped to the roof of the next building, continuing over the course of a number of buildings.

One of the buildings had piping all over the roof. He jumped over one, then vaulted over another and slid underneath a third. Turning right, he climbed up a brick chimney and launched himself toward the next building. He hit the roof, rolled, and kept running.

The last building in the row ended at an intersection. Ren vaulted over the side of the building and landed on the fire escape stairway. He climbed down all the way until his feet reached the ground.

Crossing the intersection, he dodged in and out of buildings for the next two miles until he reached the shopping district. The buildings on both sides of the street were two to three stories tall. People sold their food and goods from the front of the stores where everyone could see the products. With the way it was set up, it appeared more like an open-air market.

Ren leaped from building to building, blending into the shadows as he moved. His search for the fruit stand quickly drew him closer and closer to his target. When he finally found them, he stopped. But before he could slip down off the roof, his target started moving.

Out in the open, Ren finally got a good look at him. He clearly sensed the presence of a shade within him.

Sticking close, Ren followed him from the rooftops, never losing sight. His target kept himself on the move. If he knew Ren was onto him, Ren didn't know. It was unlikely, but not impossible. If he did, then he was a smart one.

Leaping to another rooftop, Ren saw the target turn down an empty street. He still couldn't tell if the target was on to him, but this opportunity was perfect. Ren dropped to the ground below, shooting forward with a blast of speed. He intercepted the target, picked him up, and took him into an alley faster than he or anyone around could see.

Still carrying his confused target, he leaped and ran up the back of the building until he reached the roof. He flipped the target over and slammed him down on his back, knocking the wind out of him. Unable to properly respond, Ren drew the dagger at his side and slit his target's throat as fast as he could blink.

Black energy surrounded the target's body before shooting out in all directions, staining the roof beneath the body. With the death of its host, the shade inside of him had been destroyed. Now, he only needed to get rid of the body before someone found it.

A scream broke him from his thoughts. Instinct took over, and he ran in its direction. Taking to the rooftops again in hopes of saving time, he caught the presence of another shade. A living shade, the same as his target. He prayed that whoever was against them at least wasn't human. A normal person didn't stand a chance against a shade.

Come on, come on. Make it in time, he thought.

The moment he sensed the shade directly within reach, he acted without even thinking. In a desperate attempt to save a life, he jumped off the building and drew his heaven's blade. He landed on the shade's back, driving his blade into it and crushing it beneath him. The shade within them returned to the oblivion with the death of its host.

Ren looked up and saw the figure of a person. A girl sat on her backside, only a few feet away. No doubt she was the one who'd been attacked, a terrified expression on her face. His eyes widened with immense surprise when he saw her. The one who'd been attacked, among anyone it could have been, was none other than Kelsey herself.

Eight

The Birth of a Star

Kelsey woke up early that morning. Her parents were already awake and preparing breakfast. It was a warm start, the air thick with humidity.

Her mother asked her to head to the local market and secure ingredients for dinner, as well as pick up her altered dress. She waited until after lunch to start, grabbing the list of ingredients and the location of the seamstress from her mother. She slipped on her shoes, grabbed her car keys, and headed out the door.

The shopping district wasn't that far from her house. She parked, grabbed the list, and locked the door behind her. Before getting the groceries, getting the dress was first on her list. That way, she wouldn't have to carry the food around all day.

The vendors here always had the best-tasting food. Fruit, vegetables, spices, you name it, all homegrown and natural with no pesticides.

As she walked, she found herself thinking of Ren. It had been a couple of days since she'd last heard from him or seen him. It was the weekend; he couldn't be working, could he? On the chance that he wasn't, what could he possibly be up to? She wanted to see him.

Her stomach got butterflies thinking about it. The more she thought about it, the more she found the need to whip her phone out and call him right there. No, she couldn't do that. If he was busy, she didn't want to interrupt him. She'd call later, probably after dinner.

Kelsey continued her trip around the shopping district until she bought the last of the items on her list. Having secured her mother's dress and the groceries, she headed back to her car.

Out of the corner of her eye, a stand caught her attention. A middle-aged man in a tank top and shorts sat behind a table filled with cases containing jewelry made of different types of stones. The man behind the table made eye contact with her but only smiled with a slight nod, a simple hello.

It was strange. For a Saturday afternoon, the market was basically dead right now. It was never this empty. Kelsey didn't make it very far when she felt a firm grip grab hold of her arm. Her assailant yanked her into a side street before she had the chance to even try and escape or fight them off. One hand held her tight and the other went over her mouth.

They turned right down a back alley, and when they were far enough away from anyone's sight, the person threw her to the ground. The sound of a weapon immediately being drawn drew her attention. Standing over her was the man from the jewelry stand, a knife grasped loosely in his hand.

"That was even easier than I thought," he said. "Kelsey Rose, yes?"

"Who are you, and how do you know my name?" She backed up from the man, trying to put distance between them. Now that he was armed, she was in a whole different situation.

The jewelry man started laughing. "Girlie, you're seriously out of the loop. Or is it possible, has he really not told you anything?" He? Who was he? Her confused expression made him laugh again. "This couldn't get any better!"

"Touch me, and I promise I won't go down without a fight. You'd better be prepared to sacrifice something."

The man gave her a lopsided look. "Relax. You're not the one I'm after; you're just the bait. The only thing I need from you is a tiny bit of your blood."

"Blood! Stay the hell away from me!"

The man sighed. "It's not a lot, about this much." He held up two fingers in a rough measurement. "You're special to him. Even with only that small of an amount, he'll come running."

When he stepped toward her, Kelsey threw her bags at him. They struck him in the face, causing him to stumble backward. Kelsey turned to run, but the man grabbed her. She screamed and kicked, and he yanked her to the side, placing the knife to her throat.

"If I were you, I wouldn't move around so much. We wouldn't want this to slip and cut your pretty throat, now, would we?" He gestured with the knife.

Kelsey knew he was right. He had her, and he could kill her with ease in the position she was in. She figured the best thing to do was whatever he said. If what he said was true, then he wouldn't harm her, hopefully. Unfortunately, playing the damsel in distress was never Kelsey's way of doing things. She preferred to hit hard and strike faster.

Drawing her arm back, she rammed her elbow into his stomach, pushing the knife away with her other hand. Then she turned and struck him in the nose. Blood rained down onto the pavement following a loud crack. The man howled in pain. Kelsey stepped back, holding her injured hand.

"Now you've done it bitch!" Kelsey couldn't believe what she was seeing when a black mist appeared around the man's body. "I told you; you weren't my target. All you had to do was do what I told you. Now I'm going to kill you and take your blood by force. Imagine that bastard Nightwalker's face when he sees your bloody corpse."

"Nightwalker? You mean Ren Nightwalker?"

Consumed by blinding rage, he didn't even recognize her words. He lunged at her and pinned her arms to the side. She lifted her knee and rammed it into his groin, then kicked him off her. "Come get some, asshole!" She turned to run away, but he threw the knife at her. It hit the wall in front of her and fell to the ground with a clang.

The man rolled over onto his front and began vomiting. It was then that she recognized the pain. Blood trickled down her arm, visible by the cut in her sleeve. The blade had grazed her arm.

Almost as if it had a mind of its own, the black mist around him started to move, growing larger. Suddenly, she was sent flying as something slammed into her. Fear had long since taken over her conscience. Whatever just happened to her wasn't normal. This guy wasn't someone she could handle. In fact, she wasn't even sure he was human.

Slowly, anger started to replace her fear. The fact that she was about to die pissed her off more than it scared her. She didn't want to die, especially not like this.

The man was standing now, his breathing heavy and ragged. Sure enough, getting kneed in the groin worked wonders. He was barely able to stand. It almost made her chuckle. She was a fighter, and she was damn sure going to fight. "Bring it on. I'll hit you even harder this time," she taunted.

The man took a step forward and was suddenly crushed beneath a person. The mystery assailant came out of nowhere, landing on his back. A golden sword stuck out of him, its wielder gripping the handle tightly.

So many emotions ran through her that she didn't know what to feel. Scared that she almost died, happy that she was alive, grateful to the man who saved her, or conflicted that she just saw someone die terribly right in front of her eyes. All she knew was that she couldn't take her eyes off her savior. His long bleach-blond hair hung down, flowing over his face. Wait a minute, why did he look familiar, not just the hairstyle?

Her savior looked up at her. His cobalt blue eyes were intoxicating. There was no way she wouldn't have recognized him. It was Ren Nightwalker in all his bleach-blond-haired glory.

"Kelsey!" he said, shocked. He didn't know what to do. He was too surprised to react, perhaps even more than she was. He never expected to see her, especially like this.

He sighed again, then pulled the golden sword out and sheathed it behind him. "Are you okay?" he asked her, but she said nothing. "Kelsey! Are you okay?" he asked louder, grabbing her shoulders. When did he get in front of her? She didn't even see him move.

"I-I, I don't…." She was in shock. It was understandable, given she had almost been killed by a living shade.

"Who was that guy?" she finally managed to ask. "He said he was after you. Why?"

"It's, hard to explain," he said. He was hesitant to tell her.

"Hard? Hard? After everything that just happened, hard is the least of it!" she yelled. "He wanted my blood. And there was this weird black mist around him. He was going to kill me!"

Ren suddenly tightened his grip on her shoulders. His dark expression shocked her out of her fear. "Black energy. You saw it?" he asked. She nodded silently. "Humans shouldn't be able to see ki. How did you see it?"

"I don't know; it just came out of him. What does that mean, 'humans'?"

Ren placed his hand on the side of her face, gently running his thumb across her eyes and blotting away the tears. Then he had his arms around her in a warm embrace. She gripped the back of his jacket tightly.

"I'm sorry you had to go through that, Kelsey," he said to her. "That never should have happened. But it's over now, and I promise you're alright. You're safe with me, and I'll always be here for you."

Kelsey released a halfhearted laugh. "Always?" She pushed him away from her. "You used to say that when we were kids, and look what happened. You left without even so much as a goodbye. Who knows when you'll just up and disappear on me again?"

Ren should have expected this. He had hurt her by leaving; he knew that. But he had hurt her more by not contacting her. It was a mistake he regretted every single day. But now that her emotions were amuck, she had no filter, and he was finally able to hear what she really thought. He had hurt her even worse than he realized.

Ren bit back a silent curse. What a piece of shit he was. Kelsey literally meant the world to him. He cared more for her than anyone else. And what did he do? Gave her the worst kind of wound possible: a broken heart. He'd abandoned her, and he'd never be able to forgive himself.

"You owe me the truth. And I'm not letting you go until I get it." Ren stared at her, deciding if he should tell her the truth. Her eyes won him over. He couldn't win against her. But then again, he never could.

He helped her to her feet, gently holding her hands in his own, as if she would disappear if he let go.

"That was a shade. A living shade, to be precise. Shades are evil spirits brought back from the dead. They have no mind, no physical body, and act only according to their instincts. They have no thought process, so they act purely on instinct, hunting and killing. Living shades, however, are different. They are far, far stronger."

"Living shades are, in a sense, exactly as they sound. Living creatures possessed by a shade. Where they are similar stops there, though. Better put, a living shade is a monster, a real monster, who has been possessed by a shade but managed to overpower it and stop themself from being taken over. In doing so, they gain all the shade's power but retain their mental state. For humans like you, unless they decided to show their power, you would never know someone was a living shade."

"'Humans like me.' That's the second time you've called me human."

Ren nodded. "It's the reason I carry this sword, the reason I can do the things I do. I'm like that shade. I'm not human."

Releasing his hands, she stepped away from him. Her expression — it wasn't one of fear; it was one of confusion. No doubt she had no idea what he really meant, nor could she wrap her head around it.

Ren was quiet for a moment. "Come with me," he told her.

"Where are we going?"

"To where I work. You'll understand once you get there," he said before she could ask. "I'll explain everything; you have my word. And I'll put an end to all of this." Kelsey only nodded, letting him lead her.

Temporarily turning his attention away from her, he looked over at the lifeless body of the living shade and noticed something tattooed onto his left hand. A square with a red border. In the center of the square, a red angel sat on her knees, looking up with closed eyes, her hands clasped together in prayer.

Ren's eyes widened when he saw the tattoo. He grabbed the hand, staring at it intently, gauging its authenticity. Only as soon as he saw that it was real did the situation get three times worse. "Oh shit," he said.

"What?" Kelsey asked. "What is it?"

"Look away!" he told Kelsey. But she didn't. Ren drew his heaven's blade and sliced off the shade's hand with one clean cut. Kelsey nearly vomited. Then he removed his shirt and wrapped the hand in it. "We're leaving, now." He grabbed her bags of groceries and her mother's dress, handing her the dress.

Taking her hand, Ren led Kelsey all the way back to where his car was parked. He walked over to a door, holding a card underneath a red light. It turned green and beeped, then he opened the door for her to enter, closing it behind him once he passed through.

Kelsey recognized the familiar silver of Ren's Lamborghini. They set the groceries and her mother's dress in the back seat before he opened the door for her, closing it once she was in. Turning the car over, Ren pulled out of the parking space and made his way to a metal overhead door. He put the card underneath another scanner, and the door opened up.

Ren drove down to the ground level, finally stopping in front of a guard pole. A man in a security uniform sat inside the booth to his left.

"I need a second," Ren said to Kelsey. "It's about what happened earlier." She nodded, and he got out of the car. The security guard opened the door to his booth when he saw him, and Ren stepped inside.

Kelsey waited silently in the car for near ten minutes before Ren left the security booth. She watched him get back into the car with a serious, if not concerned, expression on his face. To which she returned with her own concerned look. After everything that had happened today, if everything that he said was true, what was going through that head of his to give him such an expression?

"Ready?" he asked. She nodded, and he pulled forward once the guard pole went up.

Kelsey was quiet the entire drive to Trinity. Ren wasn't sure what she was thinking, but he never pressed her for it. It was better that way. She needed time to take everything in. He just drove in silence, not even listening to the radio.

They pulled into Trinity's parking lot, and Ren parked in a spot with his name on a sign. This section of town didn't have very many people in it. Why there was a bar out here, Kelsey had no idea. Or maybe it wasn't really a bar; it just looked like one.

Ren walked around to the front of the building, and she followed him. There was no name, only a glowing orange sign in the shape of a phoenix. Ren opened the front door and grinned. "Welcome to Trinity."

Nine

When Reality and Fantasy Collide

"Come on in," Ren insisted. Kelsey carefully walked inside, unsure of the situation. As soon as she was through, Ren closed the door and was at her side. He put a hand on the base of her back. His touch made her jump. "Relax," he told her. His tone was serious now. "Do not lose control of your emotions. Do not get intimidated. You must be strong."

She nodded in understanding, but that didn't stop her hands from sweating. Ren must have sensed her nerves because he grabbed her hand and laced their fingers together. Her nerves almost settled completely. How long had it been since they had held hands?

Just like that, all her nerves disappeared. She would walk in there confident and in control.

They walked in, hand in hand. All heads turned to them, and the place went dead silent. Most of the people were adults in their late thirties to fifties. She saw a few people who looked around their age. All of them gathered around tables or booths.

Ren let go of her hand and put it back on the base of her back. "Take a seat at the bar," he whispered into her ear. She nodded and took a seat. Ren stood next to her, leaning against the countertop with his elbows.

A big man with a large stomach, long white beard, hairless head, and tattoos running down the length of both arms stood up. His face was set into a deep scowl. He took a step forward, then stopped. Ren shot him a glare so cold it could kill. His eyes conveyed everything he wanted to say; 'take another step, and I'll obliterate you.'

The man stepped back, sweat beading down his face as a wave of fear washed over the entire bar. Kelsey couldn't blame them. She was terrified herself, and she wasn't even on the receiving end. It was then that she noticed the blue energy bubbling off his body. She swallowed, sweat beading down her forehead.

"I haven't seen that expression in a long time," said a familiar voice. Kelsey turned to see the last person she expected walking toward them; Marcus Allagash. "You can lay off the glare now, Ren. You're scaring the hell out of them," he said, stopping next to Ren. "Calm down and give us an explanation. What's happened? Where did your shirt go?"

"Marcus?" Kelsey asked, shocked.

Marcus looked past Ren at Kelsey. "I was wondering how long it was going to take for him to bring you here. Welcome to Trinity, Kelsey."

She didn't know what to say. "Um, thanks," was all she could think of.

"I hadn't planned on bringing her here directly, actually. But the situation has changed." Kelsey looked back at Ren. His gaze went around the room. "Here's the way things are going to go. If any of you so much as moves an inch without my permission, there won't be anything left when I'm done with you. Do you understand?"

Everyone except Marcus dropped to one knee. "As you command, Your Highness." *Your Highness?* Kelsey wondered. She watched as the blue energy around him faded, then disappeared.

"Everyone, this is Kelsey Rose," Ren introduced. The others beamed with delight.

"Wait, you mean the Kelsey?" the big man asked. "What the hell Ren? Why didn't you just say it was her from the start? We've all been dying to meet her, you know."

Hold on a second. They've been dying to meet her? Something didn't sit right with Kelsey. She assumed Ren had already told them about her, but how much exactly? This guy, along with the rest of the people in here, looked like they wanted to rip her apart at first. But now their expressions were the exact opposite.

Kelsey looked from him to Ren and gave him a, *what the hell is going on?* expression. "I promise to explain," he said. "But first, I have something important to discuss with everyone. It's about what happened earlier."

Earlier, as in when she was attacked by that guy, or monster, living shade? Whatever the hell it was, she didn't even know anymore. Ren seriously needed to start explaining things to her.

"What happened earlier?" Marcus asked.

Ren turned to face the bartender "Jay, Jack on the rocks," he said. A glass filled with his drink slid across the counter and into his hand.

"Um, Ren," Kelsey started to say. "Kelsey, order a drink if you want one. It's on me. We have more than alcohol. Jay, whatever she wants. Put it on my tab."

Ren took a sip and set it down on the counter. He sat down facing everyone, one leg crossed over the other.

"Alright, explanations. The reason I brought Kelsey here today and for the sudden urgency is the same. Earlier today, Kelsey was attacked by a living shade." The entire bar suddenly went quiet. Even Marcus had an unbelievable look on his face. Kelsey felt uncomfortable with all the stares.

Marcus looked up, Ren's story catching his interest. "He attacked her in broad daylight? They're getting aggressive."

"That isn't the issue anymore. He attacked her, but he was after me. The enemy knows she's close to me and wanted to use her as bait. I can only assume that our enemy has information on all of us. Our families, friends, lovers, even daily tasks."

"Even still, why would he attack her, a human?" someone asked. Julie stood up from her seat. "To a living shade, she's like an insect. Oh, no offense."

"Kelsey was never good at being the damsel in distress. And she's damn stubborn when she wants to be. Knowing her, she fought back, and he didn't like that."

"So, he attacked Kelsey to get to you, but for what reason?" Marcus wondered. "Did he honestly think he could use her against you?"

"To be honest, I don't really think it matters. Whether he expected a win or a loss, the situation we find ourselves in just got a whole lot worse. I think he was under orders," Ren said.

"Orders? By whom, Verin?" Marcus guessed.

Ren removed his rolled-up shirt from his jacket and unwrapped the severed hand. The entire bar turned white when he handed it to Marcus, displaying the angel tattoo on it. Marcus released a long vile of curses.

"As of this moment, we can assume that Verin has allied himself with the Radiant Church," Ren said.

Marcus was so furious he launched the hand as hard as it could. Kelsey expected it to smash against the wall, maybe break a couple of bottles. She did not expect it to burst through the wall like a piece of iron, leaving a giant hole in its wake.

"Is this some kind of sick joke?" Marcus yelled. "Are our lives just a game to them?"

"I wish I knew, brother. I wish I knew," Ren said back. "Unfortunately, regardless of their reasoning, they appear to have joined forces. For us, that's about as bad as it gets."

"Bad, bad?" someone in the bar asked. "It's hard enough on us to handle one of them at a time. Now we have to worry about both of them together? We can't handle all of that by ourselves."

"My father and I have a plan," Ren said. "Marcus has already been made aware of this. Unfortunately, it's one only those of us wielding a heaven's blade can partake in. We're going to take down Verin's four generals." If everyone was shocked before, it was nothing compared to their expressions now.

"Now, I believe I promised you an explanation," Ren said to Kelsey. "What do you know about monsters?"

"Depends on what you mean by monsters," she said back. "You mentioned only not being human, but to be honest, that could mean a lot of things."

"No, that pretty much fits the bill." He took a heavy breath, contemplating his next words carefully.

"Okay, we'll start with the basics. Witches, warlocks, zombies, werewolves, vampires, that kind of thing."

"Wow, talk about your Halloween fetish."

Ren raised an eyebrow at her. "They're not fetishes, Kelsey. And they're not myths either."

"There is a world, separate from this one, where all the things you call myths live and thrive. Your kind, humans, call it the demon realm. It's a concept especially popular in eastern stories. My kind call it Nexus. Eastern myths, Western, American, European, Asian, African, all the monsters humans have come to invent as myth and religion are real. And just like how all the inhabitants of Nexus are monsters, so too is everyone here in Trinity."

Kelsey's eyes went wide. In a sense, she was more surprised than terrified, though.

"We live amongst you in secret, with the ability to take on human form, living our lives like normal humans. You would never even know we were the things you read in books and fairy tales."

"And you're one of them, a monster. This whole time?" she asked. He nodded. "Then, that means, this whole time, I thought—"

"Just because I'm not human, doesn't mean the time we spent together wasn't any less real," he said, cutting her off. "So don't go start thinking it is. Besides, when I met you, I technically was human. Up until about three years ago, that is."

"You were human? Wait, three years ago? That's when you left for India." Again, he responded with a nod.

"Trinity was founded by my father as a means of stopping a powerful monster, one we've been at war with for centuries. Our enemy is a necromancer named Verin, and a very powerful one. He summons the dead to do his bidding by spreading fear and chaos."

"Shades," Kelsey realized.

"Exactly. And where fear and shades spread, so too does death. Verin is creating an army of shades, we believe, for the purpose of overthrowing Nexus. That's why Trinity was formed. We're the resistance. And, we have another enemy as well. A religious organization that's existed for nearly a millennium. The Radiant Church."

"Their members extend to all religions in this world, and their influence greater than any government. Wars, famine, slavery, revolts, terrorism, if it makes the news, you can bet they're the cause of it."

"Because they believe so heavily in religion, they consider our kind to be just as you'd expect, demonic, the end of the world. Their only goal is to destroy every monster until none of us are left.

Ten

Turning the Tide: The Stones of Sun and Moon

"So, essentially, you're fighting a war on two fronts," Kelsey understood.

"Precisely. And we barely hold out with so little of us. Many support the cause, but it's not enough. Our forces are spread too thin, and our enemies are too powerful."

Kelsey took a deep breath. To be honest, she needed a ventilator and a notebook to write all this down. But the part that hit her hardest was learning Ren was one of them.

"So, if you're one of them, then what kind of monster are you?"

"Before I can answer that, you need to know about our rank system," he told her. "Monsters are given a rank based on their species from F to S. The stronger the species, the higher the rank. Of course, there are those who exceed the strength of their species and receive a higher rank. Everyone in Trinity is at least B- rank.”

“In Trinity, the stronger you are, the higher risk and rewarded jobs you take?”

“Jobs, as in, killing shades.”

“Yes, no, sort of. That’s not all we do.”

“What else do you do then?” she asked, curious.

“Assassinations.”

Kelsey nearly dropped her drink. The look she gave Ren was full of horror. “You kill people?”

“We don’t kill humans, only monsters, but yes,” he confessed. “Very bad people.”

“There is no good or bad, Ren. Murder is murder; it doesn’t matter who the person is. That you can’t even see that, I don’t know what to think.”

Ren didn’t blame her for feeling this way. It was a logical response. “No, that’s not true,” he told her. “There is such a thing as good or bad. However, it’s easier to see if we put it into terms of bad and worse. The bad do their best to live good; the worse are just awful, cruel, and disgusting.”

“As in, murderers?” she asked, indicating him.

“Yes. As in murder, slavery, drugs, arms deals, human trafficking, children included in all of that.”

“Children?” the thought petrified her. Truly? Children?

"Yes. I've taken out a few organizations who were using children in their ranks. Killing is killing Kelsey, I admit that. And you have a right to hate me for it."

She shook her head. "I could never hate you. Not for anything. But this, I just…."

"I understand, believe me, I do. But the United States government doesn't really care about all that after the target we're assigned has ended up on the top of their most wanted list."

"Wait, hold on. You're saying you kill monsters for the government?"

"Shade-related issues are sourced privately. But we have supporters of Trinity, monsters, very high up in the government. Like, having dinner with the president high. The government is our main and our biggest contractor."

Ren gently placed his hand on her cheek, rubbing the tears threatening to spill over her eyes away with his thumb.

"Are, are you good? At it, I mean," Kelsey wondered.

He grinned in response. "Really good," he said with a cocky tone.

"Show off!" Marcus coughed into his hand. The rest of Trinity, and even Kelsey, started laughing.

"So, the ranks," Kelsey said, suddenly interested in getting back to the topic.

"Right, the ranks. You asked what kind of monster I am. I'm an S-class monster, the strongest rank. I'm a vampire."

"Ren is being bashful," Marcus said. "Because he doesn't want to scare you any further. But Ren is one of those that have exceeded his species rank. Someone so strong he's feared by other vampires even. A third-generation S+ super monster."

"I told you earlier that when we met, I was basically a normal human," Ren said to Kelsey. She remembered that. "There's a reason for that. Eighteen years ago, we suffered an accident on the job. Many of us were injured, my mother included, in her attempt to protect people. Fearing for her, my father had her go into hiding, blending in as a normal human. But she would not do it alone. So, I made the hard decision to go with her."

"My vampire powers were taken from me when we moved here to Florida. With my powers gone, my body underwent a regression, and with a little help from the magic department, I was turned back into an infant. My mother and father believed it was the best way to stay hidden, as a single mother with an infant child."

"As a result of my transformation, my memories were taken from me. They were stored away, along with my powers, with my father in a safe location. Roughly three months later, I met you, and with no powers or memories, I grew up as a normal human. After my mother died, my father brought me back to India, where he gave me my powers and memories back. After that, I rejoined Trinity."

It was such an unbelievable yet amazing story; Kelsey didn't know what to think. All she could do was try and keep the pieces of the puzzle together in her head.

Kelsey looked over at Marcus, who was leaning against the bar stoically. "So, if you're here, that means you're a monster too."

He nodded in confirmation. "I'm a werewolf." Oh, now that one really interested her! "Like vampires, werewolves are also S-class monsters. And like Ren, I, too, am a third-generation S+ super monster."

"So, you two have been working together this whole time?" Kelsey asked.

"Three hundred years, though it feels more like days. We've been together since we were kids. Five, if you can believe it."

Kelsey nearly fell out of her seat. "I'm sorry, did you say three hundred years!" Marcus nodded silently.

"We did say we were third-generation elders. For monsters, every one hundred years grants you the title of elder."

"So, you're telling me you two are three hundred years old?"

"Three hundred and twenty-one and three hundred and twenty-two, to be precise," Ren said, indicating himself and then Marcus.

Kelsey ran a hand over her face making Ren laugh. They all realized that Kelsey's mood had changed over the course of the conversation. She was no longer angry, sad, disappointed, or horrified. That was a good thing, a real good thing.

"But you look like teenagers," Kelsey said. "That whole eternal youth thing is real?"

"In a sense, yes. Certain species of monsters age physically at prolonged rates. Werewolves and vampires included. In one hundred years, I'll look like I'm in my mid-twenties."

Where previously Kelsey looked at him with horror or amazement, now she only looked at him with an entirely different and new expression: disdain.

"I hate you," she said. Ren burst out laughing. Where before, she said she'd never hate him for anything, didn't hate him even learning that he was an assassin. Now, that was proven to be inaccurate once she found out that he retained his youth. She was envious.

"Even our positions in Nexus are only slightly apart," Marcus continued. He looked at Ren. "I think it best if this comes from you. She needs to know this, especially now that she's aware of our identity." Ren could only agree with him.

"Kelsey, there is one more thing you need to know about Marcus and me, one crucial thing," Ren began to say. Kelsey started getting nervous again. What bomb was he going to drop on her this time? "Marcus and I aren't just normal monsters, besides our rank. The truth is we are both heirs to two powerful monarchies. We uphold the position of eventual control over them and the citizens who live within."

Admittedly, that one actually took Kelsey a second to wrap her head around, much more than the other stuff she'd learned thus far. "Hold on. You're saying you're a prince? An actual prince?" Ren nodded in confirmation.

"The Nightwalker clan I belong to has been a powerful vampire clan since ancient times. We've always held immense prowess beyond just physical like magic and combat, but also in politics, economics, and trade."

She held it in, but inside, Kelsey wanted to scream. Her head felt like it was about to explode. "Okay, I understand everything, but why didn't you tell me? I thought we were supposed to be friends. I thought you trusted me."

"We are friends, and I do trust you. You mean the world to me, Kelsey; you always have. But this is different. This is beyond even you. Humans don't take well to things that aren't like them. They reject it and pretend it doesn't exist to console themselves. How would you have felt if I told you I was a three-hundred-year-old vampire prince?"

"Okay, good point." She had to admit, it was tough to hear that. But he was right. She would have likely thought him insane.

Ren opened his mouth to say something else when he was interrupted by Jay's cell phone. He listened silently before a sudden outburst surprised everyone.

"What? Hold it, back up. Are you serious? You actually found it?" He turned silent as the person on the other line spoke and began writing furiously on a napkin. His conversation continued for several minutes before hanging up.

"Everyone listen up; I've got news!" Jay yelled. "That was James on the phone. Hold onto your seats when you get a load of this."

Ren and Marcus sat up straight, now thoroughly invested.

"Who's James?" Kelsey asked.

"He's an old friend of Ren's father and an advocate supporter of Trinity. His name is James Wilson," Marcus started to say.

"But you might know him as your high school principal," Ren finished.

"Principal Wilson is a monster?"

"Yes, and a powerful one. He's one of the few monsters whose power surpasses his race and achieves a higher rank. His power is what keeps the shades from destroying your school and killing you all."

"Well, like usual, James comes through for us in a moment of need," Jay went on. "He thinks he found the location of the map to the sun and moon stones." The entire bar suddenly went dead quiet. Even Ren was so shocked he dropped his glass, spilling the contents all over the counter.

Jay handed Ren the piece of paper he was writing on while on the phone. Marcus leaned in to look at its contents. A set of numbers, 40° 45' 9.8136" N, 73° 58' 38.0244" W.

"Coordinates?" Kelsey asked. "Where to?"

"Don't know, but I'm about to find out," Ren responded.

He pulled out his phone and searched the coordinates using his map app. The map blew up in scale as it zoned in on the location of the coordinates. Details came up on the side, along with a picture, but he didn't even need them. It was perhaps one of the most famous places in the city, so he knew the building as soon as he read the title. "Grand Central Terminal."

"Seriously? Grand Central? Of course it's there!" Marcus said. "It makes sense, but maybe that was on purpose."

"What does that mean?" Kelsey asked him.

"Grand Central is one of the most famous train stations in the world. It's also been designated a national and historical landmark, not just for the city, but the country. The number of people that use the terminal is monumental. It was built as a need for expansion, among other accompanying needs. No doubt a flex of power and wealth as well. But, if these coordinates are accurate, and the station really is the location of the map, then the expansion may have just been used to conceal its real purpose. Grand Central was a cover-up."

"If the map really is there, then we have to find it. If we can get those stones, we might seriously have a chance at winning this war."

"I'm coming with you," Kelsey blurted out. Honestly, she said it before she truly thought about it.

"No, you're not." Ren told her.

"It's not your decision, Ren; it's mine. I want to come."

"Actually, as the one with the most authority here, it is my decision. You have no say or business in taking this quest. In all likelihood, you'll just end up getting yourself killed. This isn't your war to fight."

It didn't matter to her what Ren said, she was determined, and he knew exactly how stubborn she was.

"It's none of my business? You have no right to say that. They attacked me. I'm a part of this now. If you didn't want me in all of this, then you shouldn't have told me the truth about you." She crossed her arms in victory.

"Told you the truth. I think you misunderstand," Ren said. "I brought you here to tell you the truth. I never said I would let you leave with it." Her confidence immediately exploded. What was Ren planning on doing with her?

"You don't belong here. You're not one of us. You're just a human. And you never should have been attacked. In fact, you never should have gotten involved with me. Coming back into your life was a mistake because it only put you in more danger. I brought you here so I could take care of that for good by erasing all forms of our existence from your life."

A deep chill ran through Kelsey's body as she felt her whole world collapse around her. The thought of a life without him terrified her.

Ren walked toward her and held out his hand. Kelsey got out of her chair and backed away, suddenly overcome by fear. He continued forward, and she fell to her backside. She was surrounded, with nowhere else to go. Ren knelt in front of her, placing his fingertips upon her forehead.

"Don't worry, it won't hurt, so long as you don't struggle. It'll be over before you know it. When you wake up, you won't remember a thing. Trinity, shades, monsters, or me." Her eyes went wide. "We never should have gotten involved in your life. Knowing about us will only bring you trouble. Erasing our existence from your memory is the best thing for you. You can continue with your life and grow up ignorant of everything. Leave all of this to us."

No. This isn't what she wanted. She didn't want to forget. Ren had an expression that she couldn't make out, but he looked hurt. More a human than a vampire. She realized he didn't want this either, but he was doing it to keep her safe. He knew the dangers otherwise.

"Farewell, Kelsey." There was no way she was going sit there and accept this. Not Ren. She wouldn't lose him again. She couldn't.

Kelsey suddenly went on the offensive, throwing her arms around him. Her surprise attack pinned him down only momentarily, but it was enough.

"No! I refuse to be separated from you anymore." Ren could only look at her with eyes muddled with different emotions. "I don't want to forget; I don't want to be separated. We've been together since we were little, or I was little; I don't even know what to call it anymore. But you know more about me than anyone else. Those three years you were gone felt like a lifetime. I can't go through that again."

"You won't even know. All these emotions you're feeling, they won't exist. You will have nothing to fear, nothing to worry about, no reason to not want to be separated. You'll never even know I exist. All of this will simply fade away painlessly."

"That's nonsense, and you know it! You are a part of me, Ren. Just as I am a part of you. You have always been a part of my life. You're part of what makes me who I am, and the moment you came back, so too was all of this, the truth. This is *your* world, and I want to be a part of it. I don't want to forget, even if I could. A life without you in it isn't a life at all."

He stared at her for a few moments before finally letting out a deep sigh. "This is a bad idea. Trust me when I say this is too much for you. You could die. Do you understand that?" his voice was soft and comforting, no longer the furious tone it previously held. "It's not worth it to risk your life. If I have to watch you die, I'll destroy it all. I'd rather be separated and out of your life forever so long as I knew it meant you were safe."

Death. That really made her think about what she was trying to get herself into.

"Then protect me. Protect me where I can't protect myself. And in return, I will protect you where you can't."

The determination in her eyes was resolute, and there was no getting rid of it. She wanted him to be a part of her life, to be a part of his, and he wanted her to be too. Kelsey was his everything, and he would always admit that.

"Ren," one of the people in the bar spoke up. "It's alright. Maybe you should let her in. We want to coexist with humans, right? This is it. You don't have to be alone anymore."

Ren looked into Kelsey's pleading eyes. They were desperate to hold onto him. "You have to promise to stay within my sight the entire time. You are not to go anywhere on your own. Always have Marcus or me with you at all times. Even when we stop to rest."

"Promise," she said.

"… Okay," he finally gave in. "But we have to leave the day after tomorrow. Ideally, I'd like to leave as soon as possible, but you've been through a lot today."

"Actually, Ren, I'm expecting a mission to come in either today or tomorrow," Marcus said, "so that actually works out."

"I see. In that case, you can stay at my place tonight," he said to Kelsey. "I'll take you home so you can drop off your bags. Tomorrow we'll gather everything you'll need."

Eleven

The True Meaning of Courage

Ren shifted gears and switched lanes. They'd left Trinity and were headed back to Kelsey's car, which was still parked at the shopping district. The entire drive, Kelsey thought about everything she'd just learned. Part of her thought she'd gotten in over her head, but the other part told her not to care and forced her legs to swim to the surface.

"Where are you parked?" Ren asked, breaking the silence.

"Keep going a little farther. It's a dark green Jeep," she said. Ren continued until the white-blue headlights of his car hit a dark green Jeep Wrangler and pulled off to the side behind it.

Kelsey got out and into the driver's side of her Jeep. She pulled out in front, and Ren followed behind her to her house. He knew Kelsey was having a tough time digesting everything, but looking at that house, he couldn't help but smile. It was the same as it had been three years ago and all those years prior.

Ren grabbed her groceries and her mother's dress from his car and handed them to her. He thought it best not to step inside right now. It was already three o'clock. Kelsey had been gone almost four hours. She couldn't believe how fast time had gone.

"Kelsey, is that you?" her mother asked from the kitchen. "Where have you been? I called, but you didn't answer." Then she noticed Kelsey's weakened state. "Are you alright? You seem kind of out of it."

"Sorry, some things came up." She set the groceries down on the kitchen counter. "I'm alright. I've just got a lot on my mind. Some crazy things happened today. I'm still digesting it all."

"Kelsey, you really don't look good. Why don't you go lie down?"

"I'd love to, but I have to go. A friend needs my help. It has to do with why I was so late. I'm sorry for not being able to tell me more, but you have to trust me on this. It's important that I do this. I'll be back tomorrow. I promise."

Kelsey and her mother exchanged only a few words before she walked outside, despite her mother's protesting. Thought it was far from proper, she had given her an explanation, and why she needed to leave for the night.

Ren looked at her when she hopped back into the passenger seat of his car, recognizing the heaviness of her eyes.

"You look exhausted," he told her. "Try and sleep, and I'll wake you up when we get there." She nodded, then leaned her head against the seat, slowly drifting into the deepness of sleep.

Ren pulled out of the driveway and headed home. He called his father along the way to let them know he was on his way.

"Kelsey. Kelsey," a voice called. It was soft and soothing, the kind of voice that calmed her nerves. She opened her eyes to see Ren's on her. Those beautiful cobalt blue eyes of his.

"We're here," he said. Kelsey said nothing back, only taking in the view. A large gate with a tiger on each post swung inward. He continued down the single road with a line of pink trees on both sides. Her jaw dropped when she saw the Spanish-style mansion. This was his house? It was many times larger than her own.

Ren parked the car in the garage and led Kelsey inside. He opened the door and stepped inside, holding it for her.

They walked into the living room, and Kelsey looked around at the tan leather furniture, the large rug on the floor, the dark-stained TV stand with a fireplace, and the large seventy-inch television.

Ren's father and Ellie were playing some sort of board game. Suddenly, he slapped his forehead with the palm of his hand. "This is the tenth time in a row I've lost. How are you so good at this?" he asked her.

Her face lit up when she saw Ren. "Ren!" she shouted. She ran and jumped into his arms.

"Hey, munchkin," he said, holding her up. Kelsey thought the whole thing was sweet but was so confused.

"Welcome home," Ren's father said. Kelsey took in his appearance. He had a goatee and short bleach-blond hair like Ren, along with the same golden skin tone. Only he had green eyes instead of blue. They looked just like each other.

"Hello, my dear. Welcome," he said to Kelsey.

"Hello," she said nervously. "I'm Kelsey. Kelsey Rose."

The man smiled at her. "I know very well who you are, my dear. Ren never stopped talking about you. The last time I saw you, you were only three years old."

"Kells, I know you don't remember him, but this is my father, Leo Nightwalker."

"Really? It's nice to finally meet you," she said. Then she remembered what Ren had told her back at the bar. He was the heir to a monarchy. "Your Highness."

Ren and his father both looked at her in surprise. Then his father set the exact same eyes on him. "Actually, Kelsey," Ren said. "It's majesty for monarchs. Only the heirs are highness."

"Oh, I'm so sorry! I didn't mean to offend you."

Ren's father surprised her by laughing. "It's fine; no harm done," he said. "Please, call me Leo. Ren and I do not use our titles here in the human world unless we need to, and only when dealing with our own kind."

Ellie pulled on Ren's shirt. She moved, so she hid behind him, leaving only her face visible.

"Ellie, this is Kelsey. Kelsey and I have been friends for a long time."

"It's nice to meet you," Ellie said, still hiding behind Ren.

Kelsey heard a whine, then what sounded like a large object coming toward them. She nearly fainted when a fully grown white tiger walked into view. Ren knelt down and rubbed the side of its neck.

"Hey bud. I was wondering where you'd gone. Kells, come here," Ren said. She shook her head. The tiger's eyes were locked on her. They were nearly the same shade of blue as Ren's.

Ren let out a light chuckle, then he and Nidar looked at each other. Ren rubbed him underneath his chin and nodded. He took Kelsey's hand and dragged her over to his side. Placing one hand around her in comfort, he gently eased her hand over Nidar's head but never let them touch.

They waited for Nidar to lean and touch his head to her hand. Kelsey scratched the top of his head, in front of his ears, and under his chin. She could hear his purring as she scratched. His fur was smooth and soft to the touch, like a thick winter blanket.

"Kells, this is Nidar." Keeping his eyes on Kelsey, she looked better than earlier but still drained. Today had more to digest than she was capable of.

"I know there's too much to take in. For now, sleep and let it pass. I'll show you to a room," Ren said to Kelsey. "Follow me." Kelsey bid Ellie and Ren's father a good night, then followed him. He showed her to a room and returned to the living room once she was situated.

"So, you told her then," Ren's father said.

"Yeah. I kind of had to." His father gave him a confused expression and Ren grinned. "We need to talk," he said.

Twelve

Sendoff

Kelsey woke up with sunlight shining through the window. The first thing she did was check the time on her phone: eleven in the morning. She threw off the covers and went into the connected bathroom to shower. Time got lost; she was in there so long. But when she finally got out, she felt refreshed. The exhaustion from the night before completely faded.

Ren was in the kitchen when she walked in, popcorn on the burner. He ran his fingers through her long copper hair. "Good morning, Kells."

The popping from the popcorn soon ended, concluding it was finished. "Ellie and I were going to watch a movie, hence the popcorn. Care to join? I'll make you something to eat."

Kelsey only gave him a half-baked nod before Ren opened the fridge, grabbed a handful of ingredients, and started cooking. He finished up quickly, then grabbed the popcorn.

"Come on," Ren said to Kelsey. She followed him into another room. "Ellie! Nidar!" he called. Ellie and the tiger walked into the room from another. Kelsey scratched the side of Nidar's face, and he started purring. She still hadn't gotten used to the animal, but she was getting there.

Ren led them through the house and down a set of stairs into an open room. Mounted on the wall was another colossal television. Not quite movie theater big but bigger than your typical household television. In front of the TV on a raised platform were two curved black leather sofas facing it with a small countertop wrapped around from one side to the other. Behind the two curved sofas was another straight one.

Kelsey followed Ren onto the platform, her feet sinking into the soft carpeting. He grabbed drinks and took a seat on one of the curved couches. Kelsey sat to his right and Ellie to his left. Nidar jumped up and plopped down on Ren's lap, making him groan and enticing a laugh out of Kelsey and Ellie.

"I'll get yours, so could you get off?" he asked. Nidar got down, and Ren went to the corner, grabbing a piece of furniture that looked like the footrest of a recliner. Ren positioned it in front of them, and Nidar jumped up.

Ren sat back down and grabbed the remote. He hit two buttons, one to turn off the lights and another to start the movie. He broke open the popcorn and handed it to Ellie, who dug her tiny hand inside.

Halfway through the movie, Ellie got up in search of a drink. Now just the two of them, Kelsey snuggled closer to Ren. "She's cute," she said. "Does she know? About what you are, I mean."

"She knows. Marcus and I saved her from a monster."

Ellie returned sometime later with a drink in her hands, and they went back to watching the movie. Once it ended, Kelsey used the remote to turn on the lights. Nidar had his head on Ren's lap, who was scratching him in front of his ears.

"You two are close, huh?" Kelsey asked.

"I found him when he was just a cub, while on a mission. He was wounded and abandoned. I refused to leave him to die. We've been together ever since."

"How long ago was that?" Timing wise, it couldn't have been more than the three years they were apart. And Nidar was an Indian white tiger.

"A couple of months after I arrived in India. Speaking of arriving, we should be getting back to your house soon. There's still a lot to prepare."

Ren grabbed a couple of items from his room before heading to the garage. This time, he unlocked the car doors to the second car in his garage.

The exterior was solid black with a high spoiler on the back. The interior was all tan leather with a touch screen consul and black leather gear shift. The tan leather steering wheel which housed the car's control features on the side had white wood on the top and bottom. Kelsey had only ever seen pictures of these before, but never actually been in one. A McLaren.

"I've never seen you drive this," Kelsey said.

"Yeah, I don't take it out for street driving. I mainly use it for jobs, or in this case, quests. This car's interior is actually different than it should be. It's a P1 GTR, but I had it modeled after the 570s interior," Ren explained. "I didn't like the GTR's original interior."

Ren opened the door for Kelsey, and she got in. Ellie had to sit on her lap, and Kelsey buckled them both in. As soon as Ren started the car, it roared with life.

The garage door opened, and Ren backed out. With one shift, they were on their way.

Ren pulled into Kelsey's driveway and parked. He turned off the car and went around to Kelsey's side to open the door for them.

"Mom, Dad?" she called as they walked inside. The room was empty, and the silence that followed almost made it seem like no one was home.

"Kelsey?" A man with the same green eyes of a darker shade walked into view.

"Dad, where's Mom and Alexis?" Kelsey asked him. Her hope was that they hadn't left.

"In the kitchen, why—" he stopped when he saw Ren standing beside her with Ellie. "Hello," he said, unsure of what to say, or do, really. "Are you one of Kelsey's friends?"

It was clear her father didn't recognize him either. That made things a little more awkward, unfortunately.

"I am," Ren said. "We've been friends for quite some time now. It's good to see you again," Ren said. He could tell it went right over her father's head. "With your permission, why don't we get reacquainted. It has been a long time."

Kelsey led Ren to the couch, where they sat down. Her father walked off to find her mother. Moments later, a woman with the same copper hair came into the room holding a glass, and a little girl bounded into the room happily. Alexis, Kelsey's younger sister.

Kelsey's mother stopped when she saw Ren sitting on the couch, his arm behind Kelsey, and a little girl sitting next to them.

"Hello there," she said, cheeks-stained red.

"Hello," Ren said back. Okay, he didn't want to admit it, but he was enjoying this. Even Kelsey couldn't hold back her laughter, seeing her mother's expression. Apparently, Ren had that effect on every female, regardless of age.

"Man, this place is exactly as I remember it," Ren said. "I wish my father could be here. I know he wanted to get back in touch with you guys. Still, aside from Alexis getting so big, you two haven't changed a bit," he said to her parents. "It's been a long time, Jacob, Ella."

Kelsey's mother and father exchanged glances, suddenly putting the pieces together. Past the long hair, the rippling muscles and height, they recognized the familiar smooth voice and cobalt blue eyes of the young boy they'd known for so long.

"Ren?" Kelsey's mother asked. He smiled at her, giving a light nod of his head and she crushed him in a hug. "We weren't sure we'd ever see you again. You just disappeared. Kelsey said you texted her that you were going to India, and we never heard from you again."

"I'm sorry for that. I had my own reasons, but, well, let's just say Kelsey already scolded me pretty good." Kelsey's cheeks suddenly burned with the heat of embarrassment.

"I know that things were rough for you after… after your mother died. We tried to help, but regardless, that must have been tough," her father said. "When did you get back?"

"Losing my mother certainly took its toll, yes," Ren admitted. "I returned earlier this week. I'm here working for my father."

"And the girl?" Jacob asked.

"I'm her guardian. She's living with me. I've got my own place. I came here to let you guys know I'm back. But there's something else I need to discuss with you concerning Kelsey."

Ren looked at Kelsey. "Go ahead and get ready. I'll be up in a few minutes." She nodded. "Ellie, why don't you go with Kelsey." Ellie hopped off the couch and followed after Kelsey.

Once they were out of view, he turned to Kelsey's parents. "So, here's the deal," he started to say.

"Hey, almost ready?" Ren asked, walking into the room.

"Almost done. What did you tell them?" Kelsey asked him, overly curious to know how they reacted. And what exactly he told them.

"That we're going on a trip for my job, and I needed your help," he said.

"And they believed that?"

"Well, I used a little magic to help persuade them. Nothing dangerous. Of course, I assured them that I wouldn't let you leave my side the entire time. That was our deal."

"That's one problem solved, then. What about school and my job?"

"Handled. I already talked to James. He'll take care of your leave from school. As for your job, it shouldn't matter. You work for Trinity now. We've already had your employment terminated."

"Oh, I guess you're right. You did offer me a position. Albeit not this exact one. But I forced myself into this. This means we're all set then," she said.

"How are you feeling?" he asked her. She recognized his question was not in regard to her physical condition.

"I can't tell if I'm more nervous or excited," she confessed.

"You know, this is your last chance to back out. Are you absolutely sure about coming? It's going to be dangerous."

"Yes, I'm sure. And nothing you say can change my mind."

"I've long since passed trying to change your mind. But I am worried you won't be able to keep up, or that something will happen to you."

Ren moved her hair out of her face and stared into her beautiful emerald-green eyes. His eyes moved to her lips. He felt the overtaking urge to kiss them but fought it back. Instead, he settled with touching his forehead to hers. After a few moments of contact, he moved his head away and handed her some more clothes to put in her suitcase. Once it was filled, she zipped it closed.

"Do you have hiking boots?" he asked. She shook her head. "Then we have to go get some. You'll need them."

Ren grabbed Kelsey's suitcase and followed her out of the room, closing the door behind him. She grabbed hold of his free hand and Ellie's. He took her bags outside and put them in the trunk.

Kelsey and Ellie sat down in the passenger seat. Ren walked around and got in the driver's seat. He started the car and revved the engine. Kelsey's parents were waving from the front door, to which she responded by mirroring the gesture.

Ren backed up and drove off. Their next stop was for hiking boots and other gear. From what Ren had heard in stories, the stones were located in the most remote places in the world. They had to prepare for everything.

They pulled into the parking lot of an outdoor recreation store. Ren looked for equipment while Kelsey looked for hiking boots. When he returned, he found her trying on a pair of tan hiking boots with black soles and brown laces. He carried a circle of rope and harnesses around his shoulder, as well as some other equipment.

Ren paid for her boots and the equipment and loaded what fit into the trunk. The rest he squeezed behind the seats.

"That's everything we need right now. I have plenty of equipment at home already," Ren said. "Let's get back and pack everything up."

Returning home after shopping, Ren grabbed the bags while Kelsey opened the door, and he placed them in the living room.

Kelsey seriously underestimated the involvement of this quest. There was so much gear it took them hours to sort it out and get everything loaded into the car. Thankfully, Ren's proficiency made stuffing everything into the small trunk much easier.

Kelsey was lying on the couch, exhausted, when Ren walked back inside. "I warned you," he said.

"I know. Just give me a minute," she said back.

"Why don't you come to bed? You'll feel better tomorrow after a full night's sleep."

Kelsey yawned and nodded. "Good idea." Ren was about to take Ellie to bed when a sharp pain ran through his head. A fit of dizziness fell over him.

"Ren, are you alright?" Kelsey asked. "You're bleeding."

Blood dripped from Ren's nose onto his hand. "Just… just need a minute," he said. He got up, his body shaking, and managed to walk to the doorway. He turned and went to his room as fast as he could manage.

At the foot of the mini fridge in the wardrobe, Ren collapsed. With shaky hands, he managed to open the fridge and take out one of the bags of blood. He ripped the top off and chugged the contents. Once he drank the blood, he waited for his condition to subside, closing the wardrobe and tossing the packet.

"Are you alright?" Kelsey asked. She stood in the doorway nervously.

"I'm fine," he said. "It happens sometimes."

Six minutes. That's how long it took for the side effects to subside this time. This wasn't good. They hadn't even left yet, and already things were off to a bad start.

Thirteen

Into The Darkness

The first streaks of sunlight were just passing over the horizon when Kelsey first stirred. Ren was sleeping soundly with his arm still around her. It took her a moment to remember they had slept in his room last night. His presence relaxed her, and she was able to sleep soundly.

The next time Kelsey woke, Ren wasn't in bed. Sunlight shined through the windows. She quickly brushed her hair, then went to see if she could find him.

Walking through the house, she was drawn by the sound of music. She followed it into the kitchen, where she saw a shirtless Ren and his father cooking breakfast while listening to rock music. She greeted his father politely. With Ren, it was easy to forget he was a vampire prince. But with his father, it would take time for her get used to him and be more comfortable around.

Kelsey asked Ren if they needed help, to which Ren told her she could help set the table. So, she rummaged through the cupboards for glasses, napkins, and silverware, setting them in place at the table.

"Do you drink coffee, Kelsey?" Ren's father asked.

"Yes sir. Cream, no sugar, please."

"Creamer is in the fridge, dad," Ren said. "Left side, third drawer down on the door."

Leo poured the creamer into the coffee and handed it to her. Kelsey took a whiff and let the heat and smell fill her. As soon as the food was done, Ren filled the plates and set them on the table. He wrapped another for Ellie and put it in the fridge.

"You two are leaving today, correct?" Leo asked. "Ren already told me about the quest. I'm sure you've already heard it enough, but I cannot stress how dangerous this will be. Are you absolutely sure about this, Kelsey?"

"This isn't your mission, nor is it your war to fight. Honestly, I would much rather Ren had erased your memory to save you from all of this. You're human, you're not one of us. The dangers you will face on this quest will be unimaginable to you. Is there anything I can do to convince you otherwise?"

"You're right; I have no idea what to expect. I have no idea of the dangers, and I have no doubt that I will experience severe hardship. Like you said, I'm not part of your world. But I want to be. More than anything, Ren and I need each other. I will never have a chance to do something as great as this in my life again. I have to take this opportunity, no matter the dangers. I want all of you in my life, and I want to be a part of yours."

Leo released a heavy sigh. "I see. Very well, then. I will not stop you, but if something should happen to you, Ren will be crushed, and I don't want to lose either of you. Now that Verin's making moves, this quest is even more important, and even more dangerous."

"Which is why we need to get these stones," Ren said back. "And we will."

"Verin's generals may be strong, but even they can't take the top two ranked Heaven's Blades at the same time," Ren said. "I know it's a desperate ploy, but it's all we have left. Leave this part of the battle to Marcus and me. You have to believe in us."

"I do believe in you. In both of you. I know exactly what you're capable of, and when you two work together, you're unstoppable. But that doesn't mean I don't fear that something will go wrong. And in a fight against Verin's generals, even the smallest mistake is guaranteed death."

"Marcus and I haven't made a mistake in over a hundred years. Like I said, we've got this."

Leo let out a deep sigh. "You're right; it'll work. It has to," he said, taking a sip of his coffee.

Noon hit, and Ren and Kelsey were ready to leave. He changed into his usual outfit. Leather jacket, black pants, belt, combat boots, white and brown mixed shirt, and black fingerless leather gloves. Kelsey wore a black tank top, brown short cargo shorts, and her new hiking boots.

Kelsey's new look was a little off-putting to Ren. He had told her to dress comfortably, but perhaps that was a little too comfortable. It was exactly the opposite of battle ready.

"I'll be back soon," he told Ellie. "Shouldn't be any more than a couple of months. Listen to Leo, and I'll call you whenever I have the chance."

"Bye, Ren. Come home soon," she said, putting her arms around him in a hug.

Ren's father handed him a metal briefcase. "Be safe."

"We will. Watch over the house." They embraced, then it was Nidar's turn. The white tiger put one arm over Ren's shoulder and rested his head on his other. "Be good while I'm gone. Be sure to protect Ellie and Leo." The tiger whined. "I know. I'm going to miss you too, but it won't be for too long. I'll be back before you know it." The tiger licked him, and Ren kissed him on top of the head."

"Let's go," Ren said to Kelsey. He opened the passenger side for her, then got in the driver's side. He pulled out of the garage, and they were on their way. Grand Central was already programmed on his GPS. It would take over sixteen hours to get there.

The drive was long and quiet. Save for the music, neither Ren nor Kelsey spoke much. When they did reach their destination, instead of heading straight for the terminal, Ren ventured into the city.

When Kelsey asked why they were going out of the way, he told her the importance of discretion. If they parked somewhere secluded but occupied, should their enemies make an appearance, it actually made escaping easier. True, it would take much longer, being so far from the car, but they could slip away much easier using the entirety of the city. Nor would they be followed.

Ren found a parking garage in the city and found a spot in the middle levels. Crossing his golden sword over his back, he holstered his pistols and sheathed a dagger at his side. With a snap of his fingers, the weapons disappeared.

"Magic," he said before she could ask. "I've rendered them invisible so no one can see them. That be human or monster."

They took an elevator down to ground level and headed to the terminal.

It was an hour's walk to reach the terminal, but it stood proudly. The classical architectural design vastly different from its lavish interior. Kelsey couldn't believe how busy the place was. It was almost dark out, but there were still so many people.

Ren was at her side and they entered the terminal. It was beyond words to someone like Kelsey had never been there before. She'd only ever seen it in moves.

"The food court is this way," Ren said. "Let's get something to eat."

As they walked, Ren caught on to a presence. It maintained pace with them the entire time.

"Kelsey," he said calmly. "Give me your hand."

"Okay, but why?" She grabbed hold of his hand.

"Stay calm. We're being followed."

She looked at him with wide eyes, and he squeezed her hand. "Is it that necromancer, Verin? Or those Church guys?" she asked nervously.

"I don't know," he confessed.

She turned her head to look. "No!" he said quickly. Her head snapped back. "Don't look back; that will only draw attention. Just keep walking; act like you don't know anything. No matter what, don't draw attention to yourself, or it'll set them off."

"So, what do we do, start looking for the map?" Kelsey asked.

"There are too many people here. Besides, we're still waiting on Marcus. We'll have to bide our time for now. Then we'll need a distraction to keep everyone away."

"And how are we supposed to do that? Pull the fire alarm or something?" she asked. "There are so many people here. They'll catch on if we cause a scene."

"There are plenty of ways to cause a scene or a distraction without causing notice to ourselves. We have magic at our disposal too. For now, let's find something to eat and wait for Marcus."

The sun had long since faded from the horizon when Ren and Kelsey got a message from Marcus. Ren checked his phone for the time. "Ten o'clock," he said. "Let's go. We're meeting Marcus at the clock."

Kelsey pushed her chair in, following him after throwing out her trash. By now, most of the restaurants were closed, including the one they had ordered from. The number of pedestrians traveling through the building was nowhere near close to empty, despite that. They must have passed hundreds of people on the way to the service desk alone.

From the antique design to the use of materials, Kelsey saw the terminal in a completely different way. She was mostly familiar with the main lobby, where the central clock and service desk was. The same one they were to meet Marcus at.

Ren said something that Kelsey didn't make out. She was too busy looking at the marble floors and decorated walls.

"Kelsey. Keep focused," he said, finally getting her attention.

"Sorry. How are we supposed to find a map in a place this big?" she wondered.

"I don't know. They must have left something when they built the terminal. If they really did use this place to hide the map, there will be a clue somewhere."

The information booth clock was the first thing to come back into view after returning to the main concourse. Above, the green vaulted ceiling with the twelve zodiacs inked in gold floated above them.

Ren walked off, leaving Kelsey to herself. So, she decided to search somewhere else. She walked along the right side, inspecting the walls and columns. She found nothing. Ren checked out the back of the place, examining the columns, the walls, and the floor for anything. But like Kelsey, he, too, found nothing.

"There are too many people here," Kelsey said, when Ren found her. "I don't even know where to begin looking. I know we started here because we're waiting on Marcus. Do you think we're missing something?"

"I have no idea," he said. "The truth is, I can create a barrier and empty the place out. But I don't have enough magic for that, even with my heaven's blade. I need Marcus's help to do it."

"You guys look like you could use the help," said a familiar voice. Marcus walked toward them. "Ask and you shall receive."

"Hey, good, you're finally here. We're trying to find the map, but we've come up empty," Ren said. "There are too many people. We need to clear this place out."

"Then let's send these dear passengers on their way, shall we," Marcus said back. Ren nodded, and they each said something in that pretty language of theirs.

The area around them suddenly went silent, almost frozen. They unsheathed their heaven's blades and placed the tips on the ground. An invisible sphere shot out around them, expanding to cover the entire terminal. The pedestrians inside slowly filed out, almost as if bewitched. Soon, the once busy terminal was abandoned.

Together, the three of them spent the next several hours searching the terminal. They searched beyond the main concourse to the other concourses, but still turned up empty. Marcus was still scouring the main concourse when he returned to the information desk and clock for the umpteenth time. There was something here, he was sure of it. Its location, the feel of magic it emanated. The clock was the clue.

Marcus called Ren and Kelsey and told them to meet him back at the clock. Ren was the first of the two to arrive, Kelsey coming minutes later.

"Ren, come here and check this out."

"What's up? Find something?" Ren asked, jogging up to him.

"I think so. Do you feel that?" Ren stopped next to Marcus, unsure of what he was implying. "Magic," Marcus said. "I can feel traces of it emanating from the clock."

"What does that mean?" Kelsey asked. "Helpful?"

"It means this clock is the clue," Ren answered. He walked around the lock and the desks. Inspecting every part of them, along with the floor. He tried to focus on the magic Marcus said he felt. Sure enough, Ren felt the steady stream of magic pouring out. "I don't see anything. But I do feel magic emanating from somewhere."

Kelsey sighed and leaned against the information desk, trying to think. She looked down and noticed something off about one of the panels, kneeling to get a better look. She called them over, and Marcus knelt next to her.

Ren got three steps in before a sudden pain flooded through his head. His vision faded and started to blur. *Damn it!* he thought.

"I need a minute," Ren told them. He walked to the bathroom, turned on the water, and splashed it onto his face. His breathing was getting heavy. He reached behind him and took one of the vials of blood kept on his belt.

He uncorked the vial and quickly drank the blood, his senses returning and headache disappearing. Breathing out deeply, he corked the vial and put it back in its loop on his belt, heading back over to where Kelsey and Marcus were.

"This might be it," Marcus said. Ren knelt down to get a look. One of the panels near the floor had an empty gap just big enough to fit their hands into. For something so meticulously designed, it was much too out of place.

Ren placed his fingers in between, but the panel didn't budge. "Marcus, help me with this," he said.

Marcus reached his hands in and grabbed the panel. Together, they pulled as hard as they could. It sprung out toward them, rotated from its original orientation. Ren returned it to its previous state and pushed it back into place.

They heard a single click, but nothing happened. Kelsey backed up to get a better view of the source, then preceded to walk around. On the other side of the information desk was another panel sticking out from its previous spot. It required Ren's and Marcus's help, but they managed to turn it back and push it into place.

There was another click followed by a ticking sound. Something on the top of the clock raised into view. It looked like a button.

Ren and Marcus exchanged long glances. Could it really be? Was Grand Central really a cover-up? How had no one noticed?

Ren started climbing, careful not to damage the desk or the clock. Inside, he could see the emergency staircase for the workers at the desk. Gently, he pressed the button at the top of the clock, and it fit perfectly into place, seemingly unnoticeable. The sound of gears turning was followed by a grinding noise. All the doors swung open, and they descended the service stairs used only by the workers.

At the bottom of the stairs, a hatch the same material as the floor sat open, revealing a ladder that led down into a hidden passageway. Were it not open, no one would ever realize it was there. It was truly unbelievable.

"Come on, let's get this map," Ren said.

They climbed down the ladder, leading down into the passageway. Once they reached the bottom, all the doors and the hatch above closed shut, sealing them in, and enveloping them in darkness.

Fourteen

That Which Guides Hope

It was pitch black in the passageway. The sound of a pebble hitting the floor made Kelsey jump. She couldn't tell who, but she landed in someone's arms.

"Kelsey. *Sab theek hai*?" Ren asked. "Is everything alright?"

"Sorry, I guess I'm a little nervous since we're sealed off and it's so dark."

Light suddenly filled the room. Ren held one arm around Kelsey, and the other held his heaven's blade. Marcus had drawn his as well. "There, now we have light."

Kelsey was mesmerized looking at the golden swords. They radiated golden energy and light.

"They're called heaven's blades," Marcus said. "In case you didn't know."

"I know about the Heaven's Blades, but no one has ever explained anything to me," she told him.

"The thirteen strongest monsters who have proven themselves are given one of thirteen divine blades. No one knows who actually created them, or why. The holy magic they contain is how they got the name. Those who receive and have the honor to wield one are given its title. Heaven's Blade, literally, a warrior of heaven."

"Keep up, you guys," Ren said. "Fall behind, and we could be separated." Marcus and Kelsey hastened their pace. Although dark without the light of their heaven's blades, the passageway was relatively straight, making it easy to navigate. They followed it for a long time in silence, Ren in the lead and Marcus bringing up the rear.

Kelsey slowed down to walk beside Marcus. "Something on your mind?" he asked.

"I guess I'm just curious to learn more about it. The whole Heaven's Blade thing, I mean."

"Heaven's Blades are ranked based on the abilities of their wielder, not of the weapon. As far as ranking goes, I'm hitting second."

"Second! That's amazing."

"Well, it does coordinate with our rank in Trinity, remember? I'm second-ranked. That's because I'm the second-ranked Heaven's Blade."

"Oh, so that means Ren's top-ranked?"

"Ren? He's the best of us. He's rifted more shades than anyone in Trinity, ever. His count is so high that if you put the number of rifts of everyone in Trinity together, they would just about match up."

"So, Ren is stronger than you, then. I guess that fits with the whole the strongest species rules in your world."

"Mmm, yes and no. Ren might be ranked first, but our power is about even. Ren is ranked first for another reason. Truth is, Ren doesn't have access to all of his powers. If he did, far and few would be able to stand a chance against him."

Kelsey stared at Ren. He still walked ahead of them, too far to hear their conversation. What was it like to wield that much power?

They walked for what seemed like hours until Ren came to a stop.

"Do you hear that?" he asked them. "Listen."

Marcus's head twitched slightly. Kelsey wondered what that was about, only to realize he was listening and reacting to sudden changes in sound. His hearing was impossibly acute.

"Water. Probably a river. It's coming from below," he said.

Kelsey took the lead, walking ahead of them. "I can't believe this has been hidden beneath grand central the whole time."

"Kelsey, wait a minute," Ren said.

"We need to keep going," she said. "I seriously doubt any water—" She stopped when the ground beneath her shattered, and she fell through a hole. Her backside hit something solid and she was sliding fast.

"Kelsey!" Ren shouted. He jumped into the hole and slid down after her.

Kelsey realized fast that the slide was coming to an end, but it was so dark she couldn't see anything around her that wasn't lit by Ren's sword. All she could make out was where the slide stopped and met the void.

"Kells, Grab my hand!" Ren yelled. Kelsey reached out and grabbed hold of him as they reached the end of the slide. Ren dug his sword into it, bringing them to a stop.

With Ren's sword lighting the way, Kelsey could make out her surroundings a little better. The slide was an actual slide. A downward slope made of dirt. They hung off the edge, inside of a chamber with stalagmites hanging from the ceiling and wet rocky floors. They would have been torn to shreds if they hadn't stopped. The sound of running water was now easily visible, indicating that there was, in fact, water below.

"Ren!" Marcus called from above. "Don't let go!"

"No shit!" he yelled back. Despite the situation, Kelsey couldn't control her giggling.

"Grab my shoulder and hold on tight, Kells. I'll get us out of this in a minute," Ren said to her. With some effort, she managed to grab it from behind. "Now, the other."

"What? No way. I'll fall!"

"I've got you, trust me." He raised the hand she held high into the air. The force took Kelsey with it, her body rising into the air.

She grabbed Ren's shoulder, and he put his now free hand under her to stabilize her. "Wrap your legs around my waist," he told her. She did as he said and crossed her legs in front of him at his waist.

Ren looked around the cavern. Off to the side, he spotted a set of stairs. They had to lead somewhere. Perhaps they were a way down, or back up. "Marcus, there's a set of stairs!" Ren shouted. "I'm going to blast an opening. See if you can find it!"

Ren drew the dagger at his side with his free hand and drove it deep into the dirt slide, twisting it to secure their position. He took his sword out and raised it into the air. The glow and energy coming from it increased.

"Lend me your help with this one, Shadow Hunter."

He swung the sword down, and a blade of golden energy shot toward the stairway, blasting apart the cavern walls around it. Only a large hole remained.

In this attempt to climb onto the slide, it began to crack. With their combined weight, it wouldn't hold out much longer. He needed to think. Marcus was on the move; they could wait. No, waiting was not the right option. Who knew how long it would take him to reach the stairs, or if he was even able to reach them? He had to be careful of Kelsey, who held on to him tightly, but he simply didn't have the time to wait on Marcus.

Ren's only choice was to use magic, but as he wouldn't see the bottom until they were too close to it, the chance of them getting injured or worse was high.

"Kelsey, we're going to drop," Ren told her.

"Drop!" What the hell was he thinking? Had Ren finally lost his mind?

"I just need a little more time to cast my magic. The higher we are, the more of it I'll have. You have to trust me. Now hold on tight."

Kelsey tightened her grip on him. He could feel her shaking. She was scared, and he couldn't blame her.

Gripping his dagger tightly, he gave it a hard yank. The edge of the slide gave way, and they were falling. Kelsey failed to hold back her screams.

Ren sheathed his dagger and spun around, gathering his magic. Wind whirled around them, quickly picking up speed. Soon, Kelsey realized they were no longer falling. Daring herself to peak, she opened one eye. Ren's palm faced down, the other held his sword. No longer were they falling to their deaths. Instead, they floated in place, the wind keeping them upright. The only light was the golden glow of his sword. Ren flexed his magic and slowly forced them to descend.

When his feet touched solid ground, he knew they were in the clear. He gave Kelsey a tap, indicating that she was free to let go. Slowly, she unwrapped herself from around him. Her legs shook like mad, the fear of falling still imminent in her memory.

Ren saw her wobble, and he put a hand on her waist to steady her. It took her a minute to regain her bearings.

"Thanks. I'm okay now." Ren nodded and released her.

Looking around, he took in their surroundings. The water they'd previously heard was only ten feet from where they stood. It moved at a substantial pace, but the water itself was relatively shallow. *More like a stream than anything else,* he thought.

"Hey! You guys, alright?" Marcus asked. He came down the stairs as they crossed the stream and ran over to them.

"We're fine," Ren said, intrigued by the stream. "This has to come from somewhere. It could prove beneficial if we can the source."

"The slide aside, someone built those stairs I took for a reason. They wouldn't have done so otherwise."

"Perhaps Kelsey falling through that hole was a saving grace. I think we're on the right track."

The three of them walked to the other side of the cavern. Where previously unnoticed, with the combined light of their heaven's blades, they saw a crack in the wall. It arched at the top, maintaining its smoothness and thickness. That wasn't just a crack; it was a door.

"There's got to be a way to open this," Ren said. Kelsey checked out a circular extension of rock next to the door. A slit was cut into it.

"Looks like we need some sort of Key," Kelsey said. Ren drew his dagger and rammed it into the keyhole.

"Or you could just do that."

He turned the knife, and the extension followed. Once it could be turned no more, it stopped, but the door still didn't open. Ren pushed in on the stone, and the extension slid back into the rock wall.

One side of the door released, and it slid inward. It was only a slight movement, never clearing the stone, but it was enough. Ren and Marcus put all their weight against the door and pushed. The door slid open, revealing another larger passageway beyond.

Passing through the doorway, they headed down the passageway until they entered a large dome-shaped chamber. In the center lay a large pool of water. The light of Ren's and Marcus's swords reflecting off the water cast a light teal glow around the room, but the water was still clear enough that you could see to the bottom. Above them, a circular ledge spanned the entire size of the chamber.

"Well, looks like we found the source of that water," Ren said.

"Look," Marcus said, pointing.

In the center of the water was a stone podium with a single parchment lying flat against it. A solid stone walkway connected to a circular platform where the podium was.

"Marcus, watch Kelsey," Ren said.

"Whoa, bro, don't you think someone else should do this instead? Let me cross."

"I've got this." Reluctantly, Marcus nodded, inching closer to Kelsey.

Ren made his way across the walkway to the podium, gazing at the worn piece of parchment. There it was; the map to the stones. He picked up the map, feeling the material against his fingers, then returned to where Marcus and Kelsey stood. "Come on, let's get out of here before we read it."

"It's far too late for that," said a voice. Seemingly out of nowhere, dozens of people filed out from above onto the ledge. Every one of them wore animal masks over their faces. They dressed in white robes with a red angel on the front. She knelt on her knees in prayer, a red border around her. Auroras. The Radiant Church had found them. They were surrounded.

Fifteen

Pray, My Angel

"Look at what I've caught," said the voice from before. A man with a large stomach addressed them, clearly superior to the rest of the clergy on the ledge.

Though he wore the same robes, a tall white hat sat upon his head. In his hands, a golden staff with the same angel as their robes, only this time her arms were held out above her head, and she looked to the sky. He wore a silver mask on the left side of his face, exposing half of it.

"A vampire, a werewolf, and a… oh my, a human? Talk about an unexpected combination. What in the world are you doing with these two, my dear?"

"That's none of your business," she said.

"What are the likes of you doing here, Arron?" Ren asked. The man sneered at the sound of the name. "Why don't you go crawl back into whatever hole you came out of? I take it then that was you guys following us earlier?"

"The only hole I will be crawling into is the one I'll be burying your body in, Ren." They knew each other's names. From the way they spoke to each other, it was apparent that not only did they know each other, they had history.

"You know, my dear, you really shouldn't associate yourself with someone like him," the man said to Kelsey. "The Blood Prince isn't someone you want to have as your company. He's nothing but a monster above monsters."

"I'll decide who I keep as my company," she said.

"You really don't have the right to talk about the company you keep," Ren said to the man. "Not now that you've allied yourselves with Verin."

"Oh, I assure you, it's only a temporary thing," said the man. "We'll deal with him thoroughly after we've gotten what we need. That includes you and the girl too. If she's allied herself with you, then she'll die alongside you."

"Really? That's so sweet of you. Can we be buried together too?" Ren asked sarcastically. "Let me guess, you want the map?"

"Precisely. If we can find the stones, then we'll have the power to destroy you. Even the infamous Nightwalker Clan will not be enough to stop us." Then he turned his eyes on Kelsey. "I see you've seduced yet another innocent girl into assisting in your dirty work."

"Seduced isn't exactly the word I would use."

"And yet, you haven't even told her about the stones, have you?" Ren was quiet. "I knew it. You've put your faith in the wrong man, my dear."

"Searching for the stones without even knowing their use, let alone their value, is aberrantly stupid. The Sun Stone, a stone with the ability to bring life and prosperity. Those who basked in its presence were granted love, and their desires fulfilled. And the Moon Stone, a stone of darkness. Used to take lives and wreak havoc upon the world. Those who dare to enter upon its sanctum are met with death and despair. Poverty, illness, terrible luck, and loss of their sanity. But when they are brought together, the two stones create miracles and grant wishes. They grant order and freedom, and above all, limitless power."

"So, what your saying is you want to use the stones to enact a genocide, while we want to use them to save lives?" Kelsey summed up.

"I care not what any of you think. Nor does it matter which side you choose. I will not allow you to get your hands on the stones." He pulled an old colt pistol from his robes and pointed it at Kelsey. "Because you're human, I will kill you first." He pulled the trigger, and instinctively, she closed her eyes. BANG!

That was the last sound Kelsey heard. Everything was quiet, then she realized she was still alive. She felt around her body but found nothing. Opening her eyes, Ren stood in front of her, his arm raised to his chest.

"Ren!" she said frantically.

"Stay back, Kells," he said. She stopped herself mid-step at his words. Ren looked at her, then turned his gaze back at Arron. "You're going to have to do much better than that."

"How is this possible? That was a silver bullet," the priest said. Against a silver bullet, there was no way Ren should have been able to escape unscathed. No matter how powerful he was.

"Really, Arron? You know silver only works when it penetrates." He opened his hand, and a bullet dropped to the ground.

"You caught it? No way could you have reacted that fast. It's a gun!"

"Dude, magic, duh. Besides, that's not a gun; it's an antique." Ren pulled out one of his Beretta's. "This is a gun," he said, and fired.

The colt flew out of Arron's hand, dropping into the water below. "Ow! Damn it, Ren, that was my favorite gun!"

All of a sudden, a dense fog rolled through the room. It collected at their shins, growing higher bit by bit. "What is this? Where did this fog come from? We're in a cave for God's sake!"

Nice timing, Marcus, Ren thought. They exchanged glances and nodded. The fog was at their waists now.

Marcus dove left, and Ren dove right, taking Kelsey with him. He drew his heaven's blade and released a blade of golden energy that ripped through half of the balcony. The clergy fell into the water as Ren grabbed Kelsey and sprinted for the exit, Marcus at their side.

"Marcus, take Kelsey," Ren said. He picked Kelsey up as Marcus's form changed. He got taller; the view of his muscles replaced by thick light brown fur. His nose elongated into a snout with razor-sharp teeth, and ears appeared in his head. His fingernails extended into razor-sharp claws.

Before Kelsey could protest, Ren threw her to Marcus, who caught her in his arms. "Hold on," he told her. At least his voice was the same. He helped her onto his back, and they took off at speeds faster than Kelsey thought possible.

Ren drew his second pistol, turned around, and fired away. The clergy of the Radiant Church dropped like stones. A wave of white energy barreled past him, just barely missing. Arron.

Racing after Marcus and Kelsey, he continued firing, emptying more clips into the Church's clergy. It was clear his bullets were getting nowhere, not with Arron's powers. Changing tactics, he holstered his guns and gathered his ki, the energy within his body. In one ferocious attack, the tunnel crumbled behind him as he ran.

Looking behind, the last of the tunnel collapsed, and the remaining clergy were sealed. No escaping from that.

Marcus and Kelsey were waiting by the door at the entrance to the tunnel when Ren caught up to them. Marcus had his ice bow drawn, an arrow nocked and ready to fire. When he saw Ren coming, he fired. The arrow flew past him and struck the ground behind him. A wall of ice shot up to the ceiling.

"Just in case," Marcus said when Ren stopped next to them. "No normal person or monster would be able to survive, but Arron isn't exactly normal."

"We slowed them down, at least. Let's get out of here," Ren said to him.

The stone steps Marcus took entering the cavern stood strong. An opening waited for them at the top. Climbing the stairs, they entered into the passageway they'd come from. They turned left and started running again.

"Why are we running?" Kelsey asked. "They're trapped."

"The staff Arron has is enchanted," Ren said. "One only those of quincy-rank can use."

"What's a quincy?" she asked. The name was completely foreign to her, including the Church's ranks.

"The Radiant Church has four ranks in its clergy. Auroras are the lowest rank. Above them are high priests. Then, there's the quincy, like Arron. There are very few quincies in the Church, and the only rank below the paxon, of which there is only one. The paxon is the head of the Radiant Church. Not to mention Arron's capable of generating their ki like us. On the chance he managed to escape, we need to get out of here as soon and as fast as possible."

"Ki? What's ki?"

"Internal energy. I'll explain later. For now, just focus on running and getting out of here."

They continued down the passageway in silence. As they ran, Kelsey realized the only footsteps she heard were her own. Ren and Marcus didn't make a sound.

"How are you doing that? I can't hear your footsteps."

"Habit," Ren said. "Quiet footsteps are a necessity in assassinations."

"Werewolves are known for their speed," Marcus told her. "As such, we have the ability to mask the sound of our steps. We're quite famous for it, actually."

"My father taught it to me, and he learned it from Marcus's father," Ren added. "Heads up, I think I see the exit up ahead."

"How can you tell?" Kelsey asked. "All I see is darkness."

"A vampire's sight is far better than a human's. And I'm picking up traces of fresh air."

It took longer to get to the entrance than they expected. After ten more minutes of running, Kelsey had to stop to catch her breath. Ren swept her off her feet, and they continued running.

Eventually, the passageway came to a stop. Thanks to the glow of Ren and Marcus's swords, they could see around them. Built into the ceiling was a wooden door.

"Give me a boost," Kelsey said. Ren knelt down.

"Hop on," he said. Kelsey put one leg over his shoulder, then the other one. He stood back up, holding her securely so she could work without worry of falling.

Opening the door took a little finagling, but she finally got it. Pushing up slightly, it lifted enough for her to get a peek at the surroundings. "It's clear," she said back.

Ren sent out his senses, using his vampire powers to sense blood flow. He sensed no indications of life.

"I'm not hearing any pursuers behind us either," Marcus said. "We're clear. Go ahead." Ren nodded and let Kelsey down. He walked to the wall and started walking vertically.

"Okay, that's creepy," Kelsey said. "Is that a vampire ability?"

Ren stopped moving, standing upside down on the ceiling. He cupped Kelsey's cheeks with both hands. "It most certainly is," he said. "Comes in handy, actually."

Switching back to all fours, he pushed up on the door. It flipped over, and he climbed out. "Come on," he said to Marcus. They grabbed hands, and Ren pulled him up.

Finally, it was Kelsey's turn. Ren grabbed her hands and pulled her up.

Once they were all out, he closed the door. The dim light of the moon barely lit their surroundings, and they didn't draw their heaven's blades for light either.

Kelsey walked around and came upon what looked like a door. "Guys, I think I found an exit." She tried to open it, but it wouldn't budge. "It's locked."

"Move, I'll get it," Ren told her.

"Hey, did you guys hear that?" asked a voice. It came from outside. The three of them stopped dead. "I swear I just heard voices. It sounded like it came from that building."

Beads of sweat dripped down Kelsey's forehead. Ren waved Marcus off. He nodded, then snuck away without making a sound.

"You're hearing things, man. Come on," another voice sounded.

"No, I'm telling you I heard voices. I'm going to check it out," said the first voice.

Ren looked at Kelsey. The footsteps were drawing nearer. He put Kelsey up against the wall and grabbed the nearest object he could find, tossing it out a window. The shattering of glass, followed by the impact of the object, was enough to scare off whoever was outside. They waited for several minutes, and when no other sounds or movement came, they determined it safe.

Marcus crept out from his hiding space. "Nice cover," he said. "Luckily, this place is full of stuff."

Ren placed his hand over the door handle. He cast another spell, and they heard the sound of the door unlocking. He turned the handle and pushed the door open, then stepped into the night.

Sixteen

The Lost Language

Kelsey crashed face-first onto the hotel bed. "It's already three in the morning," Kelsey said.

"Get some sleep," Ren told her.

"Yes, Your Highness."

"Hey," he said, indicating her use of his title. She knew he hated that.

Kelsey laughed into her pillow, but she could tell their conversation with the clerk at the front desk was still heavy on his conscience.

When Ren pulled into the hotel parking lot, Marcus was already waiting. They checked in with the clerk at the front desk, a man in his later forties. As he worked his fingers on the keyboard, Ren noticed something about the man. He had an aura inside him.

"What race of monster are you?" he asked. "I can sense your monster energy. You're not exactly hiding it."

The man didn't look surprised. It was true that he wasn't hiding his energy. "I'm a centaur." A centaur, a B-rank monster.

"Really? You guys are rare in the human world."

He shrugged. "Nexus just suits us better than the human world. But there are so many monsters in this city, it might as well be overrun. What about the other two?"

"Monster and human," Ren said. "Don't worry, the human's with us. She's a good friend of mine. She already knows our secret."

"I see. Is she trustworthy?"

"More than any other human I've ever met. If I can't trust her, then I can't trust anybody, even other monsters."

The man nodded, satisfied. "For a fellow monster, I'll give you a dis—" he stopped as soon as he saw Ren's name on the computer. "Ren Nightwalker?" he asked in shock.

The man quickly dropped to one knee. "Your Highness, please, forgive my rudeness for not recognizing you. That must mean this is Prince Allagash," the man said, bowing to Marcus.

"It's alright, no harm done. It's been a while since we've last been to Nexus anyway. This world is a big place."

Kelsey got Marcus's attention discretely. "Dose this happen to you two a lot?" He nodded back.

"As the princes of the two most well-known and powerful races, we're shown the proper respect. Nexus is feudal based, so this is a common occurrence for us."

"Your Highnesses, if I may be so bold as to ask, what are your current actions? The last I heard, you were with Trinity leading the resistance."

"We are. We're on a quest right now. I'm afraid I can't tell you more. You never know who's listening. Word could get out. Well, I guess it already has."

"If you're asking about my allegiance, it doesn't lie with Verin. I have family in Trinity, and of course, support the resistance myself."

"Who?" Ren asked, suddenly curious. Normally he wouldn't care, but coming from a centaur, it was different.

"My half-brother, Harley Fierro."

Ren and Marcus looked at the man in shock. "Harley! Then you must be Nicola." He confirmed with a nod.

"Who's Harley Fierro?" Kelsey asked.

"He's another Heaven's Blade, rank eleven," Ren answered. He and Marcus exchanged a nod. "If you're Harley's half-brother, then I think we can trust you. Do you have a place we can talk in private?" Nicola nodded, and led them to the back room, locking the door. They grabbed a seat at the small table in the middle of the room.

"For starters, have you heard anything about what's going on lately?"

"Yeah. James Wilson is an old friend of mine. We used to be on the same team, acting as guards for your father. He's kept me up to date on everything. Is it true he thinks he found the map?"

Ren nodded and pulled the map out from inside his jacket. "We just got back from retrieving it. And we had a run-in with the Church in the process."

Nicola rested the palms of his hands on his forehead. "So what James said is true. The Church has allied themselves with Verin."

"Maybe not," Ren admitted. The Church's resources are extraordinary, but they don't seem to be totally on the same side as Verin. It seems they're only working together to stop us from getting the stones, that's all. Their actions seem to be independent of each other."

"Is that so. Maybe all is not lost then. Have you already looked at the map?"

"No. We'll look as soon as we get to our rooms."

"In that case, I'll get your room keys and call James to let him know you've found the map."

"Thank you," Ren said. "If you're making calls, do you mind letting Harley know as well? Having as many Heaven's Blades up to date on the status of our quest will be helpful."

"I'll do that. Good luck Your Highnesses." They shook hands, then went to grab their gear from the cars.

Outside their rooms, Marcus opened the door, and they walked inside. Ren and Marcus set the gear down on the inside space between the beds.

Kelsey plopped down onto the bed nearest to the door. Only now were the effects and length of the day taking its effects on her.

"I'm going to look at the map. I'll tell you what I find tomorrow morning," Ren said.

"I'm not so tired that I can't focus on our quest, Ren," Kelsey said back. "But if it's alright, I'd like to shower."

Ren couldn't argue with her, so he let her return to her own room.

Kelsey felt refreshed after taking her shower. She threw on a pair of pink and white cotton shorts and a white t-shirt, her usual nightwear.

Exiting her room, she knocked on the door to Ren and Marcus's room. The werewolf in question opened the door and let her inside. She sat down on the edge of one of the beds.

Ren could hear Marcus and Kelsey from the bathroom. His hands shook as he lifted the last vile of blood to his mouth, making it difficult to drink, especially without spilling it. With some effort, he managed to drink the blood. *Damn, it's getting worse,* he thought. *One vial a day now.*

When the effects first hit, Ren had grabbed the briefcase his father had given him. He set it on the counter and opened it. The entire case was filled with packets of transfusion blood. *Thanks, dad.*

He refilled his empty vials with one of the packets and exited the bathroom with the case. Kelsey found herself unintentionally staring at him. He wore tan cargo shorts and was shirtless.

Ren set the briefcase down and grabbed the map, sitting next to Kelsey, then spread the map out on the bed. They all leaned over to get a good look at it. The parchment looked so old Kelsey thought it would turn to dust any second. It showed the world as a common map did with geographic designs. A marker was visible on the eastern part of the US, New York City.

The rest of the map had writing on it that Kelsey couldn't read. A mixture of symbols and letters blended together.

"What the hell is this?" Marcus asked, indicating the symbols. "Some kind of ancient language? No one said anything about the map being in a strange language."

"You can't read it?" Kelsey asked. She had really hoped he or Ren would be able to given that she couldn't.

"This is unexpected," Ren said. "I recognize this language, though I can't read it. I never thought it'd appear on the map to the Sun and Moon Stones of all things."

"You know what language this is?" Marcus asked. "Then do you know who can read it?"

"Perhaps. This is the ancient language of the vampires. It makes sense that you wouldn't know it. The problem is, most vampires now can't as well, myself included. It was lost millennia ago. I can make out a few words, but that's it. Most of the ones who could died ages ago. The rest are mostly in hiding somewhere in Nexus."

"So, then we've got no way to read it," Kelsey assumed.

"I didn't say we were out of options," Ren said, still eyeing the map. "I know the location of someone who can read them. Someone who lives in the human world. The one who trained me."

"Isn't that your father?" Kelsey asked.

"No. My father taught me some of my abilities, like silent steps, but most of what he taught me was about running the kingdom. It was another vampire who taught me all of my vampiric abilities and how to use magic. I was told to keep his existence a secret, but given the situation, I think it's necessary to reveal it."

"He's here, in the human world?" Marcus asked. "Where? I thought he never left Nexus." Marcus was aware of Ren's vampire teacher; however, he had not seen him since he was ten.

"The peak of Mt. Whitney. The highest summit of the Sierra Nevada," said Ren.

"Where's that?" Kelsey asked.

"California," Ren answered. "However, the journey up the mountain isn't a pleasant experience. We'll head out tomorrow. It's going to take three days to get there."

"Three days?" Kelsey asked. She released something between a sigh and a moan. "Alright, I'll see you guys in the morning," she said.

Ren watched as Kelsey left the room.

"Are you alright?" Marcus asked. "You don't show it, but something's wrong with you."

"I'm fine. But my craving for blood is getting worse. I need one vial a day now."

Marcus was quiet for a minute. "Ren, maybe you should think about—"

"Don't even finish that sentence!" Ren said angrily, his ki bubbling off his body.

Marcus raised his hands in defeat. "Alright, alright, forget I said it. Just so you know, though, if you're ever in need, I'll be there for you." He went to the other bed and turned off the light. "You can't keep running away," he said.

Kelsey lay in bed, unable to sleep. Thoughts plagued her mind, and every time they changed to Ren. She felt the uncontrollable urge to be with him. She wanted him next to her. She wanted his arms around her. Why now was she feeling like this? She had never even thought about it when they were kids, and they used to take baths together. But ever since he came back from India, she couldn't control herself. Her face burned, and she covered her head with a pillow.

Finally, she couldn't take it anymore. The urge was too strong. She grabbed her room key and went to Ren's room. But standing outside the door, she was frozen. What should she do? Should she knock, or use her phone? Would they still be up? She didn't want to wake them.

All of a sudden, the door opened, making her jump. Marcus stood there. He raised an eyebrow. "Um…" she started to say. Her words disappeared. Why couldn't she think of anything?

Marcus rolled his eyes. "Here," he said, handing her his room Key. "I could smell you standing behind the door. You smell like strawberries. It's your shampoo." Kelsey ran her fingers through her hair. Marcus let out a quiet chuckle. "Good night, Kelsey."

"Good night," she said and handed him her room card.

Kelsey walked into the room and closed the door behind her. Now that she was in there, she was suddenly more nervous than when she stood outside the door. Stepping on the balls of her feet so as to not make any noise, she walked over to where Ren lay and sat down on the edge of the bed. The rise and fall of his chest could just barely be made out from the light of the moon. Gently, she ran her fingers through his hair.

"What are you doing, Kells?"

She snatched her hand back. "I'm sorry; I didn't mean to wake you."

He grabbed her hand and pulled her down next to him. With her back to him, he put an arm around her. "This is what you wanted, right?"

Kelsey had no idea how he knew, but it suddenly didn't matter. With his arm around her and the warmth of his body, she was quickly consumed by sleep.

Seventeen

The Peak

Kelsey woke up with sunlight streaming through the window and birds chirping somewhere outside. Ren sat on the edge of the bed, his fingers gently sliding through her copper hair. She used to get teased about her hair when she was younger, but Ren once told her how much he loved her hair. Since then, she'd learned to love it herself.

Ren gave her one of his heart-exploding smiles. Damn him and that smile. "Good morning, Kells. Marcus and I are about to go down for breakfast."

Kelsey sat up, rubbing her eyes. "Now? Alright."

Ren couldn't take his eyes off Kelsey. Her emerald eyes were dazzling, and her lips were intoxicating. How he wanted to kiss those lips. He was good at being stoic and keeping to himself, but when Kelsey was around, he lost all control.

Kelsey got out of bed and threw on her shoes, then they headed for the elevator. Ren hit the lobby button, and down they went. Kelsey leaned against him until the doors opened.

Marcus was already waiting at a table when they arrived. A cup of coffee sat in front of him.

"What time did you get up?" she asked him.

"Early enough," he said back. She didn't even want to guess what time that was, for it was already far too early.

"Have you eaten anything yet?" Ren asked Marcus.

"No, I was waiting for you two."

"Then let's go; I'm starving." Ren grabbed Kelsey's hand and led her toward the buffet. Marcus watched as he led her and smiled before heading over himself. Ren filled his and Kelsey's plates, even after she told him it was too much.

Ren wanted to discuss their trip to California, but in light of any supporters of Verin or the Church being there, he held off. He didn't want anyone else knowing his master's location.

After eating, they gathered their gear, and Ren drank one of the vials of blood. If he drank it now, he wouldn't have to worry about the effects of not feeding later.

From the hotel, it was pretty much a straight shot to their destination. Forty-two hours of driving, this was going to suck.

"Hey, can I ask you a question?" Kelsey asked. He nodded and she jumped right into her question. "The things you hear about vampires, their abilities and weaknesses, I mean, are any of them true?"

"For the most part, no. What brought that on?"

"I've just been thinking. From watching you, I don't see anything you hear about vampires. You seem more human than anything."

"That's a common mistake. What you hear and watch in movies is mostly untrue."

"Then, the whole turning to ash in the sunlight thing isn't true. I thought perhaps you were one of those Daywalkers."

Ren surprised her by laughing. "Actually, that myth is the one I hate the most, because it makes no sense. For the same reason Marcus can transform any time he wants. Where do you think moonlight comes from, Kelsey?"

"The sun. Where else would it come from?" That's when she realized what he meant. "Oh! Wait, that really is stupid."

"My point exactly. People seem to forget that moonlight is just reflected sunlight."

"For your information, I like garlic. Some of us don't, but that's just a personal preference. We do show up in mirrors, silver only affects us when it physically penetrates our body, and as you saw, I can walk vertically and upside down. On any surface, really."

"The sunlight concept is actually the only one that didn't come from a myth, though. Several thousand years ago, a human came upon a man who could not enter the sunlight. This was the first contact between humans and vampires. Well, he took it as vampires couldn't survive in the sun, but that's not true. That vampire just happened to have Erythropoietic Protoporphyria."

When Kelsey tried to ask him what he was talking about, she found that she couldn't say the name, causing Ren to laugh at her, which she wasn't amused at.

"It's basically considered being allergic to the sun. They pretty much can't go outdoors without being protected from the sunlight."

"At some point, through interactions with each other, the common myths you know of now were created. Well, they've changed as time goes on. But since most humans think we're myths now, it doesn't really bother us. There used to be a time when humans and monsters of all races lived together in peace, but those days are long gone."

"Were you alive back then?"

"No. It was when my master was a kid. My father mentioned something like it when he was younger, too. I wish I could have seen it, a world where we can live among each other openly."

"As far as weaknesses go, water is pretty much it, save for the silver part. We're weak against its purifying powers. It's why we have to purify it first with herbs and such. Holy water works well against us, but only if it's blessed by a priest who can actually use magic. Typically, that extends only to the Radiant Church, specifically those of high priest or higher. Otherwise, it's no different than regular water."

They spent the rest of the day in silence. Both nights they stopped at motels, grabbing two rooms. These times Marcus and Ren shared a room.

Kelsey's backside and legs hurt from the constant sitting, as did Ren's and Marcus's. But being more accustomed to it, they pushed through it.

After nearly three days, the Sierra Nevada was in sight. The Mountain range pierced the sky, the highest peaks coated in a lush white powder.

Ren was going to tell Kelsey they were almost there, but she slept quietly in the passenger seat. He shifted, and the speedometer jumped up, and the range sped towards them.

✝

Ren and Marcus pulled off to the side of the road in front of the base of a mountain. They parked well away from public parking. This way, they weren't spotted. Ren looked at the sun. It would be setting soon. Kelsey was still asleep. She looked so peaceful. No longer able to hold himself back, he leaned down and gently brushed his lips against hers, letting them linger for a brief moment.

✝

Kelsey woke to the sound of someone calling her name. Ren stood next to her, looking down. The door was open, and they were parked on the side of the road. The base of the mountain was across the street. "We're here. Come on. We need to get moving."

"Sorry, I fell asleep."

"It's alright. Better you got your rest. It's going to be a long and difficult hike."

Kelsey got out of the car and stretched. Ren closed the door, then grabbed the rope from the trunk.

"You might want to put his on," he said, handing her a jacket and pants. She slipped the pants on over her shorts, then zipped up the jacket. It was incredibly soft and warm.

For some reason, her lips seemed to tingle. She'd dreamt of Ren earlier. They watched the sunset over the water, and she finally got the big idiot to kiss her. She guessed it was the cause.

"Let's go," Ren said. He shouldered the bag of gear and walked to the base of the mountain. The incline was gradual at first, but then it got steeper. Sometimes they hiked through trees; other times, they were in the open.

Ren jumped up and grabbed a ledge. He pulled himself up and over, leaving Marcus and Kelsey to follow closely. Kelsey's legs burned as they continued up the mountain. On the other hand, Marcus and Ren didn't even look tired. They leaped from place to place, grabbing onto ledges and footholds. *Yup, they're monsters, alright,* she thought.

After another hour of climbing, they reached the face of a cliff. Ren tied one end of the rope around her waist and the other around himself. "Just in case," he said. Then he grabbed hold of a handhold and started climbing.

"Wait, we're climbing without any equipment?"

"We don't have of a choice," Ren said. "There are no bolts in the rock to anchor ourselves to, even if we did have it."

This is absolutely insane, Kelsey thought. She grabbed the handhold and started climbing.

Maybe we should have taken a different way, Ren thought. *I have to remember Kells is human. I did warn her beforehand, and I tied the rope to both of us, but still. She can't do the things we can. If something happens to her.*

Ren glanced at Kelsey. She was looking at the holds, focusing on climbing. Next, he looked over at Marcus, who was looking up at him. He motioned down with his head. Ren nodded, sending him a silent thank you.

Marcus climbed up as Ren moved to the side. He started making his way down to Kelsey. Her arms were on fire. She didn't know how much longer she could keep going. Looking around, she spotted a ledge large enough to sit on. It was just a few paces up.

"Ren, Marcus, I need to rest on that ledge for a minute."

"Wait, Kells," Ren warned. "You don't know how stable that ledge is."

Kelsey moved above the ledge and lowered herself. Her feet touched down, and she felt instant relief. It was large enough for her to walk on. She sat down, letting her feet dangle.

CRACK. *What was that?* she wondered. There was another crack, and the world flew past her. She didn't even realize she was falling until she saw the look of horror on Ren's face. "KELSEY!" he shouted.

A jolt ran through Kelsey's body as the rope straightened, and she stopped. Ren's hand slipped as he was yanked, but he managed to hold on.

"Ren, Kelsey!" Marcus yelled.

"Kelsey, grab the rope!" Ren yelled. Kelsey grabbed the rope with both hands. Holding onto the rope with one hand, Ren tried to pull her up, but when he did, the handhold he was using to support himself cracked. *Think,* he told himself. *Think!*

Foolish and dangerous as it was, he came up with a plan. He knew for sure that Kelsey wouldn't like it.

"I've got a plan," he said. "But you're not going to like it."

"I hate it when you say that!" she said back.

"I'm going to swing you. When you get close to the cliff, grab hold of anything that you can."

"As stupid as I want to call this plan of yours, I don't think I have the strength left to even stay in place."

"Just hold out long enough for me to get to you."

Marcus climbed down next to Ren and grabbed hold of the rope with one hand. Magic started pouring into it, strengthening it all the way to both ends. "I'll help guide you in. Trust us, and you'll be okay."

Kelsey looked up at them and nodded. She could do nothing else but trust them in her situation. Strangely enough though, even hanging in midair by a rope, with only Ren to support her, she wasn't scared.

Ren and Marcus swung the rope back and forth, gaining enough momentum for Kelsey to reach the cliff. They had to be careful she didn't go too fast and missed her target though. When she got close enough, she reached out. Her hand clasped the rock but slid away.

"Damn it. Just a little more; I almost had it." Ren and Marcus swung the rope again. On her second attempt, she managed to grab on and hold herself against the cliff face.

"Go, I've got you," Marcus said to Ren.

Ren immediately descended to Kelsey as quickly as he could. He got there just in time before Kelsey's arms gave out. Carefully, he wrapped one arm around her waist. "Grab hold of me. I won't let you won't fall, I promise."

Kelsey's first arm wrapped itself around his shoulder, then her leg, followed by her other arm, and then her final leg. True to his word, Ren was a statue. The guy didn't even budge. Now with her holding onto him, he grabbed hold of the cliff. With all four limbs, he was much more stable.

"You, okay?" he asked her.

"Fine," Kelsey said back. And it was the truth. "Just need to settle my nerves. How much further to the top?"

"We're almost there," Ren interjected. "Once we get to the top, you can rest. You'll have plenty of time while the map is being translated."

Ren and Marcus started climbing again. It was clear that even with Kelsey attached to him, climbing was no more difficult for Ren than doing it without the extra weight.

Kelsey knew they'd reached the peak when she could see the ledge above them. Ren and Marcus grabbed hold and climbed over. The view was breathtaking, a vast landscape spread out before them. In the distance was the entrance to a cave.

Ren let Kelsey down, and she felt her legs shaking. Not from fear, but from the strain of climbing for so long.

"That was close. Good thing we had the ro—" Ren cut her off by pulling her into a strong embrace. "Ren?" She felt him shaking. It seemed even he got scared. She wrapped her arms around his waist, returning his embrace.

"I thought I lost you," he said. Kelsey put her hands on the sides of his face and made him look at her.

"I'm alright," she said. Time, she needed just a little more of it to settle her emotions and aching muscles. They were at the peak; it wasn't time to stop now. Taking his hand, she helped him to his feet.

Walking into the cave, Kelsey got an ominous feeling. If Ren and Marcus felt it, she didn't know. It sure didn't stop them from continuing deeper into the cave. The inside was pitch black, and Kelsey couldn't see a thing. Only the feeling of Ren's and Marcus's presence gave her any sense of security.

After minutes of walking, the cave brightened. They entered a large chamber, lit blue with a pond at one end. Sitting on a mat was an older man, deep in meditation. Ren stepped forward and knelt on one knee. "I have returned… master."

Eighteen

Keepers of the Lunar Treasure

*S*o, this is the man we came to find, Kelsey thought. He certainly looked older, closer to his late forties. She wondered how old he really was.

"Fourteen hundred, my dear," he said to Kelsey.

"Excuse me?" she asked back. The number aside, she truly had no idea what he was talking about.

"My age. You were curious."

"You're fourteen hundred years old?" He nodded.

"Time has been calm. You'd be surprised just how quickly it goes." For the first time since entering, the old vampire opened his eyes, setting them on Ren.

"Lord Vaylor," Marcus greeted, giving a light bow. "Marcus Allagash. The little pup has grown. I know why you have come. Follow me. I shall take a look at the map."

The man motioned them to sit at a wooden table, one large enough to fit six. He went behind another curtain and came out several minutes later with a tray of Japanese teacups, handing one to each of them.

"Now let's see that—" he stopped, resting his eyes on Ren. His sudden stop surprised them all. "Ren. Oh no."

He placed his hand on Ren's chin, forcing him to look into his eyes. "I feared this would happen. How have you lasted this long?"

"I told you I would never do it, and I stay with my word. No matter the consequences."

Kelsey was confused, but the gears in Marcus's head were turning. Ren couldn't fool him. But he needed to hear him admit it before he determined himself correct, no matter how sure he was.

"Now, as for the reason we're here," Ren said, pulling out the map. He laid it on the table and unrolled it. His master put on a pair of glasses and began looking it over. Kelsey saw his mouth moving, no doubt reading the writing, but no sounds came out.

"The location is very close. Come, Ren, take a look." Ren got up and walked over to read the map. He looked at the writing, and his master helped him determine its meaning.

"Hearst Castle, in California," he translated. Marcus raised a curious eyebrow in response.

"Why don't you all rest for a bit? No doubt the climb was long and difficult. Ren, come with me," his master ordered.

Ren followed him behind another curtain and down a hallway. The cave was enormous.

A long silence passed before his master spoke. "Are you sure about this? Is this really your decision?"

"It is," Ren said. "I will stay true to myself until the very end."

"How much time do you have left?"

"I'd say about six months."

His master let out a deep sigh. "I knew this would come, but how I hoped it wouldn't."

"It'd be a lie to say I don't have any regrets, but I've accepted my fate, and I'm content with the consequences."

Ren reached into his backpack and pulled out a dagger. A tiger was imprinted on the blade. "I'm entrusting this to you. I'd give it to Marcus, but truthfully, I don't think he'd make it in time, and my father wouldn't even consider holding it. So, I'm leaving it with you. If I end up losing control of myself towards the end, I want you to be the one to kill me. I know you can do it."

His master pulled him into a tight embrace. For an old man, he had a hell of a grip. "You have my word. Good luck Ren. May you find happiness, in this life and the next." Ren nodded, giving him a silent thank you.

"Rest here for the night. You've got a drive ahead of you."

"Thank you. Farewell, master." Ren exited the room and made his way to the others.

"Farewell, Ren," his master said, but Ren was already out of earshot.

Marcus and Kelsey were still sitting at the table amidst a conversation. "Let's get some rest," Ren said.

"Did something happen?" Marcus asked.

"No, I just want to rest so we're ready for whatever comes our way. It's been a difficult day and I want to get the stone as quickly as possible."

I'm running out of time, he thought. *We have to get both stones, before it's too late.*

The next morning, all three of them exited the cave in silence, aware of the lack of Ren's master's presence. They reached the edge of the peak, sunlight raining down on them.

"Just out of curiosity, how are we planning on getting down?" Kelsey asked.

The wind started to pick up around them. "Like this," Ren said. He put his arm around her waist and pulled her in close. She wrapped her arms around him, and he jumped.

✝

Ren pulled into the parking lot below the castle. The view from the long road up was incredible. The two steeples pierced the sky with astonishing grace.

{175}

The incredible thing about the castle, the parking lot was only half full. And the tour only took up to six people. That meant they had a lot of leeway.

Per the rules of the estate, they weren't allowed to drive up to the castle. They could only board a bus after booking a tour of the castle. Their tour guide met them at the castle's entrance. Before entering, their guide broke off into talk of their itinerary and a brief history of the castle.

"I wonder what it looks like?" Kelsey wondered. "The stone, I mean."

"No idea. But you'll know it when you see it," Ren said back.

"Gee, so helpful."

Ren shuffled in place, feeling the familiar presence of Shadow Hunter, his heaven's blade, on his back. He and Marcus had already hidden their weapons with magic.

Finally entering the castle grounds, the tour guide took them through the various parts of the castle. Their first stop was an outdoor pool. Surrounded by Roman columns and statues, it was by far one of the most beautiful pools any of them had ever seen. But being so open, they saw nothing of the stone.

After the pool, the tour passed through the gardens, the main hall, the dining area, several other rooms, and even a theater. Ren, Marcus, and Kelsey scanned each one down to the smallest detail, but they saw nothing that resembled a stone, for it was all concrete, wood, and plaster.

"It's incredible, isn't it?" someone asked. Ren turned to see a woman in a dress standing next to him. With a quick glance, he caught Marcus and Kelsey on opposite sides of the room.

"Yes, quite," he said back.

From the corner of his eye, Ren caught movement. But he couldn't make it out, and just as soon as it was there, it was gone. His instincts started to kick in, and he was suddenly on high alert. Something wasn't as it should have been.

Moving on to the final location on the itinerary, a massive indoor roman pool. Ren had to admit, it was beyond impressive. The whole castle was, really.

The tour guide was deep into the history of the pool when he noticed a dark figure hiding in the corner, out of everyone's sight. The figure seemed almost ghostly. *Shade*, he thought. Conscious of the woman from before who still stood next to him, he gave her a smile. He sensed no magic, nor ki, nor any death. For all reasons, she seemed human. But Ren knew better than that.

Concentrating, he focused his energy on her, pushing through the surface layers and into the depths of her being. That's where he felt it, the aura of a shade coming from her body. The woman was a living shade. One who had hidden herself impeccably well.

Now that he focused, looking around the room, he started making out auras. Several people on the tour, workers, even the tour guide. His instincts were right on the money, as usual. Not good. Not good at all. This place was full of shades, both living and non. There were far too many of them in one place, acting the part of regular people doing their jobs. This was a trap.

Getting the stone would never be that easy. But before they found it, he needed to deal with the shades.

"Why don't you and I have a little talk," Ren said to the woman next to him. "About what your plan is luring all these humans here."

The woman's eyes went dark. Ren put a hand around her waist and pointed his dagger at her side. "Walk," he ordered her. "Not a sound."

Ren and the woman snuck out of the room and into an empty side room.

The woman released a heavy sigh. "Will you put that thing away? I have no interest in harming you, Ren Nightwalker." Ren was hesitant but seeing her lack of movement, he sheathed the dagger at his side. "You know, I may be a shade, but that doesn't make me evil. For the record, I hate Verin and the Church. Not all of us choose to become shades, you know."

Well, that was new. In three hundred years of rifting shades, this was the first he'd ever heard of a living shade not choosing or wanting to become one.

"So, you're plan? What's with all the shades?" Ren asked.

"Plan? There is no plan. The person who heads all the tours and caretaking here is like us. They gave living shades like us, ones who want nothing to do with Verin, a place to work, free from his control. We've no contact at all, and certainly not from the Church either. It's not the dream job, but here we can live like ordinary people."

Ren focused on the flow of her energy, listening to the sound of her heartbeat. Both were even and regular. *She's telling the truth.*

"Alright, then we part ways here. Stay out of my way, and I'll stay out of yours."

"That was the plan," she told him.

✝

Ren snuck out of the room without being seen and searched for the tour group he'd left. They needed to find that stone and fast. Marcus and Kelsey were together in one of the rooms when he found them, searching for the stone, no doubt.

"There you are," Kelsey said. "We've been looking everywhere for you. We can't find the stone. I don't think it's here."

"It's here; we're just not looking in the right area. We've only searched the lower floors, not the upper ones, and we need to find it fast."

"Why the sudden urgency?"

"Because we've been caught in a trap," he said. "This place is crawling with shades. The workers and even the people in the tour."

Marcus reached for his sword instinctively, ready to engage in combat. Ren stopped him by placing a hand on his wrist. "Not here. The truth is I talked to one of them, a living shade. Apparently, all the shades here have no connection to Verin."

"That's impossible," he said, in complete disbelief. There was no way a living shade wasn't loyal to Verin.

"That's what I thought, but the shade I talked to definitely wasn't lying. Nevertheless, we need to move now in case I was wrong."

"Follow me; I saw a staircase leading upstairs," Marcus said.

The stairs were surrounded by people entering and leaving the castle. When the coast was clear, they ascended to the second floor. Between the second and third floors, they searched every room in the castle, careful to avoid detection from any tours or staff. Not one of them contained anything like a magical stone.

Marcus punched a desk in one of the rooms out of frustration.

"Are we absolutely sure it's here?" Kelsey asked. "That's what the map said? You didn't mistranslate it?"

"No, I'm positive. It's here."

"Where? If it's here, then where is it?" Marcus wondered. "We've checked every room in this castle.

The only other place it could be is somewhere on the grounds. With as large as they are, we'll surely never find it."

Ren looked out the window and saw the two steeples in the distance. They were the most prominent parts of the castle from a distance.

"Actually, that's not necessarily true." He motioned to the steeples with a nod of his head.

"You're insane," Kelsey said. "How are we even supposed to get up there?"

"How else, from the outside," Ren said.

He walked out of the room and down the hall, entering another room they'd previously searched. At one end was a door that led to a balcony. Rather than leap down to a lower-level roof as Kelsey thought he would, Ren climbed onto the railing, then stepped on the wall.

Marcus and Kelsey watched from the balcony as Ren walked vertically up the wall and climbed onto the roof above. Next to Kelsey, Marcus changed into his werewolf form, then knelt. "Climb on." She climbed onto his back, and he began to climb, digging his claws into the wall.

From the castle roofs, the view all around was breathtaking. The fading sun almost disappeared beyond the horizon, a full moon in its place.

Where previously unnoticed, now a purple glow came from the very top of one. Kelsey swallowed loudly, knowing what awaited her. It was her decision to come on the quest, so she couldn't complain, but that didn't settle the drop in her stomach.

Using the roofs, the three of them reached the steeple with the purple glow and started climbing. Luckily for them, both steeples had ladders spanning up to the second level. They only had to climb up to the top level, using the columns and ornate railing for support.

The purple glow came from a single sphere the size of a softball. It was built into the bell but never more out of place. Ren grabbed the stone and pried it free before holding it up. In the light of the full moon, its true colors became visible. It was mauveine purple with swirling white lines. Kelsey noticed the white lines didn't just look like they were moving; they actually were. They moved all on their own just beneath the surface of the stone, intersecting and crossing. It was almost as if the stone was alive.

"That's it, the Moon Stone," said Marcus.

"It's otherworldly, isn't it?" someone asked. The three of them turned to see a figure leaning against the railing on the other side of the belfry. They stepped out of the darkness and into the light of the moon.

"I tried to get it myself but couldn't get to the top of the tower. I owe you my thanks." Ren and Marcus were bombarded with a blast of evil ki. A living shade, and a powerful one. "Hand it over, please."

"Rot in hell," Ren said back.

"That's not nice."

"Neither is this." Ren drew Shadow Hunter and slashed. A golden blade of energy flew at the shade, but they dispersed it with a blast of magic.

"Go, now!" Ren shouted at Marcus and Kelsey. He unleashed another attack, but it was only a diversion, following up with another slash of his sword. This time it cut right through his opponent's magic, slashing through their arm. They howled in pain and kicked Ren in the chest, knocking him to the ground.

Quickly getting to his feet, he fired a blast of magic that struck his opponent in the chest. It gave him enough time to leap off the railing. He used Shadow Hunter as a handle to slide down to the roof, quickly catching up with Marcus and Kelsey.

Ren's attacks were not enough to kill whoever their assailant was, but it would slow them down and buy them time, time needed to escape. Their fifteen-minute bus ride to reach the castle was much longer on foot; however, their assailant never returned to counterattack.

As soon as all three of them made it to the parking lot, they jumped in their cars and put them in gear, the wheels screeching as they shot forward.

Nineteen

Beneath the Brightest Moon

Ren and Marcus dodged cars and sped through lanes while Kelsey held on for dear life. They drove like their lives were on the line.

As soon as they were clear of the castle, Ren and Marcus pulled over and stopped at the side of the road. No one crowded the streets so late into the night.

Kelsey's entire world was spinning. "I think my brain's been squished," she said back.

They got out of the car, and Marcus met them in front of the trunk. Ren pulled out the map and opened it. Some of the words had changed to Lazarus, the main language of Nexus, no longer ancient vampire.

"Seek the brightest night. Let the moon guide your future," Ren read. Marcus and he started racking their brains around the meaning of the words. "Brightest night," Ren repeated.

"The brightest night is a full moon, right?" Kelsey asked. "It has to be that."

"Actually, the night sky is brightest during a supermoon," Marcus corrected.

"No, Kelsey's right," Ren said. "The supermoon only occurs around four to six times per year. We don't know when the next one will happen, nor do we have time to wait. A full moon is still one of the brightest things in the sky. It'll have to do."

Ren held the map up, letting the full intensity of the moon shine down on top of it. Nothing happened.

"It has to be the stone," Ren and Kelsey said simultaneously.

"Kelsey, hold the map," he told her. She took the map and held it up to her chest in the moonlight.

Ren held the stone up in between the moon and the map. The moonlight hit the stone and amplified. Purple light bathed the map and the words began to glow. When it faded, the words had been translated to Lazarus.

"Kells, since you can't speak the language in Nexus, leave reading the map to us," he said.

"What are you talking about? The map is in English." she responded. He and Marcus looked at her like she was crazy.

"No, it's not," they said.

"Yeah, it is. See, right here, Hearst Castle, San Simeon, California."

Ren and Marcus looked at each other like the world had imploded. The map was definitely in Lazarus for them, but it appeared in English to Kelsey.

"It must be magic cast over the map," Marcus assumed. "It makes it readable to whoever finds it."

"But then why didn't it work the first time?"

"We didn't have the stone the first time. It must have been the key to activating the map's powers."

Laying it flat, they gazed over the map. "Looks like our next destination is Taormina," Ren said.

"Taormina. Italy!" Kelsey said. "Great. How are we supposed to get to Italy? We don't even have passports."

"Marcus, call in Greg and Johnathan," Ren said. "The pilots of our private jet," he told Kelsey, before she could ask. "Well, it's my father's, technically, but he lets us use it as needed. As for the passports, I think we may be able to get by that one. I have a few friends who live in Italy, and one of them works in a private airport. If we explain the situation, he'll let us through."

"They're on their way," said Marcus. "They'll be landing at the private airstrip in L.A. at four. We have to get in the air right away, though. It's after midnight now."

"Then let's get out of here." Ren rolled up the map and put it and the Moon Stone in his bag. They got back in the cars and sped off at full speed. Marcus maneuvered and drove up next to him. Together, they stuck close to each other nearly the entire way there.

Ren, Marcus, and Kelsey waited in their cars until the plane landed. A white tiger was detailed on both sides. Kelsey looked at him like, 'really, dude?' "What, I like tigers?" *Yeah, no kidding,* she thought.

The door to the plane opened, and a man appeared in the doorway. "Ren, Marcus, sorry for this, but we're running a tight schedule, so we have to hurry. We'll be landing at the private airport in Milan. Luigi will be there to let you pass. Did you really find it?"

Ren took the stone out of his bag. "Pay up," the man said to the other guy in the cockpit.

"Damn it!" the guy in the cockpit said. He fished into his pocket and handed the other pilot a hundred-dollar bill.

Kelsey took a seat as Ren and Marcus descended the steps. The jet's interior was all brown leather and a dark stained red oak. There were two rows of leather seats in the front and back on both sides facing forward, with another four around a small table. The ground was all carpeting. There was even a leather couch.

Ren and Marcus returned and set their gear down as two helicopters landed. Each one had an empty shipping container attached beneath. Ren and Marcus drove their cars into the containers before boarding the jet.

Kelsey watched from the window as the two containers were reattached to the helicopters and carried off. Minutes later, she felt the plane move as it drove to the runway. It shot forward, and then they were weightless as they rose into the air.

Twenty

Den of a Thousand Eyes

The was little turbulence the whole way to Italy. Kelsey and Marcus fell asleep in the chairs, which extended into recliners, Ren on the couch. A sudden shockwave shot through Ren's body, and he shot up.

An intense pain pierced him. Sweat cached his body, and his canines elongated into his fangs. His vision turned red and his pulse raced like a rocket. All he could hear was the beating of his heart and the flow of his own blood.

It had been almost two days since he last drank blood. Now, the effects were hitting him with a vengeance. Blood, he needed blood. His case.

Shaken, weakened, and with all the strength quickly draining from his body, he got up and walked to the back of the plane where the bathroom was.

Ren downed the first vial, but his condition didn't improve as it usually did. He drank another vial, and the effects slowly receded. *It's getting worse,* he thought.

For a moment, he pondered drinking another vial to be safe but sided against it. He didn't want to drink too much; in case he lost control.

Returning to his seat on the couch, he retrieved his heaven's blade, laying it across his lap. Ren closed his eyes and tuned out all the noise and sights of his surroundings. Then, he felt his consciousness being pulled into the blade. Suddenly he wasn't on the plane anymore. He was in an opening in a forest with a stream that flowed into a deep crystal blue pond with a waterfall.

A man with long golden hair threw his head back and out of the water, leaving him exposed from the torso up.

"Shadow Hunter," Ren greeted.

Shadow Hunter walked out of the water and snapped his fingers. He was instantly dry, his hair tied into a long ponytail, and he was clothed.

"Ren," he greeted back. "Everything alright?"

"No, not really. I'm slipping."

Shadow Hunter locked his gaze on him. "I know. Your rate suddenly spiked. I can still feel the tingling. I'd say you've got months left."

"It's taking more and more transfusion blood to contain my urges. Two a day now. I was tempted to take three but decided against it. We have to get the stone, before I run out of time."

"It's only going to get worse," Shadow Hunter told him. "You've been fighting a losing battle from the second you started. I really wish you would feed. I rather like you as a partner."

Ren said nothing back; he couldn't. Shadow Hunter could sense his feelings, so there was no need.

"You coming here actually works out. I've had a vision."

Like every other heaven's blade, Shadow Hunter could see bits and pieces of future events. The visions were brief, usually warning of what was to come, or answers to questions previously asked.

"He's coming for you. One of Verin's generals." A chill ran through Ren. "I don't know which one, but he's definitely one of the four."

"I see. So it's finally time. Good. Let's get it done then." Shadow Hunter raised an eyebrow, waiting confidentially. Ren rushed forward and immediately engaged him in hand-to-hand combat.

Ren kicked at Shadow Hunter's head. He blocked it but slid across the ground. "So, any advice?" he asked Shadow Hunter.

"You're referring to the general. Or perhaps the stone. Either way, seek out Hades. He's the head of an organization called ReZellion. They can provide assistance on your quest."

Shadow Hunter was silent for a few moments before he spoke again. "You'll be landing soon. You should get going. We should meet more often as your battle draws nearer."

Ren nodded, his growing exhaustion nipping at his consciousness. "Thanks, Shadow Hunter."

And just like that, Ren was back on the plane. Shadow Hunter lay in his lap, a thin veil of energy surrounding the blade. Looking out the window, the landscape below was bathed in mountains and farming. Every so often, he saw the burning of crops, the smoke rising into the bright blue sky.

Marcus stirred and sat up. "Are we there?" he asked.

"Not much longer," Ren said back.

"Have you been up all night?"

Ren nodded. "It's getting worse. I had to take two vials last night, almost three."

"That's not good, Ren. That's seriously not good. This is getting too dangerous." But Ren said nothing back. Only focusing on the world outside the small plane.

They spent the rest of the plane ride in silence. Ren heard the opening of a hatch, the signal the landing gear was being lowered. He felt the light bump of the wheels hitting the runway and the plane slowing down.

He moved to where Kelsey slept in her chair. "Kells, Kells," he called. She stirred, then opened her eyes. "We're here," he said. She yawned and stretched her arms and back. Ren grabbed their gear as the plane turned and came to a stop. The staircase was lowered, and they exited the plane.

Marcus and Kelsey followed Ren as he headed toward the terminal. They bypassed the empty customs line and headed into an office, where a brown-haired man sat behind a desk with a computer.

"*Ciao* Luigi," Ren said in greeting. "*Come stai?*"

"Ah, Ren, *mi amico. Bene, bene*." They embraced. "When I heard that you were coming, I had everything prepared for your arrival," he said in perfect English. "Did you really find it?"

Ren handed him the Moon Stone. Luigi examined it, looking closely at the details. "*Mio Dio*," he said. "I didn't think it was true, but they really do exist."

"Yeah, and the Sun Stone is in Taormina."

Luigi handed the stone back to Ren. "So, what are you going to do next?"

"We have to find ReZellion. The leader Hades will be able to help us get the stone."

Luigi looked stricken. "ReZellion! *Mi amico*, I would highly advise against going there. They're very dangerous. The whole organization is filled with Cyclopes."

Ren was momentarily taken aback. "Cyclopes? I'd rather not mingle with them if I didn't have to. Unfortunately, I don't think that's an option. Shadow Hunter told me to find their leader."

Both Luigi and Marcus exchanged glances. Kelsey grabbed Marcus's shirt to get his attention, and he shot her a look that said, 'I'll explain later.'

"If shadow Hunter told you to find them, then there must be a reason. In that case, you should go," Luigi agreed.

"Any idea where we can find them?" Ren asked.

"They have a base in Genoa. Look for the blue lobster symbol. Good luck guys."

Luigi let them pass through customs and any other checkpoint without stopping. Exiting the terminal, Ren's and Marcus's cars were waiting out front.

Kelsey's mind was so focused on Ren's heaven's blade that she didn't even remember getting into the car. Shadow Hunter had told him to an organization of Cyclopes. As in, directly told him?

They drove through Milan in silence. Kelsey watched all the people, taking note of their surroundings. All the buildings were tall and packed tightly together, with balconies and windows on each floor.

"It may not look like much now, but it'll grow on you," Ren said, indicating the layout of the city.

"Well, Milan aside, I've always wanted to visit Italy," Kelsey said back. "Next, I'm going to France."

"Paris, I remember."

"Mmm, that didn't get lost in India?"

"No, it didn't. Remind me to take you the next time I have an assignment."

Kelsey sat up, now severely interested. "You've been to Paris? Oh, you better take me. "

Ren chuckled at her demand. She knew he couldn't deny her, given their worlds blending. But now that she had him talking, perhaps this was a good time to ask.

"So, how much haven't you told me?" she asked. "Earlier, you said Shadow Hunter told you to find this place we're headed to. As in physically told you? I thought it was just a sword. Is it not?"

"Yes and no," he answered. "It's complicated."

Ren was about to say something else when he pointed ahead of them. "Look, one o-clock. The truck two cars ahead of us."

Kelsey strained her eyes to see the truck. It looked like any regular truck. Then she noticed the blue lobster on the license plate.

Ren used his car's touch screen to contact Marcus. "There's a truck a few cars in front of us," he explained. "It belongs to ReZellion."

"Then let's follow it. I'll be right behind you," Marcus said back.

The phone call ended, and Ren looked over at Kelsey. "Ready to enter a den of Cyclopes?" he asked.

"No, not really," she confessed. The only thing she knew about Cyclopes were from Greek stories. And if they were true, it terrified her.

"Neither am I."

They followed the truck into the town. From a distance, Ren spotted a building with a wooden sign hanging from it. The sign had a blue lobster painted on it. He pulled off to the side of the road, people stopping to stare briefly before moving on.

Kelsey could feel the number of eyes on her. She hated it. On the other hand, Ren looked stoic as usual. He raised his arm and locked the car. "Let's go," he said.

Kelsey noticed Marcus walk up beside her. She had Ren to her left and Marcus to her right, protecting her from anything that might happen. Having the two of them on either side of her, the closer they got to the building, the more nervous Kelsey got.

"Stay calm, don't show any fear," Ren said. "Just like at Trinity. You must remain calm. Cyclopes are more aggressive than most species of monsters. They will not hesitate to kill you, especially since you're human."

Ren opened the door to the building and stepped through first. Kelsey went next and Marcus last. The inside was poorly lit and damp. At the back was a display of fresh seafood with a few tables, all of which were occupied.

"*Benvenuto. Cosa posso portarti?*" asked a man behind the counter.

"*Stiamo cercando* Hades," Ren answered. All eyes turned to him, and they didn't look happy.

"Americans? And what do you want with the boss?" he asked, switching to English.

"We were told he would be able to help us on our quest."

"Quest? You guys are monsters, then?"

The people sitting stood up. Kelsey thought they might be gearing up for a fight. The man behind the display held up his hand. He studied them for a few moments; as if deciding what to do with them. "Come with me. I'll take you to the boss."

Kelsey swallowed, but Ren just nodded. "Stick close," he whispered.

They all followed the man through a doorway and down a set of stairs. Just like the entry room, the stairs were poorly lit. Made of stone, they were carved right out of the ground. The walls changed from concrete to sandstone the lower down they went.

Finally, they entered a large room bustling with Cyclopes, all in their monster form. The room went quiet as soon as they entered. "Wait here," the man said. He walked down a tunnel off to the side.

The gazes of the unhappy monsters pierced them. One big Cyclops got up from his seat, knocking his chair over, his gaze intense. Kelsey swore she saw him look at her. Ren stared at the big Cyclops, stoic as usual.

Marcus released a deep growl, ready to rip the big guy to shreds with his claws. Ren held his hand out in front of him. "Don't. You know the rules. Even if this is the human realm, it's still their territory." Marcus ceased his growling, but still looked ready to kill at a moment's notice.

Ren shot the big Cyclops a glare. He stepped back in fear, tripping over his fallen chair and landing on his backside. He scooted back, but Ren held his gaze. It was full of murderous intent. When it came to sticking fear into people's hearts with a single glance, Ren had mastered the technique.

"My, my, what intense bloodlust," said a new voice. A man in a black trench coat walked toward them. His black hair hung down on all sides, the back reaching his shoulders. He looked young, but the circles under his eyes and the streaks of gray running through the sides of his hair gave his age away.

Ren switched his glance to the man. "Alikshaw tells me you're here to see me. I am Hades. Why don't you explain yourselves?"

Twenty-one

The Price for Protection

Ren's eyes swept across the room, sending another wave of fear through the Cyclopes. He searched for their monster energy, seeing the familiar blue aura appear around them all, indicating that none had been possessed by a shade.

"My name is Ren Nightwalker. I'm here seeking assistance with my quest."

At once, all the Cyclopes bowed, and the man in the trench coat who had indicated himself as Hades, spoke up.

"Your Highness, welcome to our den. Might I ask what kind of quest you're on?"

"Do you know of the situation going on with Verin's army?" Ren asked.

"We've had no news as to his advances, unfortunately. Word doesn't really get to these parts that fast," Hades informed them.

"Then I suppose I should bring you up to date, but you're not going to like it. Although they work independently of each other, Verin has allied himself with the Church." Hushed conversations filled the room, and Hades held up a hand, silencing them.

"That's why we're here. We're looking for an ancient artifact; the Sun Stone." If learning of the alliance was a shock, it was nothing compared to what he just told them.

"We already have the Moon Stone," Marcus said. "We had a run-in with the Church and Verin's shades while retrieving it. Luckily, we've got the better of them so far. But we can be absolutely sure they're working independently of each other."

"So, they're searching for the stones too? Wonderful. Though I'm not surprised. So now you're here looking for the Sun Stone."

"The map says the Sun Stone is in Taormina," Ren said.

"Taormina, huh? If you don't mind me asking, Your Highness, just who told you to come find me?"

"Shadow Hunter. He had a vision."

Hades' eyes enlarged, but the other Cyclopes just looked confused. "Lord Hades, who is Shadow Hunter?" the Cyclopes that manned the counter asked.

"Shadow Hunter is Prince Nightwalker's heaven's blade. He bares the title, as you're well aware. If it told you to come here, then it's for a good reason. It wouldn't do so otherwise."

"Will you be able to help us?" Ren asked. "I'm not sure what it's for, but he did send us here after all."

Hades seemed to be thinking about it, debating whether or not they should help.

"Normally I would turn you away, regardless of reason. However, considering it's you two asking for help and given what you've told us of Verin's movements, yes, we will assist you on your quest."

Hades turned his gaze from Ren to Kelsey. "And the girl? Who is she?"

"Her name is Kelsey. She's a friend and has been assisting Marcus and me on our quest."

"I see. From Trinity, I presume, then. Are you a vampire, or werewolf?" Hades asked Kelsey.

"Neither," Kelsey said back, her voice hoarse with nervousness.

"Ah. Well, Trinity has many races among its ranks. What are you then? You hide your energy as well as they do."

Ren shot a quick glance of unease at Kelsey, and she swallowed. What was she going to do? They had no idea she was human. Once they found out, they would likely try and kill her.

"She doesn't have one," Ren answered.

Hades looked at them, visibly confused. "How could she not possess a rank?"

"It's because she's not a monster; she's human."

Hades' expression turned dark, his power flowing out of him. "You brought a human to our den!"

"I told you, she's a friend. Thus far, she's been a valuable asset to this quest. We wouldn't have found the map or the stone without her."

Hades released a heavy breath, his power fading. "She's that important to you? That you would bring her into our world."

"I wasn't the one that brought her in. She was attacked, by a living shade. They were using her to get to me. So, I had no choice but to expose our existence. I had intended to erase her memories. It was her choice to stay and be a part of it."

Hades set his gaze on Kelsey. "You actually joined of your own accord? I have no reason to doubt His Highness's words. However, I need to hear it from your own mouth. Are his words true?"

"They are," Kelsey said with certainty. "Every word. Rather than ask, I more or less forced my way into your world, however. If only not to be apart from him."

"You're tenacious, young human. You have a big heart, one filled with courage. I admire that. Human or not, I will not discriminate against you, or the company Prince Nightwalker or Prince Allagash keeps."

Kelsey breathed a sigh of relief. And although they didn't easily show it, Ren and Marcus looked relieved as well.

"Ren, heads up," Shadow Hunter warned, his voice appearing in Ren's head. "Someone is coming. A sword."

A sword? When used by one such as Shadow Hunter that meant only one thing. A Heaven's Blade.

"*Ciao, qualcuno lì?*" asked a voice. "Hades, *mio cugino, dove sei?*" asked voice asked again.

A man who looked about eighteen came into view. He was dressed in black cotton pants and a dark black zip-up hoody over a red shirt. His dark brown hair was short with a brush up. On his back was a giant golden sword. Seeing him up close, he was just a few inches taller than Ren.

"*Hades, eccoti mio cugino,*" The man said.

Hades, who recognized the newcomer, immediately lit up. "Raziel!" he said back. The two of them embraced, then the man with the giant golden sword noticed Ren and the others.

"Ren, Marcus, what the hell are you guys doing here?" he asked, surprised to see them. "And who might this be?" his second question directed at Kelsey.

"Raziel," Ren greeted. "This is Kelsey Rose. She's helping us with the quest."

"Kelsey? So, this is the human? Jay got me up to speed once I got back to Trinity. I got on the soonest plane I could to come here and tell Hades. But my guess is, you've already done that."

"So, did you find the map, or any of the stones?" he asked.

"We've already acquired the Moon Stone," Ren said. He tossed Raziel the stone, who looked over it with great detail.

"So, this is a legendary artifact. I've never seen anything like it." Raziel handed Ren the stone back. "How did you find it?"

"James Wilson. He called and told us he may have found the map." Ren continued with leaving to search for the map, all the way to finding the Moon Stone and then making it there. The only part he intentionally left out was their trip to Mt. Whitney.

"I see. Sounds like you've been in one dangerous situation after another. So, what does that map say?"

"The Sun Stone is in Taormina. That's why we're here in Italy. Shadow Hunter told me Hades would be able to help us locate the stone."

"Shadow Hunter told you to come here? Interesting. Whatever is hiding that stone can't be good."

"Have you been in contact with Gram?" Ren asked.

"I have, but he hasn't said anything. He only mentioned meeting some friends along the way. I take it that's you guys."

"Perhaps then, now's the best time to mention this. I was going to wait until we got to a hotel, but with three Heaven's Blades gathered, now makes the most sense."

"Before we landed in Milan, Shadow Hunter warned me on the plane ride. He doesn't know who it is, but one of Verin's generals is on the move."

Raziel and Marcus exchanged concerned looks. "I can't decide if that's good news or bad," Marcus said. "After all, this was our plan. To take down his generals. Now one's coming right for us."

Ren crossed his arms, delving into thought. "It is, but we still need to be cautious. We've no idea which general it is, or any of their strengths. A fight with any one of them may very well kill us."

"Do you think you can beat him?" Kelsey asked Ren. "I mean, I know you're strong, but the way you guys talk about these generals, it seems like you might not be able to beat them."

"You must have faith in us, Kelsey," Raziel said. "We're not Heaven's Blades for nothing, you know." Kelsey seemed more convinced after hearing that. For a Cyclops, he was a very calming person. Just being in his presence eased her nerves.

"It's his sword," Ren said, as if he could read her thoughts. "Gram has the power to calm emotions."

"But it only works on someone when they're in an overly emotional state," Raziel added.

"Regarding your quest," Hades said, changing the course of the discussion. "If we're going to help, we'll need a plan." Ren nodded in agreement. "For starters, are there any specific requirements you have regarding your party?" Ren shook his head.

"Are you thinking about something?" Marcus asked, seeing Ren's expression.

"I think I know the reason Shadow Hunter sent us here," Ren told him. "I've been to Italy several times, but I've never spent that much time in Sicily, let alone Taormina."

"I don't think I've been to Taormina at all, only Palermo."

"Several of us have spent some time in Taormina, myself included," Hades said. "It makes sense that Cyclopes would be the best choice to assist you. In that case, I'll put together a group to travel with you."

"Thank you," Ren said. "Though it's only for a short time, we look forward to working with you."

Twenty-two

Guardsmen

Ren crashed as soon as he got into the hotel room. His flare-up on the plane had drained his stamina more than he would admit. It was only minutes before he succumbed to the darkness of sleep.

The next time he woke, it was dark outside. Marcus slept soundly in the other bed. Kelsey slept peacefully next to him. She lay facing him, giving him a glimpse of her sleeping face. Gently, he brushed a section of her bangs away.

Climbing out of bed, he walked to the balcony. He couldn't get the future events out of his head. This enemy he was supposed to face was one of Verin's four generals. Before, he would have been confident enough to defeat him. But now, with his condition worsening, he wasn't so sure he would be able to.

If it turned out he couldn't defeat this general, he knew Marcus and the other Heaven's Blades could. Yet still, the fact that he might no longer be able to defeat them unsettled him. Regardless of whether he could or couldn't, it was just a means to an end.

Ren played through all the possibilities of the battle. Even if he did manage to defeat this enemy, his time was running out. It won't be long before he'll have to leave it in Marcus's and everyone else's hands anyway. Maybe he could even convince his father to take Shadow Hunter. Better that than him being without a wielder.

Watching the stars in silence, the sounds of the city were like a late-night melody. His thoughts drifted again. He would have to start distancing himself from Kelsey. But would she even let him? That girl was more stubborn than a mule.

He also wanted to see Ellie before the battle started. She'd be sad, but she was a strong kid. She'd be able to handle it if he didn't make it. Still, he wanted to see her again. She effectively became a little sister once he took her in.

Look at me. When did I get so sentimental and high-strung? he wondered. *I knew the consequences of what I was doing. There's no point in letting it get to me.*

Maybe he really did need to distance himself. Since he'd been spending so much time with Kelsey and Ellie, he was starting to become soft. Members of Trinity couldn't afford to be soft, especially him. He was the prince of the vampires and Nexus. As the rank one Heaven's Blade and an assassin, it was in the job description.

Ren felt Kelsey's presence as she approached. "You alright?" she asked. "You look like you've got something on your mind."

"I'd be lying if I said I didn't. But I'm just getting some fresh air," he responded.

"Is it about the Cyclopes or finding the stone?"

"No, nothing like that. It's nothing worth talking about."

"If you say so," she said after a brief hesitation.

Kelsey knew something was wrong. Ren might have said everything was fine, but she knew he was trying to hide his thoughts from her. She wouldn't pry into his thoughts, but she wanted to know what was bothering him.

"Well, I'm here if you need me," she said, trying to lift his spirits.

"Yeah, thanks." Apparently, her attempt had failed.

"Why don't you come back to bed? It's late," she insisted.

"I will in a little bit." His mood was starting to rub off on her. She hated to see him like this.

She stopped at the doorway and looked back, a ghost of a smile spreading across her lips. Then she closed the door behind her and went back to bed.

Ren continued to watch the stars until late into the night. He woke the next morning before Marcus or Kelsey. Shadow Hunter's presence tingled in his mind. The sword was calling to him. He grabbed it and sat down, laying the sword across his lap.

"Alright, Shadow Hunter, let's get to work."

Ren closed his eyes and focused. He felt his consciousness get pulled and transported into the sword. Shadow Hunter sat on a large rock on the bank of the pond.

"Well done getting Hades to help you. You even met with Gram's wielder."

"Yeah, though it almost got ugly. Seeing Raziel was definitely a surprise."

"How you get them to assist you doesn't really matter. If you hadn't, getting the stone would have been extremely difficult, it not impossible."

"I figured as much. Numbers and race was the idea. So, what now?"

"Now you find the stone. Hades and five of his best men are going to be accompanying you. He'll likely want Raziel to join you, but Raziel is needed elsewhere. Tell him to go back to Trinity and prepare for battle. You're going to need their assistance with this if you are to succeed."

"How do you even know I'll succeed?"

"I don't. I know you were second-guessing yourself last night, but you must have faith in yourself. I'm not sure how, but we'll get through it. Hence why I called for you. Let's get you ready. You'll survive long enough for this fight; I can assure you of that."

Ren held out his hand. Shadow Hunter changed into his sword form and flew into it. With one swing, a wave of golden energy flew into the waterfall, then disappeared. He spent hours swinging away, his blade a furry of death and metal.

"I think it's time you stop swinging at something imaginary and instead at something that swings back," Shadow Hunter told Ren.

Energy flew off the tip of the blade and took the shape of Ren. Everything about the figure, his skin, his clothes, his hair, was jet black. Only his eyes were different, a fierce fiery red. In his hand was a solid black sword with the same shape as Shadow Hunter.

"Your greatest enemy is always yourself, Ren. Remember that. Although, in your case, it's also your eventual demise."

"Refusing to feed was a terrible mistake," the other Ren said. His voice sounded like a collection of several people, all talking in unison.

Ren raised his sword. In an instant, the two met in a clash, their swords locked together. They pushed against each other but remained locked in place.

Ending their standstill, they separated from each other, reappearing in another clash of swords. Ren hacked twice with his sword and landed a kick to the chest. His copy jabbed while Ren parried it away and swung with a backhand. The copy ducked underneath and slashed upward. Ren swung down against his sword and twirled it around. The copy's sword flew out of his hand and fell to the ground. Without any hesitation, Ren slashed him across the chest.

The copy Ren dissolved, only to reform a short distance away. His wounds were healed, and when he reached for it, the black sword flew into his hand.

Ren put up his guard, sword ready. The copy disappeared and reappeared behind him; his sword aimed straight for his back. Ren turned and blocked it, but his copy disappeared back into his shadow. Ren used his powers to sense his blood flow but found nothing.

"Trying to sense my blood?" the copy asked. His voice came from everywhere, and yet he was nowhere in sight. "Your powers don't work on me, stupid. I am only a manifestation created by energy. I have no blood."

Another attack came out of nowhere, his copy exiting his shadow. Ren avoided it at the last second, but the blade still clipped him. Blood ran from the cut on the side of his arm and the wound healed in seconds.

"You may be a manifestation of energy, but vampires have incredible regenerative powers," Ren boasted. "We're the fastest healers of any race."

"I know that. I'm you, remember? That just means I get to have fun with this!"

Ren appeared behind his copy and rammed his blade through his back. He pulled it out and, with one slice, cut him in two. The copy's face bore an evil grin before he disappeared into his shadow again. Ren parried a strike from the side, and the copy slipped back into the shadows. Another attack came from the front. Ren swung up, and the black sword flew out of the copy's hand, then disappeared as he returned to the shadows.

"Enough!" Ren said. He released a blast of ki. The blue aura radiated out from his body, and his copy was thrown from the shadows as they disappeared, the light from Ren's energy snuffing them out.

"I'd like to think I'm better than this," Ren said. "If you're really me, then I'm seriously conflicted right now." His copy scowled at him in response.

Ren took a wide stance, pointing his sword downward, and raised his free hand into the air behind him. Simultaneously, he and the copy lunged forward. The copy swung down, and Ren swung up. When their swords hit, Ren spun in a circle, moving behind his copy. The black sword broke in half, and his copy released his grip on it, his torso separated from his lower body.

Ren turned and slashed nine times rapidly. The copy's vision was split as his body was cut into nine pieces before he dissolved into black flames and disappeared.

Shadow Hunter changed back into his human form. "That was even better than I expected. I wouldn't worry about defeat just yet."

Shadow Hunter's attention was directed elsewhere momentarily. "It's about time for you to head back," he said after a brief pause. "Your companions are awake now."

"We'll continue when I return on the way to Taormina." Shadow Hunter nodded in agreement. Then, Ren's vision dissolved, and he was back, sitting on the floor of his hotel room. Kelsey yanked her hand back in surprise.

"Marcus told me I could get your attention if I touched you." The werewolf in question had fallen asleep again. "But I didn't expect you to come to at the same time. Were you sleeping?"

Ren shook his head. "I was training with Shadow Hunter." He could tell by the look on her face that she was trying to wrap her brain around it.

"You were right previously, about Shadow Hunter talking to me," he said. "Heaven's blades aren't just weapons. They all have a spirit inside of them. An actual spirit. It makes them, in a sense, very much alive. And all Heaven's Blades have the ability to communicate with that spirit. We do it two ways, verbally, or by sending our consciousness into the weapon. When we do the latter, we enter the world of the spirit inside, and can interact with it in its human form."

"And what happens when you do that? Something more than just the verbal communication?"

"It strengthens the bond between the weapon and its wielder. Plus, it mitigates any damage or energy release. But any damage and fatigue we sustain in there, we retain out here."

Ren suggested breakfast before they continued any further. It would help her focus more and understand it better. A buffet was located on the second floor of the hotel. After filling their plates, Ren made them cappuccinos from the coffee machine. They took a seat on the balcony outside.

"What a beautiful view," Kelsey said.

"Yeah, but I've got a better one," Ren said. She looked at him and realized he was talking about her. Her face turned bright red.

Two full plates and three cappuccinos later, Ren finished eating. Kelsey stared at him in awe. "Where do you put all that food?" she asked.

He lifted up his shirt, revealing his perfect six-pack. "In my line of work, Kells, you can pretty much imagine how much I keep myself in shape." He leaned over to whisper in her ear. "Besides, being a vampire, my energy is immense. I have to eat a lot to maintain it. Come on, let's go wake sleeping beauty and head over to Hades."

Marcus was already awake when they got back to the room. "Good, you're awake. We're heading to Hades' as soon as we're done changing."

"I'll be ready in a minute," he said back.

Hades and a bunch of Cyclopes were sitting inside their store drinking carbonated water when they arrived.

"Ah, perfect timing," Hades said when he saw them. "We've just finished arranging the members traveling with you." Five Cyclopes were gathered besides himself, one of them being Raziel, all of them in human form. Three of them were tall, beefy men, while the other was lean and solid.

"These men are the best we have, and they have knowledge of Taormina. Along with these five, I will also be joining you."

"We have to make a change," Ren said. "I need Raziel to do something else for me. Shadow Hunter told me to tell you to go back to Trinity and rally them for the upcoming battle. We'll need their assistance, and you're the only one capable of that right now."

Raziel looked at his cousin. "If it's from Shadow Hunter, I have to go."

"Yes, I think it's best that you leave as soon as possible. It will only take us about a week to get to Taormina."

"I'll get a flight right away. Good luck, guys."

"You too," Ren said back.

Hades selected another person to replace Raziel, and they were ready to go.

Twenty-three

Reunion with an Old Frenemy

Hades immediately broke into the plan for getting the stone, the map spread out before him.

"We'll head to Florence from here. It'll take us about three hours to drive. We can stop while we're there, but we need to be careful."

"Florence is filled with the clergy of the Church," Ren explained to Kelsey before she could ask.

"Right, so we have to be careful not to draw attention to ourselves," Hades continued. "If we're lucky, we'll be alright so long as we act like tourists."

"That shouldn't be too hard," Kelsey assumed.

"Just to be safe, we should stick with a buddy system. Groups of three should be perfect," Ren suggested.

"I think that's a good idea," Hades agreed.

"Once we get to the city, Marcus will stick with me. Kelsey, I want you to stay with Hades," Ren said. "It'll be the safest place for you since no one knows who you are. The chances of you getting caught are meager. And if someone recognizes Marcus or me, you won't be dragged into a confrontation." Kelsey nodded. She wasn't happy being separated from Ren, but she agreed.

"Your Highnesses, you don't by any chance have vehicles with you that are good for narrow terrain, do you?" Hades asked. "Chances are we'll be forced into areas not good for cars."

"We don't, but we can get them," Marcus said. "We have friends in Trinity that work for the transport industry."

"I'll call our guy and have him switch for transport. What about you?" Ren asked Hades.

"I've got a friend that owns a local motorbike store with what we need. He'll hook us up."

Ren looked at Marcus, and they nodded in silent agreement. The six Cyclopes shouldered the belongings meant to accompany them.

When Marcus went noticeably quiet, Ren looked at him and saw that he was spacing out. Then he looked up at him. "Glorious just told me disguises are useless."

"Is that so? Did he say anything else?" Ren asked.

"That the two of us need to stick together, which is what we already had planned. I asked, but he couldn't see far enough to know why they would fail. I assume either we'll be spotted regardless, or we won't be spotted at all. In which case, our little tourist act is meaningless as well."

"We'll deal with it when we have to, then. Ready to hit the road?" Ren asked.

"Let's go. You take point, I'll follow behind," Marcus told him. Ren only nodded in agreement.

"Miss. Kelsey, why don't you ride with me?" Hades suggested. "If we're going to stick together, we might as well get acquainted." Ren nodded to her when she looked at him. Then he opened his door before getting into the driver's seat. Well, that ended that brief conversation.

Hades unlocked the doors to his Mercedes and turned it over. Kelsey opened the passenger door and sat down. He followed behind Ren and Marcus at a distance that wasn't close but also wasn't too far.

"So, I have to ask, what really made you decide to accompany them?" Hades asked.

"On the quest? Or in general?" Kelsey asked back.

"Yes," was Hades' only response.

"Truth is, I've known Ren since I was a baby. For reasons, there was a time when Ren aged like a normal human, so we grew up together."

"I see. So, you two are close then." The look she had on her face, however, was one of uncertainty. "Insecurity is a failure of all relationships, My Lady."

"Yeah, well, we aren't in a relationship," she admitted.

"I never said anything about love." He gave her a sly look. She'd been caught red-handed. "There are many kinds of relationships, and I daresay yours is exceptionally unique, but love is love, My Lady."

"I find it strange that you're telling me this. You wanted to kill me earlier."

Hades was silent for a bit before speaking again. "True, but my words since have not changed either. I will not discriminate. Cyclopes have always been one to stick to our own. We're very particular about who we let in, to our den, and our lives. To defend you as they did, you must mean a lot to both of them. You willingly chose to become a part of our world. Besides, if Trinity accepts you, then that's enough for me."

"So, what's with this My Lady thing then? Where did that come from?"

Her question caught him off guard. "What do you mean? You're Prince Nightwalker's lover, aren't you?" he asked, as if it were the most obvious thing in the world.

Kelsey blushed from head to toe. "I thought I said we weren't like that! We're just friends."

"Really? I just thought you were being bashful. I see. I apologize for overstepping, then. From my perspective, it was fairly obvious."

"It's obvious?" Truth be told, hearing that made her heart flutter.

"Well yeah. I see the way you look at each other. I would never have guessed you weren't already bound. Huh, that makes it even more surprising. That he'd go to such lengths. But like I said, I've seen the way he looks at you. Even if you aren't a couple, his love for you is obvious."

"Please don't tell me you're joking," she said. *No, please don't be joking,* she thought. It may give her too much hope. Hold on, hope?

"No, not at all. Prince Nightwalker was willing to face off against a den of Cyclopes for you. I don't believe he'd do that for just anyone. To be honest, I think you two make a wonderful pair. You and Prince Nightwalker bring out the best in each other."

"I'd heard the rumors. The legendary Blood Prince, they called him." That drew Kelsey's attention.

"I've heard about that nickname," she said.

Hades nodded. "They said he was ruthless, fearless, and immensely powerful. When it came to rifting shades, he was the best, but his services weren't cheap. Word was he'd rift anyone, any shade, no matter who they were. Man, woman, adult, child, it didn't matter. He was the embodiment of death itself."

"Ren's not like that. I mean, I know he kills people, but he cares about them too, and he protects them," Kelsey insisted.

"I don't doubt that. However, suffice to say, the rumors were true." She looked at him in shock. "I saw him in action once. He was merciless. Slaughtering every shade in his path without hesitation."

Kelsey did have to admit that there was a lot about Ren she didn't know. Just when she learned one thing, three more secrets came along with it. As much as she wanted to, she was finding it hard to say Hades was wrong. He'd seen Ren in action, much more than she had. She was beginning to realize just how different they were.

Three hundred years was a long time, and a lot could happen in that time. However, that was his past, and the past was just that. It was the Ren now that really mattered to her. She only hoped he stayed that way.

After almost three hours of driving, they finally reached Florence. Kelsey and Hades talked to each other the whole time. It was a lively and bustling city with extravagant buildings and a giant church. Not far into the outskirts of the city, everyone pulled off to the side of the road.

"Everybody stay close, don't go anywhere alone," Ren said. "This place is crawling with the Church's influence. Meet back here in three hours."

"If you feel in any way that something is wrong or doesn't seem right, let the others know right away," Hades added.

The nine of them split into a group of three and four while Ren and Marcus walked off on their own.

"Think we'll run into any members of the Church?" Marcus asked.

"Not sure," Ren admitted. "It's a possibility that I'm not looking forward to discovering. As far as I'm concerned, everyone here is a member."

Ren and Marcus saw a tourist group and followed them. They walked down several side streets until they came out into an open square with a giant domed church. People were gathered on all sides, and they filled the shops on the surrounding streets. There were leather shops everywhere. Jackets, purses, wallets, gloves, and belts filled the shelves.

Ren took note of the guards in the area. They were actual soldiers from the Italian military, dressed in camouflage ACUs, black combat boots, red berets, and holding carbines. Ren never made eye contact, but his attention never left the soldiers.

No one paid them any attention as they walked around. As far as they could tell, no one recognized them. Perhaps there weren't any clergy there after all. They didn't detect even a single monster.

"Let's get a drink," Marcus suggested. He nodded toward a group of people sitting on the steps of the church. They seemed interested in their conversation, but Ren couldn't help picking up a weird vibe from them. They weren't monsters, that was for sure, which left only one thing, the Church.

"Over there," Marcus went on, pointing at a small shop with his thumb.

They walked inside, and the man behind the counter said someone would come to them. Since much of the seating was outside, that's where they went. Seven square tables were enclosed by a three-foot iron railing. There was an awning over the whole area. Ren and Marcus found a table in the corner with two chairs.

A waiter came over to them and handed them a menu. Both Ren and Marcus ordered a cappuccino with a gelato. The waiter took back their menus and their order was placed in front of them only minutes later.

They took the time to immerse themselves in their order and enjoy each other's company. It didn't get much better than eating gelato and drinking a cappuccino with your best friend in Italy.

Ren let the heat of the sun invigorate him, the light shining down on them. He had his eyes and ears peeled for any signs of the Church.

A group of Italian girls walked past the church when they saw Ren and Marcus sitting at the cafe. They held bags from extravagant shopping. The moment they saw Ren and Marcus, they immediately headed in their direction.

Ren sensed their presence before he saw them. As confidently as he or Marcus had ever seen, the girls asked them to join them on their trip.

"Sorry love, we'd love to," Ren started to say,

"But we're here on work, and with other people," Marcus finished.

"Americans?" one of them asked.

"Something like that," Ren said, switching to English, then back to Italian.

One of the girls put her hand on Ren's forearm. She continued to gaze upon him, clearly not taking no for an answer. Ren and Marcus exchanged glances, gradually becoming more certain that these girls were actually members of the Church. They weren't being picked up; they were being hunted.

Ren switched from a charming look to a serious one. His eyes pierced the group of girls. "We're not going with you. Walk away, *humans*." He said 'humans' like it was the worst thing he could think of.

At once, the group of girls stood up straight and started walking away. They made no effort to resist or argue, only doing as he commanded. Well, all but one, anyway.

"Hey, where are you going?" she asked them. Her friends continued to walk, never even recognizing that she had spoken to them.

Ren's magic, it worked. They carried no wards on them to deter or resist magic. That meant they weren't with the Church; they really were only hitting on them.

"What did you do?" she asked, turning to Ren. "What have you done to them?"

Ren gave her a look of interest. "You're not affected? Interesting. You have some resistance to magic. Is it just you, or is something protecting you?"

"Magic? Wait, don't tell me you're—" Ren grabbed hold of her shirt before she could finish.

"Say another word, and your memory won't be the only thing missing when I'm done with you," he said. The girl's face went white, but Ren's eyes were blazing. "I hate humans, and you are no exception."

"Hey, let go of her!" a familiar voice shouted. Ren looked to the side to see a man with a large stomach walking toward them angrily. He was dressed in the white robes of the Radiant Church, sporting a tall white hat on his head and a silver mask on the left side of his face. He held a golden staff with the angle on top in his hands. Arron, the quincy they'd met after finding the map.

Ren and the man locked eyes. "You!" Arron shouted. Ren got up from his seat.

"Um, Ren, maybe you should—" Ren ignored Marcus and walked around the patio. Arron raised his staff, and Ren punched him in the face, knocking him to the ground. With the quincy down, Ren planted his foot over his throat.

"That's O for three, Arron; want to go for four?" Ren asked. Arron sneered at him, and Ren pressed harder.

"Stop it!" the girl said. "Let him go!" She pried Ren off of him, allowing the quincy to catch his breath.

Arron got to his feet and rubbed his neck. A crowd had gathered around. Ren and Arron exchanged glances before Arron tapped his staff on the ground, and Ren snapped his fingers. The crowd of spectators trickled away until no one paid them any mind.

"Why don't we have a little chat," Ren said.

Twenty-four

What Really Makes a Monster

“You’re a fool if you think we’ll go anywhere with you,” Arron said.

“I wasn’t asking,” Ren said back. “Take a seat.” He sat back down in his chair.

Arron and the girl reluctantly pulled a chair up to the side of the table.

“I kind of guessed you’d survived,” Ren said. “I’m sure you reported the incident to your superiors, but what about Verin?”

“I told you, we may be allied, but we’re independent. We have no intention of working for that necromancer,” Arron said back.

“And the girl?” Ren asked.

Arron looked at the girl sitting next to him. “My daughter; Angela.” That one actually surprised Ren. Not because he had a daughter, but because of something much more complicated.

"Wow. She's gotten big. There's no way I would have recognized her." Arron nodded.

"It has been nearly twenty years. I'd more surprised if you did." The look on Angela's face indicated she suddenly had no idea what was going on, but clearly Ren and her father knew each other.

"In that case, it makes sense why she's not affected by my magic."

"I have a barrier around her at all times."

Angela could no longer sit their silently with so many questions she wanted to ask.

"Just who are you?" she asked Ren. "You're a monster, that's for sure. How do you know my father? And how do you know me?"

"That, is a rather long story. Your father and I have a lot of history together, don't we, Arron? My name is Ren, Ren Nightwalker. I'm the one… that killed your mother."

Angela's eyes widened, and she looked back at her father. "Killed? What is he talking about? You told me my mom got sick."

"She did, in a sense," Ren said back. "You should have just told her the truth."

Arron kept a poker face, but at least spoke up. "I thought it best not to at the time. She was too young. And as time passed, I didn't see the need to bring up old wounds."

"Then you should do so now. You owe her that much Arron."

"What will her knowing the truth change?" he asked. "Beyond just self satisfaction. It won't bring her mother back."

"No, it won't," Ren admitted. It's not like he had anything to combat that.

"Then if you're so adamant in telling her, it should come from you. You'll explain it better than I could anyway."

Ren was silent at first. He finally nodded before turning to Angela. "Your mother wasn't sick, in the way you'd normally think. She got possessed, by a shade." Angela visibly reacted to his words.

"Your mother went through a profound change at the end of her life. She had given up on life and turned to drinking. Verin found her and used her — warped her mind. Her weakened state allowed the shade to possess her. And the people like me who fight against shades have a duty. I was given the assignment to rift a human turned shade."

"It was on this assignment that I met your father. He was just an aurora at the time. They wanted to kill your mother, along with the two of you. With my own agendas in mind and a little pleading from your father, I wiped out the group that wanted you dead. The incident was buried after that."

"But even though I saved you from the Church, I still had my assignment. Your mother was, well, let's just say she was damn tough. The shade had its hold on her, but she refused to give up and fought against it. Given that she wasn't fully turned, I was unsure about rifting her."

"Shades are always monsters, but your mother was one of the very few exceptions to the rule. Monsters can't be changed. Once a shade, always a shade, but humans are different. Although extremely rare, if a human is turned into a shade, they can be changed back."

"Why? Why only monsters?" she asked. "Because in order to be possessed by a shade, one needs to have a solid foundation of who they are for it to be taken over. Humans normally don't possess this."

"By invoking a purification ritual, a human can be released from the shade inside them and return to normal. So, I changed my plan and decided to save your mother. I had the ceremony ready, but I was never able to carry it out. A the very end, she lost the will to fight, allowing the shade to take over."

"How could she suddenly lose her will? Especially after she fought for so long and so hard."

"Because of you. You got sick. The sickness you contracted is dangerous, and in infants like you were, can be deadly."

"We took you to several physicians, but there was nothing any of them could do. You were dying," Arron confessed.

"Your mother lost hope, fearing the worst for you," Ren continued. "There was nothing that we could do once the shade took hold of her. The malice coursing through her caused her unimaginable pain. In the end, it was too much for her to bear. So, she begged me to do it. With her last bit of sanity left, she begged me to pull the trigger. Truth is, it was one of the hardest things I've ever had to do."

"So, if I was so sick and going to die, why am I alive?"

"I healed you. After your mother died, your father feared he would lose you too. He asked me to help you, and I did. With some highly advanced magic, I was able to rid you of your sickness."

"I don't understand. You two are enemies, but you have such history. Why won't you just bury the hatchet?"

"I'm afraid it's not that simple," Ren said. "Yes, I helped you, and yes, we worked together, but the fact remains that I killed your mother. That's something that can't be forgiven. Not to mention I'm a vampire. Perhaps, in another life, we could have been friends, but fate is cruel and likes to play tricks. It just wasn't meant to be."

Ren pulled out his phone to check the time. "We should be heading back soon," he said to Marcus. Marcus nodded, and they stood up.

"Wait! I have one more question," Angela said. "Why do you hate humans so much?"

Ren was quiet for a few moments before answering. "Like you, I lost the person who was most important to me. And humans were the cause of it."

"Your species is a plague. You're greedy, spiteful, cowardly, self-centered, arrogant, and hateful. You lie, cheat, and steal as if it was second nature. And you don't hesitate to hurt, kill, and betray anyone or anything that gets in your way. And when it does, you presume the whole world is against you and that you are the victims."

"There is so much wrong with the human race that any amount of good is immediately snuffed out and ceases to exist. In the end, you will be annihilated by nothing but yourselves. Are monsters perfect? No, but at least we try."

With that hanging in the air, Ren and Marcus left the two of them sitting at the table. Marcus placed his arm on Ren's shoulder. "I'll always have you back, no matter what."

"I know. Thanks, brother."

They walked by the church, and Ren got the distinct feeling something was wrong. It didn't feel like they were being followed, but he could sense electricity crackling in the air. It made the hair on his arms stand up.

A woman with similar robes and a hat as Arron, though of a lower rank, stopped in front of them. She was tall and lean, evidence of time spent training her body. A high priest of the Radiant Church. "Would you two mind coming with me."

"Sorry, but we're late and must be going," Ren said back. He continued on and walked into a wall of white energy. Magic. "I wasn't asking," the woman said. She tapped the bottom of his staff on the ground, and a dome of magic encased them. All the people outside it vanished.

"Are you sure you want to do this here?" Ren asked.

"With the barrier I just placed around this area, we've effectively been cut off from the real world. Did you really think you could show your faces around here without being recognized? Ren Nightwalker, Marcus Allagash."

Ren moved left as the priest pointed her staff and fired a blast of magic. Ren fired his gun, and the bullet ripped right through the attack, canceling it out. Then he struck the priest in the chest with the palm of his other hand. Blue energy burst out, and the woman went flying.

A dozen auroras suddenly surrounded them. Ren and Marcus got back-to-back before they could question where they had just come from.

"Shall we?" Marcus asked.

"We shall," Ren agreed. They rushed in on the surrounding clergy. Ren aimed his pistols and Marcus his ice bow.

Ren jumped over one of the attackers, and Marcus shot an arrow into the ground at his feet. Everything around him turned to ice, freezing the auroras in place and trapping them. Ren pointed his pistols and fired away. Marcus twisted his bow in two different directions in the middle. It split apart, forming two daggers, and he sliced right through the remainder.

Having recovered from Ren's previous attacks, the high priest channeled magic through her staff, firing a volley of spells. Ren fired back, but the priest summoned a barrier, catching the bullets before they could hit.

Seeing that his attacks were failing, Ren changed tactics. The area went dark as thunder boomed overhead, and a bolt of lightning came down, striking the high priest. He kicked her feet out from under her, knocking her to the ground. Without hesitating, Ren pointed his pistol and fired. The bullet passed through her forehead.

With the high priest dead, the barrier surrounding them disappeared. Ren grabbed Marcus and immediately jumped into the nearest shadow before they were seen.

"This isn't good. They're getting bolder," Marcus said, coming out of a shadow. He and Ren stood in a back alley, next to where they had just fought the Church. "They actually attacked us in a public place filled with people, barrier or not. We have to warn the others and get out of here."

"I agree; let's go," Ren said.

Marcus dove and took them both to the ground as a blast of magic struck where they had been standing. A circle of flames danced around the destroyed area.

"Well, aren't you quite the sneaky one," Ren said to the caster. He looked around until he found him standing on top of a roof.

The attacker jumped down. "I knew those fools wouldn't be able to stop you. Why is it the weak ones never listen?"

This guy was no joke. Ren could feel the energy coming off of him from there. He was much stronger than Arron, a quincy was. Which meant only one possibility. This guy was an elite guard. The paxon's personal bodyguards, and the strongest of the Radiant Church's ranks.

"Ah, you sense it. Good, that saves me the trouble. Daniel Laresta, at your service," the guy said, giving a light bow. "I have the privilege of killing you on his grace's orders."

Ren was tempted to draw Shadow Hunter but decided against it. Using him here wasn't a good idea.

He thrust his hand out, and a ball of flames shot at the Guard. The guy held his hand out and the fire disappeared as soon as it hit. Ren tried again, shooting more flames, but the result was the same. *Alright, let's try something else,* he thought.

He used earth magic to summon spikes that shot out of the ground. Then he gathered his energy and summoned lightning to his hand. It shot out at and blasted the guard into a building, making it crumble like a Jenga tower, but the guy emerged completely unscathed.

"It's useless," Daniel told him. "This ring on my finger was a gift from his grace. All the elite guards receive one. Each one is holy and has a specific power. Mine has the ability to negate any magic that comes near me, which means your spells are useless."

Ren lunged at the guy and his fist struck the guard in the face, knocking him to the ground.

"If my magic doesn't work, then I'll just use my fists," he said.

Hand-to-hand combat was an option, but not the best in this situation. He needed something more, but the bullets in his pistols wouldn't do anything to this guy with his ring. It was a good thing he had something stronger.

On the side of both pistols was a trigger that released the ammo clips. They dropped to the ground, and he loaded a set of clips with multicolored bullets in them. They clicked into place and Ren fired relentlessly. Fire, water, ice, lighting, all sorts of magic shot out.

Daniel ran around him, closing the gap in a second. He kicked Ren in the chest, who brought his arms up to block it. Ren skidded to a stop a few feet back. The Guard whistled in surprise.

"I can't believe how well you took that." In response, he launched another blast of magic. Ren fired one of his pistols, and the magic exploded. Daniel stared at him with a grin, like he was already victorious. Large orbs of water the size of bowling balls floated above his hands.

"Mother—" the water flew at Ren. He dove right, avoiding the attack. The water splashed on the pavement. It reformed, then flew at him. He dove out of the way again as it reformed and continued to blast him. Ren just barely avoided them, but one clipped him in the shoulder. Lightning shot out around him from where he got hit. Taking deep breaths, he held back the pain and continued fighting.

Daniel laughed hysterically as Ren ran around, avoiding the water. "Run, run, run as fast as you can, little vampire." Another one came at him. Ren pointed his pistol and fired. A bullet of air shot out and collided with the water, blasting it apart.

After avoiding them for long enough, Ren had learned the timing of the spell. He matched his firing to Daniel's, canceling out the water balls. Soon, Daniel's grin turned to a deep-set frown. He fired two more shots in succession, and Ren fired three back. The first two were blasted apart, and the third one struck Daniel, blowing him through the nearest building. The Guard struggled to get back to his feet, having hit his head when he landed.

Thunder boomed. The Guard managed a look as a bolt of lightning flew at him with incredible speed. He tried to move but was too slow. The lightning ripped through his arm, detaching it from his body. He cried out in pain. The heat from the lighting cauterized the wound instantly, but the pain was agonizing.

Filled with anger and hatred, he held up his remaining arm. Water formed above him and collected, growing in size. Soon a sphere of water floated above their heads. "Die, Vampire!" He threw his hand down and the water followed. Ren turned his back to the water and covered himself with his jacket, but the water never hit. At the last second, it disappeared.

"What the hell was that?" Daniel asked. "What did you do?" It was only for a split second, but Ren saw the glow of a golden dome around him, a signature move of the Church. But there was only one person willing to shield him with it. *Arron,* he thought. The sides of his mouth twitched up into a light grin.

"Perhaps you're not as strong as you think you are," Ren boasted. Of course, he knew it was a lie. But he wasn't about to betray Arron's assistance.

"I guess the elite guards aren't all they're cracked up to be. I feel sorry for them, having you in their ranks." Lightning gathered around his hands. It struck the ground in front of him, and when it disappeared, Ren was gone. He appeared behind Daniel, and a bolt of lightning pierced through him.

Twenty-five

Reaper's Den

Daniel didn't make a move. He stood frozen, like a statue, a gaping hole in his torso from where the lightning ripped through him.

Despite the situation he was in, Daniel managed a weak laugh. "Overcome by the monsters I swore to kill," he finally managed to say. "But others will succeed where I failed. Once his grace and the Church learn of my death, they'll be coming at you with everything. Besides, we've got him on our side now."

"Who?" Ren asked. The way he said it, this guy sounded like bad news.

"Don't know his name. We call him, the Crimson Reaper." A sinister laugh escaped his lips.

"Never seen someone leave so much blood in their wake before." With the last remaining bit of his strength, the guard grabbed the lapel of Ren's jacket. "He can't be stopped." His grip released and his hand fell. The remainder of his strength, and life, now gone.

The Crimson Reaper? Ren wondered. Were they a high-ranking member of the Church, perhaps even the head of the elite guard? Or could this Crimson Reaper be the general Shadow Hunter told him about?

"Hey, you alright?" Marcus asked, jogging up to him. In response, Ren grabbed his arm, the pain scorching through him. Sparks still erupted around the wound. Marcus saw the hole in his jacket and the searing red of his skin. "Shit. You got hit."

"I'll be alright," Ren told him. He started coughing, dropping to his knees as blood came out of his mouth and nose. He felt like he'd been run over by a truck.

Marcus acted quickly, grabbing the vials of blood attached to his belt. "Hold on, Ren. Just hold on." He uncorked two of them and handed them both to him.

Ren gulped down the blood, and relief washed over him. "Thanks," he said through heavy breaths.

He recorked the vials and put them back in their place. Marcus helped him to his feet, letting him lean against him. "I'll be alright. I just a minute," Ren said.

"No, we need to get you out of here," Marcus protested. "Come on, I already called the rest of the team and told them to meet us." He put Ren's arm around his neck and let him lean on him for support.

When Ren and Marcus arrived at the cars, the rest of the team was already waiting. Marcus helped him over to his car, and he leaned against the driver's side. His arm ached badly. The wound, it was getting worse. The water may not have punctured his skin, but it didn't matter. His arm felt numb.

With a fair amount of effort and some assistance from Marcus, Ren managed to get off his jacket and shirt. Kelsey didn't have time to bother staring at his chiseled torso. She was too taken by the giant burn along his arm. It was bright red and blistered all over.

"Damn, it's worse than I thought," Ren said.

"How much did you come into contact with?" Marcus asked him.

"A small blast, about the size of a marble."

"Your jacket is supposed to protect you. Guess the force was too much for it to handle."

Kelsey was immediately at Ren's side when she saw him injured. "What happened to you?" She reached out to touch his arm, but he pulled it back, making him flinch from a sharp pain.

"Water," he said. "This is what happens when a vampire comes in contact with water. The more we come into contact with, the worse the effects. I already stopped sparking. I'll be fine in a few minutes."

Kelsey seriously doubted that. With the state his arm was in, there was no way he'd be alright in just a few short minutes. He looked to be in intense pain. And what was that about sparking?

Then it happened. She saw the wound on his arm start to heal. First, the blisters vanished, then the redness receded until it was gone.

True to Ren's words, his wound had disappeared in only a couple of minutes. She couldn't believe it.

"I told you before, vampires have incredible regenerating powers. Healing an injury caused by water takes a long time, the longest of any healing. Luckily, I didn't come into contact with a lot of it."

"Why don't you tell us what happened," Hades said. Ren quickly summed up his and Marcus's fight with the Church.

"You fought a member of the elite guards? The Church must be getting desperate. Then there's that name, the Crimson Reaper. I don't like the sound of it."

Ren put his shirt and jacket back on. "I thought the same. We need to get out of here. So, where to now?" he asked Hades.

"I'd like to make it to the end of the Tuscany region, then reach Rome tomorrow. We can spend some time there until the day after."

"That sounds reasonable," Ren agreed. "Our transport should come in tomorrow too. Rome would be ideal in that case. Let's go with that."

Sitting in the driver seat of his McLaren with Kelsey now occupying the passenger side, he pulled away from the curb, and they drove off with the others behind him. He increased his speed slightly and switched lanes. Not even ten minutes passed before Marcus's name appeared on the display screen.

"That fight got me anxious," Marcus confessed. "We need to be on the lookout for the Church. It's possible they're trailing us after the incident earlier."

"If they are, given what they just came at us with, I don't know what to expect. But I have a feeling that Arron will likely come through." Kelsey flinched when she heard Arron's name.

"What makes you think that?" Marcus asked.

"The last attack that elite guard used on me, I saw it stopped by a barrier. One made of magic used by the Church. He's not such a bad guy."

"Part of me wants to believe that his daughter was right. About you two. Maybe you really can be friends. A little more pushing is all it could take. But for now, let's be careful."

Marcus hung up, leaving Ren and Kelsey alone in silence. They drove for hours without a word. The mountain scenery was all the same but still beautiful to look at.

Kelsey was the first to spot the large house high up the side of a mountain. From his position, Ren could see that it was made of brick and stucco with columns along the front and sides. The house was large, especially Italian wise. He was ready to dismiss it merely as the strange desire of wealth, when he felt the trickle of magic emanating from it.

Getting the others' attention, he pointed to the house and motioned for them to stop. Turning onto a dirt road, he headed up the mountain. Marcus, who was close behind, followed him, leaving the Cyclopes waiting at the side of the road. Having those bikes would have come in handy right now.

The house became clearer the closer they got. They stopped right in front of it, giving it a once-over. It was a complete mess. The bricks were cracked, and the mortar turning to dust. The colors of the building had faded over time. Windows were destroyed and cracked, littering the ground with glass. By all rights, the house appeared abandoned.

Ren opened the car door and stepped out. Dead grass crunched beneath his boots as he walked toward the front porch. It wrapped around the entire front of the house. The wood making up the steps, floor, and railing was rotted and splintered; the paint chipped away.

That unsettling feeling he had when he first spotted it intensified. Only this time, there was something else. It was eerie, almost evil. A deep cold crept up his body, making his skin crawl. Dark magic. He sensed death.

Marcus held his hand up, an indication for them to stop. He walked toward the porch steps, his gaze never faltering. As soon as his foot touched the first step, it fell through. Cracks spread from the hole, and the whole step fell to the ground in pieces. *I kind of expected that,* he thought.

Looking around, he settled on the railing. A couple of pushes were all he needed to see if it was sturdy. Satisfied well enough, he jumped right over top of it and landed on the porch. He half expected to fall right through the floor, but it held.

Careful of where he stepped, he walked to the front door. Two wooden doors with lion door knockers on the front. The door handle broke right off when he turned it. Oh, great.

"Looks like we'll have to find another way in," he said to himself.

Taking a step back, he searched for another way in. Kelsey, who was curious, headed towards him. Marcus had just come up with an idea for getting inside when Ren made his move.

"Maybe we could use one of these windows to—" he stopped when he saw Ren throw a flying sidekick. There was a loud crack, followed by an even louder boom and crashing sounds, as Ren kicked the doors clear off their hinges, and they flew into the back wall, landing in a heap of broken wood.

"Or we could just kick the door down. Because, you know, that always works," Marcus said.

"You guys coming or what?" Ren asked.

"Let's go," Marcus said, looking at Kelsey. He helped her onto the deck before heading inside.

Ren searched the house. Everything was covered in dust. Cobwebs spanned the walls and furniture. Clearly, the place had been abandoned for a long time. Years, he guessed.

He wandered aimlessly, eventually walking into the kitchen. There was a table big enough for four and complete with all types of appliances. The cupboards were empty, the insides covered.

After the kitchen, he explored one of the bedrooms. The furniture was newer than most of the house but clearly unused. Nothing seemed out of the ordinary.

He was searching through the furniture when he heard Kelsey call him. He moved to close the door behind him, and that's when he saw it. A mark on the floor beneath the bed. Curious, he moved the bed as much as he could, leaving most of the mark visible. A red angel on her knees, her hands clasped together in prayer. Ren's eyes widened.

A loud crash got Marcus's and Kelsey's attention. They immediately headed towards it and found each other in the living room.

"Please tell me you heard that?" Marcus asked.

"Of course I did," Kelsey said. "Where's Ren?" She hadn't seen him since they'd split up to search.

"I don't know. I haven't seen him since we split up." So it was the same for him as well.

Ren appeared before they could make it out of the living room. He ran towards them before coming to a stop.

"We're leaving!" he said. He grabbed Kelsey's hand and rushed her out of the room. "This place belongs to the Church!" he said. "We need to leave, now!"

Marcus let his curiosity get the best of him and quickly rushed toward the bedroom Ren had just been in. He saw an angel on the floor next to a pile of rubble that used to be a bed. "Damn it!" he yelled and ran to catch up with Ren and Kelsey. He found them in the main foyer, headed towards the door.

"This place is most likely a safe house of some sort. Who knows if it's still being used," Ren said. "We need to leave before we find out the answers." He pulled Kelsey along with him, moving towards the door.

"I was wondering how long it was going to take you," came a voice. It spoke in English but reeked of malice. The voice gave Kelsey the creeps, sending chills through her. Ren stopped in his tracks.

Kelsey could vaguely identify a shape in the shadows. The figure emerged as a man, probably in his late thirties. He had black hair cropped close at the sides and bangs styled up and away from his face, with light-brown eyes.

"Algiroth," Ren said harshly. "What are you doing here?"

"I believe the nature of this location should suffice," the man said back. "I'd heard you were looking for the stones. It was only a matter of time before we encountered each other."

Ren gripped Kelsey's hand so hard she thought it would break. Now, everything made sense to him. And the name that elite guard had let slip finally made its way back from the depths of his memory.

"You traitorous bastard!" Ren shouted. "Why would you join Verin?"

"Excitement," he said with a grin. "I find life dreadfully boring. Nothing interests me anymore. Joining the necromancer has proven to be very entertaining. And thanks to our temporarily alliance, making use of the humans, the Radiant Church, has been quite beneficial."

Kelsey felt the surge of Ren's energy before she saw it. He was gearing up to fight. "The Church has ordered its forces to hunt you down, and word from above is the necromancer has sent his elite supporters after you as well. Yours truly happens to be at the top of that list. Though I admit, you were much easier to catch than I expected. How I've longed for this, Blood Prince."

"Joining the enemy was your worst and last mistake. I'll send you back to Verin in a box, *Crimson Reaper.*"

Twenty-six

Crimson Brawl

Ren and Algiroth met in a fierce clash of fists. The force blew Kelsey to the ground. Pain shot through her when she landed.

Algiroth deflected a roar of flames, and Ren moved behind him faster than Kelsey could see. He tackled Algiroth and beat him relentlessly. The force of Ren's punches sent blasts of energy outward.

Algiroth kicked Ren off him. His face looked like a train wreck but healed in minutes. He was a vampire alright.

He kicked Ren's feet out from under him and slammed him down. Ren wrapped his legs around Algiroth's arm and sent him tumbling to the ground. He pulled, and there was a resounding snap. Then he flipped Algiroth up and over onto his stomach.

Algiroth swung at Ren using his free hand, and Ren flew into the wall. Algiroth got to his feet with some effort. His body shook, and his arm hung limp at his side. He grabbed it, and there was a pop as he set it. He took a few seconds to flex and test it, allowing Ren to get to his feet as well. Blood trickled down his arm.

The blue aura surrounding their bodies was vibrant now. They lunged at each other and were thrown backward by the force of the backlash. The floor cracked, and one of the walls came crashing down. At this rate, they were going to take the whole place out.

Ren drew his pistols, and Algiroth slipped two daggers into his hands out of nowhere. Ren fired, and Algiroth deflected it with a dagger.

Kelsey had to find cover, for fear of getting hit by the deflected bullets, or worse, their energy attacks. They were so powerful; she'd never seen anything like it. She hid behind a turned-over sofa, though she wasn't sure it would be able to stop a bullet.

Ren fired one of his pistols and came around with a heel kick to the head. Algiroth deflected the bullet, then ducked underneath the kick. Ren lowered one of his guns below his leg as Algiroth ducked and fired.

The vampire fell back with a hard thud, a pool of blood forming beneath him, the bullet still stuck in his head. Kelsey fought back the urge to vomit.

Ren holstered his pistols and ran to her. "Come on, we have to go. He won't stay down for long."

"Wait, he's still alive? But you just shot him in the head."

"I told you; vampires have incredible regenerative abilities. He'll heal soon enough."

She was starting to wonder how exactly one did kill a vampire. If they can survive getting shot in the head, who knows what it would take.

Ren took her hand and hoisted her over the couch. They ran towards the door and were met by an invisible wall that sent them tumbling to the ground. They could hear Algiroth stir in the other room. He would be healed soon.

Ren got to his feet and pulled Kelsey along. They tried for the closest window or door, but everything was either blocked or didn't open.

"This way," he said. They turned left and ran the other way. Two men in white robes with the Radiant Church's symbol on them blocked their path. Ren drew his pistols, ready to fire when another member of the Church came flying and crashed into the two in front of him.

"Get moving!" Marcus said. He ran down the hall, and Ren and Kelsey followed him into another room with a connecting door on the other side that led outside.

Marcus aimed his ice bow at the door. When he drew the string back, an arrow formed, and he fired. The arrow whizzed through the air and struck the door. It exploded from an eruption of ice, leaving a large hole in the wall.

Kelsey got out first, then Marcus. Ren stopped at the door. "Ren, what are you doing? Come on," Kelsey said. He looked back inside the house. Algiroth was coming.

Kelsey reached for his hand, but he stepped back. "Ren!" Kelsey said, this time louder. "Ren get over here now!" She was shouting now. "Ren Allen Nightwalker, you get over here this instant!"

"I can't leave Kells. Algiroth would catch us in minutes. If we don't stop him here, who knows how much damage he'll cause. Besides, with the Church here, there's a chance we'll all be killed before we can make it out. Where there's one, many more follow. They probably have an army on the way, if they're not already here. You need to leave before that happens."

"But—"

"Just go!" he yelled, cutting her off. "Keep going, and don't turn back."

Ren pulled her into him, and then his lips were on hers. When she opened her eyes, he was running inside, then he turned a corner and was gone.

Marcus grabbed her hand and pulled her toward the cars. Kelsey looked back to see Algiroth shoot into the sky, a pair of large, jet-black wings on his back. In his arms was a blond-haired teenager, but Kelsey knew he wasn't really a teenager.

Algiroth spread his wings out to the side and stopped dead, then he released his hold on Ren. Kelsey watched in horror as Ren plummeted out of the sky.

Marcus threw open his door and jumped behind the wheel of his car. Kelsey sat in the passenger seat, holding on tightly as the car shot forward at insane speeds. One thing was for certain. They had a lot of explaining to do.

Twenty-seven

A Life Worth Fighting For

Ren fell towards the ground as fast as gravity would
allow. He had to act quickly before he became a
vampire pancake. Who knew how long it would take him
to recover from that — if he recovered at all. A fall at
this height might actually kill him.

He flipped over, so his feet faced the ground and
threw his hands down. Wind exploded everywhere, and
he shot upward just before impact. His feet hit the roof,
cracking it where he landed, and he rolled to his feet.
That was too close for comfort.

"You're quite resilient, aren't you?" Algiroth stated.
"The rumors do you justice." He floated down in front of
Ren, his wings flapping lightly. His feet touched the
shingles, and he tucked in his wings.

"If only you would feed. Who knows how powerful
you would become? And you would finally get your

wings. One who doesn't even embrace the rituals of his own race isn't fit to be one of us; or our ruler. You don't deserve your title."

"Maybe you're right," Ren agreed. "But even if I don't deserve my title, you sure as hell don't either."

Algiroth flew at Ren, but he ducked and spun sideways, sending him flying with a kick to the stomach. Algiroth crashed into the ground with a heavy thud. Ren jumped from the roof and concentrated his ki into his fists, crushing Algiroth under the strength of his punch. His ki reformed over his body as he stepped back.

Though he was almost out of strength, Algiroth was down. Now, Ren needed to make sure the vampire stayed down. He drew Shadow Hunter and sliced off Algiroth's wings with one swing. There was no getting away now.

Ren raised his sword, tip aimed at the small of Algiroth's back when his body turned into shadows and disappeared. "Damn it! When did he pull that off? Slick bastard."

"You really are as strong and ruthless as the rumors make you out to be." Algiroth floated in the air above the ruined safe house. "If I had been any weaker, I would have died for sure. I'll leave it at this for now. We're both out of strength. We'll finish where we left off when we next meet. Don't stop entertaining me, Ren." He turned and flew into the sun. Then he was gone.

"Damn him. I should have seen that coming," Ren complained. He spat out a vial of curses.

Entertainment, huh? he wondered. *Has he been watching us? Damn it, Algiroth. What are you really up to?*

The sound of footsteps echoed behind him. They grew closer until Ren could see who they belonged to. Twenty people, all wearing the robes of the Church. Over half of them were auroras, but that wasn't the problem. Among their ranks was one high priest, one quincy, and worse, two elite guards.

Oh, come on, Ren thought. *Now how in the hell am I going to make it out of this? The high priest and quincy aside, those elite guards are going to be a problem. I had a hard-enough time against one. Now I have to face two, and with little strength left. This could be worse than I thought. I really may not make it out of this one.*

One of the elite guards walked forward and bowed. "Your Highness, it is an honor."

"I don't suppose we could just call this a day and leave, could we?" he asked, weary from his fight with Algiroth.

"I'm afraid that's impossible. The Lord has ordered you dead, and we have our own score to settle with you."

"You've disappointed us," said the other guard. "Even we are not strong enough to go up against one of Verin's four generals single-handedly. That's why we intended to leave killing that vampire to you."

"But you failed," said the first guard. "And let him get away. It's bad enough we have to work with your kind, now we take orders from them. That's crossing the line if you ask me."

"Wait, so you're not seeking revenge for the death of your comrade?" Ren asked.

"Who, Daniel? Please. He was foolish enough to think he could take down the Blood Prince on his own. He got what he deserved."

Interesting, Ren thought. *Not all of the guards are on good terms. There's a rift between them. Perhaps I can use this.*

One of the guards drew an axe strapped to his back, and the other guard drew two hammers that hung at his sides. *That's right, come and get it.*

The guard with the axe charged. Ren swiped his hand at him, and a blast of air blew him away and knocked their remaining numbers to the ground. His next spell released a bright flash of light, blinding them.

Reaching behind him, he drew Shadow Hunter. With one swing, a wave of golden energy raged toward the clergy.

The energy crashed into them, and Ren heard the screams of dying men. The elite guard with the axe swung and dispersed the light. Only the quincy and two elite guards remained. The rest had been cut down in his surprise attack. However, the elite guard who wielded dual hammers now only clung to one. His second hammer lay on the ground, still clasped in the grip of his severed arm.

"You're no joke," the guard said. "Witnessing your power, and the power of a heaven's blade first-hand, it's otherworldly."

"Do you have any idea how much credit we'll get for killing this guy?" the guard with the axe added. "Our ranks in the elite guards will be secured indefinitely."

"Permanent placement in the top ranks of the elite guards. Sounds perfect to me."

The guard with the axe charged at Ren, who met him in the middle. His sword went up as the guard's axe came down. Shadow Hunter sliced clean through it.

Confused and defenseless, Ren kicked him in the chest and sent him flying. "You idiot, his weapon is far stronger!" the other guard yelled. He attacked Ren with his hammer, but Ren dodged all the swings.

Ren's chest heaved with heavy breaths. He still hadn't recovered from fighting Algiroth. The guard who wielded the axe came from the side and threw a fury of punches. He punched the ground, and a crater formed where he hit. Ki manipulation.

Magic came flying at him, and he deflected it with his sword. The quincy held his staff in the air and was chanting. Ren swung his sword, and a blade of energy flew at him. The energy ripped through the barrier surrounding the priest but never touched him.

The two elite guards attacked at the same time. Ren blocked their attack with his sword, and the one who wielded the axe drew a knife, slashing at him. Ren blocked or avoided most of them, but several got through, cutting his arms and face. When the blade came in again, it grazed his cheek.

Lightning came down from the sky and struck the spot where Ren stood, but he was too weak to avoid it. Suddenly, he was no longer in control of his body. He moved with incredible speed, and his arm swung his sword, deflecting the lightning off the blade.

"I've got your back, partner," Shadow Hunter's voice said in his head. He had taken over Ren's body and reacted for him.

"Thanks for the help, partner," Ren said back. He was glad to have Shadow Hunter on his side.

That lightning attack, it hadn't come from either of the elite guards. Which left only one option.

I have to take care of that quincy, he thought.

Thinking quickly, he came up with a plan. The quincy pointed his staff at him, and a bolt of lightning came out. Ren swung three times in quick succession. The first blade of energy crashed into the lightning, and the second ripped through the barrier surrounding the priest again. Now exposed, he was vulnerable. The third blade of energy struck the quincy in the chest, cutting him open. He glared at Ren with hatred before dropping to the ground in a lifeless heap.

"Looks like we're all that's left," said the guard with the hammer. "Even as weakened as you are, you still managed to kill the rest of them. I'll admit, I'm impressed."

Ren had to end this fight soon, or he would die. Shadow Hunter was taking control of his body more and more with his fatigue weighing him down.

The guard with the hammer threw it at Ren and charged. Ren dove to the ground and avoided the hammer. Rolling to his feet, he ran to the side of the safe house.

"Duck!" Shadow Hunter yelled. Ren ducked just as a boulder flew over his head and ripped through the safe house. The attack had given the one guard enough time to retrieve his hammer and block Ren's path while the other lifted another boulder into the air. They both had a smirk on their faces.

When the elite guard holding the boulder launched it, Ren punched the boulder, and it blasted into a million pieces. Hidden from the dust, he swung his sword, and another blade of energy crashed into the guard in front of him. The guard flew into the one behind him, a large gash spread across his chest where he got hit.

Ren walked toward them, his sword pointed at the ground. "*Aapaka bhagavaan ab aapako nahin bacha sakata,*" he said in Hindi. The two guards looked up at him with fear in their eyes. Ren gripped Shadow Hunter tightly and swung. The guards were obliterated in a torrent of magic.

Fatigue took over, and Ren nearly collapsed. No, he couldn't afford to pass out. He needed to get as far away from this place as he could, back to the others. Sheathing Shadow Hunter behind him, he wobbled back to his car. His muscles ached, the open wounds on his body left a trail of blood as he limped along.

Sliding into the driver's seat, he put the car in gear and drove off in the direction he had previously been heading. Even if he didn't meet up with the others, only when he was far enough away could he finally rest. Until then, he had to keep going, pushing through the exhaustion. Luckily, he could feel Shadow Hunter lending him strength.

Ren swerved around cars and trucks. There weren't many vehicles on the road, which helped him make up lost time. It didn't take long for him to get sick of driving through tunnels, though. There were dozens of them due to the mountainous geography. He longed to see the countryside. That was the best place to call in for the day. Out in the Italian countryside, no one would find him. It was perfect for hiding out.

A couple of hours into the drive, Ren finally entered the countryside. He breathed a sigh of relief. Now, if trouble came looking, it wouldn't find him, hopefully.

The drive was quiet, but Ren didn't mind the silence. In fact, right about now, he relished in it. After all that mess, and still evading people who were trying to kill him, some alone time driving through the Italian countryside was just what he needed.

Another hour passed and a notification appeared on his display screen. It was a text message. He pulled off to the side of the road, hoping it was from Marcus or Kelsey. It turned out to be from Marcus. The message was short, containing only a set of numbers: coordinates. More than likely to their location. That also meant they were stopped. Good.

Ren input the coordinates into the GPS in his car. As it turned out, they weren't that far away, only about two and a half hours. He breathed a sigh of relief, knowing they were alright and that he would see them soon.

With renewed vigor, he gunned the car forward, following the directions toward his friends.

Twenty-eight

The Deepest Wounds

When Ren fell, Kelsey didn't know what to think. All she could imagine was him lying on the ground, possibly dead. He may be a vampire with incredible healing powers, but even he couldn't survive a fall from that high up, could he?

Watching him fight that vampire, Algiroth, they looked like they were equal in terms of strength, but she wasn't so sure. That Algiroth had wings. That was a huge advantage. Ren had told her he had wings too, but then why didn't he use them? Sure, Ren was super strong, she knew that, but with an advantage like that, the odds weren't in his favor, and in Ren's world, that meant death.

The urge to vomit crept up on her. The thought of Ren lying there dead made her sick. She didn't want to admit it because she'd tried to be strong and independent her whole life, but she needed him, wanted him there with her. Having Marcus with her helped ease her nerves, but it wasn't the same. He wasn't Ren.

She was on this quest with him because she didn't want to do nothing while he faced danger and could end up dead. And yet that's exactly what happened anyway. Ren had promised to be there for her and watch out for her, and he had. But when he needed her, she wasn't there for him. Kelsey could do nothing as she was taken away with the others, leaving Ren behind to fight a losing battle. She felt utterly useless.

Marcus's touch shook her away from her thoughts. "He'll be alright," he said reassuringly. "Ren's not dead; you can be sure of that. If he was, then we'd all be screwed. Without Ren, there's little to no hope of winning this war."

"If you say he's alive, then I'll believe you," Kelsey told him. "I just hope you're right."

"If you don't believe in me, then at least believe in Ren. Have faith in him."

"Faith has never been my strong suit."

"Then that makes two of us. But when it comes to Ren, I've learned to develop some."

Kelsey tightened her grip on the seat, and Marcus switched lanes. She wasn't very religious, unlike her parents. Still, she sent out a silent prayer to any god who was listening to have Ren return safely.

After an hour and a half of driving, Marcus pulled over to a small rest stop on the side of the road. Whatever their reason for stopping, Kelsey didn't know. The only thing that mattered was that the place had food. It sold all kinds of sandwiches, drinks, and snacks.

The churning of Kelsey's stomach made her grateful they had decided to stop. She hadn't eaten since Florence, and it was only something little. Not to mention the sun would be setting soon. If he knew that she was hungry, or if they all were, she wasn't sure. Hopefully, it would take her mind off Ren's current situation.

Marcus ordered for himself and Kelsey since she didn't speak Italian, which she was grateful for. She really needed to learn more languages.

A room in the back filled with tables and chairs connected to the main store. All the Cyclopes worked together to put tables together and secure the correct number of chairs.

Kelsey found an open spot and sat down. Marcus sat on one side, and Hades found her other. However, Marcus's chuckling distracted her from her sandwich.

"I haven't been to one of these since Ren and I worked a job together in Italy ten years ago. Really takes you back."

Ren. Just hearing his name made Kelsey's stomach sink with worry.

"He'll be alright, My Lady," Hades said. "Let go of your worry. You'll only make yourself sick."

"He's right," Marcus told her. "Ren's alright. He's probably speeding down the highway as we speak. Keyword speeding." His comment made her chuckle.

The eight of them ate through stories told around the tables. It took the better of an hour before they were ready to leave. Long after they had finished eating.

Marcus returned to the front counter with a rolled-up piece of parchment in his hand, the map to the stones. "*Avete una mappa?*" Marcus asked the man behind the counter.

"*Si signore,*" the clerk answered. He brought out a map of the area. Marcus asked for their location in comparison and the man pointed to a part of their map before saying something back.

It turned out they weren't far from the edge of the region. Only about three hours from Perugia. "*Grazie signore,*" Marcus said.

"*Prego,*" the clerk said back

While Marcus rolled up the map, the clerk looked at Kelsey. "*Americano?*" he asked. Kelsey nodded back. "How, you, like, Italy?" the man asked in rough English.

"It's beautiful," she said.

"*Bene, molto bene,*" the clerk said, happy with her response.

"*Buonasera,*" Marcus said to the clerk, who responded with the exact same phrase.

Outside the store, the Cyclopes were waiting to leave. They were in the middle of deciding where to settle for the night when Kelsey noticed something strange in the distance. Dark shapes, and they appeared to be moving. What's worse, it looked like they were coming closer.

"Um, guys, I think we have a problem," Kelsey said. She pointed to the dark shapes, directing their attention to them.

"Damn," Marcus said. "Shades. Dozens of them. Hades, Gary, with me. Kelsey, stick close to the others. If you need to, take the car and leave."

"But how will you get back?" she wondered. He'd have know way of knowing where she'd be.

"I know your scent; I can track you," he said back. It dawned on her that she'd forgotten just how strong his nose was.

Hades and Gary ran to intercept the shades. Marcus drew the string on his ice bow and an arrow appeared. Releasing it, the arrow whizzed through the air and struck one of the shades in the chest, freezing it solid.

Drawing and creating another arrow, he aimed and fired. This time, it struck the ground in front of a group of six shades. A wall of ice erupted, encasing the shades. His next shot struck another in the chest and took out the shade next to it.

While Marcus fired away, Hades and Gary smashed the shade Popsicles to pieces with clubs. Any that got near and Marcus didn't pick off received a hard smash to the head.

Kelsey was standing by the car when she heard shuffling noises behind her. One of the shades was headed toward her. She had no idea how it had gotten through and come from behind. It was the first time she'd seen a nonliving shade up close. Its body looked like it was made of black mist. It had no noticeable features other than the claws where its hands would be, and it didn't have a face except for two piercing eyes, which were jet black.

As close as the shade was, there was no way she was going to be able to get away without it catching her. She needed to get clear of the thing. The problem was how. She didn't have any weapons. Instead, she settled with what she had and smacked it in the face with her backpack. It was doubtful that the bag would do anything at all to the shade, but it was all she had. It surprised her when the shade fell to the ground. She half expected her bag to pass right through it. Apparently not.

Two Cyclopes came from behind and quickly disposed of it while it was down. With the shade gone, she hopped into Marcus's car, ready to leave. Screams poured from the store, stopping her. Marcus had told her to leave if she needed to, but she didn't care. Grabbing her bag, she ran inside and found the skeletal figure of the clerk behind the counter. It looked like he'd been sucked dry.

A loud crash from behind made her turn rapidly. Three shades stalked toward her before one of them ran at her with incredible speed. She tried to kick it, but it was much too fast. The shade tackled her to the ground, digging its claws into her sides. Pain barreled through her body, and she cried out.

The shade opened a mouth she had no idea was there, revealing rows of razor-sharp teeth and a needle-like tongue. She had to act quickly; otherwise, she'd die. She struck the shade in its left eye. It reared back, ripping its claws out of her sides. The sudden burst of pain took away her breath.

Fighting through it and ignoring all the signs her body sent her to stop, she got to her feet. She touched her side and looked at her hand. It was covered in blood. At this rate, she'd be the one to die instead of Ren.

Kelsey backed up to the counter, and the shades surrounded her. Just within arm's reach was a small basket. She grabbed it and threw it at one of the shades. The basket hit it in the head, and the other shades turned to look. The distraction gave her just enough time to move around the counter and try to outmaneuver them, but they were too fast, and she was in too much pain.

Just like that, the shades were encased in ice, then slashed to pieces. Marcus ran over to her, his bow back into its dagger form. As soon as he grabbed her, she collapsed from the pain. With the shades gone, she could no longer fight through it.

"Kelsey! Stay with me, Kelsey." He slid off her tank top, exposing her wounds. Her sides were covered in blood, the holes in her flesh the sign of the shade's claws entering her body.

Marcus placed his hands over her sides without physically touching them, and a golden glow appeared around them. Kelsey felt the pain begin to vanish, along with the cloud looming over her consciousness. When the glow stopped, he pulled his hands back. Her wounds had closed, leaving not even a scar.

"Here, drink," Marcus told her, handing her water. He raised her up gently. She took the water and gulped down the whole thing. She hadn't realized how thirsty she was.

"What did you do to me?" she asked.

"I healed you with magic," he said.

"Thank you," she said. If not for him, she may very well have bled to death.

"Don't thank me. I shouldn't have let you out of my sight. If I had kept you with me, you wouldn't have gotten hurt."

She shook her head. "It's not your fault. I ran in here with no one to help me. It's my own fault."

Marcus disappeared into the back and reappeared a bit later with a wet rag. She used it to clean the blood off and put her tank top back on. "Ren's still going to kill me for this," Marcus said. That made her laugh.

"Come on. Let's get you out of here," Marcus said. Extending his hand, he helped her to her feet. "We're close to the border. Unfortunately, there aren't any places to stay around here. Those shades cost us the time we needed to make it to a town. We'll have to camp out for the night."

"Any idea where?" Kelsey asked.

"No. But we need to get away from here in case more shades appear. Keeping ourselves moving is the priority for the moment. We can make it into town early tomorrow morning."

Marcus kept track of the time and their location as they left the store. They came to a stop next to a dirt path that led off the road and into a dense patch of trees. With such a thick brush, it was the perfect cover for them. And the much-needed time to rest was easily acquired.

After Marcus's handy magic trick and a little rest, Kelsey felt back to one hundred percent. But sleep was starting to overpower her consciousness. When Marcus stopped the car and slid out, she matched him, and they split up tasks for erecting a camp.

With eight of them working together, the camp was up in no time. Tents were pitched, and a fire was already started.

"Let's see, where the hell are we?" Marcus wondered. Using the GPS and mapping on his phone, he was able to find the coordinates they were currently camped at. Whatever Ren's current position was, he still didn't know. But he sent Ren a message and included the coordinates in it. Hopefully, that would help lead him right to them.

Kelsey was sitting on the ground, leaning against a tree when Marcus found her. From the looks of it, she was already halfway to falling asleep. The girl was exhausted, and Marcus couldn't blame her. She didn't have their stamina.

"How you feeling?" Marcus asked, sitting next to her.

"If you're talking about my wounds, then I'm fine. Just tired." Marcus nodded back.

"Do you mind if I take one last look?" She shook her head, and he lifted her tank top up, exposing her stomach and sides. Gently, he ran his fingers over her skin, where the wound from the shade used to be.

"Do you feel anything? Any pain, irritation, numbness?"

"No. Just your fingers."

"Good. It looks like it healed properly. Sometimes wounds from a shade can reappear after they've been healed due to the dark energy they possess. They are evil spirits, after all. I just wanted to make sure that didn't happen."

"Thanks, Marcus. Without you, I'd be full of holes right now." She leaned her head against his shoulder, gaze focused on the fire that burned mere feet away. Its heat danced upon her skin and cast an orange glow over the area.

She recalled the times she went camping with her parents when she was younger. It perhaps gave her a warmer feeling than the fire. Then she felt the heavy dread of sleep creeping up on her. Unable to fight against it any longer, it took over, and she closed her eyes to the darkness.

The crackling of the firewood stirred Kelsey awake. She was lying on the ground next to Marcus, his back to her. Damn her for falling asleep. Her plan was to wait up until Ren arrived, if he arrived. She gave a quick look around, but there was no sign of him. Clearly, that didn't happen.

The fire continued to blaze in the middle of the camp. Its flames had died down prematurely, but not enough to burn out anytime soon. That meant she must not have been asleep for long. Nevertheless, she grabbed a few sticks from their pile and threw them into the fire, watching the flames roar up. With the blaze returned, the area was once again cast in an orange glow.

A rustle in the trees made her jump. It came from a distance but still sounded close. An animal, or maybe Ren, she hoped. Or worse, what if it was a shade or the Radiant Church? Then what would they do? She doubted she'd be able to wake everyone up before they were killed.

Kelsey grabbed Marcus's dagger, which lay next to him. She stood, ready to fight and wake him at a moment's notice. The cause of the rustling appeared out of the tree line, a man, his bleach blond hair turned orange in the light of the fire.

"Ren!" she said excitingly. Ren stumbled forward, and Kelsey dropped the dagger before she caught him. He was covered in grime, his hair was a mess, and his clothes were shredded. Ren managed an exhausted look at her. She could see how worn out he was just from the sunken state of his eyes.

Kelsey helped him over to where she had been sleeping. With all of his strength seemingly sapped away, she practically had to carry him there before setting him down. Those oh-so-beautiful eyes, they were barely able to stay open. And yet, she wanted to get lost in them.

Gently, she placed her hand on his abdomen and Ren placed his hand over hers, lacing their fingers together. He found comfort in her touch, knowing that she and the others were alright.

"I missed you," Kelsey confessed. "I was so worried something happened to you. I feared the worst, even though Marcus told me otherwise."

Ren squeezed her hand lightly. "I understand your concerns," he said. "It's not right to just expect you to understand and feel the way we do because of our experience. But you should have more faith in me than that. I've been in bad situations before. It's part of the job description."

Kelsey focused on his wearied frame, the fading of his voice, his heavy breathing. He needed to rest; otherwise, he may genuinely fall into a precarious state. But, despite everything, she surprised even herself when she leaned in and pressed her lips to his. He was warm and smelled of pine and tree sap.

She drank him in, pressing closer against him. When they finally separated, Ren held her gaze, fixing his cobalt blue eyes on her. It was intoxicating.

With pain and fatigue sinking their fangs into him, he lay down, soaking in the warmth of the fire. Kelsey added more kindling before lying down next to him. Draping his arm over her, she scooted as close to him as possible, feeling his embrace. One last time for the night, his lips found hers, then they closed their eyes and quickly fell into sleep.

Twenty-nine

The Origin of Power

Ren woke with the sun high in the sky. Kelsey still lay next to him, his arm around her as she slept. She sat up and looked around. With the light of the sun shining down and the blue sky overhead, everything was completely different. It was a new day, and he was alive. They all were. And luckily, everything seemed to be normal.

Kelsey opened her eyes and saw Ren looking around. "Morning," she said. "What is it? Has something happened?"

"No, I was just checking. Even with Marcus here, you never know what could happen while we're sleeping. We've been caught off guard before."

"What does that mean? How is Marcus supposed to know if something happens while he's asleep?"

"The guy's a werewolf, Kells. His hearing is beyond anything you can imagine. He'd wake up instantly at the first sound of trouble."

"Then why didn't he wake up last night when you came back?"

"He did."

Her head snapped to Marcus, who still lay on the ground with his back to them. He sat up and raised his hands in defeat. "Guilty," he said, raising his hands. She couldn't believe it.

"Wait, you really didn't know?" Ren asked. "I figured he would have given you a signal or something."

"Why didn't you say anything?" she asked Marcus.

"I didn't think I needed to. I knew it was Ren before I even heard him approach. His scent came in much earlier. Besides, it got so steamy between you two I figured I'd best leave you to yourselves."

Kelsey's face burned bright with the heat of embarrassment. "Does that mean you heard everything?" she asked him.

"Would you feel better if I said no?" he asked back.

"Oh, my, god!" She covered her face with her hands, trying to hide her embarrassment. Not that it did any good.

"So, care to explain how you ended up like you fought an army again?" Marcus asked Ren. Wait, again? That one didn't go unnoticed by Kelsey.

"If you consider the numbers I went up against, I suppose you could compare the two," Ren said back.

Marcus and Kelsey sat there silently as they waited for him to explain.

"I'll admit it was a close call by the end of it. Algiroth is strong, much stronger than he used to be. Our fight didn't lead to any results on either side. In the end, he escaped. I wasn't able to bring him down. And in his wake, he left me against the squad of the Church's clergy he commanded."

"He commanded them?" Marcus asked. Ren confirmed with a silent nod.

"And you won't believe who made up their ranks either. Most of them were auroras, as expected. But among them was one high priest, one quincy, and two of the top-ranked elite guards." Marcus's face turned white. The widening of his eyes gave away his complete surprise.

"All of that, alone," Marcus said. Again, Ren nodded.

"If Shadow Hunter had not lent me his assistance, I hate to admit that I wouldn't be here right now."

This time, it was Kelsey's turn to react. Her stomach seemed to drop into a bottomless pit.

"And to make matters worse," Ren went on. About half an hour after I got your text, I was ambushed by a horde of shades."

Marcus gripped his hands so tight his knuckles turned white, his hands threatening to bleed. "I should have stayed with you. I knew it. It was foolish of me to leave you behind like that."

"There's no way you could have known, Marcus. You took care of Kelsey; despite any distraught situations you may have found yourself in."

Marcus suddenly lowered his head. A sense of shame overcame him as he realized that Ren already knew of Kelsey's injury.

"Marcus, I would never hold you accountable," Ren told him. "I know you did your best. Don't put the blame entirely upon yourself."

"No, it's entirely on me, Ren."

"I seriously doubt that, brother. I know exactly how Kelsey can be."

"And just what is that supposed to mean?" Kelsey asked.

Ren gave her a lopsided look. Like she didn't know. "I'll get the whole story once everyone has woken up," he said. "Right now, though, I want to eat. I need to replenish my strength. Where's my bag?"

"With mine," Marcus said. "Hold on, I'll grab it." They watched as he walked off toward where he kept his and Ren's bags safely out of reach from being taken or ransacked. He returned moments later and handed it to him.

Ren sifted through for any food he brought in case he got hungry or they camped. Seeing him eat, Kelsey and Marcus decided to eat themselves. Kelsey could see the muscles in his torso, and compared to last night, they were relaxed. She found that incredibly satisfying.

The three of them ate in silence, only opening up to conversation after they were finished. "Ren, Marcus, I was wondering if you could tell me what your world was like?" Kelsey asked. Her sudden question caught them off guard.

"Why? What's got you suddenly curious?" Marcus asked.

"Actually, it's not sudden. I've wondered about it for a while. I just didn't bring it up because I didn't see the right time. We've been pretty non-stop with our pace up until now."

Marcus and Ren exchanged glances and gave each other a silent nod. "Alright. In hindsight, we probably should have told you sooner. Nexus is a feudal society, as you already know. It's ruled by kings and queens, not presidents."

"I've been thinking this for a while now, but despite your world being so undeveloped compared to this one, it seems like our world is influenced by yours more than we realize."

Ren surprised her with a grin. "Then you'd be right. Your race gets more influence from us than your own kind. The reason we don't advance ourselves is simply because we choose not to. Certainly, we could become much more advanced than you, but it would cost us for too much."

A grim thought flashed through Kelsey's mind. "How long until you return?"

"As of right now, we're not sure. Truthfully, I was hoping to return after we found the stones. That will have to wait a little longer until we defeat Algiroth. He's too much of a threat to leave be."

Her dejected expression gave her thoughts away, causing Ren and Marcus to chuckle. "Want to come along?"

Her entire face brightened. "Yes! Can I?"

"You can. If you truly want to. Now that you know of our existence, but most importantly, want to be a part of it, you have the right to visit Nexus and see all that it has to offer for yourself."

"I'll warn you; it'll take some getting used to, though. You may find yourself bored at first until you settle into life."

"With you two there, I hardly doubt I'll even have time to be bored."

"Is that an insult?" Marcus joked. "I think you just dissed us," he said, causing them to laugh.

"Speaking of technology, have you talked to your parents recently?" Ren asked Kelsey. She nodded.

"I talked to them when we were at the hotel in Genoa."

"Good. Best not to forget and go too long without contact. They'll get worried, and we don't need extra baggage weighing us down."

One by one, the rest of the group started waking up. It turned out Cyclopes were heavy sleepers, which was not really that surprising given their toughness. They were A-ranked monsters, after all. It only took them a few moments to recognize that Ren was no longer absent from their group, having joined them sometime during the night. What that meant for the enemy, though, they didn't know.

"Is everyone rested?" Ren asked once everyone was awake. A compiled group of nods confirmed his question. "Good, then we can cut right to the chase; breakfast can wait. Someone explain to me how Kelsey ended up injured."

The sudden switch in the tone of Ren's voice caused a nervous sweat to break out from everyone but Marcus. Kelsey had been dreading this conversation, but it was unavoidable. So best to just get it over and done with.

"So, she told you, as expected," Hades responded.

"No, no one has told me anything. When I arrived last night, not only did the smell of blood linger on her skin, but her flow was also off, indicating she had been injured. So, start talking."

Kelsey knew she needed to speak up but didn't know what to say. Ren didn't seem mad, unless he was hiding it, in which case he was doing an amazing job. But she needed to be careful with how she explained what had happened.

"I am mad," he said, as if he read her thoughts, "but I'm sure Marcus did everything he could to protect you. We can't be everywhere at once, despite our strength. Even we have limits. It's why we work as a team. I told you I would protect you, and I meant that."

"You did, and you have been," Kelsey said back.

"Only because I knew Marcus would be coming with us," he confessed. "If he had not come along and it was to be just the two of us, I would never have let you come, no matter how much you begged or held your ground. Fighting enemies and keeping an eye on someone is difficult for even the most experienced and strongest monsters." She nodded in understanding. Man, was he going to be mad when he found out she ran off on her own.

After a long silence, Marcus spoke up. "We were attacked by shades. After we left you to face Algiroth, we figured it was best to head for our original destination and rest there for the night. Along the way, we stopped for dinner, and we got more than we bargained for."

"Kelsey spotted the shades first. They came at us from everywhere, over two dozen of them. I had Kelsey hold back by my car had she needed to get away while we dealt with them. A couple of shades got by somehow without us knowing and ended up inside the store. But by then, well. She was gone by the time we looked back.

I found her inside being attacked by them, but she had already sustained her injury."

Ren looked at Kelsey, his silent but piercing eyes indicating he wanted to know more from her. "I heard sounds of a struggle coming from the store. Everyone else was busy fighting the other shades and didn't seem to notice. I was concerned about the clerk that was still inside. He died before I could get there, though. And without any weapons or ways to beat them, there wasn't much I could do to defend myself."

Ren pinched the bridge of his nose, letting out a heavy sigh. "Why must you find the need to put yourself in danger like that?" he asked Kelsey.

"I'm sorry," Marcus apologized. "This is my fault. If I had kept my eye on her and paid more attention, Kelsey wouldn't have been injured."

"No, don't apologize. Like I said, I don't hold you accountable. It was Kelsey who ran off on her own. I know very well how stubborn she is, and so do you by now." Marcus nodded in agreement. The girl was exceptionally hardheaded.

"All things aside, I believe there is merit in this," Hades said. "Now Miss Kelsey has a clear understanding of the dangers and consequences of going up against a shade, especially unprepared and untrained. But now that she has encountered them, she knows better, and you can use this to teach her."

"Teach her?" Ren asked.

"I believe it was too arrogant of us to believe that she would just sit still at all times. This instance has only proven that we never know what could happen. Whether or not this kind of situation happens again, there is always the possibility of her having to face off against them again. Which is why she should be taught how to combat shades."

"As much as I know you don't want to hear this, I think Hades is right, Ren," Marcus said. "I know you want to protect her, but next time, or the time after that, you might not be able to. If she is going to be a part of our world, she has to learn to face its dangers as well, and shades are just one of those. I think we should teach her. She was curious about how to use ki anyway."

Ren looked over at Kelsey before releasing another heavy sigh. He was right, they both were, and the look in Kelsey's eyes proved that she was interested. She wanted to learn. Perhaps it was for the best that she did.

Kelsey had a clouded expression on her face when he took her hand, like she couldn't decide if he was angry or not, or if she was to be happy or disappointed. Ren raised her hand up and gently planted a kiss upon her fingers.

"Perhaps you are right," he said. "There is merit in teaching her. If she is going to be a part of our world, as you say, she'll need to learn to face its dangers."

Kelsey placed her free hand overtop of his. "Thank you," she said, planting a lingering kiss on his cheek.

"Ren, if you don't mind, I was wondering if we could change topics and you could tell us what happened to you after we left. The last we saw, Algiroth dropped you out of the sky." Ren nodded and proceeded to retell what had happened after they left. For Kelsey and Marcus, this was a recount, which is why he added in finer details that he had previously left out.

"I think this could be my first lesson," Kelsey said. "What you always talk about, that blue energy. I've seen it several times, and not just around you, either. Can all monsters use it?"

"Yes, and so can humans, actually. That energy is called ki," Ren told her. "Ki is the energy inside every living thing. Have you heard of chi before?"

"You mean the Chinese energy?"

"Yes, that. Well, the Chinese adapted that name after they discovered it from us. They were the first race of humans to master and control it, which is why it's a commonly learned term and often used in works of fiction."

"Ki flows through the body and the soul. All the energy you need to live, perform tasks, anything you do, your ki is the energy that powers it. Nature has been using it since the dawn of time, as it always will. Monsters eventually learned to harness and control it, as you've seen."

"From what I have explained and what you've seen, it shouldn't surprise you to learn that monsters were the first beings to be able to manipulate their ki to such fine degrees as we have. But since ancient times, the use of ki by other species has decreased significantly, especially in humans. Nowadays, most of your kind only know it by the adopted version. Out of every human in the world, only a handful can actually use their ki."

"Why can't we use it anymore?" Kelsey asked.

"Because you turned towards other forms of survival. You became technologically dependent, and that dependence only increases every year. Eventually forgot about it, and now you've lost the ability to use it."

"That's why you guys don't adapt technologically in your world!" Kelsey realized. "You rely on your ki and your abilities to survive. If you advanced yourselves, you'd lose the ability just like we did."

"Correct. That's why the Radiant Church is so powerful. Their members having the ability to use their ki is extremely dangerous and makes them a threat."

"Then, could I learn? Would you or Marcus or someone teach me?"

"Yes, we can. And we will. You'll need to learn how to manipulate your ki if you're going to fight shades. But not now. It takes a while to learn to control one's ki properly, and time is something we don't have a large amount of. Right now, I say we finish breakfast and get moving. I'd like to sleep in an actual bed tonight, and I'm still exhausted from yesterday."

"It's already past eleven," Marcus said. "We've got another four hours to Rome, and the sooner we get there, the sooner we can rest." The others nodded and hastily gathered their things, ready for the next part of the journey.

Thirty

In the Lands of the Ancients

Kelsey climbed in the passenger seat of Ren's McLaren. Their next stop was Rome, one of the places Kelsey had always wanted to visit. Now she got to visit and be with Ren at the same time. Talk about lucky.

Marcus came from the side and drove up next to them. He pointed to the sky, then tapped his wrist with one hand and held up three fingers. Ren made the so-so sign with his hand, and Marcus shrugged.

The GPS on Ren's car had them pegged a little over three hours outside of Rome. Of course, that was with a route without tolls.

"We should reach Rome around two, two thirty at the latest," Ren said to Kelsey. "So long as we keep pace. Let's hold off on the quest until tomorrow. We need to check the map too."

"Good; that means you can accompany me around the city," she said, causing him to laugh.

Marcus snuck glances at Ren and Kelsey from his driver's seat. Unable to contain his emotions, he found a smile had formed on his face. Seeing his friend happy gave him hope for the future. Ren had always held a candle for her, long before he got his memory back. And before yesterday, the issue was how long it was going to take Kelsey to realize her own feelings. The way she looked at him made it painfully obvious, but the girl had a head of iron. But she was special. She made him human.

Marcus's biggest concern right now wasn't Ren and Kelsey's infatuation with each other though. It was Algiroth. The vampire took up all the available space in Marcus's head.

Ren kept his eyes on the road, keeping a lookout for anyone that might be following. Shades, the Church, or worse, Algiroth, could be on their trail. Who knows when they will run into them again? He just hoped they wouldn't run into any trouble while in Rome. There were too many people, any of whom could get dragged into the conflict. That was the last thing he wanted.

So far, he didn't sense anything out of the ordinary, nor did he detect any bloodlust. Of course, that didn't mean he could relax. It looked like they were in the clear, for now.

They entered Rome at around quarter after two. Kelsey looked at the graffiti-covered buildings. Made of brick and stucco, they were a mixture of old and new buildings. The town was bustling; cars and mopeds drove everywhere, but the number of people walking dwarfed the amount of transportation.

Partway through the city, Ren, Kelsey, and Marcus split up from the Cyclopes who had their own place for accommodations. Thus, the three of them were left to find their own, but that didn't prove to be any trouble for them.

Ren drove through the city, clearly knowing exactly where he was headed. Being so popular, Rome had plenty of hotels to spare. He figured the best one would be the hotel he and Marcus usually stayed at when they came to the city.

Kelsey leaned her head on the window, watching the world go by. Rome was beautiful. They passed by buildings that amazed her. Large structures were lined with columns. She saw fountains all across the city, some large, some small, all equally as amazing.

Ren and Marcus stopped in front of a rather modern hotel. It was huge, with six stories and large expanses of glass. The hotel had a private parking area in the back that was secured behind a locked gate. Marcus held a card beneath a scanner, and the red light turned green. The gate swung open, allowing them to pass through.

The parking was mostly empty, leaving ample room for their choice of parking. The privileges of being Royalty. And having allies of Trinity working at the hotel also helped.

Marcus was out of his car first, then Ren and Kelsey.

"I'll go check us in," Marcus said. "Can you grab our gear?"

"I've got it," Ren said back. "Kells, you go in with Marcus."

"Won't you need help? You can't carry everything by yourself."

"I'll be fine. I'd rather you go in with Marcus. We've been to this hotel before, so they'll know us. Several of the workers and a few managers are monsters and supporters of Trinity."

Kelsey shouldered her bag, giving him an understanding nod. "Come on, this way," Marcus said to her, tossing Ren his keys.

They walked inside the hotel and up to the front counter. A woman with her brown hair tied into a bun stood behind it on the computer.

"Marcus!" she said excitedly. "Welcome back. And who's this?" she asked, indicating Kelsey. "A new face."

"Hey Laura. This is Kelsey. She's new to Trinity. We're on a quest and she's helping out."

"Congratulations," she said to Kelsey. "Is Ren not with you then?" she asked Marcus.

"He's grabbing our gear. He should be coming inside any second. Oh, there he is."

✝

Ren grabbed the gear from his car before grabbing the rest from Marcus's. Locking the door behind him, he double-checked for anything missing before heading for the front entrance.

Outside, Ren saw Kelsey and Marcus at the reception desk. He walked through the double set of doors and heard Marcus say, "Oh, there he is."

Ren walked into the reception desk and handed Marcus his keys. "Hey Laura," he greeted.

"Hi, Ren. What happened to you?" she asked, noticing his torn clothing.

"I'll explain in private. Is Cecilio here?"

"He's in the back."

"Get someone to cover and come with us; you'll want to hear this."

She walked away from behind the counter and returned a few minutes later, leading them past the desk and through a door that was for employees only. A man with gray hair was sitting at a table with a cup of coffee and reading some documents. The man looked up when they entered, seeing Ren and Marcus with Laura, and a girl he hadn't met before.

"Hey guys, on another assignment? And why aren't you up front, Laura?"

"I had her get someone to cover for her for a few minutes. She'll want to be here. You guys need to hear this."

Ren quickly briefed them on their quest and the events they'd encountered thus far, including their battles. Laura was shocked, but Cecilio just sat there, his hand on his chin, eyes downcast at the table.

"So, then the rumors are true," Cecilio finally said. "Verin and the Church have joined forces, and the stones of legend are being sought out."

"Word is a fight is brewing, and it's going to be one of the largest and most destructive battles yet," Laura added. "The war is turning, but in whose favor remains to be seen."

"Our people are divided, Ren. Luckily, they're taking our side," Cecilio said. "More and more of us are supporting the cause. You guys at Trinity have done wonders and earned the respect of some very powerful people."

Ren nearly spoke up when his vision suddenly turned blurry. A pulse ran through him, along with the unshakable desire to consume. His urges, they were hitting again.

"Sorry to cut this short, but we should get going," he said. He needed to get to the hotel room fast. "But before that, let me introduce you two. I didn't do it earlier. You've already met Laura. Kelsey, this is Cecilio Donaghan. Cecilio, this is Kelsey Rose."

"It's a pleasure to meet you," Cecilio said.

"Likewise," she said.

They got up and exited the room after Cecilio handed them their room Keys. Their room was on the top floor.

Ren unlocked the door and stuck the key in a slot in the wall, then turned on the lights. The room was big and modern, with two beds, a recliner, a desk and chair, and a TV on top of a dresser. Kelsey found the mini fridge built into the wall where the closet was.

Without hesitation, Ren hurried into the bathroom and ripped open the briefcase filled with blood. He uncorked the three vials at his belt and downed them all at once. His urges stalled momentarily before returning full force. He ripped open one of the full pouches in the case and finished it in three big gulps, yet still, nothing changed. He was losing control.

A knock on the door snapped him out of his state. "Ren, are you alright?" Kelsey asked.

"I'm, I'm fine. I'll be out in a minute," he answered with difficulty. He put a hand on his head and took deep breaths.

The truth was anything but. He wasn't fine, and he knew it. The transfusion blood no longer sustained his urge to feed.

Over the course of the following three minutes, Ren had to fight against the urge until the effects slowly disappeared. His headache disappeared, his vision cleared, and his breathing settled.

In a fit of frustration, he slammed the side of this fist against the countertop. *Damn it!* he cursed in his head. It was even worse than he thought. The rate of his decaying was increasing so rapidly that he couldn't even tell how long he had left. For all he knew, he could drop dead tomorrow.

When Ren finally exited the bathroom, he found Kelsey sitting on the bed with a nervous look on her face.

"What's wrong?" Ren asked her.

"You were in there a while, and it sounded like you were struggling."

He sat down next to her and put an arm around her waist. Ren's lips met hers, and a wave of calm washed over her. His sweet smell filled her nose.

When they finally separated from each other, Kelsey handed him another pair of clothes. "I grabbed these from your bag. Good thing you have spares."

"There's a reason I keep them, save for my jacket. It's custom-made."

Ren took the clothes and quickly changed into them, leaving his jacket on the chair. "Come on, let's take a walk," he said, taking her hand. "You'll love Rome."

Before leaving, they let Marcus know they were headed into the city. He told them he'd keep his ears open should anything happen and give them a call.

They took the elevator down to the lobby. Laura was back in her position at the front desk again. "Laura, we'll be back later," Ren said. "If anyone contacts the hotel looking for us, forward them to Marcus for me, will you."

"Will do. And Ren, be careful," she said back. "Both of you."

"We've always got our eyes out," he told her. "Besides, we're not defenseless." He pointed to his back, indicating Shadow Hunter's concealed presence.

Laura gave him an unrelieved nod. Clearly the rumors and the movements from Verin and the Chruch alike had her deeply unsettled. But she said nothing more as they exited the hotel.

Having to walk made Rome feel ten times bigger than being in the car. No surprise there. Ren took Kelsey around the city as much as they could in the time they had. They visited the Colosseum first. It was one top of Kelsey's list. After, they moved on to the Roman Forum, then the Pantheon, one of Ren's many favorites.

With the final streaks of sunlight dancing just along the horizon, there was only one place left to go, dinner. Where didn't matter. Ren had his preferred places that he usually visited when he was in the city, and they would all do just as well. So, he took her to his favorite.

The great thing about being on a date in Italy, the drinking age was sixteen for certain beverages, such as wine. Incredible food, combined with wine and a great ambiance, made for the most romantic dinner they had ever had together.

Staying silent while they ate just wasn't on the cards. There was too much to discuss, given their mission. So, they talked about their next plan of attack to find the Sun Stone. Ren suggested their next stop would be Crotone. It's on the southern coast and about an eight-hour drive. They could check the map there before moving on. From Crotone, it was a little over four hours to Taormina. Four hours to the end of the line.

Thirty-one

Altering the Path

Kelsey woke early in the morning. The first thing she noticed was Ren wasn't in bed. She looked at the time on her phone; eight twenty-six.

Sitting up, she swung her legs over the bed. The bathroom door opened, and a shirtless Ren emerged.

"Hey, did you just get up?" he asked.

"Yeah, how long have you been up?"

"Just now. Had to use the bathroom."

She laid back down while Ren climbed back into bed and slipped his arm over her. She looked over at him, planting a soft kiss on his lips.

Neither of them fell back asleep. They simply lay there in silence, and Kelsey let the sound of his breathing comfort her. When nine hit, they woke Marcus up, and all three of them went down for breakfast, finding a spot outside.

Halfway through their meal, Ren's phone started ringing. He recognized the number which belonged to Hades. Their conversation was brief, only to discuss their next move.

Ren told him about traveling to Crotone before heading to Taormina. And now that they were in Rome, they needed to switch out their cars. The other vehicles they had prepared would have been delivered already. Hades' only suggestion was that they stay outside the town. It would be better for them should they attract any unwanted attention.

Ren relayed the plan to Marcus, who agreed. The sooner they got the stone, the better.

After finishing breakfast, they grabbed their gear and headed for the lobby. Laura and Cecilio stood at the front desk as they had the day before. The moment they saw the three of them, they approached.

"Here to see us off?" Ren asked.

"Something like that. Can I talk to you in private for a moment?" Ren nodded and followed him away from the others. When they were finally out of earshot, they stopped.

"Listen, Ren, I've got family in Sicily," Cecilio said. "They're not in Taormina, but they probably know people who do live there. I'll give them a call and see if they can help on your quest."

Cecilio's sudden silence secured Ren's curiosity. "Cecilio," Ren said, forcing him to speak his mind.

"How long do you have?" Cecilio asked.

"Sorry?" Ren asked in confusion.

"How long do you have left, Ren?" It was then Ren realized what he was talking about.

"You knew?"

"I can sense it within you. Your ki is waning. You're losing control." Ren said nothing back. All he could do was nod in silence.

"No matter what or how, be sure to come out of this alive. Too many people need you. It would break their hearts."

"I wish it were that simple," Ren said back. "But I can't fight it anymore, Cecilio. The urges are just too strong. Now, it's just a waiting game."

Cecilio was quiet for a few moments before speaking again. "Ren, you need to be careful. Rumors about your condition are starting to spread. It's not only Verin or the Church you have to worry about anymore. Monsters that want you out of the way will start hunting you, seeing a chance. The weaker you get, the worse the situation gets."

Great, another problem to worry about, Ren thought. *Now my own people are out to kill me.*

"I understand, and I'll be on guard. Thanks for the heads up." Cecilio pulled him into a tight embrace before Ren returned to where Marcus and Kelsey were waiting.

Ren's situation was indeed grave. He had people trying to kill him on three fronts, and he still had to find the Sun Stone, not to mention the little remaining time he had left. Things were looking worse for wear.

Marcus looked at Ren, a concerned look on his face. He, too, was wrapping his brain around their current situation and trying to come up with solutions.

"Hades isn't that far from here, about twenty minutes west. He's in a low-end district of Rome," Ren said. "We'll pick up our bikes afterward."

It took them half an hour to reach Hades' hotel with all the traffic and lights. In such a famous city, they really had to be careful about pedestrians.

Hades and the rest of the Cyclopes were outside waiting when they got there, and with new transportation. Unlike Ren and Marcus, they had already exchanged their cars for new two-wheeled vehicles.

"Everybody ready? Nothing forgotten before we leave? It's a long drive to Crotone," Hades said.

"Follow us. Our transport should be here," Ren said.

Ren and Marcus led the team to a shipping depot close by. Sitting in the yard out back were two shipping containers. Inside one, secured to the sides and bottom were two stands. Each contained one vehicle, the motorcycle Kelsey had seen in Ren's garage, his Ducati 1299 Panigale, and a Suzuki GSX-R 750.

They freed the bikes and wheeled them down the ramp before driving their cars inside. One of the depot workers assisting them closed the containers and locked them.

"We will hold them for you at our depot," the man said. "When you have need of them, let us know, and we'll deliver them."

"Thank you. I suspect we'll be switching them back out once we get to Sicily," Ren said. He and the man shook hands.

"Sicily it is. Good hunting, Your Highnesses."

Mounting the bikes, Kelsey nervously climbed on Ren's Ducati. Like they knew it would be, the drive was indeed long. Within the first half an hour, they were outside the city. The landscape changed from brick and stucco buildings and concrete and pavement to mountains and trees.

The further south they traveled, the fonder Kelsey was growing of Italy.

Ren switched lanes into the far left, and Marcus followed behind him. They still brought up the rear, which was odd. They'd been in front this entire trip.

Kelsey was smart enough to know that something must have happened, something that put them on the lookout. Were they being followed? Was it more shades, the Radiant Church, or even worse, what if it was that vampire Ren fought back in the Tuscany region? Algiroth. Just the sound of his name sent chills down her spine.

They rode for a while longer in silence before Kelsey got Ren's attention again. "How far along are we?" she asked.

"Almost halfway there, give or take."

"Can we stop at the next place? I have to go to the bathroom."

"Yeah, but I'm not sure when the next rest stop is. Hold on," he told her, and gunned the Ducati forward. They caught up to the others and he lifted the visor of his helmet. "Bathroom break, next stop!" he yelled.

"Roger!" Hades yelled back.

The next rest stop they came across was an hour away. It was huge, and sat on the side of the road, tucked neatly into the landscape. Outside were pumps for gas. Inside, the store carried a vast selection of small items, from food to electronics.

Ren slowed down and pulled into a parking space. The parking lot was enormous, given that it had spaces for cars and an area for buses and trucks. Marcus pulled up next to them and parked in the space, and the rest of the team parked on both sides. They all dismounted and headed inside.

Kelsey looked around for Ren when she came out. He was sitting on the seat of his bike, the map spread out in front of him across the handlebars. "Woah," he said. The others hurried over.

"What's wrong?" Marcus asked.

"See for yourself," Ren said, showing him the map. Where previously blank, a new marker was now displayed.

"What the hell? When did this happen? This wasn't here this morning when we looked."

"It was there when I opened it. My guess is it appeared either because we're close to it, or because we're closer to the stone."

Ren continued to scour the map. "Luckily it doesn't appear that we missed anything along the way."

"What would have happened if we hadn't stopped?" Marcus wondered.

"Who knows? But we should keep a lookout. Perhaps more locations will appear the further down we go."

Ren read over the new inscription, his mind an ocean of curiosity. Paestum ruins, Salerno, Italy. The Sacred Key.

"I don't understand. Why would the map send us to some random ruins in the middle of Italy?" Marcus wondered. "And now, there's something about a key."

"Your guess is as good as mine," Ren said back. "But if the map is telling us to go there, it's for a reason."

"What in the hell is this map leading us into?"

Ren put the ruins into his GPS and let it guide him to the ruins. They knew they were near when they spotted the first Greek temple. It wasn't until they actually reached the ruins that they discovered how large they were, though.

Ren pulled off to the side of the road, dismounting the bike.

"So, where should we start looking?" Marcus wondered. "They key could be anywhere. That is, assuming we're looking for an actual key."

Ren was looking at his phone when he pointed to one of the ruins in front of him. It was the largest of all the temples they could see.

"We start with the temples," he said. "If we split up into groups of three, we can each search one."

"Ren, Kelsey, and I will take the smaller temple," Marcus said. "Hades, Leonardo, Francisco, you three take the larger one. Gary, Jemson, Carlos, you three take the remaining temple."

"As you wish, Prince Marcus," the group said.

"This'll be fun," Hades said sarcastically.

It was a short walk to the smallest of the three temples. "So why this one?" Kelsey asked.

"According to what I read, this is a temple of Athena. She's the goddess of wisdom. It seems fitting that if we were to find something, it would be in her temple," Ren said.

"I'd like to know what a Greek temple has to do with the Sun and Moon Stones. Or this key."

"So would I."

When they reached the temple, they had to sneak inside since it was restricted. Marcus was the first to spot something on one of the marble columns at the front of the temple. An inscription, written in the language of monsters. It was carved only a couple of feet above the ground, almost as if it were inscribed while sitting. "Guys, come check this out," he said.

Ren and Kelsey followed him, now equally curious.

Marcus ran his fingers over the inscription. It was worn and faded from time, making it difficult to read. He and Ren had to work together to piece the inscription together.

Minutes felt like hours, yet it only took fifteen minutes until Ren and Marcus finally solved the inscription. The translation sent chills through Kelsey's body.

"Maximilian III, 1326. To all those that seek the stone, I leave you this warning. Proceed no further, or suffer the fate of all those who came before you."

Thirty-two

The Queen's Temple

Marcus and Kelsey looked at Ren, and Kelsey felt a hole form in the pit of her stomach. The words inscribed on the temple made her skin crawl. She could almost feel the unfamiliar touch of death on her skin. Suddenly Kelsey didn't want to continue this quest. She wanted to just leave Italy, leave this quest, return home end this whole thing. But the looks on Ren's and Marcus's faces told her that wasn't an option.

Below the warning was another inscription. In truth, Ren and Marcus weren't sure what to think. The ominous tension in the previous inscription was enough to mentally shake them, even but a little bit. They'd come across enough warnings like while on other jobs for trinity, and even other quests, to know not to take them lightly.

Ren recalled the last time he ignored a warning like that. Two years ago, in the Jungles of India. Back then Marcus had been with him, and even then, they'd lost their entire party. They'd seen the warning and ignored it, as they had many times before. Eleven people died that day as a result.

"The key to the stone of heaven must be won, not found," Ren and Marcus read on. "A challenge none have succeeded at, and one I, too, have failed. If you possess the strength necessary to succeed, know that the path to the key mirrors the path to heaven. But to enter the heaven's, one must first pass through the underworld."

"Find the legend, defeat the guardians. Defeat the guardians, find the legend. May fate smile upon you, that our sacrifices were not in vain."

"Well, I'm severely creeped out," Kelsey said. "Did either of you understand a word of that?"

"Not really, no. We'll just have to figure it out as we go," Marcus said. "We don't have the time to sit here and play twenty questions."

"We're lucky this Maximilian left this message," Ren said. "Without it, I'm not sure how we would have found our way to the key from here."

"Exactly what part of that was helpful? All I heard was proceed and you die."

"The message said the path to the key mirrors the path to heaven. The path to heaven is synonymous to the

Sun Stone. We find the key the same way we found the location of the stone."

"The map," Kelsey said.

"Not quite. A map, not our map."

"That still doesn't—" her sudden stop came at a realization. "The Moon Stone," she realized.

"The stone will show us the path to the key," Marcus surmised. "The question now is, where's this new map? With the Moon Stone we already had the map first."

"That, my friend, is where the power of the stone comes into play," Ren said back.

Ren pulled the stone out of his bag. In the light of the moon, the moving white lines were unworldly. Even if it wasn't a full moon, the stone bathed its surroundings in purple light.

Raising the stone above his head, they waited for the power of the stone to light the way. It turned out they were only in for more disappointment. The stone didn't react to anything. It merely continued to cast its glow on the temple.

Kelsey took the map from Ren and opened it. She hoped that it would prove useful this time as well, perhaps even update as it had previously. More disappointment only followed.

The inscription wasn't carved as part of the quest. It was simply the whim of a fellow seeker who had failed in his mission. No, if the map were to react, it would be to something else. Something they weren't seeing.

Marcus and Ren exchanged glances before turning them on the stone. "Well, this isn't working," they said in unison.

"I had hoped we wouldn't need to scour the ruins to find our way," Marcus wished.

"If only it were that simple," Ren said back.

Ren started walking. His feet carried him through the entire temple. Each piece of the floor, each column and wall was caught in the light shining off the Moon Stone, yet they found nothing.

Continuing to search the temple would prove pointless, so they changed locations, moving south along the west side of the ruins. What once dominated as the living quarters and a burial ground for the ancient city.

Passed the living quarters were two more temples, much larger than the first temple they had started at. Ren was wandering around the largest of the two when the moon stone suddenly started to glow. A beam of purple light shot out, striking the floor of the front of the temple. A feint white glow appeared from a piece of stone carved into a perfect circle. He walked to the stone and the light from the stone changed direction. Another circular stone outside of the temple glew.

Ren got everyone's attention while he moved to the next stone. It made up part of the road through the ruins. Again, the light from the Moon Stone changed, lighting up another stone along the road. The same pattern continued until Ren stopped at a stone archway. The entrance to the amphitheater.

On the inside of the archway, a patch of stone began to glow when the light from the Moon Stone hit it. Ren put his palm over it, but nothing happened. At first they stood there confused. At least, until the entranceway began to shake, and an opening appeared as a section the size of the door broke open. Beyond lie a dark passageway with a set of stairs leading down.

"Oh great, another set of stairs in a dark passageway," Kelsey muttered.

Ren and Marcus started chuckling, and Kelsey sighed as everyone walked down the steps and descended into the tunnel. It was long, much longer than they expected.

Marcus sniffed around, searching for anything he could that would help to guide them.

"Smell something?" Ren asked.

"I'm not sure. I do smell something, but I'm not sure what it is. What about you? Sense anything?"

Ren used his powers to do a scan of the area but found nothing. He shook his head. "Let's find out where this leads." He took off running, Marcus at his heels.

Even in darkness, it was easy to tell when the room opened up into a larger chamber. In a place like they were at, Marcus, being a werewolf, was now their most valuable asset. His senses grew ten-fold. Even Ren couldn't see in the dark like he could.

Marcus looked at the ceiling and noticed something above. "There's something hanging from the ceiling. It looks like a chandelier."

Shooting forward, he sprinted up the back wall and launched himself at the hanging object. His magic swallowed it and the object blazed to life, casting the room in an orange glow. It turned out the object was, in fact, a chandelier,

The room was small. Just large enough for the nine of them and maybe two more. And the ceiling was higher than it looked at nearly two stories high.

"Not to be the bearer of bad news, but does anyone else realize that there's no other way out from here?" Kelsey asked.

"I wouldn't be so sure of that," said one of the Cyclopes. "If there's a way in, there has to be a way out." He pointed to the wall on the left from where they came in. "And if there is another exit, then there must be a way to get to it. We're Cyclopes, remember. Earth magic is our specialty."

"We have to be extremely careful. Who knows how strong the foundations for this place are? It could collapse at any second," Hades mentioned.

"It doesn't matter," Ren said back. *"Chalo bas chaabee dhoondhate hain."*

"Where do you think it is?" Marcus wondered. He was the only one there that spoke Hindi and therefore understood whatever Ren had just said.

"No idea. There's got to be something around here, though."

"I believe our way out lies there," Hades said. On the wall at the far end of the room was a glowing key symbol. It was made of brick and clay, clearly man-made. He touched the symbol, but nothing happened. The key symbol glowed on the surface of one of the bricks. What's more, the mortar holding it in place was nearly nonexistent.

Ren drew the dagger at his hip and cut around the brick. He gently pulled it out from its place and stuck his hand inside. His fingers touched solid stone. What's more, he felt a small gap between the wall and surrounding bricks.

All nine of them worked to remove the bricks, only stopping when a pile lay at their feet. By then, enough brick had been removed to reveal the surface beyond. Stone formed into blocks, similar to modern concrete masonry units. Their staggard appearance was nothing unordinary at first, but then he focused on the crack following the blocks. They weren't natural.

Placing both hands on the stone, Ren felt for any shifting or anything that could be used as a lever or handle. He noticed the slight movement when he pushed. Using more force, he pushed again, but the block was just too heavy.

"I need help!" he said. Marcus walked up next to him and placed his hands on the block. They exchanged a quick nod before pushing together. A large section of block swung inward, exposing another room beyond. The opening was wide enough for two people to fit through side by side.

Marcus stepped through the doorway and sniffed the air. I'm smelling something up ahead again. It's the same smell from before, and it's getting closer." They watched as his body started changing. He grew larger, his nose and mouth elongated, he grew ears and a tail, and his body became covered in light brown fur.

This was the second time Kelsey had seen Marcus in his werewolf form. Marcus ran his claws along the side of the wall. There was a loud scraping sound like metal on metal and sparks. Kelsey swallowed loudly. Man, those were sharp, and the size of her fingers.

"I see a set of stairs," Marcus said. "About one hundred feet out. Then it drops, but everything beyond is too dark for me to see."

Ren put a hand on the ground and closed his eyes. It was silent for a few moments then he stood up. "I'm not picking up anything magical or otherwise. And as far as living things, we're the only ones."

Ren was quiet for a moment before speaking again. "Kells, slow your heartbeat. You need to relax." She realized he must have read the pace of her heartbeat with his powers as a vampire.

"I'm going down to take a look," Marcus said.

"We'll be right down," Ren said. Marcus took off running, then jumped and disappeared. Ren pulled Kelsey against his body. "Hold on tight," he told her. She wrapped her arms around his neck as he picked her up. Kelsey's stomach dropped as soon as they started falling. She held on for dear life as the wind whipped her hair into a frenzy. Moments later, Ren's feet touched the ground with a light thud.

They couldn't see a thing it was so dark. Ren drew Shadow Hunter, and the light of the golden blade illuminated their immediate surroundings. Yet even still, parts of the cavern were pitch black, too far out of reach. The only sounds came from Ren and Kelsey's breathing and the movement of the Cyclopes from above as they descended the cavern.

Both of them stared into the darkness when a pair of golden eyes appeared out of nowhere. Marcus emerged and walked over to them.

"This way, I found a room," he said. They followed him into a small room attached directly to the chamber. It was completely empty and seemingly darker than the adjacent chamber.

In the darkness, two orbs of light appeared: one blue, and the other brown.

The lights expanded and changed, taking new forms. The blue light became a man with a long beard, braids, and a toga. The brown one became a woman with short hair that curled at her neck, wearing a dress.

"Welcome mighty heroes. I am Oceanus," said the man, "And the woman is Tera." She gave a light curtsy to them.

"We are spirits of the past, once faithful devotees to the gods. We protect the sacred temples, and shall for an eternity."

Ren coughed into his hand and whispered to Marcus. "Not to say you haven't noticed, but you do realize who these two might be, don't you."

"Defeat the guardians," Marcus whispered back, referencing the inscription on the temple.

"Why have you disturbed our slumber?" Oceanus asked.

"Our apologies. We never meant to disturb you," Marcus answered. "We seek something precious and believe this to be the way to it. The Sacred Key."

Oceanus and Tera flinched. "Sacred? You know Sacred?" Oceanus asked.

"Do we know Sacred? I don't understand," Marcus said.

"Brother, I bet they're working with him in an attempt to take our treasure," said Tera. "You never should have come entered this cavern." Ren's and Marcus's instincts kicked in when the female spirit's hands suddenly burst to life with golden flames.

Thirty-three

The Guardians of Tomorrow

"It's unfortunate, but if you're acquainted with Sacred, then your lives are forfeit," Oceanus said. "Grudges, personal issues, you understand."

"Actually, I don't," Ren said back.

Tera shot a blast of flames at them. All nine of them dove to the side to avoid the flames.

"Resistance will only make this worse for you," Oceanus said. He held out his hand, and a blanket of ice covered the ground. Marcus jumped into the air, avoiding the ice. However, the rest of the team was too slow, and they found their feet frozen to the ground.

Marcus charged at Tera, but she disappeared. He turned and slashed at Oceanus with his ice daggers, but his hand passed right through.

"Marcus, move!" Ren said. He held out a finger, and flames gathered at the tip. Oceanus raised his hand, and Ren was frozen solid before he could fire.

There was a crack, and the ice surrounding Ren exploded. He held out his fingers again and shot a blast of flame which ravaged the small room. Oceanus froze the flames solid in a second, but Ren was already on the move. He appeared next to him and brought his back leg around. Just like with Marcus, it phased right through.

He jumped back and drew his pistols, firing at them. The two spirits just stood there, the bullets passing through them harmlessly. Not surprising, so Ren dropped his empty clips and loaded his magic bullets. The two spirits sensed the magic in them and Tera put up an earth wall to defend. Ren continued to fire away, blowing the wall to pieces.

"Go, now!" he said to the others. Everyone but Marcus turned and ran into the adjacent chamber.

"I've got the rear; go," Marcus told Ren. He reached for his heaven's blade, the golden sword sliding cleanly out of its sheath. With one swing, a blade of golden energy sliced the spirits in two, but only infuriated them further.

Marcus ran up the stairs along the side of the room, his sword lighting the way for him.

As soon as they all reached the top, they ran toward the entrance of the chamber, and Ren summoned a wall of earth behind them.

"I'm not sure if that'll hold them, but hopefully, it'll at least buy us a few minutes," he said.

"What now, then?" Hades asked. "Anyone got any ideas on how we can defeat two ghosts?"

"We can't. Not without purification magic," Ren answered.

"That's going to be a problem then," Hades said back. "None of us are persists, or able to use holy magic."

"We may not need to. I'm certain that those two are guarding the key."

"That inscription on the temple, it mentioned a challenge, one none have succeeded at," Kelsey said.

"Right. If we want the key, we have to defeat those two, the guardians," Ren added.

"In case no one realized it, but not even our heaven's blades work on them. How are we supposed to defeat them otherwise?" Marcus wondered.

"I got some weird vibes from that room where the spirits first appeared," said Hades. "It's much larger than we thought. The room keeps going, but there was definitely a wall at the back end. There may yet be an answer beyond it."

Marcus looked at Ren. "Hundred bucks says it's an illusion," he said.

"Deal," Ren said back. They shook hands.

"I'll applaud you for your efforts. Not many have ever been able to get the best of us like you have," came a voice. Oceanus and Tera phased through Ren's earth wall. "Did you have enough time to chat?" Oceanus asked.

"Actually, we did," Ren said back. "My furry friend there is incredibly fast, and ferocious. Now, allow me to show you what I can do."

Ren held his hands out to the side, and a light sparked. Then the room was lit bright as day as a bolt of lightning crackled between his hands.

"Get down!" Marcus yelled.

Everyone ducked as Ren fired the lighting from his hands. It rocketed at the two guardians faster than Kelsey could blink and blasted them away.

Kelsey had seen Marcus use lightning before, but this was her first time seeing Ren use it. Something about the two was different, though. Unlike Ren, when Marcus used it, he appeared physically drained. For Ren, that didn't appear to be the case. He looked utterly unfazed.

"Go, now!" Ren yelled. Everyone but him took off running.

Oceanus stirred, and his sister stumbled before finding her footing. "Come on, let's see what you've got," Ren taunted.

"You will regret that," Oceanus warned. More electricity crackled in Ren's hands in response.

At the bottom of the stairs, the team ran for the room where the guardians first appeared. Marcus ran full speed at the wall. He swung his sword, but instead of blasting it to pieces, he passed right through.

"Ha, called it!" Kelsey heard him yell from the other side.

"God dammit!" Ren yelled from above. Suddenly, Kelsey found herself unable to hold in her laughter.

"Come on, I think this is the way," Marcus said, poking his head through the illusion.

"What about Ren?" Kelsey asked.

"Right behind you," Ren said. They turned to see him running toward them. "Don't stop; I think I made it worse." He jumped through and kept running. Seconds later, Ren turned a corner and was out of sight.

They followed him around the corner, only to see him turn left down another tunnel. It opened into a large room lined with candle sconces along the walls. In the back was a stone altar with a single bronze dagger placed atop it.

"I'm willing to bet that's our ticket out of here," Ren said.

"Then you would be correct," said a voice.

They turned to see a man sitting on a throne that was covered in cobwebs and needed some serious refurbishing.

"Welcome young ones, to my chamber."

"Your chamber? And just who are you?" Kelsey asked.

"Truly? You came here without knowing? How mysterious. My name is Sacred."

Sacred? Suddenly, everything made sense. They had it all wrong. Sacred wasn't a thing; it was a person. Memories of an old folk tale flooded Ren's mind. Why hadn't it occurred to him before?

"Now I get it. You're Sacred Norwest, aren't you?" Ren asked.

"My reputation precedes me," the spirit said.

Glorious came out of its sheath faster than anyone in the room could see. The blade stopped dead in front of Ren, the handle tight in Marcus's hands as he protected his friend from the spirit in front of them.

"Move an inch, and I swear I'll reap you," Marcus told him, a dangerous edge to his voice.

The spirit raised his hands in defense. "Hey, easy there. You're the one who came looking for me, remember?"

"If we had known who you were beforehand, rest assured our party would be much smaller."

Sacred stared ahead, not at Marcus, but at Ren. They appeared to be reading each other's expressions, trying to discern what the other was thinking, what intentions lay behind their expressionless faces.

"Ren, you and Marcus know who this guy is?" Kelsey asked.

"I'm afraid so," Ren said. "His achievements have now turned into legend, but the wounds are still healing for some. In his day, Sacred Norwest was a legendary vampire hunter."

A vampire hunter! As soon as he said that, Kelsey jumped in front of Ren, placing herself between him and Glorious as a second layer of defense. This time, all the Cyclopes took action, readying their weapons.

"It was around four hundred years ago or so," Ren continued after pausing temporarily, "but Sacred Norwest was known worldwide for his abilities, and most of all, his kill count. He was the best hunter of his time."

Sacred and Ren never lost eye contact with each other. "A vampire, huh? That explains why they rushed in to protect you."

Marcus stepped forward, and Kelsey slipped her hand into Ren's.

From inside the tunnel, they could hear the voices of the two guardians. "Look, we're not here to start a fight with you," Ren said.

"We just need to borrow your knife. We'll give it back when we're done and be on our way."

"You damned monster, you can't hide from us! Your death will be slow and agonizing!" the two guardians said.

Sacred let out a whistle. "Is that Oceanus and Tera? Wow, are they mad. What did you do?" he asked.

"I hit them with lightning, knocked them off their feet a couple of times, and I may have thrown an insult or two in there, not really sure," Ren said.

"Really?" Marcus asked. His expression said, 'were the insults really necessary?'

"I was in the heat of the moment, okay," Ren said back.

Sacred surprised them when he started laughing. "You two are interesting; I like you."

"Look, I don't mean to rush, but those two are going to catch us any minute. We need your knife. Can we borrow it or not?" Ren asked.

"Sure," Sacred said. He held out his hand, and the blade flew into it, then tossed it to Ren.

"That's it? Just like that?" Ren asked.

"Just like that," Sacred said back. How utterly strange. Usually, something was required to gain whatever they needed on these kinds of quests. That's always how it went. He expected some trial in order to get the damn thing.

Sacred turned his attention back to the raging guardian spirits. "Hey, can I get in on this?" he asked.

"Get in?" Marcus asked back. What did he mean by that?

Sacred held one hand out and drew his other back. A magical bow appeared out of thin air as Oceanus and Tera came into view.

"There you are!" Tera yelled. "Sacred! I knew you were behind this, you conniving bastard!"

"Tera, lovely as ever," Sacred said back. He released a magical arrow that whizzed by and struck Oceanus in the shoulder.

Oceanus collapsed, gasping in pain. Tera turned, distracted by her fallen brother. Ren took the opening and threw Sacred's knife. The blade cartwheeled through the air with incredible speed and struck Tera in the back. She screamed and collapsed, her body bursting into flame before disappearing.

Oceanus pulled the arrow out from his shoulder, gripping it in pain. Ren was already on the move, running at him before he could recover. He picked up the knife and jammed the blade into the spirit's chest. Oceanus cried out before his body exploded in a wave of energy, and he, too, disappeared.

"Damn!" said one of the Cyclopes.

"Yes, impressive indeed," Sacred said.

Ren spun the knife so he held the blade in his hand and handed it back to Sacred. "Thanks," he said. "I wish it was that easy before."

"Well, that's because you didn't have this," Sacred said back, holding up his knife. "It's the only way to defeat those two. Well, they'll return, eventually. They always do. A guardian can never truly be defeated. Let me guess, you're looking for the key? No one ever comes here unless it's for that."

"That's right."

"I figured. So, the power of the stones is finally being sought out after all this time. The last person who tried looking for it came around three hundred years ago, but he wasn't very adept at fighting and died before he got the key."

"I'm surprised," Ren said. "I'd heard about you in legends. I expected you to be more intent to kill me the second you laid eyes on me."

Sacred shook his head. "I didn't kill vampires at random, only those who committed evil acts or harbored malicious intent. The ones that didn't stray I left alone, much like yourself. I don't sense a drop of evil in you."

"I suppose that's rather believable now that we've actually met you," Marcus said. "You lent us your knife without any tests or protests after all. You didn't try to kill Ren either."

"You're not the first to believe that, and you won't be the last either, trust me. But it's been a long time since anyone has believed in me. I only wish there were more."

"Your knife really was what we needed," Kelsey said. "You don't happen to have the key either, do you?" she asked.

"Afraid not. Your task was to get my knife in order to defeat Oceanus and Tera. The location of the key can only be revealed after they were defeated. That is where I come in."

"Find the legend, defeat the guardians. Defeat the guardians, find the legend," Ren said. "Those were the words someone who once sought the key and failed carved into one of the temples. You're the legend."

"You are correct, vampire. Very intuitive. Now, do you have the map?"

Ren handed him the map to the stones. Sacred spread it out and placed his hand over it. A piece of it began to glow as a new spot appeared. He handed it back to Ren, who looked it over with Marcus. A pained expression surfaced on Marcus's face.

"At least it's not cold," Ren said back. Marcus gave him an annoyed look in response.

"Well, there's good news and bad news," Ren said. "The good news is, the location is in Sicily. So we can continue on as we normally would have."

"And the bad news?" Kelsey asked.

"The key is located inside Mt. Etna."

Thirty-four

How Light Begins to Fade

"Mt Etna, a volcano? Great, as if things couldn't get any worse," Kelsey retorted.

"I wouldn't be so sure of that," Sacred said. "The journey to the stones, not to mention the key, is designed to test the very limits of your mortality. They're designed to do so."

"Are you sure of that?" Kelsey asked. "I don't mean to offend, but I'm not even a monster, and honestly, this journey hasn't been as hard on me as I expected, especially to the point of the 'very limits of my mortality.' If anything, it's been more tedious with the empty searching."

"I have to admit that she's right," Marcus agreed. "The only real trouble we've had came from our enemies interfering. The most curious thing has been locations."

"You're questioning why we're here," Ren surmised. "From the States to Italy. Why the human realm no less." Marcus confirmed with a nod.

"The locations of the stones change," Sacred said. "With the exception of the Sun Stone, which is sealed. Hence the purpose of the key."

"The map was hidden on purpose. New York makes sense, given the history and density of the city," Ren said. "But a castle-house in California, on the other side of the country? A ruined city in Italy, and a volcano. None of those locations relate, or seem even logical."

"Oh, I assure you, it's very logical. Your journey and trials thus far have been for a reason. Take that to heart. And most importantly, take caution. If you find the Sun Stone, you will understand."

Sacred waved his hand, and an opening appeared in the wall. Stairs carved directly from the earth around it.

"Those stairs will lead you to the surface. Take heed young heroes, and may fate smile upon you. I wish you the best of luck on your quest." Sacred faded and disappeared, leaving the rest of them alone in the room.

"We're going to need it," Ren said under his breath.

"Allow me to take point," Hades suggested. "The six of us can search the surroundings with our magic at the same time."

Hades ascended the steps with two of the Cyclopes. Ren, Kelsey, and Marcus followed behind them in the middle, the remaining three Cyclopes taking up the rear.

As soon as all nine of them were through and started up the stairs, the opening Sacred had made disappeared.

"Looks like a one-way trip," Ren said. "Let's keep going."

Only the light from the combined magic of all eight of them made ascending the steps possible. It was so dark, even with all that light, they couldn't see more than five feet ahead of Hades. It was a good thing he had offered to take point.

Ren wasn't sure how far below the surface they were. They had taken so many tunnels before and only gone down. Sacred had said the stairs would lead them to the surface, but they had no way of knowing how deep they actually were, or even where they were.

"I think we should take another look at the map when we get to the surface," Marcus suggested. "Just in case." He walked directly to Ren's side, making their ascent rather tight. But it kept their conversation close to them and away from anyone else's ears.

"I agree," Ren said back.

Ren's attention wandered while they ascended to the surface. Marcus noticed, Kelsey noticed, and the three Cyclopes behind them noticed.

"En… Ren," Marcus called. Ren was torn from his thoughts at the sound of his name. He looked at Marcus. Though the werewolf said nothing verbally, he and Ren appeared to have their own private conversation just through an exchange of eyes.

"We've no time to dally," Ren said back, pressing on.

They knew they had reached the surface when the ground above them flattened into carved stone. One square sat directly overhead. Hades put his hands on the stone. Two of the other Cyclopes helped him push the slab up and slide it over.

A sky burned pink from the rising sun greeted them when they exited the stairway. They had come out underneath the largest of the three temples. On the slab that they had pried open, a piece of stone in the shape of a perfect circle shinned before fading. The same stone that had first led them on their path.

No longer confined underground, the breath of fresh air was invaluable. It made them want to stop the quest right there and soak it all in forever.

"It's a couple of hours past daybreak," Ren said. "And four and a half hours at the fastest route until we reach Crotone."

"I can manage another four and a half hours. If the rest of us can as well, I say we rest once we reach the city," Marcus suggested. "Are you tired?" he asked Kelsey.

"Surprisingly, no," she said back.

"We can continue as well," Hades added, before they could ask.

Ren took out the map and looked it over quickly. He saw no alterations since Sacred's chamber. "Nothing's changed on the map. Alright, let's get to Crotone. We'll make camp once we're there."

Three of the Cyclopes slid the slab back into place. Once again, the stairs were cut off from the world. Who knew when they would be found again, if they were ever found?

Careful of any curious eyes, they returned to their vehicles. The drive was quiet, as expected. If there would ever be a good chance for Kelsey to ask Ren about his state of turmoil in the stairway, she didn't know. So, she decided to break the long silence and just go for it. If he said he didn't want to talk about it, she would drop it.

Using the Bluetooth in her helmet, she called Ren's phone, which connected to his own. "Kelsey, what is it?" he asked when he answered. Admittedly, she had to force herself to be courageous enough to ask him once the time actually came.

"What happened down there? When you spaced out, I mean? If you don't want to tell me, that's fine, I won't pressure you, but it's been a long time since I've seen that look on your face."

Ren remained quiet. Just when she thought he wasn't going to answer, he spoke.

"I was thinking about my mother. Sacred said that there was a reason why the stones are located where they are, why the key is located where it is. He said it's for a reason. It made me think of my mother, when she died.

Was it for a reason? Was it for something more than murder?"

Kelsey couldn't believe what she was hearing. This was the first-time Ren had talked about his mother since she died, to her at least. After the case was closed, Ren stopped talking about her altogether, and then, he just shut himself off. Losing her had changed him.

A part of her always believed that the Ren she knew before the fire was gone, and as it turned out, she was right. Sure, she was blown away at the whole vampire thing, but that was just one piece. Good or bad, people change, even her, and she was going to have to live with it.

"Kells?" Ren asked. His voice snapped her back to reality. "Are you alright?"

"I'm fine, just thinking."

"Thinking about the past or me?" She gave him a smug grin from behind the face guard, not that he could see. "Both, actually," she said.

"Those were the days, weren't they? Remember we used to go to the amusement park? You wanted to ride that big roller coaster over and over," he said.

"And how worked up our moms used to get when they did the bumper cars," she added. "We can't go back to those days anymore. They're long gone."

"Our time as children may be gone, but our time together has only just started. She may not be there physically, but you can be sure my mother will still be with us. They're never truly gone, Kells. Remember that."

After four hours of driving, they neared Crotone. As they drove through the mountains, they could see the Mediterranean in the distance, just at the horizon.

A half an hour outside the city, in the town of Cutro, Ren pulled off to the side of the road.

"What's going on?" Marcus asked him. The others gathered around.

"We have a problem. I searched Crotone using the map on my phone and only found one spot that could hide us. It's about fifteen minutes from here. We can make camp if everyone agrees to it, or we can try to find a hotel in town."

"How far from Crotone is it?" Marcus asked. "If there are properties that close, then it's best we don't go near, lest they catch wind of us. This isn't Nexus. We can't just camp out and expect people not to bother."

"We'll still be about half an hour from Crotone. The same as our current position. No residents, as far as the map shows."

"Then we take it. So long as it hides us, I see no issue."

Ren led the way to their campsite, following the GPS on his phone. They pulled over to the side of the road in front of a grove of trees and rolled the bikes inside to a spot suitable to make camp. All nine of them worked to set their tents up and get a fire going.

An hour and a half passed since they made camp and Ren's eyes shot open. After setting up, he had found a spot to rest, only to be awakened to a searing pain. His head throbbed terribly, and his heart beat rapidly. Next came the coughing. It continued until blood spewed from his mouth.

It had been a while since he had last taken any blood, and the effects were finally starting to show. Only this time, there was nothing he could do. He could feel it, just like before, but worse.

Ren crawled away from the others until he was far enough that they couldn't hear him and rolled over onto his back, gasping for breath. Turning to the side, blood splattered against the dirt. He had no idea how long the side effects would last — if they stopped at all, or how long he would even last against it.

Shortly after, he regained his breath, but the rest of his condition remained. He had no idea how long had passed when the effects finally subsided, but it was apparent now just how little time he had left.

He sat up and put a hand to his head. Everything was spinning. His breathing was heavy but regular, at least. He loathed having to go through that again, especially if it was worse.

With some difficulty, he took a few minutes to rest before walking back to the campsite. When it was in view, he heard Marcus speak. "Can't sleep?" Ren shook his head. They sat down next to each other, just a little ways away from the others but still within earshot.

Marcus kept his gaze centered on Ren. He looked sick, deathly so. His skin was paler than it ever had been.

"I've had my suspicions for a while, but you never said anything, so I left it alone. Seeing you now, though, I can't let it go anymore." Ren said nothing. "You're dying, aren't you?" He was quiet again, then finally nodded in return. "I see."

Marcus looked up to the sky. "The prepared blood?" he asked.

Ren shook his head again. "It doesn't work. They no longer sustain my urge to feed. I'll be lucky if I can get through the quest. If the effects hit even one more time, I have a feeling it's going to be my last."

This time it was Ren's turn to look to the sky. "We need to get the Sun Stone as fast as possible before it's too late. I'm running out of time, and for once, fighting isn't really an option."

Thirty-five

Into the Fire

Marcus kept his eyes focused on the sky. Hearing his friend finally admit it didn't make it any easier. Ren was the textbook definition of stubborn, and now that stubbornness was literally going to kill him.

"I pretty much realized it by your third vial. It was only a matter of time. Especially with your condition declining so fast." Ren nodded in understanding. There was no way his demise would have gotten past Marcus.

"I know you don't want to hear this, but maybe it's time you finally gave in to your instincts," Marcus told him.

"I'm not feeding," Ren snapped.

"So you always say. But things are different now, Ren. You're not alone anymore. You have Kelsey and Ellie now."

Ren kept his gaze ahead, recognizing the truth in his friend's words. "Drinking blood goes directly against my principles. I've met plenty of vampires who lose themselves in their lust and become true monsters. I refuse to let that happen to me."

"Not even for mine?" Ren looked at him rather uncertainly. "What if I give you my blood?"

Drinking Marcus's blood had crossed Ren's mind before. He knew his friend would be more than willing to volunteer, but the thought repulsed him. What would Kelsey think of him if she knew?

"If you're worried about what Kelsey will think, don't be," he said. "Believe me when I say it'll be of little consequence to her. If she were bothered by your instincts, she wouldn't be here right now." He was right, and Ren knew that. But could he push aside away everything he felt and give in?

"Too many people are counting on you Ren. And too many lives are at stake. Our world needs both of us, together, if we are to set it free. I can't do this without you. There is no shame in being what you are. You say you don't want to become a monster, don't want to lose yourself, then don't. Fight it, and to all those who didn't believe in you, prove them wrong."

Ren felt the weight on his shoulders only grow. He had too many concerns, but he knew more than anything that this was the best for him right now. Doing this might just give him enough of a chance to defeat Algiroth after all. Marcus was right. It was time for him to stop running away.

"Alright, let's do it," he said. "Once we reach Taormina, we'll give it a shot. I'll need my strength if we're going to get this last stone."

Relief flooded through Marcus, even if only temporarily. He lay down and closed his eyes. "You'd better get some sleep. You're going to need it. I've got your back."

"Thanks," Ren said back. He closed his eyes, letting his need for rest wash over his senses until he finally fell asleep.

"You can't escape," said a voice. "You will burn, just like her." Ren recognized the voice; it was Algiroth's. The vampire's wicked laugh filled his head. Images flashed through his mind; his friends lying on the ground, covered in blood, a fire, and his mother. He saw his apartment in flames, then exploded.

The next thing he knew, he was fighting Algiroth. Algiroth landed a hit to his stomach, then sliced his body with a blade, covering his torso in wounds. Finally, he rammed it into Ren's stomach, his hand gripped tightly around his throat.

"Your time is near Ren Nightwalker. Say hello to your mother."

Ren woke with a start. He lunged forward without thinking and drew his pistol, pointing it down. "Wait, wait, wait! Don't shoot!" someone said hastily. Ren's senses came back to him. He had pinned Jemson, one of the Cyclopes, down with his pistol pointed at his forehead. His breathing was erratic, Jemson's face a mixture of emotions.

In a swift and angry movement, Ren got off Jemson, holstered his pistol, and walked off, smashing a tree with the side of his fist. Marcus sighed, then dropped the items in his hand and walked off after Ren.

Kelsey watched the scene play out through fearful eyes. There was no denying it; something was definitely wrong with Ren. She just had to get him to admit it.

The only problem with trailing a werewolf, trailing a werewolf. Marcus was fast when he wanted to be. By the time Kelsey had caught up to them, he and Marcus were engaged in conversation.

"I can't do it!" Ren shouted.

"What makes you so sure?" Marcus asked calmly. He was leaning against a tree with his arms crossed.

"He completely destroyed me. I've got no shot of winning. I'll waste away without accomplishing anything worthwhile on this stupid quest!" He punched another tree, and his ki exploded. The tree was ripped in two at the trunk and came crashing down.

Kelsey stepped forward, her footsteps giving away her position. Both Ren and Marcus turned to look at her. Her face gave away everything she was thinking. She had a million questions, but she couldn't ask. When she tried, no words came out.

Ren sighed and ran his hand through his hair. He walked over and embraced Kelsey. She grabbed fistfuls of his shirt, burying her head into his chest.

"Don't worry, I'll figure this out," he assured her. "I promise. One way or another, we'll find a way to beat him." He kept her secure in his arms, doing everything he could to ease her worry. "Besides, it's personal now."

"It was always personal," Marcus said. "He was one of us, and he betrayed us."

"No, that's not what I mean," Ren said back. "The way he spoke to me, it wasn't a coincidence. I think Algiroth had something to do with my mother's death."

Ren's words surprised them both, not just Marcus. Actually, now having admitted it, it surprised even himself. Perhaps it just hadn't registered before.

"Algiroth has a lot to answer for. I've got more than one reason to stay in this fight. I'm not giving up yet, even if it were hopeless. So don't count me out yet, understand?" Kelsey nodded back, her face still buried in his chest.

Back at their vehicles, Ren checked the map one more time. With no new changes, he and Kelsey mounted his Ducati.

"Everyone stay close. We're picking up the pace," Marcus warned. "If you get left behind, you're on your own."

Ren turned the handle, and they sped forward down the road. This time Kelsey was sure he was speeding, not that it mattered. Whatever was happening to Ren was urgent. And now, with this news of Algiroth, they were even more pressed for time to get the stone. A little speeding was nothing compared to that.

Twenty minutes of driving passed before they reached Crotone. Then from Crotone, it was almost five hours to Mt. Etna.

The long drive finally came to a stop at the end of a dock. They were behind two cars stopped side by side. In front of them was a large boat that was open at the back.

"It's a ferry," Kelsey realized.

"And the only other way to Sicily other than by plane or train. This is one of the many that go back and forth bringing people across," Ren told her. "The ride takes half an hour to reach Sicily, so everybody goes up for some air and to watch the boat as it crosses. Stay close to us. If you get lost, there's nothing we can do, and you may get left behind."

"I don't know where I'm going anyway, so believe me, I'm not leaving one of you," she told them.

Everyone loaded onto the ferry, and Kelsey followed Ren and Marcus up a set of stairs to the top deck. She leaned her forearms against the front railing, taking in the expanse of the view. Ren appeared behind her and placed his arms on either side of hers, using his body as a barrier.

Sicily was in sight before long. Watching from the deck, thirty minutes felt more like ten. As the ride neared its end, everyone on board returned to the bottom deck. Kelsey held Ren's hand while he led her down the steps and to the bikes. Slowly, they started moving, and soon they were off the boat.

The GPS lead them the rest of the way toward the volcano. Kelsey was so busy staring at the Mediterranean she didn't even hear Marcus when he pulled up his face mask.

"I've been thinking. Before we actually drive up the volcano, we should take a look at the map. Etna is a tourist spot, so it's safe to assume the location to enter the volcano isn't anywhere around the developed areas. The map might reveal the location of the entrance."

"You're right. We'll take a look once we get to the base."

"You can go up the volcano?" Kelsey asked, finally ripped away from the view.

"Yeah, there's a restaurant next to a couple of craters and a path that goes further up the mountain, but you have to take it on foot," Marcus said.

Time flew by, and before long, they were at the base of the volcano. For some reason, the last couple of days had gone by in a flash, especially the driving.

Ren pulled out the map of the stones and looked it over, but there were no changes. "Damn it," he cursed.

"This is going to be a pain in the ass finding the entrance," Marcus said.

"Let's see what we can find after heading up," Kelsey suggested. In agreement, they started up the winding road up the volcano and pulled into parking spaces next to a small wood building.

"We'll scout around and see what we can find," Hades told them. The group of six Cyclopes walked off.

"Let's check the restaurant," Marcus suggested. "Maybe we can find some information."

All three of them entered the restaurant, and a waitress told them to seat themselves. When she finally returned, Ren acted first.

"Excuse me, love. Do you know where we can find some information?" he asked in a different language. The same one he used when he cast spells, like the invisibility spell back at Grand Central.

The waitress just gave him a confused look. "I don't understand," she said, shaking her head.

"Never mind," he said, switching back to Italian. She took their orders and walked off.

"Well, she's out," Marcus said. "Just a normal human. Let's keep asking. If there are any monsters here, hopefully, they'll help us out."

They asked all over but found nothing. They didn't find any monsters, and none of the humans had a clue as to a way into the volcano.

Deciding to take a break from gathering information, they returned to the restaurant and found Hades outside.

"Ren, Marcus, Kelsey, we've got something," he said. "We did some searching, and I ended up running into an old acquaintance of mine. According to her, supposedly, there's a secret entrance into the volcano near the peak. As far as we know, though, it's just a rumor. She didn't know anything else."

"That's fine; it's a start," Ren said. "Where's the rest of the team?"

"Inside. I haven't told them anything yet, though. I decided it best to tell you first."

"Then we start our search there. Have everyone join us here and we'll go together."

Hades disappeared inside the restaurant, returning minutes later with the rest of the team in tow. He was already debriefing them.

"I'll hold your bag," Marcus said to Ren.

"Thanks," he said, handing it to him before crouching. "Kelsey, climb on."

"I can walk perfectly fine, you know," Kelsey said back.

"It's not that. We're going to be traveling fast. You won't be able to keep up with us." She knew with certainty that that was true. So, she leaned against his back, letting him carry her.

Faced with a long path that continued up the mountain, all eight of them took off running. Even though he was carrying Kelsey, Ren ran as easily uphill as on flat ground, and at a pace as fast as her sprinting.

Kelsey looked to the side to see Marcus running alongside them on all fours. The rest of their team was right behind them. In their human forms, it was easy to forget they were A-ranked monsters. Cyclopes were powerful, but you would never have guessed they were fast too. They kept up with Ren and Marcus with little difficulty.

The path went all the way up the mountain. As they reached the end, they stopped, and Ren let Kelsey down.

"Let's split up," he said. "We'll cover more ground that way. The entrance must be around here somewhere. Kelsey, you're with me," he told her.

"What's wrong, don't want me out of your sight?" she asked smugly.

"We're at the peak of a volcano. No, I don't." She slipped her hand into his.

"Then we're together."

Ren used his magic to scout the area and try and locate anything that could pass for an entrance. Unfortunately, he found nothing. Even his vampiric powers didn't help. Meanwhile, Kelsey checked the slope of the peak, but like Ren, she, too, found nothing.

Seeking a better option, Ren found an open spot and sat down. He laid Shadow Hunter over his lap, then closed his eyes and concentrated. His conscience entered the sword.

Hades found Kelsey looking around. "Anything?" he asked.

"No, nothing yet," she said, a little downbeat. "Ren and I split up to cover more ground, but there's been no results. Where is he anyway?"

They looked around until they saw him sitting down with Shadow Hunter across his lap. "What's he doing?" Kelsey asked.

"He's talking with Shadow Hunter," Marcus said, walking over to them. "He's probably trying to see if he knows where the entrance is."

Marcus unbuckled Glorious from his hip and sat down in front of Ren. "I'll ask Glorious if he knows anything either."

Ren opened his eyes just as Marcus was about to enter into his sword. He found him sitting there, Glorious lying across his lap.

"Anything?" Marcus asked.

"He doesn't know," Ren said. "Only that the key is located deep in the heart of the volcano. What about you?"

"I haven't asked yet. You came to just as I was about to. Give me a minute."

Marcus closed his eyes, and his consciousness entered his sword. Several minutes passed before he opened his eyes. "He doesn't know either," Marcus confessed. "But he did say to check the map."

Ren pulled out the map and spread it out along the ground. Sure enough, Glorious had been right on the money. A new location had appeared at the top of the volcano, right around where they were.

"We're in the right spot, at least," Hades said.

"So we just keep looking," Kelsey said. "Exactly where is the marker located?"

"Over there," Ren pointed. The nine of them walked to the location marked on the map.

Ren and Kelsey were searching with Marcus this time when Ren noticed something in the ground. He walked a few feet to the right and knelt down, brushing away dirt with his hand to reveal a stone the size of his forearm. However, it wasn't the stone itself that called to him; it was what was on it. An inscription, written in Lazarus, the language of Nexus.

"Hey guys, I found something," he said. Marcus and Kelsey knelt next to him as the rest of the team made their way over. Kelsey found the stone perplexing.

"Are those supposed to be words?" she asked.

"Yeah. This is written in Lazarus," Ren answered. "Enter the soul. Into the fire," he translated. There was a rumbling sound, and a spot in the slope fell inward to reveal the entrance to a tunnel.

Thirty-six

The Key to Power

Marcus stepped through the tunnel first. He heard nor smelt anything out of the ordinary, just dirt and rock. "Clear," he said.

Everyone else entered the tunnel, certain that it was safe. Once the last person was through, the top of the tunnel came crumbling down, trapping them inside. With only one way left, they headed deeper into the tunnel.

Mere minutes into their descent, the tunnel opened into a large room. Fires burned in bowls that sat on pedestals along the left side of the room.

On the right side of the room, a pool of water flowed into a river that passed through a grate in front of them. On the other side was a door built into the grate, with a walkway that was carved from rock. It was smooth to the touch and carved in segments, forcing it to appear like a sidewalk.

Ren pulled at the door in the grate, but it didn't budge; locked.

"Kelsey, knife," he said. Kelsey handed him his dagger, and he jammed it into the lock. With one twist, they heard the satisfying sound of a snap, and the door opened.

"You could have used magic to open it, you know," Marcus said.

"No point in wasting my ki," he said back. "Better to save it, just in case."

Kelsey took the knife back from Ren, and they walked through the gate, continuing down the tunnel with the river at their side.

"Good news is we have a supply of fresh water for the time being," Marcus said. "We can use it to cool ourselves until it stops."

"Yeah," Ren agreed, only half paying attention. The other half was focused on their descent into the volcano.

The walk through the tunnel was eerie but uninterrupted. Over time it gradually increased in its descent, the river picking up speed. The deeper they progressed, the worse the temperature inside the tunnel got.

When the heat got too unbearable, Ren and Marcus put up a barrier to protect everyone. Kelsey stuck close to them, careful to stay inside. Only their Cyclops companions appeared unphased.

Cyclopes are resistant to fire and can handle such temperatures with ease. Ren and Marcus knew this but used the spell on them as a token of good faith.

After what seemed like hours, the tunnel finally flattened out, and they entered a large chamber. Even with the spell in place, the room was disgustingly hot. The chamber glowed bright red and orange. Located in the center was a large pool of magma.

Kelsey looked up, but she couldn't see the top of the volcano.

"Look," Ren said. He pointed to the pool of magma.

Sticking out of the center was a gathering of black crystals. They varied in size, their interlocking nature creating solid ground, almost like an island. They neither burned nor melted and contained smooth polished edges. A walkway connected the crystals to the edge of the chamber in front of them. The magma reached just shy of the surface, threatening to spill over at any moment.

Ren squeezed Kelsey's hand. "Stay here," he told her. She nodded, perhaps much too quickly. That was one thing she wasn't going to argue with. No way was she crossing that.

Together, Ren and Marcus made their way across the walkway to the crystals. The small island barely fit both of them, and was one of the most incredible things either of them had ever seen. In the center, the largest crystal of them all stretched up at an angle. A slot had been carved into the side, facing them.

The object resting inside was wholly unexpected. Not a key as they had thought, but a single polished stone of blue and green. It weighed and sized closed to that of a river stone. The way the two colors flowed together, it was clear that they were moving, flowing about the surface, just like the Moon Stone.

"That's the key?" Marcus wondered.

"Worry about that later. Get ready," Ren told him. Marcus nodded and got ready to sprint back across the walkway. So far, getting here had been easy once they actually found the entrance.

Ren took the stone off the platform. He expected something to happen, but nothing did. He slipped the key into his pocket before walking back across the walkway with Marcus at his side.

Shadow Hunter's voice appeared in Ren's head once he made it back to the other side. "Ren, did you get the key?"

"We got it," Ren said back. "It was just as you said. The deepest part. Although, it's not much of a key."

"That shouldn't have come as a surprise. The possibility of it being anything but should be fairly high. I was able to catch some of it from your eyes, but I wanted to check in with you regardless. My sight has been changed before."

"We should be out of the volcano in a little while."

"Then I'll take my leave. Just call when you need me."

Ren felt Shadow Hunter recede from his mind. It was then that he realized something important. The entrance they came through was sealed. That meant they needed another way out of the volcano.

He looked about the chamber for anything before returning the way they had come. Directly in front of them, on the opposite side from where they were standing, was the opening to another tunnel. One which Ren guessed was their way out.

"This way. Everyone stay close," he said, leading the way to the other tunnel. His decision to travel to the other end came at the confusion of the rest of the group.

"Um, Ren, the way out is that way," Kelsey said, pointing.

"The way out is sealed," Ren reminded her. She had totally forgotten about that, as had many of the others. "We can't go back, which means we can only go forward. And that tunnel is likely the only way."

Ren headed for the tunnel, forcing the others to follow. Just like the one on their journey down, they came across a river. It was a mirror image to the other one, only located on the opposite side of the tunnel.

The river flowed out from a room identical to the one at the entrance, only also mirrored on opposite sides. The yellow glow of the setting sun shined inside through an opening in the wall ahead of them.

"Ladies first," Ren said.

"Why thank you," Kelsey said back.

"I was talking to Marcus."

"Oh, screw you," Marcus said back.

Laughter overcame them as they walked outside. The exit was down below the peak, on the side of the volcano. Ren immediately checked his phone for the time but got more than he expected.

"Damn it," he said. "It's seven-thirty."

"Seven-thirty isn't too bad," Marcus said. "Taormina's only a few hours from here. We can get there later tonight. What's the problem?"

"The problem is it's been two days since we entered the volcano."

"That's impossible," Kelsey said. "We haven't slept or eaten anything while we were in there. At most, it had to be half a day."

"The Key," Marcus said. "Time must flow differently around it. It felt like hours, but we were in there for two days."

"Which means our timeframe has just been successfully thrown astray," Ren added. "We need to get to Taormina now so we can get that stone."

"I'll make arrangements for a hotel. We'll have to look for the stone tomorrow."

Heading down the volcano from the exit was another path. They took it all the way back to the restaurant area, where their bikes were waiting. Kelsey took her place behind Ren on his Ducati, pulling the helmet over her head.

"Is everyone ready?" Ren asked, halfway on the bike. The rest of the team gave him a thumbs up. "Good, then let's go."

Pressing the start button, he turned it over, then put it into gear and began the descent down the volcano. Once they reached the bottom, Ren cranked the handlebars. The bike did a one-eighty into the other lane, and they were off.

Thirty-seven

The Sicilian Pearl

Ren and Kelsey could see Taormina on the horizon. Beyond it, the Mediterranean sparkled in the sunset.

"Oh wow," Kelsey said. Ren chuckled from under his helmet. He didn't even need to see her face.

As planned, they headed for the transport depot their cars were being held and switched out their bikes, securing their delivery home.

When Ren pulled up to a hotel right on the water, well, I'm sure you can guess the rest. The nine-story structure seemed to rise from the depths of the sea behind it.

"Stay close, Kells. I'm sensing a lot of monsters, and maybe some shades, too. It's getting hard to tell with so much energy. Just keep cool and follow our lead. The energies haven't been confirmed hostile." Kelsey nodded, and they got out of the car.

Marcus walked over and whispered something into Ren's ear. He was checking the energies, and as far as he could tell, they were harmless — for now.

Each of them walked on either side of Kelsey as they crossed the street. Hades and the others stood by the cars in wait. They passed through a rotating door into an enormous lobby. Ren checked their surroundings by searching for ki or blood flow while Marcus sniffed the air and tuned his ears for anything out of the ordinary.

When they found nothing, Ren turned around to face the others. He made circles in the air with his index finger, and they crossed the road and entered the hotel.

"I'll go check us in," Ren said. "You stay here," he told Marcus, who responded with a nod.

He walked over to the service desk and spoke to one of the attendants. He came back a few minutes later with key cards. He handed them off to the others while he kept the one for his, Marcus's, and Kelsey's room.

"Don't let your guard down," he said. "Things appear safe, but that could change at a moment's notice. I'm still sensing a lot of different energies. Keep your guards up just in case."

"We'll keep a lookout," Hades said.

Ren handed one of the keys to Marcus. "You two go up to the room. I'll grab our gear. Everyone else, meet in our room in half an hour."

The others trailed off on their own before returning to their rooms. Following their lead, Ren grabbed his,

Kelsey's, and Marcus's gear and brought them up to their room on the top floor. His knuckles rasping against the door got their attention inside. Kelsey opened the door, freshly changed. Her long copper hair was braided and laid over her exposed shoulder.

Kelsey went into the bathroom to wash her hands, and Ren set their gear down next to a chair before taking a seat. Outside on the balcony, he could sense Marcus's presence.

When Marcus and Kelsey returned to the room, they found Ren asleep where he sat. His palm supported his face, his breathing light and regular. Kelsey fingered his bangs out of his face.

There was a knock on the door, and Marcus answered it, putting a finger to his lips. The rest of the team walked into the room quietly. When they saw Ren's sleeping face, they instantly understood. He wasn't alone. They were all exhausted.

"He's been going nonstop," Marcus said. "Aside from that little bit back in the camp, he's barely slept at all lately. And he's been using his powers constantly without a break."

"We all need some rest," Hades said. "I talked to one of the staff at the front desk. Dinner will be served in the dining room on the first floor soon. Those that want to eat can. As for me, I'm going to get some sleep. We can discuss getting the Sun Stone tomorrow when we're all rested."

"I agree," said Marcus. "I'm going to get some rest too. We'll talk tomorrow."

The others left the room to go about their business. Marcus laid down on top of one of the beds and Kelsey sat down next to him. He turned on the television and flipped through the channels until he found one he liked. It was a cheesy Chinese martial arts movie, dubbed in Italian, obviously, but had subtitles in English. It wasn't Kelsey's favorite movie, but the channels were limited. Still, it was better than nothing.

Kelsey's eyes fluttered open. It was dark outside, and the TV was still on. When had she fallen asleep? Next to her, Marcus slept peacefully, wrapped in the shadows of the night.

She sat up suddenly, a little taken aback. She looked around the room, but Ren was nowhere to be seen. Oh no, Ren.

Getting to her feet in a hurry, she heard Ren's voice. "Are you sure? Alright, sounds good." She couldn't tell where it came from, but it sounded close. Then she saw movement on the balcony.

"How are things on your end?" Ren asked. "Alright... okay... yeah, we got to Taormina earlier today. We'll start looking for the stone tomorrow. It's been pretty hectic, and everyone's exhausted."

Kelsey opened the sliding door to the balcony and stepped onto it. It was monumental and furnished. Ren turned and looked at her.

"Sure, you got it. I'll let you know what happens. Thanks again, Raziel." The phone call ended, and Ren set his phone down. "What's up? Have a nice nap?" he asked. He didn't sound upset, but she wasn't sure if he was doing it on purpose.

"Ren, I," she started to say, but Ren's laughter cut her off.

"I'm sorry," he said through his laughter. "Your face. Your expression was priceless."

"I'm trying to apologize, and you're making fun of me?"

"Apologize for what? So, you fell asleep with Marcus, big deal. It's called trust. I've known Marcus for over three hundred years Kelsey. That back there, that was nothing. Trust me."

"So, I was worried for nothing."

Ren started chuckling. "You get so worked up over the smallest things," he said. "Come sit down. I was going to call home next."

Kelsey took the chair next to him, and he held up the phone as it rang. When the ringing stopped, Ren's father's face appeared on the screen.

"Ren, how are things going? Are you doing alright? Any trouble? Do you need me to send you something?"

"I'm alright; relax. We all are." Kelsey waved to his dad. "Marcus is inside sleeping. I was just calling to say hi and let you know our progress." His father seemed to relax and breathed a silent sigh of relief.

"So, how's it going?"

"We're in Taormina now. We'll start looking for the Sun Stone tomorrow. The map should reveal its location."

"That's good. The sooner you get the stone and come back, the better. Things are happening over here too. The shades have are on the move. I think Verin's is planning something."

"Something is an understatement. We meet one of Verin's four generals." His father's jaw dropped. "It gets worse. The general I met… it's Algiroth. Algiroth has defected."

"Of course it is!" he shouted.

"We've met many supporters along the way. The word traveling around is that our sides are about to clash. Algiroth seemed to confirm that as well. Which means Verin is definitely putting his plans into motion. No doubt the shade issue is his doing. I'd say that Algiroth is gathering them for battle."

"I'll let the others know tomorrow what you told me. For now, I'll let you talk to Ellie. Be careful getting the next stone. I suspect it will be much more difficult than the first."

"I figured as much. We already expect something, or someone, to interfere. Unfortunately, we don't know what yet, but we'll be cautious. Thanks, dad."

His father's face disappeared as he handed the phone to Ellie. Her little face came onto the screen. "Ren! Kelsey!" she said in excitement.

"Hey Munchkin!" Ren said. Ellie was so excited to see him she talked for near ten minutes without a break. She updated him on everything. It also proved to him that she was completely fine after he saved her. He wouldn't have to worry about it anymore.

"Ellie, dinner!" his father called.

"Coming!" she said back. "Sorry Ren, I've got to go."

"It's alright," he said back. "I'll talk to you tomorrow. Go eat, and tell Nidar I said hello."

"Nidar, Ren says hello!" she shouted. Ren heard Nidar growl in the background and started laughing. Ellie ended the call, and her face disappeared. Ren stared at the blank phone and breathed a sigh of relief. She was alright.

A loud yawn escaped Kelsey's mouth. She was still tired, and in desperate need of more sleep. She led Ren inside, and they climbed into the free bed. It wasn't long after that that they were lost in the darkness of sleep.

When Kelsey woke, it was almost nine-thirty. She looked around. Ren and Marcus weren't in the room. She checked the balcony, but they weren't there either. She decided to take another shower. Who knew when the next one would be?

✝

Ren and Marcus walked into the room and heard the shower running. Admittedly, bad intentions filled Ren's mind.

"I know you guys are technically a couple now, but don't go getting ahead of yourself," Marcus warned. "Remember, you're a lot more experienced than Kelsey is."

"Don't remind me," Ren said back. "It's bad enough that we're different species."

Kelsey exited the bathroom sometime after Ren and Marcus had returned to the room.

"I thought I heard you guys come back," she said. "What time did you get up?"

"Around nine," Ren said.

"You guys have been gone a while?"

"Yeah, sorry, we had some things to deal with. Work stuff," he lied.

In truth, work had never been the talk of their discussion. Rather, it had been the potential of Ren's new feeding habit. Marcus had offered him his blood, and their plan to make him drink had some things that needed to be addressed before they deemed it safe to try. Of course, there was no way either of them was going to tell her that, for a number of reasons.

"Indeed, you did," said a voice. It came from Ren, but it wasn't his. It was a little higher pitched, more steady, and smoother. It was also warming, just like his.

Looking at his face, Kelsey saw that it was different. His left eye was gold, just like Marcus's. It sparkled under the sunlight that shone in the room.

"Given our current state in this quest, I'd say it was rather overdue," it said.

"What's happening right now? Who are you?" Kelsey asked. She felt like her head was going to explode. Was Ren possessed?

"Do you want to introduce yourself, or should I?" Ren asked.

"Allow me," the voice said. "It's a pleasure to meet you, Miss Rose. Although you've heard my name, this is the first time you've heard my voice. I am Shadow Hunter."

Kelsey was completely taken aback. She knew that Ren and he could communicate, but not like this. "You can talk through Ren?" she asked, amazed. "Ren told me that you two could communicate, but he never told me you could talk like this."

"Indeed. The physical communication that he mentioned is not just between weapon and wielder. It extends beyond to the physical world as well."

"A heaven's blade is able to communicate with others, like how I'm talking to you, by borrowing the body of their wielder. The bond goes beyond physical communication through telepathy. It's possible for the two to either share the body like Ren and I are doing now, by which both of us may be present and speak at the same time, or switch between each other."

"Another way would be for one of them to relinquish their control entirely and switch with the other. If that were to happen, either the spirit or wielder gains control of the body."

Gains control of the body. That phrase didn't go unnoticed by Kelsey. "You can control him?"

"Yes. For example, if Ren was to completely switch his consciousness with mine, then I would get full control of his body as if it were my own, and his consciousness would remain inside, as mine does normally. He can hear and see what's happening, just not speak or interact when I'm in control unless I relinquish it."

"But there's a condition for that," Ren added. "To protect each other."

"Correct," Shadow Hunter said. "In order for the wielder and his weapon to share a consciousness and a body and switch in and out, both must agree to let the other have control."

"And that's important?" Kelsey asked.

"Extremely," Shadow Hunter said back. "Without mutual consent, one could, for instance, take control of the other and commit any acts of atrocity in the name of the other. That's why trust is so important to a Heaven's Blade. We are partners, not master and servant. We work together, we train together, and we fight together, as one."

"Shadow Hunter and I have been partners for a long time, over two hundred and sixty years. He's also saved my ass countless times. I trust him completely," Ren added.

"If only more of us were like you," said another voice. It was deep, much deeper than Marcus's, Ren's, or Shadow Hunter's.

"I was wondering when you were going to show up, Glorious," Marcus said.

"Greetings, young Kelsey," the spirit said.

It was apparent that the spirit was there given the tone of his voice, but unlike with Ren, she couldn't tell by Marcus's eyes because they were already gold.

"What Ren and Shadow Hunter neglected to mention is amongst all the current Heaven's Blades, they are one of the only pairs that can switch between each other. It's actually a lot more difficult than it seems. A bond like they have is one that takes ages to earn and countless battles. Including Marcus and I, there are only four of us that can switch with our wielder."

"Yes, but we've also been with our wielders a lot longer than most of the others, too," Shadow Hunter said. "Even longer than you and Marcus."

"Oh, Ren was a Heaven's Blade first?" Kelsey asked.

"Ren became a Heaven's Blade a couple of years before I did," Marcus said. "At the time, I was offered but refused. I felt I wasn't ready, nor was I a good match for the weapons to choose from. A Heaven's Blade doesn't just get a random weapon. The spirit in the weapon has to choose the wielder, just as the wielder has to choose the weapon. Most can tell which heaven's blade is meant for them because you will feel it. Our energies resonate with the weapon, like it's calling to us."

"A lot of times, the weapon the wielder chooses is the one that best fits them, the one they work the best with, so that helps with the bond," Ren added.

He looked at the time. "We should head downstairs for breakfast. None of us have eaten since yesterday, and we still need to go over the map with the others."

"We'll retreat for now. Let us know if you get the stone," Shadow Hunter said.

"Yeah, you got it," Ren said back. His one eye returned to its normal cobalt blue.

"I'll give the others a call and let them know we're going for breakfast," Marcus said. "The sooner we get the stone, the sooner we can get back to Florida. And the sooner we face Algiroth."

Thirty-eight

Crystallic

Ren didn't even bother with the vials of blood before they left. Instead, he went right for the whole pouch and downed it in three big gulps. The slight relief of his urges being soothed disappeared after only a few seconds.

Not too long afterward, Ren emerged from the bathroom looking no better nor worse than before. Marcus looked his way, and all he could do was shake his head. Another failed attempt to levy his inevitable doom. Perhaps Marcus' plan truly was the only option.

Breakfast was served in the same room as dinner, in the first-floor dining area. By the time they arrived, Hades and the rest of the Cyclopes were already waiting.

Kelsey found an open table for the three of them before joining Ren and Marcus at the breakfast bar. It sat four, surrounded by the rest of their team, leaving one chair open for any stragglers.

All three of them took their seats just as one of those said stragglers joined them. Francisco.

"Morning, guys. Do you mind if I join you?"

"Please, go ahead," Ren said.

"Sleep well?" Marcus asked, digging into his food.

"Yes, very. It was a much-needed rest for all of us."

"It gets rough, believe me. Ren and I have been on plenty of missions like this before. It definitely takes its toll."

"I don't doubt you. If anyone would know, it's you two. And, truth be told, this is actually my first real quest."

"That's unfortunate," Ren told him. Francisco's response to Ren's comment was a quiet chuckle, clearly amused; it wasn't not understandable. "And, with regards to our own, it's time we finish what we started. Where's Hades? He's the only one not present."

"He's over there," Francisco said, pointing to the coffee machine over in the corner.

Hades refilled his drink and sat back down in his seat.

"We can all look at the map as soon as we finish here," Marcus said. "Once we find the Sun Stone, we can return to Trinity. Which means we'll be saying our goodbyes."

Ren heard Shadow Hunter's voice in his head. "Ren, switch with me." Ren closed his eyes. When he opened them, they were golden, indicating Shadow Hunter's presence over Ren's own.

"There's something else everyone should know," Shadow Hunter said. The Cyclopes all stared wide-eyed.

"Shadow Hunter," Hades said, mouth ajar. Up until now, they had never actually interacted with Shadow Hunter beyond his physical form.

"We have a problem. I contemplated sharing with Ren alone but determined it best to inform everyone. Rather than have him explain it, I figured it better to just tell you myself. Although I'm not sure where, I have seen the location of the Sun Stone."

"Really? Where?" Marcus asked.

"Close. The stone is kept in a shrine, undetectable by humans and most monsters. It's why you went through all that effort to get that key; it's needed to unlock the shrine."

"That's good," Kelsey said. "Then we can get the stone even quicker."

"Perhaps not," Shadow Hunter said back.

One of Ren's eyes suddenly turned blue, and the voice that came out of his mouth was his own. "What did you see?" He could tell something was wrong. Shadow Hunter was never so roundabout.

"The shrine containing the stone, it's underwater."

All eyes were now on Ren. Everyone seemed to be thinking the same thing, but Ren just sat there wearing a poker face. Bringing his cup to his lips, he took a sip off his cappuccino, letting the taste roll through his like he had no cares in the world. What, was the guy made of stone or something?

"Before anything, we need to look at the map. Then we'll start making decisions," Ren said.

"He's right. It might turn out that the way to the shrine is clear, and only the shrine itself is underwater, like in a pool or something," Marcus said.

"I agreed with Marcus," Kelsey said. "Let's see what the map says before we do or assume anything. Worst case scenario, Ren stays behind."

A security guard was stationed in the hotel lobby on their way back after breakfast. Ren and Marcus quickly realized that he must have been waiting for them because he stopped them and asked to speak to Ren and Marcus in private. Not only was it suspicious, but neither Ren nor Marcus were certain of any solicited acts they had committed.

Was it a setup? Perhaps he, and any if not all of the hotel staff, worked for Verin, maybe even the Church.

Ren gave Kelsey his key card and told her to bring the others up. They'll return when they finish dealing with whatever matters had befallen them. Kelsey looked from the security guard to Ren and Marcus, a nervous sweat breaking out. Then she nodded and took the elevator up to the room.

Both Ren and Marcus still had their heaven's blades on their person. Albeit invisible through magic, should anything happen or attempt to, they would be able to act quickly.

"Relax, you're not in any trouble," the guard said. "The manager of the hotel wishes to greet you, Your Highnesses." He gave a light bow. "It is an honor. Please follow me."

The guard led them to an office in the back behind the service desk. A lone man sat in a chair, looking over a short stack of documents. As soon as Ren and Marcus entered, he got up and moved to bow before them.

"Prince Nightwalker, Prince Allagash, it is an honor to be in your presence. Thank you for choosing to stay at our hotel. My name is Mario Dillutino. I am the manager of this hotel."

"My family and I are supporters of Trinity. When I heard you were staying here, I had to meet you. However, I was away on business and unable to greet you until now. If there is anything I can do to help you, please, just ask."

Ren used his powers on the man, searching him for any signs of lying or manipulation. Any affiliation to Verin or the Radiant Church. When he found nothing, he knew the man was telling the truth. He was indeed a supporter of Trinity.

"Thank you, we appreciate it," Ren said. "Any assistance may prove to benefit us, especially given that we are foreign here. If that's all, we'll be going. We're actually here on business ourselves."

"Of course. Thank you for taking the time out of your day to honor my desires."

The manager gave another bow as Ren and Marcus walked out of the room. Behind them, the security guard bid them farewell, and they returned to their room. Everyone else was already inside when they arrived. Hades sat at the desk with the map spread out in front of him.

Kelsey got up from the bed and ran over to them. "Hey, what happened? Did they interrogate you?"

"No. The manager of the hotel only wished to extend his greetings," Ren explained. "He's a supporter of Trinity. With luck, he can help us to get the stone." Kelsey breathed a sigh of relief.

"What's it say?" Marcus asked Hades.

"Shadow Hunter was right. It's close, very close. The Blue Grotto, a tourist attraction, actually. Which means more than likely, the stone is buried underwater the entire way."

"We've heard of it," Marcus said. "People take boats in there. And because it's a tourist attraction, things may yet work in our favor. This is where using magic comes in handy."

"Let's go down to the beach and gather some information. I'll see if I can make some calls and get the manager to help," Ren suggested.

"In that case, we shall prepare some things that may come in handy," Hades said. He and the rest of the

Cyclopes left the room, leaving Ren, Marcus, and Kelsey alone.

Immediately, Kelsey started rummaging through her bag. "You told me to prepare for anything. I'm glad I decided to bring it," she said.

"Bring what?" Marcus asked.

"My swimsuit."

Ren's mind started to drift as he envisioned Kelsey in a bikini. Marcus slapped him on the back of the head. "Hey, focus," he said.

"Sorry," Ren apologized.

"Got it," Kelsey said. She walked into the bathroom, putting her swimsuit on beneath her clothes.

"Kelsey, can you give Marcus and me a minute?" Ren asked when she emerged. "Wait for us by the elevators. We'll just be a minute."

"Sure," she said after a brief pause. Her recognition of their intentions did not go unnoticed. It was clear she suspected whatever they needed to discuss was important, which she understood. At the same time, though, them leaving her out of the conversation stung worse than she'd like to admit.

After Kelsey left, Marcus lowered his voice to a whisper and raised his arm. "Alright, let's give this a shot. With the Sun Stone underwater, it's best that we have you in the best shape we can."

Ren was still hesitant but ultimately agreed. This was a risk he needed to take. Fresh blood was the most dangerous, but also the most rejuvenating and powerful. Thankfully, he and Marcus had come up with a plan that satisfied them both.

Inside his head, Ren heard Shadow Hunter's words of encouragement. Hearing his partner, whom he trusted as much as Marcus, gave him an incredible amount of courage. Plenty enough to risk what they were about to do.

He was already over three hundred years old and the only vampire in the entire history of monsters to go just as long without feeding. If he failed to overcome his status as a slave to his desires now, then he didn't deserve the title of Heaven's Blade. He didn't deserve to be the prince of Nexus. He didn't deserve the name Nightwalker.

Marcus grabbed a cup from atop the coffee machine and cut the palm of his hand with his dagger. Clenching his fist, he held it over the cup to let the blood drip inside.

Ren stared at the viscous crimson liquid resting comfortably in the cup. The smell hit him like a truck. It drove his vampiric urges wild, almost uncontainable. If just the smell did that to him, what would happen when he actually drank it?

"Here goes nothing," he said. "Let's hope this works." He tilted the cup and poured the blood down his throat. The taste of iron and the sweetness from Marcus's breakfast hit him full force. His ki surged within him, his magic running wild beneath his skin.

All of his senses suddenly went into overdrive. He could hear everything, see everything, taste everything. Then came the burning pain in his throat. It lasted only for a moment, but it felt like a nuclear bomb had gone off inside of him.

Instantly he dropped to his knees and grabbed his throat. The empty cup hit the ground, and through his intense coughing, Ren heard the sound of a heavy crash on impact. It was too much.

Marcus was at his side without a moment's hesitation. "Ren, you alright, man? Talk to me. Whatever's happening, whatever you're feeling, fight it."

Shadow Hunter's presence occupied a portion of Ren's mind. He could feel his friend and partner lending him strength, assisting him in overcoming the strain. He refused to fail. Refused to let his instincts overpower him. He refused to become a monster.

Gathering all his energy, all his senses and feelings, he subdued them, forcing them to submit to his will.

Ren looked at Marcus, and his eyes turned blood red before returning to their original cobalt blue. His coughing ceased, and he shook his head, as if to force out any lingering ailments.

"Did it work?" Marcus asked. Ren nodded back, but Marcus didn't let himself lose the tension encasing his body. "How do you feel?"

Ren's ki bubbled off his skin. "Better than you can possibly imagine." No, he was more than better. Not only were his senses back to full strength, but his powers had returned in full as well. Even the highest quality transfusion blood paled in comparison.

Marcus could feel Ren's monster energy roaring out and relief flooded through him. "Well, at least we know it works."

"It was worth the risk," Ren said back. "Thanks, Marcus. It means more than you know." Marcus nodded, and they exited the room.

Kelsey was waiting by the elevators like they told her. She was leaning against the wall talking on the phone. "Okay. They just came out, so I'll call you soon. Love you too, mom. Bye."

Kelsey put the phone in her back pocket. Her eyes focused in on Ren. Something was different about him. She could see it. He looked alive again.

The elevator took them down to the lobby.

"You guys go on ahead. I need to make a phone call," Ren said. He walked off and sat down in a chair.

Marcus and Kelsey passed the dining room and out a large entryway onto a patio. To the right was a bridge connecting to the large pool, and to the left was a set of stairs leading down to the beach.

From his seat, Ren dialed his father's number. "Ren," his father answered. "Any update on the stone?"

"Yeah, it's why I'm calling. We found the location of the Sun Stone, but the problem is it's underwater. I need to get some crystallic lotion. Do you know anyone over here that supplies it, or can help get it?"

"Damn. The worst possible place it could be. I know a guy who runs a shop for monsters over there, but are you sure you want to do this? You can always leave this one to Marcus."

"Not this time. I can't let him go in alone. Not while knowing what awaits us, or what it is we're after. Even if the others are there."

"Alright then. You seem set on your decision. Let me make a call."

Ren set his phone down on his lap and waited for his father to call back. Minutes later, it began to ring.

"Good news, he does have some crystallic lotion in stock and would be more than happy to give it to you." His father gave him the name of the shop and its location. "Good luck, Ren."

"Thanks for all the help, dad."

Ren got up from the chair and walked over to the front desk. "Excuse me, can I see the manager? Tell him Ren Nightwalker wishes to speak to him," he said in Italian.

"Just a minute," the attendant said back. She got on the phone. "Mr. Dilluto, there's a Ren Nightwalker here to see you." She was quiet as she listened to the manager. "Very well, I'll send him in."

She hung up the phone and looked at Ren. "He's waiting for you in his office."

"Thank you," Ren said back. He walked around and opened the door to the manager's office.

The manager got up from his chair and walked around to the front of his desk, and bowed. "Your Highness, you wished to see me?"

"I need your help," Ren told him. "I need to get my hands on some crystallic lotion. I have the location of a place that has some, but I don't know how to get there. I was wondering if you could give me directions?"

"Your Highness, please, allows us to go pick it up in your stead. You have more important matters at hand, do you not?" Ren realized that he knew the reason they were there. "I received word," he said, recognizing Ren's expression. "Where is it?"

"The grotto." Ren gave the manager the location of the shop that sold the lotion. The manager confessed he actually knew the owner. The man was a local broker for monster-related items and information, one of the only in the area.

Ren thanked the manager one last time, then exited the room. The manager got on the phone and had someone from the hotel staff leave to pick up the lotion.

With the problem of the lotion solved, Ren made his way down to the beach. A shirtless Marcus was leaning against a circular brick planter with trees just before the path took them onto the sand.

"Let me guess, you're getting your hands on some crystallic lotion, aren't you?"

"Better safe than sorry. I don't want you facing this alone. Especially knowing what we're up against."

"I'd do the same for you. Come on, Kelsey and the others are already down there."

Ren followed Marcus as he started walking. Despite having been to Italy before, neither of them would ever get over how blue the Mediterranean was.

Walking down the path, Ren saw Kelsey. She was dressed in a black bikini that made her copper hair and emerald-green eyes pop. It was then that he noticed the two guys she was talking to. Oh boy, fresh meat!

"You guys lost?" Ren asked. Kelsey turned to see Ren and Marcus approaching. "If I were you, I'd start walking. In case you haven't noticed, she doesn't speak Italian."

Whether he was confident or just plain stupid was unknown. But he responded to Ren's warning by slipping his arm around her waist.

When the guy put his arm around her, Kelsey didn't hesitate to make the first move. She raised her fist and brought it to his nose, hearing the satisfying crack of broken bone.

The guy dropped to his knees, clutching his face as he howled in pain. Blood ran down his face and through his hands. Seeing Kelsey punch the guy must have awoken something in his companion because the guy immediately grabbed his friend and ran off at breakneck speed.

Thirty-nine

Submergence

Ren grabbed Kelsey's hand and looked at it. "Are you alright?" he asked.

"I'm fine," she said. "Besides, if it was you, he'd be dead."

"I was thinking about it," Ren said back. "Considering you broke his nose, that's good." He ran his fingers through her long copper hair. "Good thing you're tough as nails, huh?"

"I'd have to be in order to handle being around you."

"Okay, now that was definitely a dis," Marcus said. She gave him a cocky grin in response.

"That was one hell of a punch, My Lady," Hades said. They turned and saw him approach easily over the sand.

"Saw that, did you?" she asked.

"Quite clearly. Anyway, I wanted to discuss getting to the grotto. Many people not only take boats but scuba dive as well. Diving would be best as it give us cover from tourists."

"So, we need to get our hands on a boat and scuba gear," Ren said.

"Already on it," Marcus said, placing his phone against his ear. "I've got an old friend here that rents boats and does scuba diving lessons. I'll give them a call and see if they'll help us."

Marcus was on the phone for only a few short minutes before he hung up. "They're on their way."

"How long until they get here?" Ren asked.

"A couple of hours at most."

"That works out then; I'm waiting for the lotion anyway." Marcus nodded.

Lotion? Kelsey wondered. She decided against asking; she'd find out later anyway.

"In that case, we have time to kill," Ren said. "Let's try not to attract any unwanted attention. Especially if it draws Verin or the Church to us."

A chance to relax was always welcome. Especially on such a quest as they were. There was no way Ren was going to waste the opportunity. He found a lawn chair and sat down, letting the sun kiss his skin as he closed his eyes.

"Aren't you going to put any sunscreen on?" Kelsey asked. She sat down on the side of the lawn chair.

"Do I look like I burn?" he asked back.

She rolled her eyes. "Right, says the guy who's supposed to turn to ash in sunlight."

"I told you that was a myth. We have the opportunity to relax. Let's take it while we can. Besides, I'm not going anywhere near that water yet. I've got something made for vampires on the way. It allows us to touch water without generating a lightning field in the process."

"Then we don't go near the water. We're still at the beach, though. Come enjoy it with me."

Ren raised an eyebrow at her. "Okay," he said, giving in. "Let's go." She took his hand, and they walked the beach together.

One of the hotel staff approached Ren on their way back and handed him a small package.

"Your Highness, here is the crystallic lotion you requested."

"Thanks a lot. I appreciate the assistance."

"I was more than happy to assist." He smiled pleasingly, then wished everyone a good day and left.

Ren opened the package and held the lotion in his hand. "Crystallic lotion. When applied to the body, the lotion acts as a barrier that blocks the water from making contact with us. But it only lasts twenty-four hours. Which means we need to get the stone or get out of the water before then to reapply."

Kelsey sat down on a lawn chair in wait. When Ren returned, it didn't look like he had applied the lotion at all. She placed her hand on his arm, feeling his skin. It sure didn't feel any different.

Ren chuckled lightly. "It's a lotion made for vampires, Kells. It's got magical properties."

"Yeah, when you put it that way, it makes sense," she said. "Well, at least you can enter the water now. Though I have to admit I kind of wondered if you, or vampires in general, were afraid."

"It depends. It's common to fear one's weakness. As for me, I'm used to this. This isn't the first time I've had to enter the water, so it doesn't bother me. Besides, my mom used to love it, even though she couldn't enter. When I didn't have my powers, she'd often take me swimming. Though I do remember her entering the water with me a lot, so I suspect she was using the crystallic lotion."

Ren's reached into his pocket for his phone to check the time. "We'd better meet up with the others. Marcus's friend will probably be here any minute."

His phone barely made it halfway into his pocket before it went off. He looked at the number and saw his father's, but as a video call. At first, he was curious, but then remembered the night before. With all the commotion, Ren had totally forgotten that Ellie was supposed to call.

One of the Cyclopes called Ren's name, so Kelsey answered for him when he handed her his phone. She sat down, letting the tide wash up beneath her.

Ellie's face appeared on the screen when Kelsey answered. "Kelsey! I thought you might not pick up."

"Yeah, we cut it a little close there, sorry. Ren and I were in the middle of something, so we almost missed you."

"It's okay. A friend from school came over. Is Ren there? You guys can say hi."

"He'll be back in a minute. Someone called him away."

Ellie handed the phone over and a new face appeared on the screen. It was pleasing to know that Ellie was making friends. After what Ren had told her, Kelsey, too, had concerns over her mental health in the beginning.

"Hey, what did I miss?" Ren asked. He placed himself next to her, getting a look at the screen. "Ellie was just introducing me to her friend."

"Hey munchkin'," he said. "Sorry I almost missed your call. Someone needed help. We're actually six hours ahead of you, so It's past noon here."

"How's the kid?" Ellie heard someone say through the phone.

"Come see for yourself," Ren said back, looking away. Ellie was curious when Marcus's face appeared on Ren's phone.

"Hey, Ellie. I thought they may be talking to you."

"Marcus! Are you guys done with your quest yet? I can't wait for you guys to get home."

"Almost. We should be home soon. A couple of days, max."

"Finally." He, Ren, and Kelsey chuckled in response.

"Marcus!" a woman called. The three of them turned to see a woman in a dark blue one-piece waving at them. The suit was opened at the sides and hugged the curves of her body. A logo was imprinted on the front.

"Sorry, Ellie, we have to get back. I'll call you as soon as I can," Ren told her.

"Come home soon, Ren. Bye Kelsey, bye Marcus."

The call ended, and Ren put his phone back in his bag. Marcus quickly called the rest of the team and had them gather at their location.

"Liana, it's been too long," Marcus greeted. They hugged, and she kissed him on the cheek.

"Two years, I think," she said in perfect English.

"Liana, this is Kelsey and Ren," he introduced. Liana shook Kelsey's hand and sized Ren up. He just stood there, eyes fixed on her, his mask on his face.

"So, this is the great Ren Nightwalker. I've heard much about you. Never got the chance to meet you though. Marcus already told me you don't like being called by your title in the human world, so I'll call you Ren like everyone else."

"Much appreciated," Ren said back. Liana extended her hand, and Ren shook it.

"Is it just you three? Marcus said there were nine of you."

"The others should be here any second," Marcus said.

Marcus was right on the money. The others came walking up, snacks in their hands. Two of them carried a metal trunk that it contained all of their gear, which Hades took the liberty of gathering.

A light breeze blew through the air. Ren looked out to sea. The sun would be setting soon. "Ren… Ren," Marcus called. "What's up? Something wrong?"

Ren had a serious look on his face. "The sea, the winds are beginning to shift. We're running out of daylight too." He heard Shadow Hunter in his head. "Shadow Hunter says he saw Verin's forces mobilizing. They're gearing up. We need to hurry; we're running out of time."

"Does anyone here not know how to dive?" Liana asked. Three of the Cyclopes raised their hands. "I'll give you a crash course on the boat," she said. "Let's get going."

Liana led them passed a series of large rocks on the beach. There was no dock but anchored at the base of the beach were three boats.

"This one's mine," she said. It was lower than the others, with a white base and red decal. Marcus climbed on board and helped Liana up. Ren was next, followed by Kelsey and the rest of their group.

Liana raised the small anchor and backed the boat up. She drove out a bit before coming to a stop.

"Alright, let's give you guys a little crash course," she said.

"It'd be best if you gave it to them on the way," Ren told her. "You teach them how to dive. Marcus, you help them with equipment."

"Then who's driving the boat?" she asked. Ren walked to the front, pushed the lever up, and the boat moved forward. He increased the speed, and soon, they were flying over waves.

Marcus moved up front with Ren while the others were in the back with Liana. She was teaching them how to control their breathing. He leaned against the front window with his arms crossed while Ren drove.

The boat slowed to a stop as they neared the entrance of a cave. It was dark inside, and the fading daylight didn't help.

"We're here," Ren said. He joined the rest of the team in putting on a wetsuit.

"I didn't know you could dive," Marcus said to Kelsey as they put their gear on.

"I went a few times with my parents. It was when Ren was in India, and never bothered to call once," she said, a little louder at the last part. Ren winced, and Marcus laughed.

"She's never going to live that down," Ren said.

"If you really didn't call once, then I'd say you deserve it," Liana said.

Once everyone was ready, they started falling into the water. Soon Ren and Marcus were the last ones left. "Be safe," Liana said, embracing Marcus. He put his regulator in and tumbled into the water.

"Don't worry," Ren told her. "No matter what happens, I'll make sure he makes it out alright. I give you my word."

"Thank you," Liana said back.

Ren put his mask on and his regulator in, then stepped off the boat and sank into the blue depths below.

Forty

The Shrine of Fire

Ren swam deeper, slowly catching up with the rest of the team. They coasted halfway below the surface and the sea floor before swimming into the cave.

Hades tapped Ren on the shoulder and motioned upward. Ren nodded, and the whole team swam to the surface. Once everyone had surfaced, he removed his regulator.

"The map showed the entrance to another cave, but didn't display where it actually was. We can only guess that it's somewhere below."

They put their regulators back in and submerged again. Ren swam down, going deeper and deeper until he hit bottom. He scoured the floor, looking for the entrance. Likewise, all six of their Cyclops companions dove to the bottom and dug their hands in the sand, using their powers to search for the entrance.

One of them swam ahead a few feet and started brushing the sand away until he saw something a glimpse of wood and metal. He motioned for assistance and another Cyclops helped him clear away the sand. They stared at a square door made of planks with an iron ring door pull. The door was just large enough to fit one person through at a time.

Clasping both hands on the ring, he pulled, but the door didn't even budge. That's when Hades came up beside him. they pulled together, and the door barely cracked open. With the weight of the water, and as old as it was, it was just too heavy, even for them.

Marcus was the third to join, but even with all three of them, they barely got it halfway.

Ren swam over and held his hand over the lock. The water around them began to alter, and they felt magic stir around them. A pocket of air formed and together, the three of them pulled on the ring. Finally, they managed to lift the door up and over.

Marcus swam inside, and everyone else followed. Once the others were through, Ren swam inside, letting the door close behind him, enveloping them in complete darkness.

Seconds later, their surroundings were lit with a green light. Hades held a glow stick in his hand. He handed one to each of them and light quickly enveloped the area.

There was nowhere to go but straight, so they swam forward, uncertain of what lay ahead, like always. The area opened into a cavern, the glow of blue coming from above. They swam to the surface and found themselves inside another cavern, lit blue by the mountain of glowworms that covered its walls and ceiling.

Ren spotted a bank and swam to it. Once everyone was out of the water, Hades opened the trunk they had brought and they changed out of their wetsuits.

Marcus stood in front of the trunk with his hands extended. Suddenly, a black plane as thin as air appeared, and the trunk vanished inside of it. It was astonishing, but the effects it had were noticeable. His breathing was heavy and sweat dripped down his brow. Whatever he just did completely drained him.

Ren put a hand on Marcus's shoulder and his ki poured out of his body before transferring to Marcus. Ren removed his hand and Marcus took a deep breath. "Thanks," he said.

"Don't mention it," Ren said back.

"If that was so draining, why do it?" Kelsey asked.

"Did you want to carry it back?" he asked. "That was transfer magic, Kelsey. I literally just bent space to connect two points. Try and imagine that. Besides, so long as Ren is here, I'm good."

The remaining seven of them all looked at Ren, who, like usual, maintained his stoic expression when it came to this stuff. Then they started walking through the cave, guided by the light of the glowworms.

Ren stopped suddenly, causing Kelsey to bump into him. She moved to see in front. The path split into three directions.

"Why is there always a fork?" Ren wondered. "I'm growing really sick of this."

"You're telling me. We almost died that one time in Brazil," Marcus said.

"Hey, the giant centipede was cool," Ren said back. Marcus only shrugged in response.

Giant centipede? Kelsey wondered. She shuddered thinking about it. Clearly that was a story for another time.

"We'll have to split up," Ren said. "There are three tunnels, so three groups of three."

Ren grouped everyone up, taking Kelsey and Marcus with him like usual.

"We'll take the middle," Marcus said. "Come on. Kelsey, stay close." He and Ren drew their heaven's blades and started down the tunnel.

As they walked, they heard the sound of the stream beside them. That meant it was somewhere close, just hidden.

They pressed on further into the tunnel. Eventually, it opened into another chamber with a door on the opposite side.

"I'm getting a bad feeling," Kelsey said. "Something feels off about that room." Ren and Marcus exchanged glances, then looked at her. "What?" she asked.

"How can you tell?" they asked.

"I don't know. I can just feel it."

"We were thinking the same thing," Ren said. "Perhaps being under the stress you have been because of the quest has caused your body's senses to open up, much more than other people's."

"Is that a good thing?"

"Yes. It means you're harnessing your body's energy and becoming more aware of your surroundings. This is the first step to gaining control over your ki. In any case, let's be cautious."

Ren held Shadow Hunter tightly and stepped into the room. It was dark and dreary, and soaked with humidity. Yet the room was cold. It gave Kelsey the creeps.

Marcus and Kelsey followed behind Ren as he led the way through the room, but they never lost the tension in their bodies. Strictly speaking, it was just too damn quiet. And for a room that cold to be that wet, there had to be water somewhere. The only question was, could they get to it?

The room continued for a while, seemingly endless. They followed the stone pathway carved naturally over time when Ren came to a stop.

"Here that?" he asked Marcus.

"Yeah, I noticed a while ago. There's a waterfall up ahead."

Several more minutes passed before they could see the waterfall. Kelsey heard it before she saw it, but it didn't take long for the edge to come into view. The water fell thirty feet into a pool.

Ren and Marcus took in the size of the room. It was massive.

"Oh man, I hope we don't have to go in the water," Kelsey said. She looked at Ren, who was staring at the pool.

"The crystallic lotion is still in effect. If we do have to swim, I'll be fine."

"I don't think swimming is the intent," Marcus said. He pointed straight ahead. On the other side was an opening in the wall that continued on, lit blue at the ceiling. And in between them, vines hung from the ceiling.

Ren and Marcus exchanged looks and grinned. Oh no, Kelsey hated it when they did that.

"Just like Brazil," Marcus said.

"You read my mind," Ren said back.

He pointed one of his pistols at the longest vines and fired. The vines snapped at the ceiling and dropped until they hung vertically.

"I'll go first," Ren said. "Be ready, Kells. When I come back, I'm taking you with me." Kelsey swallowed and nodded.

Ren took a step back then ran and jumped. He grabbed hold of the first vine and swung forward. When he swung back, he reached out with one hand and wrapped it around Kelsey's waist, taking her with him.

He used their momentum to increase the speed of the vine and let go. Kelsey felt weightless as they flew through the air. Ren grabbed hold of a second vine. They swung forward, then back, then forward again. Their feet were only inches off the ground when Ren let go of the vine. They touched down with a thud, the momentum taking them forward several feet before they finally came to a stop.

"All clear," Ren said to Marcus.

Marcus ran and jumped. He swung to the other vine, then landed next to them.

"Well, that was fun," he said.

"It always is," Ren said back.

The tunnel eventually opened into another chamber. It was circular in shape, with a single opening on the other side. Then came the voices. They came from both sides, and the rest of the team walked into the room, surprised to see everyone. There was never a need to split up at all.

One of the Cyclopes stepped into the room, heading for the other end. However, something felt off to Ren. It was far too empty for what they just went through.

"Wait," he said. "Something's not right."

The Cyclopes stopped, and his foot touched one of the square stones that made up the floor. The square lowered in place and they heard a click.

"Oh crap!" Ren said.

The room started rumbling. Chunks from the ceiling started falling down. "Run, Run!" Ren yelled. They all ran for the other end of the room as more of the ceiling began to collapse around them. Just before they reached the entrance, the ceiling crashed down in front of it.

"Oh great, Now what?" Kelsey asked, fear gripping at her voice.

Scatter," Ren said. Everyone moved out of the way as the ceiling collapsed where they had been standing.

"We have to get out of here," Marcus said. He and Ren turned their heads when they felt the rush of ki. Francisco knelt in the center of the room, his hands on the ground. The rubble in front of the tunnel turned to sand and opened up.

A large rock fell down and struck him in the head. He fell to the ground, struggling to get back up. Blood dripped on the ground. Ren tried to get to him, but the collapsing ceiling made it impossible.

"Go, hurry!" he shouted. Another rock struck him in the shoulder. Francisco cried out in pain; his arm hung limp at his side. "GO!" he yelled.

Ren and Marcus started for the tunnel, dragging Kelsey with them. They reached the tunnel and saw the others hurrying toward them.

"Francisco, come on!" Carlos yelled. A large chunk of the ceiling landed in front of the tunnel. Francisco gave them a sad smile.

"Get the stone. Don't let them win. Everyone's counting on you."

Francisco held out his hand, and a mound of rubble came down, sealing them in as the room collapsed.

Carlos dropped to his knees, the others lowering their heads. How long had it been since they lost one of their own? Too damn long. And now, Francisco. It was his first real quest, and he had lost his life because of it.

"We have to keep going," Ren said, his poker face set in. "We can't delay. Francisco gave his life for this. I'm not going to let it go to waste." He started off down the tunnel, Marcus behind him. Kelsey and the rest of the Cyclopes remained in place, still in shock at the loss of their companion.

The tunnel came to an end not too far ahead. It opened into a room filled with water. Down below the surface was a small shelter. No, not a shelter, a shrine.

Ren dove into the water and Marcus dove in after him.

They swam down until the front of the shrine was in front of them. Moving forward, careful of any traps, they approached the entrance when gravity took hold. They fell and landed on their feet on the inside of a transparent surface. The inside was clear of any water, yet they could reach out and stick their hand through it, feeling the water on the other side. They realized there was some sort of air pocket surrounding the shrine.

They walked toward the shrine and climbed the steps to the platform it rested on. Entering the shine, they came into a single room with carpet down the middle and candles that burned red.

In the back, atop an altar, was a glass display box with an impression in the middle of two doors. Its size was the exact same as the stone meant to be the key. And inside the display box was a spherical stone the size of a softball. The stone was bright red with swirling and intersecting gold lines.

Ren inserted the glowing blue and green stone into the impression. The glow brightened before the doors opened. The impression with the stone remained attached to one, the other free of it completely.

Please don't let there be a trap, he thought. He picked up the stone and breathed a sigh of relief when nothing happened.

"And that's two," Marcus said. Ren nodded. Even for him, it was a little hard to believe. "Now let's get the hell out of here. Time to take the fight to Verin."

Not bothering to put the stone in their bag they exited the shrine and swam back up to the surface. Marcus grabbed the key from its spot in the impression on their way out.

On the surface, Kelsey was antsy. She was all over the place, moving about randomly merely to keep from being still. Ren and Marcus broke the surface causing her to jump back.

They climbed out of the water and all eyes turned to the red and gold stone in Ren's hand. "And that's how we roll," he said. He opened his bag to put it inside when the stone started to glow.

The key to the shrine, as well as the Moon Stone, glowed as well now. The Moon Stone floated out of his bag and the two stones hovered in the air. They began to gravitate around each other, growing closer and closer until they finally touched in a blinding flash of light.

When the light faded, the stones were gone, along with most of their senses. Resting for several minutes was all it took to unscramble them. But the stones were still gone.

Kelsey felt a new weight on her wrist and looked down to see a silver bracelet with two stones on top, the same as the Sun and Moon Stones. And she wasn't the only one. The key to the shrine which had previously disappeared as well had reappeared on Ren's wrist as a bracelet of the same color as the key.

Surprise was putting everyone's expressions lightly. None of them had any clue as to what had just happened, or why.

Marcus grabbed Kelsey's wrist and examined it. "I don't believe this. It looks like the stones have chosen to reside with Kelsey. They've chosen her to command them. In none of the tales or writings does it say the stones will choose their owner."

"Hold it, you're saying I control the stones?" Kelsey asked shocked. Marcus nodded in confirmation.

"The stones have chosen you. That means you can wield their power."

"But that just begs the question, why Kelsey?" Ren wondered. "No offense, Kells. I only meant it because you're human."

"That is an excellent question. Why did the stones choose to reside with Kelsey, a human?"

"But if the stones are with me, then why does Ren wear the key?" Kelsey wondered. They stared at the green bracelet on his wrist.

"I don't think the key is what we thought it was," Marcus said. "I think the key is used to unlock the full power of the stones, not just the shrine. It chose him to be the one that controls the power of the stones. Which means Ren is the key, quite literally. While you can use the stones, without Ren, you may not be able to use their full power."

"I must admit, I'm a little surprised. I didn't expect it, you actually found them," said a voice. "I'm impressed."

Behind them stood the people they least expected to see. Over one hundred members of the Radiant Church, all clad in church attire. But the most shocking of all, leading the group in front of the entire remaining royal guard, was the big man himself, the paxon. Head of the Radiant Church.

"Following you to the stone was a smart decision indeed. I get to destroy you and take the stones all at the same time. The stones!" the paxon shouted.

The royal guards charged forward. Ren stepped in front and swung Shadow Hunter in one fluid motion. A wave of golden energy crashed into the guards, but they held their ground. He released another attack, then another. Relentlessly dishing out an onslaught of power that one by one ripped through the defenses of the guard and the clergy.

"Go!" Ren shouted. "Get out of here, don't let them get the stones!" One of the guards slipped through and swung a sword. Ren blocked the sword, then spun and slashed down. The blade passed clean through his neck. "NOW!" he yelled. Three guards ran at him as Marcus led the others away through a newly made tunnel by the Cyclopes.

"Wait, what about Ren?" Kelsey asked. She tried to go back but Marcus scooped her up in his arms. "We can't just leave him!"

"We don't have a choice. There's no time. Ren knows the risks. Right now, we've got to get you out of here."

"Let me go!" she yelled. She struggled desperately to escape but Marcus was too strong. "Let me go. They'll kill him!"

"They won't kill him, yet. The paxon knows how much weight Ren carries, how important he is. Before they think of killing him, they'll make an example out of him to our kind. I promise we'll save him, just not right now. Getting you out of here is our top priority."

The sounds of battle were drowned out as the rest of the team progressed further up the tunnel.

Ren was holding back the royal guards. Dealing with them wasn't nearly as difficult as it used to be now that he had regained his strength after drinking Marcus's blood. It wouldn't last forever, but his recovered strength made him feel alive again, and he was going to use it all to deal as much death as he could.

In the end, he managed to slay all the royal guards but one, and more than half of the clergy they had brought with them. Blood pooled at his feet, soaking through his now drenched clothes. The dead bodies of the Church members and guards scattered around and piled on top of each other.

As he was facing down the last guard, a blast of magic stuck him, binding his body. He watched as the paxon walked towards him, an evil grin on his face. This was it. He was caught, and there was nothing he could do.

Forty-one

The Fate of a Hero

Marcus and the remaining members of the team exited the tunnel. Sea water flooded in after it opened up just shy of the coastline, but deep enough that no one would see them emerge.

Using all his strength, Marcus kicked toward the surface, taking Kelsey with him. They broke the surface and breathed big lungfuls of air. Marcus let go of Kelsey, and they swam for shore. Soaking wet and dressed entirely inappropriately for a beach, they drew some attention but most paid them no mind, and the ones who did didn't bother with them.

Marcus hurried up the beach to their hotel, the others hot on his trail. He ran through the lobby and into the hotel manager's office. The manager dropped the phone when he saw Marcus then quickly picked it up.

"I'm going to have to call you back," he said, hanging up the phone. "Your highness, what happened?" he asked.

"Gather everyone you can, anyone who will fight," Marcus ordered. "What happened? Did you find the stone? And where is Prince Nightwalker?"

"We got the stone but were ambushed by the Church after getting it. The entirety of the royal guards and even the paxon himself. They've got him. They've got Ren."

The manager nearly fainted when he heard the news. Finally regaining his composure, Marcus told him they needed to move fast if they wanted to rescue Ren and stop the Church.

"Ren is a symbol, even if he may deny it. His death will not only end the war, but end the entire hope of all monsters. Which is why they'll use him to set an example. And they'll do it in front of the whole world. Gather everyone you can and get to the states. As fast as possible."

Marcus gave him the name of the town and even its location on a map. He also included the location of Trinity's base.

Next, he called Greg and Johnathan. His update of their location and the situation forced them into immediate action. But even at full speed it would still take them seven hours.

"I'll be in the room. I'm going to do one last training session with Glorious before the plane arrives."

"And we shall prepare ourselves before we join your fight back in America," Hades said.

Marcus ran for the room and Kelsey followed him. Hades and the rest of the Cyclopes began their preparations for the battle by gathering their armor and weapons. They sharpened their weapons and searched the nearest arms dealer for armor. A mixture of polished steel and leather.

Initially, the Cyclopes were to go their separate ways after finding the stone. But now that Ren was captured by the Church, they needed all the help they could get to free him and stop the Church. The fate of their entire world was on the line if they failed to do both or at least rescue Ren. Their separation would have to wait until after they dealt with this situation first.

Hades donned his own armor, different from the rest of the Cyclopes. Black steel with curved blades along the forearms. He strapped a war hammer to his back and a dagger at his side. The large weapon was made of the same black metal as his armor, the hilt a smooth stained oak with a black leather-wrapped grip.

Fishing into his pocket, he pulled out a wet red bandana. His eyes were glued to it for several minutes, letting himself get lost in it and the memory it provided. It was his most treasured possession, for it belonged to his late wife.

"Rosemary, my love. Watch over me in the battle to come. And should I perish in this struggle, I will see you again. Come to guide me, that we may be together for an eternity."

He tied the bandana around his left bicep. Now, all they could do was wait.

Kelsey paced the room desperately. Her anxiety was the highest it'd ever been. All she could think about was Ren. And all she could hope was that they didn't kill him before they got there to save him. Oh, gods, she was going to throw up.

She looked over at Marcus. He sat in the center of the room with Glorious spread across his lap. Energy radiated his body, more intensely than she had ever seen from him. If she got near, the energy would send massive jolts of electricity pumping through her. He must have been giving it his all in there.

Kelsey knew Marcus was just as eager as she was. Even if he tried to hide it, she could tell. Freeing Ren was the only thing on his mind.

Inside Glorious's space, he and Marcus clashed wildly. Sparks flew, and energy ravaged the landscape as they battled.

Marcus was blown back and smashed into a cliff. He climbed out and charged back at Glorious. Glorious blocked Marcus's strike but the impact sent him flying. Marcus appeared next to him as he flew and put his hand on Glorious's face. With one throw, he sent Glorious flying even farther and faster.

Glorious hit the ground, then lifted back into the air. He smashed through a boulder, then hit the ground again and continued to tumble until he finally came to a stop after crashing into the side of a mountain. The golden spirit got to his feet, his injuries healing rapidly. In moments, they were gone. He and Marcus charged back in, resuming their battle.

During their battle, Glorious took a step back and his energy faded.

"Your plane isn't far away. I suggest you get going. You don't want to miss it." Marcus nodded. "The battle to come is going to be a difficult one. If you need me, simply call and I will lend you my aid."

"Be prepared," Marcus said back. Then his consciousness faded and he was back in reality.

He got to his feet and readied his weapons. The magical bow that turned into dual daggers, and Glorious, now sheathed at his side. Kelsey was sitting on the bed nervously. She was fingering the Sun and Moon Stone bracelet.

"Come on, we need to get going," Marcus said. The suddenness of his voice surprised her. "The plane will be here soon. We still need to get to the airport. Once we get back to the states, I need to head back to Trinity and armor up."

"What about me?" she asked. Would he let her fight? She hoped he would.

"We have spare armor for you. I won't tell you not to fight, though I wish you wouldn't. Ren wouldn't want you to fight either, but I realize the fact that we need the power of the stones."

Kelsey nodded and followed him outside. The rest of the team was already waiting in the lobby, unconcerned about the gazes of the spectators. Marcus walked through the lobby and all eyes turned on him. Glorious radiated light through the room, and he resonated power, like a prince going into battle. Which of course, he was.

"Let's go," Marcus said. "As fast as you can." He handed Kelsey his keys. "You drive mine. I'll take Ren's McLaren. It's an automatic, in case you were worried, but keep up. We can't afford you getting behind."

She took the keys. "I'll be right behind you," she said.

They ran outside to their cars and Marcus climbed into Ren's McLaren. He started the ignition, switched gears, and shot forward into the lane. The airport their plane would land was programmed onto the GPS.

They drove through the airport and Marcus drifted to a stop. It wasn't even ten minutes before the sound of helicopters was overhead, and with them, containers to store the cars. At the same time, they watched Ren's private jet land and come to a stop nearby.

Marcus and Kelsey loaded the two cars into the two containers and the helicopters flew off. The seven of them ran full speed to the runway where the plane was waiting. They boarded quickly and buckled up.

The door closed, and the plane was moving. The pilot's voice sounded through the speakers.

"Your Highness, forgive us, but this is going to be the hardest takeoff you've ever had. We're going to put this bird at forty-thousand feet in two minutes."

The plane started down the runway, quickly picking up speed. In seconds, they were off the ground. The force from the lift pushed Kelsey against the seat, trapping her in place.

Finally, they leveled out, and the force pushing against them faded. The pilot's voice came through the speakers again.

"Your Highness, forgive us once again for the rough takeoff. We'll be traveling at full speed and be back in the states in just under seven hours. This ride is going to be very bumpy so hold on."

The plane shot forward, and they were on their way.

Marcus's Lamborghini was waiting for them when they landed at the airport in Florida, along with three other rental cars. "Come on, I'll take you to Trinity," he said. He hopped in the driver seat with Kelsey in the passenger seat and speed off.

Marcus drifted around corners, switched gears, and kept the car at full speed the entire ride there. Finally pulling into Trinity's parking lot, they got out of the car and ran inside.

Bursting through the door, everyone stopped. "Marcus! What the hell is going on?" Jay asked.

"No time to explain. Armor up, we don't have much time," Marcus said back. He ran down the room and disappeared behind a corner.

Still thoroughly confused, the other Trinity members continued gearing up for battle. They put on their armor and sharpened their weapons.

Marcus came out five minutes later. He wore black pants and a black sleeveless jacket with a high collar passed his jawline. The jacket opened at his chest and midriff, exposing his bare skin. The tail ended behind him at his knees. Golden gauntlets covered his forearms up to his biceps. Armored gloves adorned his hands. Golden shoulder guards, hip guards, and boots that covered his lower half. He had donned a red cape that wrapped around his neck instead of attaching to his armor.

Kelsey's jaw dropped. He looked amazing. She'd never be able to look at him the same again.

Marcus tossed her a set of plain silver armor. "Put that on, ask someone to help you. And be quick about it." She nodded and ran around the same corner he did. It led to a small changing room.

Julie entered the room and helped her put on the armor. All of Trinity was gathered around Marcus who was busy telling them what had happened. There was a loud smash, and Kelsey saw a table get blown to splinters. Standing where the table used to be was Ren's father, Leo.

"As soon as we figure out where they're holding him, we'll move out," Marcus said.

"Um, Marcus, I think I might have an idea," one of the members said. They put their phone on the table. A news reporter was reporting live from the city's main park. Thousands of people were gathering behind them. Though the reporter had no knowledge of what was happening, there were rumors that some sort of religious organization was the cause.

"The park. If we hurry, we might be able to beat them there. Kelsey, Hades, Leonardo, Gary, Jemson, Carlos, Trina, and Julie, you eight come with me. Let's go save Ren. And no matter what, we cannot let the Church reveal our existence. If the humans learn the truth, it's over. Who knows how fast mass chaos will spread."

They hurried out the door and to the parking lot. Marcus sped out of the parking lot and down the street. At the speed they went, it didn't take long to get to the park.

The news reporter was still there, commentating. "The crowd is still growing, eager to see the cause of the commotion no doubt. The rumor as to religious presence still has not been determined accurate but—" a commotion caught her attention, and she turned around. The crowd was speechless as the paxon and dozens of the Church's clergy walked into view.

"There they are. It would appear by their attire that they are indeed a religious organization. We have no further information on them at this time, however, we will update everyone immediately as soon as we learn something," she said.

Marcus watched as the Radiant Church walked forward. Behind the paxon, on a large wooden platform on wheels, was a golden cross the size of a person, and chained to the front was Ren, his arms out to the side. His head hung low, his hair obscuring the view of his face.

Next to the wooden platform was a man who Marcus recognized instantly, Arron. Arron caught Marcus's gaze and made eye contact. He didn't say anything, but his expression said all he wanted to say; 'let's free him and end this.' Marcus nodded in return. Arron had come around.

The paxon stopped and the rest of the Church stopped behind him. He raised his arms into the air.

"People of the world, hear my words!" he said in English. "The stories you heard as children are true. The existence of creatures other than humans—monsters. Behold, in true blood, a monster of the night. A vampire!"

The crowd of spectators started whispering amongst themselves. Some seemed shocked, others unsure. Most of them were debating if the guy had drunk a few too many.

The paxon held up a silver necklace. "Is that for me?" Ren asked. "Oh, I so love a man with jewelry," he said. A light laughter rolled through the crowd and the paxon scowled.

"Monsters don't exist," someone said. "Besides, vampires can't be in the sunlight. If he were a vampire, he would've turned to ash already."

"And even if monsters were real, how could they exist without us knowing?"

Protests at the paxon's outrageous accusation proliferated in intensity and volume. In response, he only grinned cunningly.

"Perhaps, were this a fantasy," he continued. "However, in reality, few of those weaknesses are true. Save for one."

Ren's eyes gazed out at the crowd before shooting an evil and intense glare at the paxon, but he just tapped Ren on the cheek.

"Now, be a good little devil, and I'll make your death quick, though not painless." He laughed and grabbed a cup of water from the only remaining royal guard.

As soon as Marcus saw the cup of water, he made his move, heading toward Ren. Before he could get there, over a dozen members of the Church blocked his way. Not good. If Ren got hit with that water, it was over. Their existence would come to light.

"Get the hell out of my way!" Marcus yelled, drawing Glorious. The Church members all rushed him at the same time. It didn't take long to put them down, but by the time he did, it was already too late.

"You had this for a long time coming," the paxon whispered into Ren's ear. Ren's eyes went wide, and he struggled to break free. He thrashed about, but the chains held strong.

"See how he fears!" the paxon shouted. "The demon knows his weakness."

"You bastard! Fine, go ahead! Give it your best shot!" Ren yelled back.

An evil grin escaped the paxon's lips. "With pleasure, devil."

The paxon dipped his index finger into the water. He pointed his hand at Ren and flicked his finger. Time slowed. A single drop of water flew through the air. The drop hit Ren's cheek and sparks shout out around his body. He grit his teeth as intense pain burned through him.

The paxon let out a loud maniacal laughter and flicked another drop of water onto Ren. More sparks raged around him. Ren stood firm, but the pain was agonizing.

The crowd of spectators were a mix of emotions. Some were horrified, some shocked, others suspicious, and some were utterly indifferent.

Kelsey blinked back tears, watching Ren suffer intense pain. To him, this was basically the same as being tortured. They had to do something. She looked over at Marcus, but he was gone.

The paxon produced a dagger from his robes. "And now, in front of the whole world, we end this."

Marcus appeared out of nowhere and came flying toward the paxon. Drawing back his fist, he struck him in the face with all the force of his ki and magic. The paxon flew off the platform and tumbled into the clergy.

Arron turned and shot a blast of energy into the surrounding clergy, giving them the distraction they needed. Marcus turned and cut the chains trapping Ren, and he fell into his arms with a groan.

"Let's get out of here before they recover," Marcus said.

He helped Ren down the steps and away from the crowd. It was complete chaos, but that very chaos provided them with good cover. Aside from the crowd gathered in the park, the rest of the city, no, the entire country, was in a stalemate. For those that believed the paxon's words and the display, there were just as many who believed it to be a gimmick, a trick, easily conjured. Perhaps they could still salvage the situation.

When they were clear from the crowd and Church, Marcus set Ren down against a tree. His face was white as paper, and he was covered in sweat. Sparks continued to erupt around him. Blisters had formed on his body, and his skin was bright red. He looked completely dead. And the pain, it had to be unbearable.

From within the trees, Arron appeared and put his hands over Ren. A golden light enveloped him, and the effects of the water began to fade.

"I've healed the purifying effect the water had on him. He needs to rest and regain his strength."

"No time," Ren said. He struggled to his feet, and with great effort, managed to stand. "Have to get back," he said.

"Back to where?" Arron asked.

"My house. There are things I need there for the battle."

"I'll take you," Marcus said. "I can open a gate to your place." Ren nodded.

"Won't that drain your strength?" Kelsey asked.

"I've got recovery drinks in the car," he said.

Marcus closed his eyes and held out his hand. A hole opened up in front of Ren, and on the other side showed his mansion.

"Give me an hour. I'll be back by then." Marcus nodded, and Ren returned the gesture. Finally, he looked at Kelsey, gave her that heart-exploding smile, then stepped through the gate.

Forty-two

Nightwalker

Ren stood on the curve of his driveway, and the gate closed behind him. His McLaren was parked in front of his house, courtesy of the transport company. He burst open the door and ran down the hall to his room as fast as his legs would carry.

Weakened as he was from the water, that didn't get him far very fast. Yet, he pushed through and continued on.

On the top shelf of a cabinet sat a ledger filled with phone numbers. Hundreds of names, all across the world, and each one belonged to the current strongest species in Nexus, vampires.

One by one, Ren poured through them, calling as many as he could. Each one was given an update on the situation and asked to aid in the fight with Algiroth.

When the last call had finished, he returned the ledger to its place in the cabinet. The rest of the cabinet below the shelf was filled with weapons. Swords, daggers, and other assortments of weapons hung from hooks along the back and inside of the doors.

"Ren," came a scared voice. Ren turned and saw Ellie, half hidden behind the door frame. He held his arms out, and she hugged him. Nidar walked into the room, and Ren put his forehead against his.

"I saw the news. Are you okay?" Ellie asked him.

"I'll be fine. It's going to take more than a little water to do me in. Listen, Ellie, I know I just got back, but I have to go fight. The others need me, and there's someone who I must defeat."

"Some people are coming here. My father will be with them. Let them in for me. I need to get ready and ready Nidar as well. When we're done here, I'm taking you to Kelsey's parent's house. I just hope they watch you until this is over. Go wait in the living room. I'll be there in a little bit." Ellie nodded and did as she was told.

When Ellie heard the sound of the doorbell, she got up and opened the door. Just like Ren had said, his father and five other people were there. Leo picked her up and sat down on the couch. The other five joined him. All of them wore armor and had weapons.

"You're going to fight too?" Ellie asked.

Leo nodded. "We have to help defend our people. If not, every one of us will die."

"Are you all vampires too?" she asked the others.

"That's right," one of them said. He gave her a warm smile. "We're old companions of Ren and Leo."

"Everyone ready?" Ren asked. He walked toward them, dressed in the same outfit and armor as Marcus. Nidar walked at his side, armor covering his head, neck, chest, back, legs, paws, and tail. The other six vampires got to their feet.

"I'm taking Ellie to Kelsey's parents," Ren told his father. "We'll stop there first, then go to the battlefield. I got word from Adonis. There are hundreds more of us on the move. They should be here soon. If we time it right, we'll be able to meet up with them."

Ren held his hand out to the side, and a portal appeared in the room. Kelsey's house appeared on the other side. They all passed through and came out at the edge of the driveway.

"Stay here," he told the others. He took Ellie's hand and walked to the front steps, then rang the doorbell. Kelsey's father answered. As soon as he saw Ren, his eyes went wide.

"Jacob, what are you doing?" Ren heard Kelsey's mom ask. "It's dangerous out there. Come inside, quickly."

Her face appeared next to Jacob in the doorway, and she jumped when she saw Ren. Alas, it was not from fear. Instead, it came off as more from surprise.

"You can hate me, detest me, fear me, whatever you may wish," Ren said. "All I ask is that you watch Ellie until this is over. I have no one else to rely on, and I can't leave her alone. Please, I need your help."

Kelsey's parents looked at each other, then nodded. Ren knelt down in front of Ellie.

"They're going to look after you until this is over. When it is, I'll come back and get you."

Ellie hugged him tightly. "Don't die, Ren."

"I won't," he promised. Then he returned to his father and the other vampires and opened another gate. They stepped through and were gone.

☦

Marcus and the rest of Trinity were gathered in the park. After Ren left through the gate, they managed to hunt down all the Church members that had gathered except for the paxon and a small handful who escaped with him. In the midst of things, the slippery bastard had managed to flee. Who knew where he was now?

Kelsey was with them, Ren's dagger in her hand. She seemed composed, for now. Hades and the other Cyclopes were there as well, along with the growing number of monsters living in the city that had decided to join them.

According to Marcus, the situation was still salvageable, and they were working on it. With luck, they could actually convince the rest of the world that what happened here today was nothing more than a performance. The only thing that could ruin their situation was Algiroth himself showing up. If he appeared, and with an army in tow, which they knew he would, there was no going back.

Moreover, by this point, they were over forty minutes into Ren's hour, and neither he nor Algiroth had shown themselves. Whether this was a good thing or a bad thing was entirely uncertain. Either way, the situation was dire.

Marcus heard them before he saw or even smelled them. A deep rumbling along the ground. Footsteps, thousands of them, and they were growing closer. Soon the source came into view. Just as he had feared. Thousands upon thousands of shades filled the streets, and leading them in black leather and silver armor was Algiroth himself. Armor covered his torso and the top of his wings, and a black helmet in the shape of a skull rested on his head.

Ren didn't make it in time. Algiroth had made his move. They were too late.

If he set his attention on the sounds of the city, Marcus could hear the terror of the humans who occupied it. Algiroth and his army had created quite the chaos as they passed through the city. Now, the sight of the shades had caused naught but a spur of fear in the hearts of those that had seen them.

"What do you think, Prince Allagash? Quite a numerous army, is it not? Thirty thousand shades in all.

It took a while to collect them, but the outcome will be worth it."

"Not while I'm here, Algiroth." Marcus drew the string of his bow and an arrow formed, aimed at Algiroth.

The vampire released an evil grin. "I can't wait to crush you. Destroy them!" he shouted.

The army of shades charged forward. Marcus released his arrow, and it whizzed through the air, striking a shade. A giant mound of ice formed and obliterated the front ranks.

Algiroth held out his hand, and the ice shattered. The shades continued forward. Marcus was about to release another arrow when a dagger came flying out of nowhere and struck the shade in front. Marcus and the rest of the forces turned to see what looked like thousands of monsters, all dressed in armor.

"It's about time they showed up," Hades said. "The cavalry's finally here."

"An army against an army," Marcus said. He aimed his bow, and a line of monsters carrying bows followed suit. "Fire!"

The arrows were released in a deadly arch of steel and magic, destroying the shades in troves. Then the rest of their forces charged.

Marcus fired arrow after arrow, picking every shade off he could. He ran, jumped, and fired. Spun around and fired again. He was like a demon, slaying shade after shade, destroying everything in his path. He rolled over a Trinity member's back and fired another arrow, striking a shade in the chest.

Surrounded by shades, there came a point where there were simply too many for him to take on with a bow. So, he twisted it in opposite directions in the middle. The bow came apart and changed into its dual dagger form.

Marcus found Algiroth amongst the army and charged. He broke through the enemy line, and they engaged in a back-and-forth battle. Sparks and magic flew as they clashed.

Marcus landed a kick on Algiroth's side and sent him flying. A group of shades surrounded him. Suddenly the group started glowing from the inside and exploded. Marcus turned to see Kelsey, her hand with the Sun and Moon Stone bracelet extended. She smiled at him, then slashed at a shade. He couldn't believe she had already learned how to use the stones.

Sometime during the battle, Marcus found Hades and they got back-to-back. "Any word from Ren?" Hades asked.

"Not yet. His hour is up, though. He better get his ass here soon. I can take care of Algiroth, but I won't have the energy to destroy the army of shades."

"You take care of Algiroth until Ren arrives. Leave the small fry to us." They shot forward and charged back into battle.

Algiroth's and Marcus's blades clashed. Just like before, it was a back-and-forth battle. In the time since they last saw him, Algiroth had gained a degree of power. How much of a degree Marcus wasn't sure, but he was definitely stronger.

Marcus slashed up and down with his daggers at the same time. Algiroth tilted his sword almost ninety degrees, and Marcus's blades grazed the surface. Algiroth's next strike was blocked, and they held their positions, their blades locked together. Both pushed against each other, gaining no ground.

Marcus slid his foot in between Algiroth's and hooked it around his calf. He pulled, and Algiroth fell backward. Driving both blades down, Algiroth rolled out of the way and got to his feet. A giant mountain of ice shot up where the two daggers hit.

They weren't getting anywhere. At the rate they were going, they'd both wear themselves out, or perhaps Algiroth would start to gain the advantage and release more power.

Marcus reattached his daggers and slid its bow form across his back, then reached down and drew Glorious.

"Ready, partner?" he asked.

"Ready," Glorious said in his head.

Algiroth blocked in front of him as Marcus appeared with incredible speed. Their blades crashed against each other, and Algiroth went flying, crashing into a group of shades

Algiroth got to his feet, his body shaking slightly. "Well, I felt that one," he said. He slammed his wings down and shot into the air. Marcus swung Glorious at him, and a wave of golden energy shot out. The vampire swung his sword as he collided with the attack and was thrown into the side of a building from the resulting explosion.

Algiroth flew out of the building and swung his sword at Marcus, who blocked and held strong.

"Well, I'll give you props for dealing so much damage. You're everything the stories say you are. But it's not enough anymore."

Marcus felt Algiroth's energy rise and responded by releasing his own. His body changed as he took on his werewolf form, and they both met in a clash of swords and energy. They battled viciously. Their attacks a constant fury of slashes and stabs. Magic shot out from time to time, only to be deflected with more magic.

Marcus distanced himself from Algiroth and looked around. Their forces were still engaged in battle. Bodies had dropped on both sides, though it appeared more shades than monsters.

"Where are you looking?" Algiroth asked. He appeared next to Marcus and swung his sword. Marcus spun and avoided the strike. He smashed Algiroth in the head with the pommel of his sword, and the vampire slammed into a tree that came crashing down on top of him. But before he was crushed, Algiroth sliced the tree in two with his sword.

As expected, Marcus was an incredibly tough opponent. Though, Algiroth expected no less. What else would the werewolf prince be if he wasn't? Preparing for his next move, his vampire senses suddenly took over, and he felt a massive flood of energy appear as if from thin air. And within them, one energy more powerful than the rest. Even more powerful than himself. A large grin spread across his face.

Marcus found Kelsey amongst the chaos, and they locked eyes for a brief second. She started making her way over to him, slashing away at every shade in her path. Simultaneously, he felt Algiroth's energy fade, and the sounds of footsteps appeared amongst the battles.

"Finally. He's finally here," Algiroth said. His words were directed at no one and yet at himself, almost in reassurance.

That's when heads began to turn. Heading towards them, a hoard of hundreds of vampires, all ready for battle. Out in front, Ren's father was covered in armor except for his head. And leading them all, astride an armored white tiger, was Ren himself.

Kelsey beamed with excitement. Looking at him, he was wearing the exact same armor and clothing as Marcus. His ki bubbled off his body. Not only that, but he seemed completely healed from the effects of the water.

Ren looked over at Algiroth and their eyes locked in a dead stare.

"You finally showed up," Algiroth said. "I was starting to wonder if you'd even make it. The Church really did a number on you. Even I struggle against the pain of water."

"Running away isn't my style," Ren told him. "Besides, you've got this ass-kicking coming to you. And I'm going to be the one to deliver."

"How I'd love to see you give it a shot," Algiroth said through heavy laughter. He held his hands out to the side. "Come, Blood Prince! Let us finish our battle, with the whole world watching!"

Ren drew Shadow Hunter and held it into the air. "For Nexus!" he shouted. Nidar roared into the air, and the hoard of vampires flew into battle.

Forty-three

A Fully Realized Vampire

Carnage enveloped the battlefield with the arrival of the vampires. Seeing it firsthand, it made sense the reason why they claimed the title of the strongest race. With hundreds of S-rank monsters on their side, this fight was already won.

Nidar jumped around, tackling and biting shades. He bit one and tossed it aside like a rag doll before continuing through the army. Ren slashed away at everything in their path. Thirty shades dropped at once, then another twenty, then another thirty. In mere minutes, he had cut down hundreds of them.

Seeing him in a real battle, it was clear why he was the best shade slayer in Trinity and had the highest rift count.

Nidar jumped on one shade and tore its head off with one twist. Another came at them from the side, but Ren sliced it clean in two. Then a third charged from behind, and Nidar jumped sideways, allowing Ren to rift it with one swing.

Marcus and Kelsey finally caught up to each other amidst the chaos of battle. She concentrated, and three shades erupted into flames.

"You're doing great," Marcus said. "Perhaps more so given you've never used them before."

"Thanks," she said through heavy breaths. "But I don't feel like it. I'm not sure how, but the ability was suddenly in my head. But I can only use the one move."

All the fighting was tiring, not to mention she had to focus extremely hard to use the power of the stones; it was taxing.

A roar from behind made them jump. Marcus knelt in front of Kelsey and pointed his sword but lowered it when he saw Ren riding up on Nidar. Ren swung his leg over and dismounted.

"Go help Hades on the west side," he told Nidar. "Take out their front lines that have dug in." Nidar turned and ran back into battle.

Six vampires ran up to them. "Your Highness," one of them said.

"You six, go with Marcus," Ren told them. "Take down the east and north flanks. Those are the most numerous in shades. We can't let them gain the advantage. If they start pushing us back, it could cost us the fight." The group of vampires nodded.

"Alright, boys, you heard him. Let's go!" Marcus told them. The six vampires cheered, then all seven of them ran off into battle.

"Kelsey, go to the south side. There aren't many shades there, but I want you to provide support wherever it's needed. Since you command the stones, we'll need you everywhere. Just know that I might need your assistance as well, so be prepared." She nodded and quickly crushed her lips to his, then ran off.

"Did you have a nice reunion?" Algiroth asked. He flew down next to Ren.

"If you're trying to bide your time, forget it," Ren said back. "Let's finish this already."

Faster than Algiroth could react, Ren drew his right pistol and fired. The bullet hit Algiroth square in the chest, knocking him to the ground. Getting back to his feet, Algiroth flew into the air, but the wound caused him to fall again. He crashed into a nearby tree, then hit the ground with a thud.

Ren drew his other pistol as a group of shades formed in front of Algiroth. He aimed both pistols and fired. One after another, shades fell. Firing shot after shot, he slowly approached Algiroth. When his clips emptied, he reloaded and continued firing.

Three shades came from behind. He turned and shot, destroying them. The shades guarding Algiroth rapidly shrank in size, dwindling down to single digits in no time.

He turned right and fired. A shade attacking one of the Cyclopes from their quest disappeared. He shot left, then again, then right, then in front, then behind. Shades continued to drop like stones. But time was running thin. With each passing second, Algiroth healed.

Ren ran toward Algiroth, firing as he went. He skidded and spun right, firing twice and rifting two shades. Then he spun around and held both arms out to opposite sides. Two more shades disappeared.

He jumped and spun left, firing as he turned, and another five shades disappeared. Returning to the front, one more shade disappeared when he fired, then started running again. He did a back handspring over a shade and fired, then jumped and spun right, firing as he came around. Still running, his feet left the ground in an aerial cartwheel, reloading while upside down. His feet touched down and, without looking, shot behind him.

Finally healed, Algiroth launched himself at Ren. Ren did another back handspring and fired while upside down. Algiroth veered left just before the bullets made contact. Ren turned and shot behind him.

There was no time to let up. Only the constant barrage of bullets as Algiroth flew through the air. Then, the vampire suddenly changed tactics and swooped down, grabbing Ren by the front of his jacket and lifting him into the air. Ren smashed him in the temple with the butt of his pistol, and Algiroth released him. He hit the ground and rolled back to his feet.

Algiroth came back in and swung with his sword. Ren blocked it with his forearm, and the blade bounced off his golden armor, forcing the vampire to retreat. He turned and shot, and the bullet grazed Algiroth's leg. Now thoroughly enraged, the vampire flew at him again, sword at the ready. Ren front-kicked, and Algiroth crashed right into it, hitting the ground hard. Before he could fire again, Algiroth swept his legs out from under him. Ren vaulted onto his feet using his hands and fired, but Algiroth flew out of the way.

Click. The slides of Ren's guns locked back in place, evidence that he was out of ammo. To make matters worse, he had used up all his other ammo clips too. Now, he was down to just one weapon, his signature.

Holstering his pistols at the side of his legs like always, he reached behind him and drew Shadow Hunter. The sunlight reflected off the golden blade and his armor, illuminating the area.

Ren jumped, and Algiroth flew at him. They met in a clash of swords and were blown back. Ren skidded to a stop, and Algiroth spread his wings to slow himself. Their subsequent attacks followed in much the same motion, resulting in explosions of energy that ripped away at the area.

Algiroth swung down, and Ren swung up, their blades colliding. Following up, Ren swung at Algiroth's side, but he jumped out of the way, then moved in and stabbed at Ren's chest. Ren knocked the strike aside and swung down across his chest.

Algiroth blocked the strike with his forearm guard and swung at Ren's side again. Ren stopped it with his armor and grabbed the blade. He slashed at Algiroth's chest, but Algiroth turned in the nick of time, Shadow Hunter only cutting his arm. Giving a heavy yank, Algiroth wrenched the blade free from Ren's grip and moved back.

On Ren's next attack, he disappeared, reappearing behind Algiroth. The vampire turned and held out his sword to block, but Ren used a feint and kicked him. Algiroth tumbled over the ground, smashing into a nearby parked car.

"Okay, that one hurt," Algiroth said. He pulled himself out of the wrecked car and looked at his sword. There was a slight crack in the blade. *It's cracked,* he thought. A large evil grin spread across his face. *Perfect.*

One swing at the air, and a blade of energy shot toward Ren. Then he stabbed his sword into the ground. The tip sank into the asphalt and cracks spread out towards Ren. The guy in question slashed at the blade of energy, deflecting it, then jumped out of the way as a column of flames shot up at his feet from the cracks.

"You're a lot more agile than you were the last time we fought," Algiroth said to him. "It's like you have all your powers back." He stood there, studying him. "And yet, you still have not fed. How interesting. Especially since, by now, I reckon no amount of transfusion blood could contain the thirst. Tell me I'm wrong." Ren never responded. "Exactly. What did you do, huh?"

And then he realized it. Exactly what Ren had done to achieve such a level of strength. "Ah, I get it now. Although not directly, you still drank fresh blood. To think that old trick would actually work."

"What difference does it make?" Ren asked. He slashed at Algiroth, and a blade of energy flew at him. Algiroth swung his sword and cut it in two. The destroyed energy exploded on both sides of him.

Ren lunged at him and swung down. Algiroth blocked the strike, and Ren continued with a barrage of attacks. He was relentless, but Algiroth still managed to deflect them all. Finally, Ren swung sideways. Algiroth blocked that attack too, but the impact sent him flying. He came skidding to a stop. As he put up his guard, the crack in the sword spread. In its current state, the weapon was unusable.

"It's over, Algiroth," Ren said. "Call off your shades, and I will grant you a quick death. Much more than you deserve." Algiroth unleashed a hearty laugh in response. His sudden outburst surprised Ren. And with it came the ocean of malice, of evil.

Algiroth stared at Ren with eyes unlike any he had ever seen. "You're right, it is over," the vampire said. "For we enter the next stage. Prepare yourself, oh mighty Blood Prince, for carnage."

Black mist crept out of the cracks in Algiroth's sword. The first chip fell, and then the second. Seconds later, the rest of the sword shattered, like shedding a layer of skin. And in place, an entirely new blade.

Red as deep as blood coated the edges of a blade as black as night, and red demonic symbols ran down the fuller on both sides. Two half-moons facing the opposite direction made up the guard, with thick jagged tips along the inside of the curves. Just like the blade, it, too, was black with red edges. And the pommel took the form of a skull with horns sticking out. Red jewels took the place of eyes. Jewels that almost seemed to glow.

A wave of evil spread over the whole city. Ren had never felt such pure malice before. It was toxic, and unlike anything he had ever faced. Only one such tool was capable of releasing such pure evil.

"A demonic sword," he said. He grit his teeth, recognizing just how horrendous the situation had now become.

"Indeed," Algiroth confirmed. "You have no idea the trouble I went through to obtain it, but the outcome is worth it. Just one demonic weapon has the power to rival a heaven's blade in its released form. A form which you, nor any of the other current Heaven's Blades, haven't acquired. You have already lost this fight. So, Prince Nightwalker, I shall bestow upon you the same proposal you offered me. Surrender, and I shall make your death quick."

Ren looked at the ground beneath Algiroth. It was as black as his sword. All the life around him had been completely sucked dry. The power of a demonic sword, known for sucking the life force of everything around them other than their wielder.

Just like heaven's blades, demonic swords contain spirits. Malicious souls who have been taken over by their own evil and power and trapped within the weapon. They were bad news.

Algiroth swung the sword, and a wave of black energy raged toward Ren. He watched as everything the energy passed over turned black and died. Ren swung his sword. A wave of golden energy crashed into the black one, but Algiroth's broke through. Ren blocked the attack and was sent flying.

So much power, he thought. *Shadow Hunter won't stand a chance against it.*

"We have to wear him down," Shadow Hunter said. "Let the energy take over him. The downside to demonic blades is their overwhelming power. They only grow stronger as they're used. Eventually, the energy will become too much to handle and cause an overload. The overload will destroy the host and the blade along with them."

"What happens if it becomes too much for me?" Ren asked.

"Then I will assist you."

"Assist how? Even you can't go head-to-head with that thing."

"Not alone, no. But together, we can."

Something about the way Shadow Hunter was talking made Ren curious. He was up to something. "Shadow Hunter?"

"You may not be a full-fledged vampire, having never fed. You may not be perfect as a person and a monster at all, but that's what I like about you. Which is why, if we truly find ourselves in a dangerous situation, as I know we will, I am committed to joining with you. If you feel the same."

Ren couldn't believe what he'd just heard. In fact, he'd long since assumed it would never happen. "Are you serious?"

"I am, so long as it's you. But there are conditions that must be met, both preset and personal."

"There are always conditions," Ren grumbled.

"Don't worry; if you complete them, I'll tell you. I just hope your body can handle it. Right now, your powers might not be enough to stabilize the release. Had you fed, there would be no cause for worry. As a fully released vampire, you could handle it no problem. I guess we'll just have to wing it and see what happens."

Ren got to his feet and Algiroth swung at his chest. Ren blocked it but was sent flying again. He smashed into a tree, and Algiroth was in front of him again, swinging mercilessly. Ren could only hold his sword out to defend himself from the onslaught of attacks.

Perhaps the worst part was the demonic energy raging around him, eating the life force of everything around it.

Another attack from the side sent Ren flying again. "Shadow Hunter, you alright."

"I'm fine. My aura blocks the demonic energy, so it doesn't affect me. Besides, his energy can't reach my spirit."

"Good to know."

With some effort, Ren managed to get to his feet. A sharp pain flared through his head. His muscles burned, and his senses went wild. Everything turned red, then white, then back to red. His energy started overflowing, and he struggled to contain it.

Marcus looked over and saw what was happening. "Ren!" Immediately, he ran over to him, getting a good look at whatever was happening to him.

"These symptoms. They're the same ones that come from not feeding. But that doesn't make sense. You drank my blood."

"It's not his doing," Glorious said, his voice appearing in Marcus's head. "See that sword the vampire is holding?"

Marcus looked at the sword in Algiroth's hand and bit back a curse, his face turning pale. "A demonic sword."

"Exactly. Likely, that sword's aura drew out the demonic energy in him, causing it to overflow. In a sense, it's causing the reaction to occur."

Ren started coughing. He put his hand over his mouth, and a deep crimson started dripping down his hand. He coughed again, and more blood came out, splattering the ground below him.

"REN!" Kelsey screamed. She ran over to him and put a hand on his back. She was covered in cuts and scrapes. Her armor was dirty and dented. "What happened? Talk to me!" Sweat dripped down his forehead and the sides of his face. He coughed up more blood. "Ren!"

Algiroth's sudden laughing caught them off guard. "Your pleading is pathetic. He's not injured. It's the effects taking over."

"Effects? What effects?" she asked.

Algiroth looked at her with wide eyes. Then he turned them on Ren. "You mean you haven't told her?" he asked him. Ren said nothing.

"Tell me what?" she asked. Again, Ren never answered. "Tell me what, Ren?" she asked again. He still didn't answer.

Algiroth started laughing again. "I don't believe this. You've been together this whole time, and yet you don't know. How much effort did you go through to hide it from her?"

"It's none of your business," Ren told him. "Keep your filthy mouth shut!" he yelled.

"Oh, but this is so much more entertaining." Algiroth locked his eyes on Kelsey. "This is what happens when a vampire doesn't feed. We lose our sense and control over ourselves, and if we continue not to feed, it will lead to our demise, just as you see before you. Ren Nightwalker, is dying."

Kelsey looked at Ren, terrified that her fears were finally coming true. "Is it true?" she asked. Ren didn't answer. "Ren! Is it true?" she asked again.

He kept his eyes on the ground but nodded. Kelsey's face turned white as paper. More so, she just didn't understand. Why was this happening? Why had he hidden it from her? And for how long?

"Because he refuses to feed," Marcus said, as if he knew what she was thinking. "Just as Algiroth said, the longer a vampire goes without feeding, the worse the effects, until he eventually dies."

"It's been a long time coming," Algiroth said. "I'm surprised he's lasted this long. He's the first to do so. Most of us feed before we turn one hundred, but very rarely, there are some vampires that go beyond that."

"However, Ren is different," Marcus said. "He's special. What you'd call an exception. Ren is the first vampire in the history of vampires to ever go three hundred years without feeding. Those who tried all died."

"You brought this on yourself," Algiroth said. "And now, your stubbornness will finally be the death of you. How joyous a day it is. I haven't been this excited in decades."

Marcus swung his sword at Algiroth, appearing out of nowhere. Reacting on instinct, Algiroth moved to avoid it, but Marcus's attack was too fast. The demonic blade in Algiroth's hand flew out in front of him and blocked the strike, the resulting collision of energy causing a massive explosion that ripped apart the area.

Ren shielded Kelsey from the blast, but all she could do was look at him in confusion. "Why would you do this to yourself? You refuse to drink blood? I don't understand you."

"Because I don't want to become a monster," he confessed.

"Ren, you're a vampire. You are a monster."

"That's not what I meant. There are many cases of vampires being unable to contain the power they gain from feeding, and it drives them mad. They become violent, ruthless, killing machines. I wasn't willing to take the risk of that happening."

"Besides, I'm selfish. If the day ever came when you found out the truth about me, I never wanted you to look at me like I was a real monster. Seeing you look at me with rejection in your eyes would kill me more than anything else," Ren confessed. "So, I hid everything from you in order to not scare you away."

Kelsey released a heavy and irritated sigh. "You know, for all the years I've known you, I just don't get you sometimes. How could you be so incredibly stupid?" she asked. "You're my childhood friend, Ren, and the boy I fell in love with. Do you really think I would just give up on you like that?"

Ren tightened his hands into fists, taking chunks of dirt with them.

"When you first told me you were a vampire, I was already under the impression that drinking blood was a common occurrence. It's in your nature as a vampire; there's no shame in that. I never rejected you then, did I? Then why would I reject you at all? Had I, it would have been the moment I found out the truth about you."

"If I had known you were torturing yourself and dying because of it, I would have offered you my blood from the beginning."

Ren's whole world seemed to stop momentarily. Only the continuous sounds of battle between Marcus and Algiroth kept him tethered.

"No!" he yelled. "I can't. I can't do that to you. I won't."

Kelsey grabbed his face and forced him to look at her. "If I wasn't willing, I wouldn't have offered. I'm not some weak little girl that needs protecting, you of all people should know that. I'm a part of your world now. Rely on me more."

Kelsey took off her breastplate and shoulder guards, then lowered the collar of her shirt, exposing her neck to him. "Take it."

"Like hell!" Algiroth shouted. He flew at them, but Marcus appeared in front of him and swung Glorious. Algiroth was sent flying through the air.

Ren's heightened senses were going wild. He could see Kelsey's blood flowing through her, hear the beating of her heart. He could even smell the iron in it. Kelsey pulled him down toward her, seeing him hesitate. As much as he wanted to, he just couldn't resist. Besides, Kelsey was willing to take that risk. If it was Kelsey, it was worth it.

Algiroth shouted, "Don't let him feed!" A group of shades charged them, but Hades and three other Cyclopes blocked their path, cutting them down.

"Do it!" Hades yelled. "Hurry!"

Ren sunk his fangs into Kelsey's neck, and she immediately felt a massive wave of pure ecstasy overcome her. She gasped and grabbed fistfuls of his hair. Heat surged throughout her body. It felt like she was on fire. Her pitiful attempt to hold in her cries of lust was immediately crushed.

"NO!" Algiroth yelled. He flew at them faster than they could react but crashed into a wall of energy that erupted around the two of them.

The air surged rapidly, blowing across the area. Lightning crackled throughout the area, and an intense heat burned through everything.

The power surging through Ren was unlike anything he'd ever felt before. No amount of artificial feeding would ever compare to this.

Algiroth was sent tumbling through the air, crashing into a nearby building. When he pulled himself back, he bit back a curse. For but a single moment, he felt an emotion he had not felt in decades, fear. It washed over him and then quickly vanished, replaced by uncertainty.

Ren was on his feet; that intense energy surrounded him, so strong it could be felt throughout the whole country. And that's when every monster in the country knew, he had awakened. All eyes were now thoroughly on him. But it wasn't his energy that drew their attention. With eyes of the purest cobalt, spread out wide on Ren's back, was a pair of large, jet-black wings.

Forty-four

The Right to be a Heaven's Blade

Kelsey stared at Ren, transfixed by his new form. When he closed his eyes and opened them again, they'd turned a deep and brilliant red, before returning to their normal cobalt blue. His large wings were spread out in full view. She felt a strong desire to be wrapped in them. Fanning her face, she couldn't tell if there were still lingering effects after being bitten.

Carefully, she placed her hand on her neck where she'd been bitten. There were two holes, but not only was there little blood, there was still almost no pain either.

"Yes!" Ren heard Shadow Hunter yell in his head. "Finally, you've become a true vampire!"

Marcus landed another heavy blow to Algiroth before retreating back to Ren and Kelsey. In his werewolf form, the two of them were more incredible standing next to each other than ever before.

"Well? How do you feel?" Marcus asked.

"Whole," Ren answered. "Thank you, Kelsey." He gave her a sly smile, but she figured he deserved it right about now.

An attack came at them when it was suddenly deflected right back at Algiroth, its sender. Ren's father landed in front of them, tucking his wings in.

"Ren," he said. Tears threatened to spill over.

"Now's not really the time to get all sentimental," Ren told him. "Save it for later, old man." His father's laugh made them all forget about their current situation for but a moment.

"Kelsey!" Kelsey turned and saw her parents running toward them, and Ellie was with them.

"No! What are they doing here?" Kelsey asked.

"Ren!" Ellie shouted. They spotted him and stopped.

"Hell yeah," Kelsey's father said, completely ecstatic.

Ellie tried to run to Ren, but Kelsey's father stopped her. "No, Ellie, you can't. If you go now, you'll get hurt, and Ren would be devastated. It's safer for you to stay here."

Ellie wanted so badly to run to Ren right at that moment, but when Ren shook his head at her, she knew that Jacob was right. She would only get hurt if she went over there.

"Move!" Ren yelled. The three of them hadn't even seen the shade heading toward them. It was right on top of them now.

Ren slammed his wings down and launched himself at them. The shade attacked the nearest person from it, Kelsey's mother. Against such a creature, she could do nothing. Then she was weightless as she found herself in the air, held tight in Ren's arms. When he landed, with one mighty flap of his wings, the shade was blown away and disappeared in a roar of lightning.

"You shouldn't be here; it's not safe. Are you asking to die?"

"We're sorry, but we couldn't just sit still any longer. Your battle all over the news." She recalled the moment the paxon flicked water onto him and Ren erupted into sparks. "So, you really are a vampire."

"I'm sorry for hiding it. If I told you, you'd think I was crazy. Humans shouldn't know about us. As much as we'd like to coexist peacefully, your race wouldn't take to it, or us."

"Then why is Kelsey here?" she yelled. "Why is she wearing armor and fighting off, whatever those things are?"

"They're called shades. And as you can see, Kelsey is fine. She may be human, but unlike you, she's no longer powerless."

"Kelsey has powers?"

"Unfortunately, it's going to have to wait. Now, leave. Find shelter, quickly."

Ellie grabbed Ren's hand, and he knelt down, wrapping her tightly in his arms.

"I'm glad you're safe."

"Ren, you look so cool," she said. He looked at her and chuckled.

"Thanks, munchkin'." He gently rubbed the top of her head. "Wait with Kelsey's parents for a little longer."

Marcus was knocked clean off the ground and landed next to them. "Yup, that hurt," he said, getting to his feet. Ren extended his hand and helped him up.

"You good?"

"Fine. If he didn't have that damn sword, this would be over by now."

"I know. I'll take care of Algiroth. You look after Kelsey. She's weakened from overusing the stones. Get someone from our side to lead everyone here away."

Marcus changed back into his human form. "You two are Kelsey's parents, correct?" They nodded. "I'm Marcus, a friend of Kelsey's. I worked with Ren and Kelsey on the quest."

Off to the side, Algiroth got to his feet, having recovered from the injuries Marcus had dealt. "Damn werewolf."

"You'd better get going. Looks like you've got work to do," Jacob said to Ren. "And Ren. Thank you for protecting Kelsey. You kept your promise."

"No. She protected me," Ren told him. He turned to face Algiroth, Shadow Hunter ready in his hand.

"Hey, Ren," Jacob called. Ren turned back to face him. "Kick his ass," he said. Ren nodded and slammed his wings down.

He rocketed into the air and collided with Algiroth, picking him up and taking him higher and higher into the air. When he finally let go, Ren flipped forward, slamming his heel down on top of Algiroth's head. Algiroth flew towards the ground but spread his wings and managed to come to a stop before impact.

Ren was about to fly at him when electricity sparked around his body. Black chains wrapped around his body, then disappeared. His wings disappeared, and he started falling. The ground came up fast and he smashed into the dirt.

Sitting up, he tried to summon his wings but couldn't. It was then he realized his power was gone. His newly attained strength from feeding had vanished.

"Hurts, doesn't it?" Algiroth asked. "Being so weak. I've sealed your powers with my demonic sword.

Algiroth flew down and grabbed Ren. He lifted him into the air, dealing heavy blows as they went. Ren fell, and Algiroth flew down and kicked him sideways, but the vampire didn't let up. A various barrage of attacks was inflicted on Ren, still unable to defend against them.

With great difficulty, he managed to get to his feet, though his body ached from the bombardment. Then,

Algiroth kicked him in the chest, and he landed hard on his back. While down, he took a kick to the side and flew into another tree, the impact sending a piercing pain through his side.

"I guess even the great Ren Nightwalker can't stand up to the power of a demonic sword without his powers. This fight appears to have come to an end, Blood Prince."

Pain shot through Ren's hand as Algiroth's blade passed through it and buried itself into the soft dirt. The pain ran up his arm to his shoulder.

Ren couldn't move. The pain drowned out everything else, and with Algiroth right there, there was no way he could take the sword out. His free arm suddenly moved on its own, and he watched as Shadow Hunter passed through Algiroth's shoulder. Algiroth roared in pain, and Ren's leg moved on its own next, kicking him off, the sword going with him. A burning gasp escaped Ren's lips when the blade came out.

"You alright?" Shadow Hunter asked.

"Thanks for the help. You saved my ass, again."

"Don't mention it. That's what partners are for. Can you move?"

"I think so." Ren got to his feet shakily. His chest felt like it had been put through a shredder, his breathing impossible to get a hold of. And his wound wasn't closing either, even with Shadow Hunter trying to stop the bleeding.

Kelsey dropped to her knees next to him. "Here, let me help." She held her hands out over his wounded hand. The green and blue bracelet on his wrist started glowing and the stones on her wrist followed suit. A rush of power flooded through her, rejuvenating her, and slowly his wound began to heal.

"You think I'll just let you heal!" Algiroth shouted. Ren saw a flash of movement, then stuck his foot out, and the vampire crashed right into it. Blood spat out of his mouth, and he dropped to his knees, holding his stomach.

Ren got to his feet and took a deep breath. Then, he lowered his hands to his sides, palms out. Lightning sparked to life, jumping between his hands. He thrust his hand out, and a bolt of lightning shot out. Algiroth blocked it with the flat of his blade, but the impact sent him flying. He hit the ground and rolled. The blade of his sword steamed where the lightning struck.

Ren summoned more lightning and transferred it to Shadow Hunter. Lightning danced along the golden blade. He attacked from behind Algiroth, and the vampire met Ren's swing with one of his own.

Their blades continued to clash. Algiroth dodged one of Ren's swings and kicked him in the stomach. Ren skidded backward to a stop, but Algiroth was already making his next attack. Black and red energy surrounded his blade. He swung, and a large wave of energy raced toward Ren. With one swing, he cut the energy in half, but the impact sent him tumbling over the ground. Crashing into something, he came to a slow stop. Kelsey held him tightly in her arms.

"Nice catch. Now get out of here. It's too dangerous now that Algiroth has a demonic sword."

"No, I'm not leaving you."

"How sweet. Then you can die together!" Algiroth said. He appeared above them and swung down. Ren covered Kelsey, leaving his back open to take the hit. He looked behind him, expecting to see the blade, and saw Hades jump in front of the blade's path. Ren watched as Algiroth's blade passed through Hades' breastplate and cut into his chest.

Hades dropped to the ground in a pool of blood. Kelsey screamed in horror. Ren moved and put his hand over the wound, but the blood just kept coming. "Hold on, Hades. Just hold on," he said. He tried using magic to heal the wound but to no prevail. The demonic power of the sword was interfering with the healing. "Heal, dammit!"

"What a completely foolish thing to do," Algiroth said. "What did he expect to happen, jumping in front of my blade just to protect you? What a pointless way to die."

Kelsey lunged at him, but he swatted her aside.

"My choice," Hades mouthed. "It's okay. I can finally see Rosemary again." He put his hand on the side of Ren's face. "Thank you for believing in me, Your Highness. His sword. He's nothing without that sword."

Ren could see the cloudiness in Hades' eyes. He was fading fast, and his breathing was slowing down.

"Rosemary," Hades mumbled. Ren watched as the light in his eyes faded, and then it was gone. He drew his last breath, and then his hand fell to the ground, leaving a streak of his blood across Ren's cheek.

Kelsey put her hands over her mouth, quelling her sobbing but not her flood of tears.

The feeling of Hade's energy disappearing traveled through the surrounding area. They immediately recognized the moment when he took his last breath. It sent a wave of grief through the Cyclopes. Hades was head of the Cyclopes in Genoa. His loss affected all of them.

"Well, that's one pest down, I suppose," Algiroth said. His eyes suddenly went wide from shock, and he cried out in pain as blood splattered everywhere. Ren stood behind him, his energy raging like an ocean storm. The demonic sword in Algiroth's grip fell to the ground along with his severed arm.

Anger continued to build within Ren, unable to suppress it. Death was nothing new to him. But watching Hades die, it broke something in him. Something that had been lying dormant for who knew how long.

He lunged at Algiroth and swung down on top of him. The demonic sword moved in front of him of its own will and blocked his strike with a shield of energy. The sword spun in a circle, and a blast of energy sent Ren backward. Putting all his energy into his next swing, the golden wave that raged toward the sword broke right through its energy and sent it flying.

Beneath the sword, the ground turned black and died, and it rose into the air again. It floated toward Algiroth, glowing red from its symbols. Algiroth grabbed the sword, and the glow expanded before quickly disappearing.

He stood in a new form. The severed arm Ren had cut off was somehow regrown. Not only that, but his chest was bare and covered in red demonic symbols. His eyes were pure red, and he had long black horns sticking out from his head.

"Oh, that's not good," Ren's father said, coming up to Marcus and Kelsey.

"What's happened to him?" Kelsey asked, wiping away her tears.

"He's fused with his demonic sword."

Algiroth rotated the shoulder of his new arm. "Well, that was unpleasant. I suppose there's no use in prolonging this any further. Let's end this. But, I think you've earned the right to know the truth. How your mother actually died."

Ren felt like he'd been punched in the face. "You were right. Your mother didn't die in an accident. The fire in your apartment was caused by magic."

He looked over at Kelsey. "I was astonished when I saw you in Italy. You were traveling with a human. What else, you seemed smitten with her. You, the human hater."

Ren's hatred of humans. It had already been brought up several times when they were searching for the stones. Kelsey was increasingly aware of it. Though he had never told her where the hatred directly stems from, she had already guessed.

"What you never realized," Algiroth continued, "was who was actually behind her murder. Humans were not responsible for your mother's death; I was. The fire sprung from my magic. You saw me that day, though you may not have been able to distinguish who I was."

All the fight had been drained out of Ren. Only Shadow Hunter's control over his body kept him standing and his sword in his hand.

Algiroth burst out laughing. "I still can't believe how easy it was too. For all that she was, your mother died as easily as the humans that you hate. And for nothing. Your entire drive for hatred pitted against an innocent race. That's the best part."

The demonic sword materialized in his hand and Algiroth set his eyes directly on Kelsey. Ren and Marcus appeared in front of her and crossed their swords, as Algiroth's blade came crashing down on them. They pushed up, and Ren kicked him in the ribs. Algiroth stepped back, looking completely unfazed.

Ren held his sword out in front of Kelsey. "So long as there is breath in my body, I will never let you touch her." He was angry. Hatred burned within him. But more than that, his desire to protect Kelsey. He had failed to protect his mother; he would not fail again.

"Ren, the last requirement has been fulfilled. Are you ready?" Shadow Hunter asked.

"Are you sure about this?" Ren asked back.

"I am. Our enemy is too powerful. We can't defeat them. Not unless we work together."

"Then let's kill this bastard."

Ren felt Shadow Hunter's energy wash over him. He felt his spirit penetrating the very depths of his soul and magic. It rushed out of him, like a waterfall. The earth began to rumble, the wind ripped trees right out of the ground, and the ground beneath his feet was forced apart.

"That's it, Ren, keep going!" Shadow Hunter said. "Give it everything you've got. We have to synchronize our energies."

Ren's eyes turned gold, and he felt Shadow Hunter's presence burn through his very being. He could feel his emotions, sense his thoughts, and share his breathing. His power wrapped Ren like a blanket, blending the two of them together. The power overcoming him was greater than any he'd ever felt. It was so strong it threatened to break him. But he wouldn't let it. That's when he felt it, the moment when their very being resonated.

"Shadow Hunter, release!" The voice that came out was neither Ren's nor Shadow Hunter's alone. It was a perfectly synchronized combination of both.

The golden energy around Ren swallowed him completely before peeling away. He faced Algiroth with an appearance that was both Ren and someone else entirely. His eyes remained golden, with a long golden ponytail down his back. But his armor lay in pieces at his feet, unable to withstand Ren's sudden change.

A thin golden coat with a long tail adorned his torso. Its cuffs were wide, and the open front left his chest and collarbones exposed. With pants to match the coat, a black sash was tied overtop at his waist, the ends left hanging. His feet were ensnared in a pair of leather shoes, and he had a golden gauntlet on his right arm that stopped at the middle of his forearm. Ren recognized the outfit, for it was the same one Shadow Hunter wore when in his world.

His outfit wasn't the only thing that changed either. In his right hand, he held a new sword. A single edge with a golden blade and a spiked spine. The guard took the form of a cross and a white handle that was wrapped in gold.

Shadow Hunter's presence was firmly molded with Ren's own now. He could tell by the state of his appearance that his release was successful. For he and Shadow Hunter had become one, though Ren still remained in control. Their transition between each other was somehow even more fluid, with heightened speed. But more than anything, the power that flowed through Ren was beyond anything he had ever felt. His previous powers paled in comparison. That was something dangerous.

When Ren spoke next, his voice had returned to his own, but with a complete lack of emotion. "Ready Algiroth? I'll end this, in an instant."

Forty-five

A Legend Is Born

"Incredible," Kelsey mumbled. The word just escaped her lips, her mouth unable to contain the awe she felt.

"So, this is the heaven's blade's released state," said a familiar voice. James Wilson knelt next to them.

"Principal Wilson!" Kelsey said, surprised. She didn't even notice him approach. Had he been fighting the whole time?

"Hello, Miss Rose," he said. "Ren told me you were helping him on the quest to find the stones. Which means you know everything." She nodded. "Well, our existence is exposed now, so I won't ask you to hide it."

Ren's father held his gaze on Ren. He looked at the emptiness in his eyes. They stared blankly at Algiroth. "His eyes have more power in them. Good. He's at a level now, where we can leave the rest to him."

Even with Marcus, Ren's father, and her principle as witnesses, Kelsey could tell that all four of them were focused on something different.

"Is that really Ren?" she wondered. "Something's different about him. Not just his appearance."

"Partially," Leo said. "Every heaven's blade has a released form. Obviously, the form varies for each weapon. The release is about the two of them becoming one, sharing their bodies and minds, and all the power that comes with them."

"It grants the wielder full control over the weapon's power. That's why their appearance and weapon transforms, like Ren's. The outfit represents the spirit of the blade, and the new appearance of the weapon is its true form. Having released, Ren has essentially become Shadow Hunter."

Marcus had all his attention on Ren when he finally realized possibly the most concerning part about the whole situation at that moment.

"What's happened?" he wondered. "I don't feel a thing. There's nothing. Ren has no monster energy!"

James focused on Ren, searching for that incredible energy that he always felt from him. Only this time, there was nothing. Marcus was right.

Seeing Ren's father's calm expression, he knew the guy must know something. There was no way he didn't. For all the guy's strength, there was just no way something like this got passed him.

Algiroth narrowed his eyes at Ren, taking in his blank expression. Something was simply not right. "Ren Nightwalker? Are you really Ren Nightwalker?"

There was a brief pause. "What exactly do you mean, Algiroth?" Ren asked back.

"Well, if you really are Ren, then I'd say, you're disappointing. I don't feel a thing. You have no monster energy. You let the final chance of defeating me slip away."

Ren looked to the air, then back at Algiroth. "It's about time you guys got here," he said.

Marcus looked up. Eleven figures were scattered around them, each one brandishing golden weapons and dressed for battle. The remaining Heaven's Blades had been assembled.

"Sorry, we took so long. It took us longer than we thought to finish our missions," one of them said.

"We moved as fast as we could to get here, but it looks like we missed all the fun," another said, which Kelsey recognized as Raziel.

"Unbelievable. I've never seen all thirteen Heaven's Blades gathered at once before," James gawked in amazement.

Ren was quiet, contemplating his next words. "Raziel, I'm sorry. I couldn't save him."

"I know; I sensed his energy disappear." Raziel looked over at the dead body of his cousin.

"We lost Francisco getting the stone, too," Ren admitted. "I failed. I'm sorry."

"I'm sure you did everything you could."

"I'll be sure to help you bury him on the hills of the capital's cemetery when this is over. Right now, I need you guys to do me a favor. Gwen, Mark, take four others and scout out the city for any remaining shades. Eliminate as many as you can. The rest of you remain here. Make sure there's not a single shade left. Marcus."

"I know. I'll secure the area here. Don't worry about Kelsey or the others," Marcus said.

Half of the Heaven's Blades disappeared. The other half scattered around the battlefield.

Ren took a step forward, and the black sealing chains appeared around his body. Flexing his muscles, his energy gathered around him, and they shattered.

"Algiroth, let's not do this here. I'd rather fight somewhere we won't be interrupted."

"Ridiculous. What right do you have to decide—" his voice was cut off as Ren grabbed his face and flew into the air.

He's fast! I didn't see him move. Such a strong grip. Algiroth swung his sword, and Ren let go. They floated in midair, their wings extended. Algiroth looked Ren up and down again. Ren just stood there stoically, his empty eyes focused on Algiroth.

"Ah, now I understand," Algiroth said. "You didn't lose your energy; you merged it. You merged your ki with your body's physical traits to greatly enhance them. Which explains your new speed and grip strength."

Ren looked left. "Your shades are dropping like stones. Guess it's time to end this."

Algiroth swung his sword, and Ren responded with a counter. Using only the right hand that held his sword, he met Algiroth's blade with his own. The energy released when they pulled away destroyed a nearby building. Their next series of attacks collided in unison, sending waves of energy across the battlefield. The damage to their surroundings was beginning to accumulate dangerously.

Algiroth pulled away with heavy laughter. "Amazed, aren't you? How incredibly thrilling this amount of strength is. Demonic swords are truly an unstoppable force."

He appeared in front of Ren and swung down on top of him, but Ren never moved an inch. Instead, he lifted his hand and caught Algiroth's blade in between his fingers, causing the vampire to look at him, completely taken aback.

He caught my blade? Impossible. I can see him dodging, but even that is a challenge with the speed of my sword. Yet he chose to catch it, absurd.

"Why so surprised, Algiroth? Is it really such an amazing thing? Yes, I caught your blade. Does that scare you? Now do you understand what it means to fight a Heaven's Blade?"

Algiroth sneered in anger. "Don't get cocky! Catching my blade doesn't mean anything. All you got was lucky. It won't happen again!"

He pulled back, and Ren released his hold on the sword. Dark energy gathered around Algiroth's body until it covered him completely, then cracked and started falling away.

Algiroth's skin was now pitch black, the red demonic symbols glowing along his body. He had three sets of wings on his back, all with a claw on the top. His face was covered by a black mask with no nose and a straight line of spiky teeth where the mouth would be. The eye holes displayed his red eyes.

Ren sensed Algiroth's spike in power. He knew that he had merged with his demonic sword, much like he had with Shadow Hunter.

"Finally. A complete fusion with my demonic sword. I didn't expect it to take so long, but the sword has finally accepted me entirely. My existence as a mere vampire has been shed."

Blood suddenly flew out of his chest, spraying the air. Ren stood behind him, his sword lowered. Then he moved and cut off Algiroth's left arm with one more swing.

"You bastard!" Algiroth turned and swung his sword. Ren deflected it, and Algiroth attacked again. He swung down, then sideways, then down again, then diagonal several times, then sideways again. Ren blocked all his swings, simply twisting his wrist.

When Algiroth appeared behind him again, Ren reached behind without looking and blocked his attack. He back kicked Algiroth in the chest, sending him tumbling through a building, then out the other side before crashing into a second.

Algiroth came flying at him out of the dust. Ren swung down, and Algiroth was blown back, smashing into the street below. With Algiroth still down, Ren raised his sword into the air. Golden energy gathered rapidly, then dispersed through the sword. Lightning the same color as his energy danced along the blade.

Algiroth got to his feet, facing Ren at the ready.

I still can't feel anything. Why? I don't understand. Where does he get all that power? Where does it come from? A demonic blade rivals that of a released heaven's blade. But I have gone even beyond that by fusing with my demonic blade, such as he. And yet despite all my power, I still cannot feel his monster energy. But if that's the case, then that means, he is at an even higher level than I am!

Algiroth gathered a massive sphere of energy and magic, then compacted it into a small ball at the tip of his blade. "Like hell I'll accept that!" He released the energy, and it blasted toward Ren.

Ren closed his eyes, letting the attack fly at him. He opened them and all the ki, all the magic, all the lightning that made up his being erupted forth in his final attack. *Helcdorn.* "Raikiri."

Ren swung his word down, and a massive veil of gold lightning erupted upwards, leaving only a deep fissure in its wake, and lighting the sky a brilliant gold. It traveled toward Algiroth, cutting his attack in half, and passing through his body, before dissipating into the sky.

Several seconds passed of Algiroth motionless, never uttering a word. Then, his body split in two and disappeared, obliterated. The demonic sword fell out of his hand, then cracked and shattered into tiny pieces, which were carried away by the currents of wind.

The battlefield was silent for the first time. The whole country was. With just one attack, Ren had changed the entire world and the fate of both humans and monsters.

"He did It. Ren defeated one of Verin's four generals. We won!" Their forces cheered loudly in victory.

Ren lowered to the ground, and his wings disappeared. He found Marcus next to Kelsey and his father. Along with the one responsible for starting their quest, James Wilson.

Ren looked over at Kelsey and found her staring at him. He smiled at her, but she didn't smile back. She couldn't get over his presence now that he had finally become a full-fledged vampire. The guy had almost died for her for it.

"Kelsey?" he asked lightly. He took a step forward, and she stepped back. His ki was suffocating. He was a straight-out-of-the-book monster, not that it was necessarily a bad thing.

"Kells, are you alright?" he asked. He reached out to touch her, and Kelsey saw a figure with long hair appear over him. The figure was ethereal but looked human, male, its hair and eyes kind of golden.

Her eyes were pinned on the figure so that she didn't even pay attention to Ren.

"What is that?" she wondered. Ren couldn't figure out what she was going on about. Meanwhile, the spirit simply looked at her. "What are you?" she asked it, realizing it could actually see her. "Some kind of monster?"

Ren's eyes went wide. He drew his hand back and looked away, a hurt expression on his face. She realized he must have thought she was talking about him. But the look Marcus gave her, it was pure hatred.

"No, Ren, I wasn't talking to—"

"Marcus, let's start counting the dead and wounded," he interrupted. "We'll need to make shrouds and give them all a hero's burial. They gave their lives for the freedom of our realm."

Ren continued to dish out orders, sending people everywhere, each tasked with a job. Their dead were gathered and counted.

He knelt next to Hades' body, Raziel with him.

"We'll separate him from the others. Marcus and I are heading back soon. We'll take him with us." Raziel nodded in agreement.

"I'll go help the others," he said. Ren repeated the gesture, and he walked away.

"We should leave sometime next week," Marcus said to him.

"Yeah, I plan on leaving then," Ren said back. "That way, we can finish up here."

"Ren," Kelsey called. "I've been looking for you." She grabbed his hand, but he pulled it out.

"Kelsey. You need to go home. Thank you for helping us find the stones, but now it's time for you to go. Marcus and I have work to do before we leave."

"Leave?" she asked.

He held out his hand. "The stones, please. We have to take them back with us." His eyes were still so full of hurt. She had to explain things to him. "Ren, listen, about what I said."

"Kelsey, the stones."

"No, listen. I wasn't talking to you."

"The stones!" he repeated.

Kelsey fingered the bracelet, but it wouldn't come off when she tried to take it off. She gave it a tug, but it still wouldn't leave her wrist. There was no clasp on the back or sides either.

"It won't come off," she said.

Ren was concerned about that, but at the moment he had other matters to worry about.

"It's fine for the time being. We have a lot of work to do. Go home for now. We'll figure out a way to get it off when we have more time."

"Wait, where are you guys going?" she asked again.

"Home," he answered. "We have to report to our people and bury our dead, but there's work to be done here before that. Once we've finished up here, we can go. Our next stop, Nexus."

ACKNOWLEDGEMENTS

It's been a rollercoaster of a time writing this book. There are many parts and contributions that make up a book. Going at it alone makes those who give their utmost in assisting even more special, and I'm forever grateful.

Thanks to all those who were willing to read and point out all of my mistakes, no matter how bad. Of course, any that may remain are simply my own folly. And, of course, how could I forget my amazing cover designer Goran Tomic for a jaw-dropping cover.

My best friend Josh, the one closer to me than anyone else and gave me the inspiration to write. You are more than a friend, you're a brother, and I'm honored to call you family. For helping me from the very beginning to the very end of the book; words are never enough, brother.

Thank you to all my friends who supported me along the way. From acting out and contemplating the design of the battle scenes to all the monster types used. Mapping out quest locations and character designs.

Without your knowledge of their origins, myths, and abilities, I could not have been able to create the world I imagined it to be.

Thanks to my grandmother and grandfather, Mike and Paula Manioci, who have always believed in me and supported me in my desire to write this book. I'm sure you had no idea what you were getting yourselves into bringing me into that first bookstore as just a preschooler and reading to me. Look how far we've come.

And lastly, perhaps most importantly, thanks to you, the reader, for picking up and taking a chance with Nightwalker. Your support makes everything worthwhile. I'm so excited to be able to share this with you.